LONG AGO ON AN ISLAND CALLED MANHATTAN...

It was a primitive toehold of civilization at the edge of a savage wilderness—barren soil for a young man with the soul of a poet and his delicate young wife, a woman of fragile beauty and artistic nature. In this harsh new land, hard work was the key to survival, not art or philosophy or literature.

And yet, as the lofty monarchies of England and France diminished next to the threat of Mohawk war and the day-to-day struggle with the land, Pieter and Christiana deKuyper realized that they had found a home in New Amsterdam. Deep in the wilderness of this magnificent colony, Europe was fast becoming only a half-forgotten memory—a memory fading in the dawn of a monumental new enterprise.

BRUCE NICOLAYSEN

FROM

THE NOVEL OF
NEW YORK
1613–1667

DISTANT
SHORES

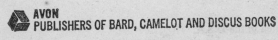
AVON
PUBLISHERS OF BARD, CAMELOT AND DISCUS BOOKS

FROM DISTANT SHORES is an original publication of Avon Books. This work has never before appeared in book form.

AVON BOOKS
A division of
The Hearst Corporation
959 Eighth Avenue
New York, New York 10019

First Avon Printing, July, 1980

For
Deirdre
friend as well as wife

ACKNOWLEDGMENTS

Maps: Tony Halstead
Three poems: Kjirsti Nicolaysen
Drawings: Karl W. Stueckland
Advice and other support: Ross Teel,
Peter Miranda, Ken and Ellen Roman, Jim and
Jill Himonas, and, most especially, Deirdre.

AUTHOR'S NOTE

Spelling in the 17th-century was hardly a precise science.

Manhattan was known as Manhatas, Manhados, Manhadoes, Mahates, Manhatec, and Manna–hatin to name but a few variations. The Dutch had a great deal of trouble with Indian place names. To make matters worse, each individual Indian usually had several names. When an Indian moved he would often take a name that was identified with his new home. Futhermore, when a Dutchman's tongue confused a word, the Indian's dry sense of humor let the mistake go uncorrected.

Concerning the use of Dutch words to identify places in New York, it seems pedantic to use "Paarl Straat" for Pearl Street and "de Heere Graft" for Broad Way. Certain Dutch words have been retained, either for flavor or comprehension. A burgher is a burgher, and a bouwrij or bouwrie a bowery. Spuyten Duyvil means "Spitting Devil"—but we know it even today by the Dutch name.

Hard money was always scarce in New Amsterdam and the people gladly accepted silver and gold coins from Holland, England, Spain, France—or any other place on earth. Actually, the most common currency was wampum—the beautiful shell-bead money of the Indians. Governor Stuyvesant once issued a decree condemning the wide-spread use of counterfeit wampum—shells that were broken or unthreaded. The second most common currency was beaver pelts.

This is a novel: but the setting and major events are historical fact. Pieter de Kuyper, Christiana, Jacob Adam and Anne are inventions of the author. But real men and women lived lives that were close to theirs, endured what they endured, and acted and talked much the way

Author's Note

they are portrayed in this book. Peter Minuit, Kiliaer
Van Rensselaer, Stuyvesant and others are historical
characters. There actually was a windmill at the site of
what is now the Battery; the celebrated purchase of the
island was made from Indians who never owned it; and
the wooden palisade built at the northern extreme of
town has left us a legacy in its name—Wall Street.

CONTENTS

CONTENTS

OUR STORY TO 1667

ENGLISH RULERS

James I	1603–1625
Charles I	1625–1649 (executed)
Oliver Cromwell	1649–1658
Richard Cromwell	1658–1659
Charles II	1660–

GOVERNORS OF NEW AMSTERDAM

Peter Minuit	1626–1632
Bastiaen Krol (interim)	1632–1633
Wouter Van Twiller	1633–1638
Willem Kieft	1638–1647
Peter Stuyvesant	1647–1664
Colonel Richard Nicolls, first governor of New York	1664–

to 1667

Huron brave — French woman

Stone Eagle 1620-

Adam de Kuyper d. 1604 (Amsterdam)

Christiana Van Venter 1607-1644

Jacob Adam 1644-

Pieter de Kuyper 1599-1667

Jan 1638 (stillborn)

Isaack Seixas d. 1661 — Sarah d. 1661

Joshua 1653-

Pieter 1627-

Anne 1631-

Paul 1658-

David de Witt 1630-

Emilie 1653-

Manuel Gerait (brother of Zilla)

Daniel 1659-

Abraham de Witt

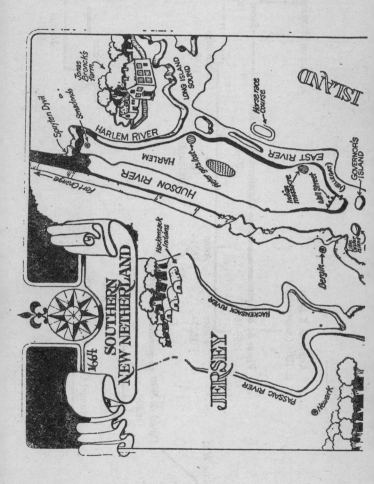

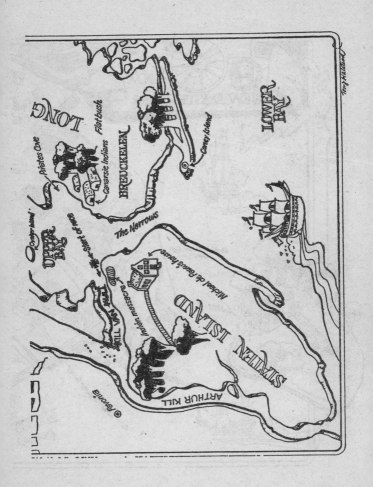

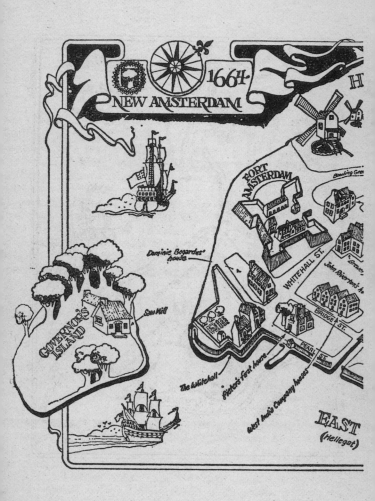

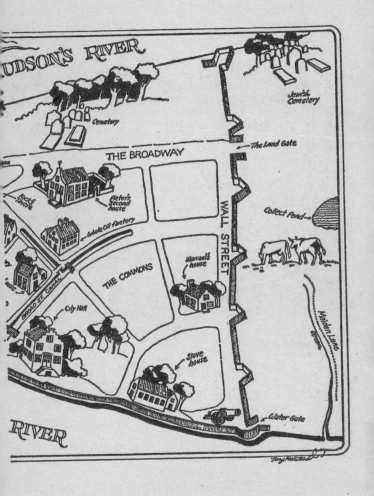

HUDSON'S RIVER

Cemetery

Jewish Cemetery

THE BROADWAY

The Land Gate

Peter's second house

WALL STREET

Collect Pond

Whale Oil factory

Manuel's house

THE COMMONS

City Hall

BROAD ST. CANAL

Slave house

Maiden Lane

Water Gate

RIVER

1

Four Huts on the Island

1613

YOUNG PIETER DE KUYPER RAN DOWN TO THE edge of the water where the men were preparing to launch the longboat. Captain Adriaen Block and five men were already aboard, and eight other sailors stood in the water, waiting to push the heavily laden boat off the pebbly bottom.

Pieter smiled weakly as the captain gave him a withering look. He climbed over the stern and picked his way through the bundles of food, casks of water, and other supplies until he found a cleared space. Captain Block nodded his head, and the men in the water heaved until the longboat floated freely in the placid waters. Two of the men in the bay pulled themselves over the gunwales, splashing and bringing water into the boat. Two other sailors manned the oars and began the thirty-yard journey to the small sailing craft that bobbed at anchor in the little harbor.

"You're always the last," Captain Block said to Pieter. "What kept you this time?"

Blushing, the boy reached into his pocket and brought forth a long strip of gleaming white wampum, the shell money of the Indians. "I got it for the smallest of trinkets," he said.

The Captain shook his head. "Someday those Indians will realize what a sharp businessman you are, then you won't get so many bargains." He couldn't help but smile.

1

Over the months they had been stranded on Manhatas, the fourteen-year-old cabin boy had developed into a trader, a true son of the merchant princes of their homeland.

It had been last fall when their ship, the *Tiger*, had burned in this very harbor. They knew she was the only ship in this area, the others already having left for Holland, and there was nothing to do but winter at the spot until the other ships returned the following spring or summer.

The first thing they had done was bargain with the local Indians for a piece of land. Captain Block offered a few guilders' worth of trinkets in exchange for "as much ground as could be encompassed by the hide of a bullock." After agreeing to this proposal, the Indians watched as the captain ordered his men to slice a large bullock hide into very thin strips. This done, the strips were tied together in a long "rope," which, laid out, enclosed a healthy bit of the tip of the land. The Indians showed no emotion at having been tricked, if indeed they thought they had been. The land claimed by the captain amounted to very little of the vastness that stretched as far as the eye could see.

Once their property was secured, the men put up four huts to protect themselves from the snows and the icy winds that howled through the night. This took a week. Another two weeks passed while they furnished the huts and made them as snug as possible. Then a week was spent on a smokehouse for the curing of meat. Just when it looked as if there wouldn't be much work beyond hunting, fishing, cooking, and essential housekeeping, the captain decided to build a boat. The keel of a forty-foot yacht, or flyboat, was laid, and the men were occupied during the months of snow in the finishing of hull, mast, spars and rigging.

The flyboat was ready to sail by the time the snow was melting into puddles, and Captain Block decided to use it to explore the nearby waterways. He figured that the other ships would not arrive for about two months—time they could use for the benefit of their employers, the merchant burghers of Amsterdam.

The longboat eased itself alongside the trim sailing craft, which bore the name *Restless*, a true reflection of

Captain Block's state of mind. The boat boasted a single stubby mast and carried a mainsail and one small jib made of bits of canvas: this much had been salvaged from the wreck of the *Tiger*.

The men tossed their supplies aboard the *Restless* and then climbed aboard. Two sailors remained in the longboat, and as soon as the others were clear, they rowed it back to the shore where the remaining twenty-three member of the *Tiger*'s crew were watching the activity. All looked with envy at their more fortunate shipmates who were getting this relief from the five months' confinement in the little camp at the tip of the land.

The sailors aboard the flyboat stowed the gear, raised the sails, and shipped anchor. Captain Block himself took the tiller, which he had carved that winter from a piece of native hickory.

He eased the boat onto a starboard tack, holding a course that pointed high into the wind. The little craft sailed around the spit of land that protected their small anchorage from the rougher waters of the open bay. The boat cleared the end of the land and the captain ordered the sails let out. The *Restless* continued on a reach until she came to the rough waters where the churning bay narrowed into a river that ran northward alongside Manhatas. When he reached the very middle, Captain Block jibed the boat onto a course that brought it before the wind. They started up the river, and the slender vessel took a liking to the combination of a following tide and the wind abaft; she picked up another knot.

"Loosen the jib!" the Captain called, and a sailor drew the line of the tiny sail from its clew and let it out until it began to flutter. He pulled it back slowly until it held taut in the wind, and then clewed it down again. The boat now ran at five knots as the turbulence of the bay increased. Its waters were being squeezed between the bodies of land on either side, creating currents on top of currents, which fought one another for space until there was a fearsome churning at the surface. Whitecaps slapped at one another, dashing themselves against the sides of the boat like angry little dogs yapping and biting at the heels of a passing horse.

"Nasty bit of water, isn't it?" the captain said to Pieter, who had taken the place on the other side of the tiller.

"The water acts as if it's displeased," Pieter said. "Maybe we're disturbing its sleep." He looked at the angry waves and turned back to Block. "Does it have a name?"

"This river? Not that I know of," the Captain said, and then he smiled at the thought in his mind. "So then it's up to us to name it. Pieter, I give that honor to you."

Pieter's young face became serious. He was a good-looking boy—blondish, with a strongly developed bone structure and a stubborn-looking mouth that betrayed his Dutch heritage. He was of normal height; a bit too slender, perhaps, but the long winter in a strange land could account for that. The most remarkable of his features were his eyes. They were large, inquisitive eyes, practical eyes but with a strange, faraway softness usually associated with visionaries and dreamers.

The boy thought for a few moments, and then he said, "She's a very untamed river. Let's call her Hellegat."

The Captain laughed. "A wonderful name. Did you all hear?" he said to the sailors. "We are sailing on the newly named Hellegat. Thanks to Master Pieter de Kuyper."

The men applauded with good nature; the boy was clearly a favorite among them. Pieter became embarrassed and stared down at the planking beneath his feet. But he was pleased.

The captain patted the young man on the shoulder. He liked this boy who adapted easily to new situations. It was the reason he had brought him along on this voyage of the *Restless*; the captain wanted to expose him to as many adventures of life as possible.

"Do you miss Amsterdam?" he asked.

"In a way, yes. The food. The markets. All the people and so many different sights to see," Pieter answered, and then he looked at the green breast of the land they were sailing past. "But I think I'll miss this place even more."

"What about your family?"

"I never knew my mother, and my father was taken by plague when I was five. I lived with my uncle, Jacob, who's an ironmonger. I was his apprentice until he allowed me to sign aboard the company's ships. I think he was happy to see me go, as he's sons of his own who want to follow him in his business." He was silent for a moment, and then he remembered something and smiled. "My uncle supplied many ship fittings. I wonder if some of his work wasn't on the *Tiger?*"

"I'd like to build a 'fitting' for that scoundrel of a shipwright who built the *Tiger*. I'd build him a coffin. The *Tiger* was a bad ship. No ship should burn as quickly as she did."

"Some good came of it, Captain."

"What are you talking about?"

"Because of it we became the first white men to winter at Manhatas."

The captain looked to see if the boy was having a joke at his expense, but no, he was perfectly serious. "Yes, but we're also the first Dutch boat not to return with a cargo of furs, which is the reason the burghers pay our salaries. And more than that, a young sailor lost his life."

For a moment Pieter had forgotten Joost Rooden. When the ship had caught fire, Joost was aboard as watch, every other man being ashore and busily trading with the natives. Joost was only eighteen years old, a boy on the threshold of his manhood. He admitted he had been asleep; by the time he woke, the fire was out of hand. He was guilty of one of the most serious crimes among men of the sea. The captain had no choice but to have him shot. It was the first execution of any Dutchman on the soil of the New World since the arrival of Henry Hudson four years ago. As Pieter thought about it, his shoulders hunched forward in shame for having forgotten poor Joost. He did not look at the Captain for a long time afterward.

And yet how difficult it was for Pieter *not* to be happy. Only since he had come to these wild shores had the world seemed to open up for him. His life in the Netherlands had been empty, dull, and, to his young eyes, devoid of all hope for the future. Of his mother he remembered nothing and of his father not much more. With his sister, Annetke, two years his senior, he had been brought to the house of his uncle Jacob and made to feel every day thereafter that he was an imposition and a burden. He believed his dour uncle begrudged him the food he ate and the warmth he took from the hearth. Even when he was old enough to work as an apprentice in Jacob's ironworks, through snide remarks and insinuations the older man let it be known that Pieter's work hardly began to pay for all the amenities he was given.

"I looked over those tackle fittings you finished today," Uncle Jacob had said one day at the dinner table, between loud slurps of soup.

Pieter waited for the next half of the statement, which was not long in coming. "No good," his uncle grumbled, "got to be done over."

Pieter stared down at the rich soup, the vegetables swimming in a thick meat broth with bubbles of delicious fat. The soup was one of his favorite meals, but now he felt he would gag if he ate another spoonful. He waited patiently until the others had finished and then excused himself. He went outside and sat on the back stoop, idly watching the chickens as they combed the tiny yard for a seed or a scrap of food. Annetke came out of the house and sat beside him.

"You shouldn't let Uncle Jacob bother you," she said. "He complains all the time, but he's really a good person."

Pieter looked at his sister and couldn't resist her smile. "I know," he said, "but he always makes me feel useless."

"Nonsense, you're learning to be a good ironworker. There's nothing useless about that. Maybe in a few years you'll be able to build something tall and wonderful like the gates on St. Maarten's Church."

"That would be grand," he said, his mind forming a picture of those stately iron structures. "And then a pair of splendid gates for the house I'm going to build for you!"

"See," she said proudly. "Now stop worrying about being useless and work hard at the forge."

She walked away, and he retained the glow of her words for less than a minute. His sister had the ability to pick up his spirits, but the effect never lasted. Reality always returned. His uncle's ironworks, modest as it was, would never come into his name. There were his cousins —boys, mere toddlers now, but Pieter knew they alone would inherit Jacob's business. He would always be a hired worker, sharing in the labor but not the profits. His dreams of becoming a master craftsman building great gates and handsome screens for the wealthy were just that —dreams, vain hopes with as much substance as smoke in a heavy wind.

In real life he trudged every day to his uncle's forge near the harbor. He spent his free time over by the docks at the end of the Prince Graft Canal or at the entrance to the Singel Canal, where the herring packers had erected their stately tower. These packers were wealthy by the standards of Amsterdam. Pieter enjoyed watching the stout men as, arrayed in heavy coats, with sashes about their waists and silver buckles on their shoes, they strode importantly into the meeting rooms of their tower to spend hours discussing, no doubt, the silvery fish that dominated their lives.

The continuous arrivals and departures of ships fascinated him, and he liked nothing better than to find a secure piling where he could rest his back and watch as the treasures of the world were unloaded from the bowels of these ponderous wooden vessels. He began to dream of sailing on one, sailing away from Amsterdam, with its drudgery and sameness, sailing away from Uncle Jacob and his stinginess and sarcasm. It was all heady stuff to a boy without money who spent long hours amid the heat and noise of an ironworks. But still, he was a boy, and to him any dream was better than no dream at all.

It was only a vague dream until Annetke went to her bed with pneumonia and died three days later. Pieter sat by his sister's still, pale form all through the night, until there were no more tears left in him. The one touch of softness and gentleness in his life had gone. The umbilical cord to Amsterdam had been cut, and now his dream of going to sea became a fevered passion. When a berth aboard a ship sailing to the New World was found, Uncle Jacob was more than delighted to free his apprentice and, incidentally, to free himself of the burden of caring for the boy. He bombarded his nephew with good advice and even gave him a small gold coin on the day of his departure. Pieter gave the coin to a blind man who was begging at the wharf where the *Tiger* was berthed. He wanted nothing more from his uncle.

When Pieter arrived in the New World he became conscious of a new freedom: here was opportunity beyond his dreams. Here, surely, was a place where a man could make his fortune.

That he was only a boy made no difference. There was more work than men to do it, and he was assigned jobs as an equal of the others. After working for Uncle Jacob, it was a delight to have a master like Adriaen Block. The captain would give him orders and then leave him alone until the job was finished. There was no carping about the boy's ability—or, if it sometimes seemed that he ate more than necessary, about his appetite. If the captain interfered at all, it was only to gently point out a better or faster way to complete a task.

"A good job, lad, keep it up," was Block's most usual comment, one ordinarily accompanied by a friendly pat on the back.

For the first time in his short life Pieter felt he was needed. As soon as he mastered a skill, the captain instructed him in another. He woke each morning with a smile on his face, overjoyed to be alive, eager to get on with the work of the day. . . .

But he had been selfish, he thought again. To be so involved with himself that he forgot about Joost Rooden was wrong. He resolved to give more thought to others, but it would be difficult to suppress the overpowering gladness that filled his mind at the thought of being here, in the New World, in this place to which God surely had meant him to come.

The boat now left behind the rough waters and entered the river proper, Manhatas on the left and the nameless mass of land on the right. A wisp of smoke trailed into the sky from a stubby hill on the nameless land, from the cooking fires of the Indians who lived there and who, no doubt, called the place by some name or other. A small village could be seen near the fires. It was a collection of only half a dozen oblong bark huts with sloping sides and flat ends. Each hut had a single opening, which served as both door and window. Some of the Indians who live on this nameless land had crossed the river to Manhatas and joined in the trading with the visitors. Furs, fruits, strange vegetables, many kinds of fish—all had eagerly been exchanged for beads, trinkets, bits of metal, and small coins whose actual value was incomprehensible to the Indians, who prized the coins because they could be used to reflect the rays of the sun.

The *Restless* moved farther up the river. The land on both sides was unspoiled, feral; trees, shrubs, flowers, and wild grasses grew down to the water's edge. Beyond

the green shoreline the men could see rolling hills covered with trees that had been growing for thousands of
years; a forest canopy harboring immense numbers of
wildlife—birds, beaver, deer, squirrel, chipmunk, mink,
wildcats, dogs, otter, raccoon, wild turkey, weasel, mountain lion, wolf, and bear. In the hills springs came bubbling up from the earth to become streams that cut
channels into the earth and meandered over the land
until they drifted into the mightier waters of the river.

The hours passed and the little boat came to a long,
slender island in the middle of the waters of the Hellegat. The *Restless* entered the channel that separated
the island from Manhatas. At one point a dugout canoe,
hollowed from the trunk of a single tree, put out from the
island. Four men paddled it alongside the sailboat at a
safe distance.

Captain Block took no precautions: he expected no
trouble from these natives. The Indians paddled along
with the sailboat for about a quarter of a mile, the seriousness of their expressions tempered by their curiosity.
Pieter waved to them, but either they did not understand
or their dignity would not permit them to return so friv-
olous a greeting. The four Indians stopped paddling and
watched in silence as the sailboat, carried by the current
and the wind, drifted onward.

They came to a fork in the river where it branched
into two narrower streams on each side of a jutting land;
the captain chose the fork to the left. But now night was
coming, and while there remained enough light to see by,
the boat was brought to a tiny inlet on Manhatas. The
rock-studded shoreline was broken by a pebbly beach,
and the men anchored the boat in the lee of a large boul-
der whose upper part extended thirty feet above the surface of the water. They secured an anchor in the shallow
water, and two men took a line ashore and tied it to a
tree. The rest of the crew waded ashore. They built a
fire and heartily ate a supper of bear meat and succotash,
a dish they had learned from the Indians. They set up
simple canvas lean-tos, smoked their pipes, and went
to sleep.

First light. Dew glistening on a leaf. The shadows recede and objects distorted into horrors by the darkness

take on their normal, commonplace shapes. Life stirs
anew.

Pieter was up, filled with anticipation of the coming
day. All the other men were in the last, blissfully still
stage of sleep.

Pieter decided to take a walk. The man on watch saw
him go; he hunched beneath his wool-and-canvas blanket,
thinking only that his watch would soon be over.

The day would not be bright and sunny, as the previous
one had been. The sky was an ominous gray. A fine mist
descended upon the land, and Pieter stayed beneath the
protective branches of the trees. It was an incredibly
beautiful world—quiet, peaceful, and yet filled with the
rustling and scratching sounds of life. Once Pieter startled
an early-rising squirrel, who raced up a tree and, from
the safety of his perch forty feet in the air, loudly scolded
the intruder.

Pieter smiled at the squirrel. It was wonderful to be
alive in such a place. The flowers, responding to the miracle of spring, were everywhere, filling the air with their
perfume. The woods smelled of pine, hickory, and oak.
Acorns dotted the ground. Strange berry bushes hinted
of the precious fruit they would soon yield, and it made
Pieter's mouth water to think of what their rich liquid
goodness might taste like.

He wandered through a glade and skirted a boggy
marsh. He noticed several narrow paths leading through
the cord grasses. A pile of cracked crustacean shells told
him that these paths were used by men. The question
was, what men?

He walked around a gently rolling hill. He crossed a
stream. By jumping from stone to stone he managed
to keep his feet dry. On the opposite bank he entered a
grove of trees with trunks so thick and dense it was not
easy to pass among them. Above, the branches inter-
mingled, creating a still-greater denseness that turned the
overcast day almost nocturnally black.

He suddenly realized he was lost.

He made his way to an open glade in order to get his
directions from the sun, but the clouds crowded one another in the sky, traveling in herds, and the fine mist began to change into larger droplets.

The rain became heavier, and he made his way back to

the protection of the tree branches. He walked ten feet into the forest—and then he stopped. His eyes widened. There were four of them: Indian braves. They were tall and straight-standing, their bodies covered with furs, tanned animal hides, and bird feathers. They stared at him with unblinking eyes for almost a full minute.

Pieter came close to panic. He wanted to turn and run, but he forced himself to stand still. He didn't know which way to run, and he had no illusions about his ability to outrun these fleet forest-dwellers. If he ran he would be inviting attack. If he stood his ground, he reasoned, the next move would be up to the Indians. He crossed his arms and forced himself to smile.

The sailors had eaten their breakfast and were ready to board the *Restless* when Captain Block realized Pieter was nowhere to be seen. The man who had the last watch told of seeing the boy embark on a walk. The sailors were sent to search the vicinity for Pieter, but after half an hour no one found a trace of him.

The captain was not happy with the situation. They were in unknown country. If they didn't know where they were themselves, how could they find the boy?

The captain divided his crew into two search parties. Each went in a different direction—one northeast, the other southeast. At midday they turned back, met where the *Restless* was moored, and spread out again to cover new territory.

They searched for all of two miserably rainy days.

On the night of the second day they returned to their camp, their muscles aching, their bodies quivering, their lips trembling with the thorough soaking they had taken. They ate a cold supper and lay down beneath their lean-tos in the sodden messes that were their beds.

The next morning it was still raining. The captain hated to abandon the boy, but there seemed to be little hope of finding him. Also, it was becoming unfair to the sailors. How many more days of this could they take? He called off the search, then took off his cap and led the men in a brief prayer.

The men wasted no time in leaving the place where they had spent such a miserable time. The *Restless* slipped anchor and headed toward the channel to the northeast. In a short time the craft had passed through the opening. It followed the curve of the land, and Manhatas was lost to view. Captain Block continued to look astern long after there was nothing left to see.

Pieter was seated on a soft fur before the fire in a long hut. He was enjoying a bowl of yockey, the soft pulpy mush beloved by the natives. From a skin he drank a refreshing liquid made of the pulp of hickory nuts and walnuts mixed with cold, sparkling spring water.

He had been in the hut for two days, and he had no idea why the Indians had brought him here. They had walked northward from the place of their encounter, coming back to the river north of where the *Restless* was anchored downstream. They continued along the riverbank until they rounded a bend and Pieter saw a much vaster body of water ahead. As they came closer, he realized it was a mighty river and the flow of its current was unmistakably southward.

Pieter tried to reason it out.

The *Restless* had sailed up the eastern shore of Manhatas on the newly named Hellegat River. (*His* name, he remembered proudly.) The Hellegat had curved to the west until it went past what was obviously the northern tip of Manhatas, emptying itself into this greater body of water. From its size, Pieter was certain this second river was the one officially known as the Mauritius, after Prince Maurice of the Netherlands; but more commonly known to sailors as the North River. (Some had also suggested naming it after its discoverer, Henry Hudson, but the Amsterdam burghers had thought this too much of an honor for an Englishman, even if he had been sailing under the Dutch flag.) Pieter suddenly understood. The rivers flowed on all sides of Manhatas, surrounding it with water.

Manhatas was an island!

He realized he was probably the first white man to discover this, and he became excited at the prospect of sharing his knowledge with Captain Block and the others. And then he was conscious again of the tall warriors who walked at his side. Captain Block and the others might never know of his discovery, for the simple reason they might never see him again.

But the Indians did not mistreat him, although they weren't over-friendly. He had been brought to their village and placed inside the hut he now occupied. It was constructed in the same fashion as he had seen among the Indians to the south. Long, slender hickory saplings were placed in the ground, evenly spaced in two long rows. The saplings were bent toward each other and tied together where they formed an arch. This basic structure was then lathed with a criss-cross of split poles. The saplings and poles had been covered with the bark of ash, chestnut, and oak trees, the smooth side inward and the rough turned toward the elements. Each piece of bark lapped over the next, creating a snug and dry interior. This hut gave Pieter excellent protection against the heavy rains. He had soft sleeping furs, and his captors gave him more food than he could eat—meat, succotash, oysters, yockey, fried fish, and vegetables he had never seen before that proved to be delicious. No, Pieter had no cause for complaint about the treatment he was receiving. What bothered him was he had been given no indication of why he was being held in the hut.

He was finished with the yockey and enjoying more of the delicious nut liquid when the fur over the opening of the hut was lifted and a warrior whom Pieter had not seen before entered.

Pieter took one look and knew this was an important man. He was dressed in furs that seemed richer than the ones worn by the others and the bird feathers in his headband were longer and thicker. The other Indians treated him with respect and deference. But what impressed Pieter most was the man's own dignity and bearing. He moved gracefully, but each gesture was measured as if it were part of a ceremony.

The chief, as Pieter immediately began to call him in his mind, moved to the fire and stared down at the boy. Suddenly Pieter knew he did not have to be afraid.

The chief sat down on the other side of the fire, and Pieter passed him the skin with the nut liquid. The chief drank, then passed the skin back to Pieter. There could be no mistaking this as anything but a sign of friendship.

The chief and Pieter spent the rest of that rainy day and most of the night together inside the hut. Though neither could speak a word in the other's language, through signs, symbols, and drawing with sticks in the earthen floor of the hut, they learned much about one another.

Pieter discovered that he had been brought to the hut because the chief wished to learn something of the strangers who were staying at the southern tip of Manhatas.

When his warriors had come across Pieter and brought him to the village, the chief had been hunting in the north; he was sorry he had not been in his village to greet the visitor. Pieter learned other things. Most of the Indian tribes were related to each other in one way or another. There was a war-like tribe to the north that was not related to them, and this tribe was always causing trouble. The location of this village was called *paparinemin*, and Pieter was told the name meant a place where the waters were always going backward and forward in confusion.

In turn the chief seemed to understand the size of the ocean and that a great land existed on the other side of it. Pieter tried to explain the large cities and the mighty kings and queens of Europe, but there was no way he could tell if the other could comprehend.

The next morning the sun was shining. The chief supplied Pieter with food and more nut liquid. He indicated that two warriors would guide Pieter to the camp of the white men on the southern tip of Manhatas.

The chief and the boy walked to the edge of the land where the North River swept past the junction of the smaller river. The chief stopped and pointed south. Then he took a delicate string of wampum shells from his own neck and placed it about the boy's.

Pieter looked at the handsome wampum and knew he had to give the chief something of equal value—not because the chief expected it, but because Pieter wished to express his own goodwill. He took the knife and scabbard from his belt and held it out to the chief. The Indian held the scabbard and slipped the sharp knife out; its surface glinted with a flash of the sun. The chief's face held no expression, but he placed his hand on Pieter's shoulder.

Suddenly the boy realized they had not learned each other's names. He pointed at his chest. "Pieter. Pie-ter."

The chief understood. He touched Pieter's chest.

"Pieter," he said, and then he touched his own chest. "Senadondo."

"Senadondo," Pieter repeated.

A figure of great calm and dignity, Senadondo turned and walked in the direction of his village. When he was hidden by the trees, Pieter stepped into the canoe and started on the journey south.

The vast river swept Pieter and his guides along, and the land they passed held never-ending delights and surprises for the young man. Animals were everywhere. He watched as a pair of beavers worked on their dam. An otter splashed and played in a stream, ignoring the men. Deer browsed contentedly but kept a wary eye on the men as they passed. Pieter watched in fascination when he saw a fox chase a rabbit from the woods. It seemed as if the rabbit would make good his escape as he bounded in one unexpected direction after another. The fox, however, knew the way of rabbits. Instead of running straight ahead, it zigged to the right so that when the rabbit made his next leap it was there waiting.

One of Pieter's guides pointed to the fox. "Senadondo," he said, and Pieter knew the warrior was telling him that his own chief, Senadondo, had been named for the crafty fox.

Small talkative brooks purred their way into the North River. Sea birds, whirling tirelessly in the sky, circled lower and lower until they dove beneath the sparkling waters, emerging moments later with wriggling fish in their sharp beaks.

They stopped to rest, and Pieter climbed a nearby hill that afforded a panorama of the interior of the island. There were forests and marshes, low flat plains, and the ridges of spiny hills. In the middle he saw a sizable lake, its surface shimmering under the sun, its border ringed with trees. Deer drank at the water's edge.

They resumed the journey and finally arrived at the southern tip of Manhatas. The left-behind members of the *Tiger*'s crew were surprised to see Pieter arrive in the company of two Indians. Their surprise turned to astonishment when he told them of his adventure and his discovery that Manhatas was an island.

Senadondo's warriors were rewarded with beads and

trinkets. They took solemn leave of Pieter and started back to their home in the north.

Five weeks later the *Restless* returned, and all the crew were delighted to see Pieter alive and well. But the *Restless* was now under the command of Captain Hendrick Christiaenson and Captain Block was nowhere to be found. Christiaenson explained to Pieter that he had come across Block and the *Restless* while he was on board his caravel, the *Fortune*—a craft sent from the Netherlands to find out what had happened to the *Tiger*. The two captains agreed to exchange ships, enabling Christiaenson to do some inland-waterway exploring of his own. Block was to spend time trading with the Indians along the shores of the new island he had discovered and sailed around. This island stretched from Manhatas far out into the Atlantic. Block had begun calling it "Long Island," and because the name seemed appropriate, others took to calling it that.

In late summer Captain Block arrived at Manhatas with the *Fortune,* her holds loaded with beaver pelts and other furs. He was so happy to see Pieter that he grabbed the young man and squeezed him until Pieter wondered if he would live to see another day.

The boy told him of his adventures, including the story of the gift of his dagger to Senadondo.

Without hesitation Captain Block took his own dagger, a handsome dirk in an ornate metal-and-leather scabbard, and handed it to Pieter. "Lose a knife, gain a knife," he said. "Here is one to be proud of."

Pieter was speechless. He examined the scabbard, which contained several jewels. He withdrew the blade. It was engraved with words in a language he did not understand.

"Spanish," Captain Block informed him. "It means 'Go Safely with the Grace of God,' and it has quite a history. Henry Hudson wore it at one time, but the Dutch East India Company claimed it was their property and Hudson returned it. It was given to me when I signed as captain with the company. And now I give it to you."

Pieter thanked him gravely and then looked again at the inscription. "But why is it in Spanish?"

"The company claims it was bought from the family of

a man who had sailed with Christopher Columbus," Captain Block said. "They say the knife was a present given to Columbus by Queen Isabella at the beginning of his second voyage to the New World. At first I didn't believe it, but I've shown the knife to several blade makers and experts on this sort of thing, and most of them believe the story to be true. The knife is the right age. The scabbard is definitely Spanish; the blade comes from Toledo, of that there's no doubt. So the story is probably true and this was actually the knife of Christopher Columbus—but who is really to know?"

Pieter decided on the spot that he would never use this knife, but would guard it as a precious possession. He wrapped it carefully in a piece of canvas and hid it among his clothing.

At the end of summer, when the air had begun to chill and the days had grown noticeably shorter, the men on Manhatas happily boarded the *Fortune* and began the long voyage back to Holland, eager to see their friends and families, pleased they were bringing back such a rich cargo for the burghers.

Pieter stood at the stern and watched Manhatas Island grow smaller and smaller as the bulky caravel made its slow way through the Upper Bay toward the Narrows. He sensed a presence at his shoulder. It was Adriaen Block.

"It's beautiful, isn't it," the captain said.

"I'm coming back."

"I'll be back next year for more furs. You may come with me."

"I mean I'm coming back to stay here."

The Captain shook his head. "There's no talk of a permanent settlement. The burghers are only interested in trade."

"This year perhaps. And next year. But one year there will be a settlement."

"The burghers must be convinced of that."

"Then I will help convince them," Pieter said with determination. "But some day I'll come back to stay."

Amsterdam seemed much smaller than Pieter had remembered it; cramped, mean, suffocated by loathsome smells, crowded with carts and animals, filled with bus-

tling men of business and with women who screeched and
argued the cost of a brace of ducks or a few stringy vegetables.

Uncle Jacob was less than delighted with Pieter's return and grudgingly gave him back his tiny attic room
beneath the sharply slanting roof. It was freezing in winter and oppressive in summer but good enough for an
orphan. Pieter was told to report to the forge at dawn in
order to pay for his lodging and meals.

The boy had other ideas. He went to Adriaen Block
and begged and wheedled until the master mariner found
him an apprentice's spot with a joiner who was building
the hull on a newly laid keel. The joiner magnanimously
offered to pay the young man a wage. It was many
months later that Pieter discovered his wage was really
being paid by Captain Block. Meanwhile Pieter worked
on the ship and handed over most of the money as board
to his uncle, an arrangment that pleased the latter and
made his tongue less sharp.

Every morning through the cold winter months, Pieter
would rouse himself from his bed before dawn and hasten
through the arctic streets to the carpentry shed, where the
hull was looking more and more like a ship. The joiner,
a kind man, carefully instructed Pieter in the skills of his
trade. The boy was a diligent pupil and rarely had to be
told twice how to do anything. Added to his knowledge
of ironworking, the skills of a carpenter would be a valuable asset to a young man who promised himself he would
someday be living in the New World.

Pieter's Sundays were days of rest, spent with his uncle's family. There was church in the morning, with a
long-winded speech by the dominie promising the fire
and brimstone of Hell to anyone who stepped as much as
an inch out of line. The dominie couldn't promise much
better even to those who didn't step out of line, because
there was a good chance that God had determined *before*
the birth of each man and woman whether or not that
soul would enjoy the happiness of heaven or the pain of
Hell. Luckily—at least the dominie thought it lucky—
there were some signs to help men determine their future.
It was God's mark of favor, the dominie said, to let those
who would enter the kingdom of Heaven prosper here on
earth. The affluent burghers, merchants, and tradespeople

looked smugly at their fine Sunday clothes and felt assured that they had been singled out by God. The poorer members of the congregation clasped bony hands over the frayed parts of their coats in an effort to make themselves less conspicuous. Pieter didn't believe everything the dominie said; he felt some men were prosperous merely by an accident of birth. He compared his own situation with that of his younger cousins. If prosperity came his way, it would be only because of his own labors. His cousins, on the other hand, would inherit their father's modestly prosperous business through no effort of their own and despite any flaws in their character. He mentioned this to his uncle one Sunday while they waited for their dinner to be served.

"Are you questioning the dominie?" Uncle Jacob asked in the mild tone he had adopted toward his nephew when the boy began paying for his board with good silver coins.

"It seems the dominie is saying rich men are more worthy in the sight of God," Pieter said.

Uncle Jacob nodded. There was no flaw in that statement as far as any sensible Dutchman could detect. The Netherlands was the most prosperous country in Europe, and pursuit of wealth was the accepted way of life. "Yes," he said, "it would seem God grants His favors in this world to those He plans to cherish in the next."

"But why should that be?" Pieter asked, setting a trap for his ponderous kinsman.

"It makes it easier for us to tell who is a good man and who is bad," Uncle Jacob said, his brow furrowing as he reached the limits of his fund of theological knowledge.

"Does it say that in the Bible?"

"I guess it must somewhere," Uncle Jacob said, "otherwise the dominie wouldn't talk about it."

"The Bible also says it is harder for a rich man to enter the kingdom of God than it is for a camel to pass through the eye of a needle," Pieter said, echoing the words he had heard spoken by Adriaen Block only this past week.

Uncle Jacob pondered this thought for a moment or two and then left the room, mumbling to himself about harboring a heathen under his own roof. But the boy

paid good board, and Jacob was not eager to jeopardize
this steady income.

Pieter went to the back of the house and sat in a corner of the kitchen, where he could revel in the delicious
smells of the dinner being prepared by his aunt, a long-
suffering woman who cooked and cleaned and sewed and
left all thinking to her husband. He took out his knife and
worked on the intricate carving he was making from a
piece of hardwood. His knife flashed as he sculpted the
hull of the miniature barque that was beginning to take
shape. He was involved in this work when he suddenly
became aware he was being watched. He looked up into
the inquisitive eyes of the most beautiful child he had
ever seen.

"What's that?" the little girl asked.

"Who are you?" Pieter asked.

"Christiana Van Venter," the child replied. "What are
you making?"

"A ship."

"A real ship?" the child said, her eyes growing wider.

"Yes," Pieter said solemnly, "and when it's finished I
plan to sail it across the ocean."

There was a long pause, and then a look of triumph
came over the little girl's features. "You are not. It's too
small," she said, pointing to the carving.

"But I'm a magician," Pieter said, managing to keep
from smiling. "When the ship is finished I'll shrink myself
down to the same size. Would you like to do that with
me?"

She stared at him for a moment; then a look of fright
came into her eyes and she scampered from the room as
if the Devil himself were in pursuit. Pieter laughed so
hard that tears came to his eyes.

The little girl, it turned out, was the youngest member
of a family that had recently moved next door. Uncle
Jacob, learning his neighbor was also an ironworker, had
invited the family to Sunday dinner. Throughout the meal
little Christiana stayed close to her mother, but her eyes
constantly wandered down toward the "magician," who
was seated at the other end of the long table. Her look
was tinged with disbelief, but she was only six years old,
none too sure of herself and not taking any chances.

When the meal was over and the families had talked

for a polite amount of time, *Mevrouw* Van Venter gathered her brood and prepared to take them home. As they said their good-byes they had to pass Pieter, who was seated on the long bench near the door. As little Christiana passed, Pieter stopped her. "I'm not really a magician," he said. "I just made that up."

"I know," the girl said, trying to be as brave as possible but still uncertain about this strange wood-carver.

"I'm just an ordinary person," he said.

"Yes."

He paused and then leaned forward. "Boo!" he said in a very quiet voice that couldn't be heard by anyone else but the girl. She screamed and ran out the door after her two brothers and her older sister.

Uncle Jacob looked sharply at his nephew, who assumed an innocent look. "What was that all about?"

"I don't know," Pieter said. "You know how little girls are."

Pieter took his wood carving to the room in the attic and thought no more about little Christiana Van Venter.

2

The Colony Begins
1626-1631

THE CAPTAIN OF THE *SEA MEW* STEERED A
more northerly course as he took his bearings from the
spit at Sandy Hook and the ship passed the tip of land the
Dutch navigators had named Coney Island. Heading
toward the end of the Lower Bay, which was marked by
the ominous jaws of the Narrows, the *Sea Mew* carried
the usual supply of trading goods and cattle, which were
kept in individual stalls on top of three feet of protective
sand. It also carried the Dutch West India Company's
newly appointed inspector-general, Governor Peter
Minuit. The governor bore funds to buy Manhatas—now
generally known as Manhatan—from the Indians, and
also a charter to establish a colony in the New World.
The entire colony was to be called New Netherland, and
the settlement on Manhatan, New Amsterdam.

There were other passengers on board, men and
women, twenty-two of them, coming not only to trade,
but also to settle as permanent residents of New Netherland. Among them were twenty-seven-year-old Pieter de
Kuyper and his young bride, nineteen-year-old Christiana.

"Look straight ahead," Pieter said as he stood near the
bow with his arm around his wife's shoulder. "Look
straight ahead through the Narrows . . . now slightly to
the right. There it is—see it? Manhatan."

Christiana squinted her eyes and finally isolated the
tiny bit of land. "It looks small," she said. Pieter caught
the apprehension in her voice.

He laughed. "Not at all. Manhatan and the land to the

23

north is vast. You could tuck all of the Netherlands in one corner and not be able to find it."

She smiled, and he felt strong and fulfilled. He had never seen a prettier woman than his wife; she could be soft and afraid, because he would be there to protect her.

The *Sea Mew* passed through the Narrows and entered the Upper Bay. The new settlers were treated to a spectacle as three whales passed on their way back to the open sea, their great backs rising and falling in the water, their blowholes spraying tall jets into the air, columns of water that were diffused by the wind and fell back to the sea as a fine mist.

Governor Minuit, dressed in his finest coat and hat, came on deck. He picked his way through the piles of lashed-down supplies and stood beside the young couple. "Well, Pieter," he said, "this is a proud day for you, no?"

Pieter's eyes remained on the island he had grown to love. "There were times when I thought I was wasting my life on a lost cause, but that's all in the past. We're here, we're really here, and we're here to stay."

"We'll build a great colony," the governor said. He grasped Pieter by the shoulders. "You were one of the few men in the Netherlands who understood the value of a permanent settlement. The others looked only at the present, not the future. But we convinced them, Pieter, we did it and now we're here!"

The Governor did not exaggerate the difficulties preceding this heady moment. Ten years ago, in 1616, Peter Minuit had proposed the establishment of a colony, but the burghers would not hear of it. Pieter de Kuyper was still a boy at the time, but soon he became one of Minuit's strongest supporters. Year after year they submitted petitions to the States-General, the ruling body of the United Netherlands. Finally the burghers, weary of Peter Minuit and this tiresome young de Kuyper, their minds more concerned with the endless wars in Europe, gave in. In 1621 they created the Dutch *West* India Company. The company's charter gave it, among other things, a monopoly on trade in the new colony of New Netherland.

After his first trip to the New World with Captain Block, Pieter had made four more trading voyages to Manhatan, the last in 1624, when the first thirty settlers had been landed on the island. However, the cattle they brought began to sicken and die almost immediately, and most of the settlers were moved about one hundred and seventy miles up the North River. There they established the colony of Fort Orange. The remaining cattle survived there, and the colonists decided to make it their permanent home.

Only eight men remained in the south, and even these did not live on Manhatan. They camped in the dense woods of Nutten Island, a tiny bit of land that stood in the bay at the tip of Manhatan and was so named because of the great quantity of acorns to be found on the ground.

Pieter was dismayed. He returned to Amsterdam. "It is all well and good to settle at Fort Orange," he told the burghers in the High Chamber of the Dutch West India Company, "but the key to the expansion of trade in the New World is the island of Manhatan. It is there we must build our main settlement."

"He's right!" cried Peter Minuit, the young, energetic Westphalian respected both as a deacon of the church and as a brilliant administrator. "Manhatan is the natural center of New Netherland. It is the hub of the wheel, and all the other settlements are but spokes extending from the hub. This wheel," Minuit argued passionately, "will turn faster and faster, creating greater and greater profits. But for the spokes to be effective and the wheel to turn, the hub must be solid and secure. The hub of Manhatan is the key to the wheel of profit in the New World!"

The burghers were impressed. Such sensible talk of profit could not be ignored, because, after all, profit was the whole reason for this venture. They agreed to try again.

In 1625 another group of settlers and their cattle arrived, but again, hardly had they landed than the beasts began to die. The remaining cattle were quickly divided. A group of settlers took half of them to Fort Orange. The other settlers took the remaining cattle and established the Good Hope Trading Post on the Fresh River, which some called by the Indian name of Connecticut.

The burghers of the Dutch West India Company were now convinced that settling on Manhatan was folly. It was Pieter de Kuyper who persuaded them to try again.

He was thin and haggard as he stood before the
burghers on their high benches; they looked smug and
secure in their black coats and white collars. Pieter gazed
around the chamber at each one. "Good sirs and lords,
only last year it was agreed in this chamber that it was
vital to our interests to establish a fort on Manhatan. That
fact has not changed. He who controls Manhatan controls the waterways of the North River and the Hellegat.
He controls the passages to the rich lands of the interior.
He controls the bays and the approaches to the South
River. Manhatan, good sirs, is as vital today as it was last
year."

The burghers nodded their heads yes yes, this much
might well be true; from a military and naval point of
view the island of Manhatan had great value.

"But," said Kiliaen Van Rensselaer, a heavyset burgher
who was one of the richest jewel merchants in Holland,
"what is wrong with establishing only a fort on the island
to control the waterways? If we have the fort, why do we
need a settlement?"

"We all know that a fort produces no profit," said
Pieter, who by now could speak the language of the
burghers when necessary. "Profits come from a colony
that grows crops and raises cattle, sheep, and hogs. Profits come from trading for furs and hides. A fort by itself
does nothing but drain the coffers of the company."

"True, true," Van Rensselaer said, paying lip service to
the god of Profit. However, he was not to be quieted so
easily. "But then our conclusion might well be that Manhatan will *always* be a drain on our coffers. In which case,
I put it to the members of this chamber, who needs it?"

Pieter was ready for this. "The French think they could
use it. Last year they attempted to land a ship on Manhatan. If our settlers had not been there to drive them off,
we might not be talking of New Amsterdam or New
Netherland, but of New Paris and New France."

"But how could the French establish a colony where we
cannot? Will not their cattle sicken and die as ours have?
Or perhaps the French have some magic elixir that will
preserve their cattle," Kiliaen Van Rensselaer said with
great sarcasm. "Are you trying to tell us that?"

"How can we build a settlement where animals will not
live?" a burgher asked in indignation.

"It's hopeless," said another.

"Foolish," added a third.

"It is neither hopeless nor foolish," Pieter said, "because I have solved the problem of the cattle. I know what to do that will allow them to land and thrive."

There was a long silence in the austere chamber. Finally, Van Rensselaer asked the question: "And just what is your solution to this problem?"

"The cattle sicken because of the long ocean voyage," Pieter said quietly. "The rhythm of the waves interferes with their digestion; when the digestion is upset it causes ague and a thickening of the blood; this, in turn, upsets the flux of their systems. With the system out of flux, they must be allowed time to readjust to normality."

"What does all that mean?" asked one of the confused burghers.

"In the past the cattle have been fed and watered as soon as they were put ashore. This is a mistake. They should not be fed or watered for two full days. By that time their systems will resume their normal flux. This causes the ague to disappear and their digestive systems will be ready to accept nourishment. I tell you, good sirs, after two days the cattle will be normal again and they can be fed and fattened, or left to die of old age, whichever is the wish of Your Lordships."

Arguments on both sides followed Pieter's statement. Doctors were brought to the chamber, and their scientific flounderings over the nature of flux and ague only clouded the issue, bringing doubt and uncertainty to every burgher's mind.

After much acrimonious debate, the burghers decided the risk was worth taking and agreed to attempt another settlement on Manhatan. Peter Minuit was appointed inspector-general and governor. In addition he was authorized to buy the island from the Indians. This was a precaution against another country's attempting to create a settlement. The talk of the attempted landing by the French had made the burghers eager to establish as solid a legal basis for Dutch occupation as possible.

As they walked from the company's chambers, their battle won, Governor Minuit congratulated Pieter on his having solved the problem of the sick cattle.

"Save the congratulations until we see what happens," Pieter said. "Just pray that it works."

"Aren't you sure it will?"

"No. I think the cattle's sickness after the first two voyages was a coincidence of bad luck. At least I hope that's what it was."

Minuit was confused. "But those things you said about the ague? And the flux? What about them?"

"I haven't the slightest idea what those words really mean."

"You made it up? All of it?"

"I had to tell them *something*."

The new governor's astonishment gave way to laughter. He slapped Pieter on the back. "You're a scoundrel, but, by God! the sort of scoundrel we need if we're to succeed!"

The voyage was planned, the settlers signed, and the cattle bought and penned near the docks, waiting to be boarded. The ship was to sail from Amsterdam, its course taking it past the Canaries and out into the empty sea, across the vast expanse of ocean to Virginia, then north until it came to the Narrows and the bay beyond. All was being prepared, and the great day was almost upon him when Pieter made an important decision.

He was going to take a wife with him.

The tiny garden behind the Van Venter house was Christiana's private joy. Now that spring had arrived, she spent many hours pruning and planting, arranging the plants and the tufts of earth until they pleased her critical eye. She was puttering about and humming to herself when Pieter de Kuyper entered and closed the back gate behind him. She saw him and smiled. Over the years Pieter had become a dear friend, and she enjoyed listening to his tales of adventure every time he returned from a voyage. There was more, of course. Pieter was a romantic figure, and she had her share of girlish dreams. How nice it would be to live in a lovely home of which she was the mistress and Pieter the master. How wonderful it would be to have supper together every night and tell each other what had happened during the day. She fantasized and dreamed, and it never went any further than that, the custom of the times prohibiting her from taking any direct action. Still, she was of age; soon it would be her duty and pleasure to join her life with a man's. Christiana had secretly determined that young de Kuyper was going to be that man. Fortunately, Pieter had come to the same conclusion on his own. Since he had first met Christiana in his aunt's kitchen, he had watched her come into the first flowering of womanhood. This beautiful creature whom he had once teased and played with, now took his breath away. Every year she grew more entrancing and it became more difficult for him to part from her even to go to his beloved America. Now the time had come when he was no longer willing to separate his two loves. He wanted both of them, together, at the same time.

"I hear you're off again on another voyage," she said, putting the trowel down and unconsciously running her hand along the side of her head to smooth her hair.

Pieter nodded but did not return the smile. His handsome features were unusually serious as he came and stood directly before her. "I've come to ask you an important question." He paused nervously, half hoping she would interrupt. But she did not, and he continued: "Will you go with me to the New World? As my wife?"

Pieter had been expecting almost anything—shock, disbelief, a demurral, laughter, almost anything except the simplicity of the answer he received.

"Yes," she said instantly, and that was all she said.

Pieter took her in his arms and squeezed the breath out of her with his strong arms. "I'll make you happy, and give you everything life has to offer."

Dear, sweet Pieter, she thought, and she knew he meant exactly what he said. But she had a nagging doubt. His stories were full of the wilderness and the wild men—how was she going to cope with them? How could she, who had never been anywhere or done anything, expect to adapt suddenly to a totally foreign way of life? Yes, she had dreamed of being Pieter's wife, but it had been a dream that had taken place here, in Amsterdam, in the heart of civilization. But she felt the strong arms about her, and the beating of his heart against her breast, and her worries vanished. She knew she was doing the right thing.

The problem arose not with Christiana, but with her father.

"Out of the question," the elder Van Venter said as he

stalked back and forth in front of the pair while Uncle Jacob stood quietly to the side. From Uncle Jacob's point of view there was nothing wrong with the proposal. He would see the last of this unwanted nephew, and that was fine. As far as the girl was concerned, Uncle Jacob had scarcely been aware of her existence, although the Van Venters had lived side by side with him for many years. "You've no right to take my daughter away to that savage place," Van Venter continued. "This is her home and this is where she'll stay."

Christiana kept her eyes on the floor. It was not her place to question her father. Pieter, however, had no such scruples.

"But I love her and she loves me. We'll be married and a wife's place is at her husband's side."

"At his side," Van Venter sneered, "at his side—in that pesthole across the water. I've heard what it's like. A filthy, dirty place with savages waiting to take your life. And this is where you want to take my daughter? I ought to throw you out of my house."

No amount of arguing could convince him otherwise. He refused to consider the possibility of Christiana's leaving for the New World. At one point the two men almost came to blows, but Uncle Jacob managed to drag his nephew from the house before the mayhem could get underway.

Christiana went to her room and cried herself to sleep while Pieter got roaring drunk at Minuit's house. Before he passed out, he vowed he would take Christiana with him even if he had to steal her from her own house. It was a foolish, belligerent idea born of alcohol, but he knew he was not beyond it.

The next day he contrived to see Christiana alone while her father was at his forge. He revealed a daring plan: Christiana would secretly pack her belongings and pass them along to him; he would smuggle them aboard the *Sea Mew* in preparation for the sailing day; at the last moment she would slip aboard and they would be far out to sea by the time her father discovered her absence. By that time there would be nothing he could do about it.

Christiana had a terrible struggle with her conscience as she smuggled her things, one by one, out of the house. To disobey her father was an unnatural thing for her to do. She avoided him as much as possible, and when they were together she couldn't look him in the eye.

Everything went as planned until the day of the sailing. The *Sea Mew* was to sail on the noontide. All Christiana's belongings were aboard. The elder Van Venter was at his forge and would not return home until suppertime. Christiana left the house on the pretext she was spending the afternoon with a girl friend. Pieter was waiting at the side of the herring packers' tower, trying to look as innocent as possible.

"Come," he said, as she hurried to his side, "the ship's leaving its berth in twenty minutes."

She stopped and put her feet together and looked away from his eyes. "I can't go through with this, Pieter," she said in the smallest of voices.

"What?"

"I know how much it means to you, and I want to please you, but I can't . . . can't do this to my father. It would be wrong." It was a lame answer and, she admitted to herself, a half-lie as well. Her deepest reason for not wanting to go was her fear of the unknown. When she dreamed of the New World it was always a nightmare filled with monsters and demons determined to drag her off to the pits of Hades. But she despised herself for her weakness and would not admit it to Pieter.

"I could pick you up in my arms and take you aboard the ship by force," he said, glancing over his shoulder and measuring the few hundred feet to the *Sea Mew*'s berth.

"You wouldn't do that," she said. He looked dejected; he knew she spoke the truth. As much as he wanted her to come with him, it would have to be her decision.

He started to speak but could find no words. He looked at her for a long time, and then the strength and optimism seemed to leave his body. His head dropped and his shoulders hunched forward. He turned and started walking slowly back toward his ship.

She watched him go almost half the distance before she realized tears were streaming down her cheeks. Oh God, she thought, am I such a fool that I will let this man go, let him disappear from my life simply because I am a coward? She fought with herself a few seconds longer and then found a strength she had never realized she possessed. She wiped her eyes, threw her head back, and ran toward the wharf. When she caught up with Pieter he was almost at the ship. Without a word being spoken, he held out his hand and the two of them boarded the vessel that was to take them to their new life.

After the *Sea Mew* cleared the landfall and her sails were set, the first order of business was the solemnization of the marriage vows of Christiana Van Venter and Pieter de Kuyper before the ship's captain. Double tots of rum were passed, and settlers and sailors alike drank to the health and happiness of the newly married couple.

Thus had begun the voyage that was now reaching its termination.

The *Sea Mew* dropped its sails, footed its anchor, and rode easily in the tiny harbor off the southern tip of Manhatan. Several longboats came out to meet her, bearing settlers delighted to welcome newcomers who brought supplies and news from Europe. The supplies were placed in the boats and the cattle lowered into the water. As each boat was rowed to shore, it towed a furiously bellowing beast. A man in the stern held a tight grip on the stout rope keeping the animal's head above water as it swam. Upon landing, the cattle were taken to a pen made of crude logs and, on Pieter's instructions, kept from food and water for two days. When the men already in the colony heard the reason for this measure, they cheered, and congratulated Pieter on his discovery. Pieter smiled, but his heart beat faster; his theory was only so much wind. But it might work, he thought to himself, and then he vowed that *it would work*.

The other new settlers came ashore. Pieter took his his wife on a tour of the settlement. It was hardly a sight to encourage the stoutest of men.

The fort—Fort Amsterdam, they called it—consisted of partially completed earthworks with no stone facing and no gates. Though only two years old, the earthwork already was falling apart. Several pigs snorted as they poked their snouts at the base, sniffing and digging for grubs and roots, helping to undermine further the pitiful fort.

From the point of view of Christiana and the other new settlers, there wasn't much to see in New Amsterdam.

But to Pieter's eyes, which had first seen the settlement when it consisted of only four rough huts—huts he had helped build—quite a bit had been accomplished. There were now twenty shelters. The settlers called them houses, but they were hardly more than huts—earth walls covered with a facing of bark or rough-hewn planks, the roofs made of sod or thatch, the floors of dirt, the walls windowless, the interiors empty and gloomy. Several streets had been surveyed and the stakes driven to mark their routes. But other than the chopping down of trees, nothing much had been done to make them proper streets. They were of loose dirt, certain to become impassable during the rainy season; also certain to be torn up and frozen by the snows and ice of winter. The main street of the fledgling New Amsterdam was de Heere Straat—The Broad Way, a wide, generous avenue, thoroughly out of scale with everything else, proclaiming the grandiose dreams of those who dared to carve a civilization out of the wilderness. The Broad Way started at the fort and ran only a quarter of a mile before it narrowed to the Indian path it had been before the coming of the Dutch.

The unmarried men were put up inside the fort, and the newly arrived couples were assigned temporary housing. Pieter and Christiana stood in the middle of the hovel that had been given to them. They stood side by side, not speaking, looking around at the blotched earthwork and the peeling bark that showed how poorly the structure had withstood the ravages of the past winter. The hut was miserable, dirty, with garbage piled in one corner and strong evidence that pigs often spent their evenings there.

Christiana's eyes seemed glazed. She was as neat a person and as good a housekeeper as anyone she knew, yet where did one begin to make such a place livable?

Pieter could no longer stand her silence. "Come," he said, taking her hand and leading her to the door. The floor of dirt was beneath the level of the street, and they had to climb through the front door on all fours.

Pieter kept her hand in his and they walked past the fort, where the old hands were getting drunk to welcome the new settlers and the new arrivals were getting drunk to celebrate the end of the tedious eight-week voyage. They crossed an empty field whose trees had been cut down; it was a wasteland of mud and dirt, rutted by the

wheels of carts and heavy wagons. Even as they walked,
they passed a trader and his horse-drawn cart, which was
piled high with furs to be loaded on the *Sea Mew* for her
return voyage. The wheels dug into the earth, and the
horse groaned and strained. The trader first used his
whip to encourage the horse and then, when he saw
that was useless, applied his shoulder to the side of the
cart.

Pieter and Christiana skirted a roped-off garden where
a few scraggly plants poked their heads through the soil.

They came to the eastern shore of the island and looked
out over the waters of the Hellegat. A long line of stakes
had been driven into the ground, indicating the path of
a new street. Back from the street were other stakes, each
blocking out a large lot that would soon be the site of
a new house.

"This will be Pearl Street," Pieter said. They walked
down the nonexistent street until they came to a set of
stakes indicating a particularly large lot. "Here's the lot
I bought from the company," he said proudly. "This is
where our house will stand."

This was much better. They gazed out at the Hellegat.
As they stood facing east, the sun was setting behind them,
its last rays flowing past, dancing on the waters of the
river, casting a golden haze on the far shores of Long
Island, bathing the world in a gentle beauty. Christiana
sighed, and a smile came to her lips. "When I was in
that hut I was afraid. But now that I see this I know
everything will be all right."

Pieter took her in his arms and kissed her on the lips.
Their bodies felt warm and wonderful to each other. He
took her face and cupped it in his hands. "We'll be happy
here. I promise you that."

"Why is it to be called Pearl Street?" she asked.

He took her hand and led her to the sandy beach along
the shore. When they came to the water's edge, he reached
down and picked up a few of the small, white shells that
covered the riverbank. He held them up in the now-faint
light. They were mottled white; flesh-colored in parts,
and pearly.

She clapped her hands in delight. "A front garden of
pearls! What a lovely place to live!"

The glimpse of the pearly shells made her fall in love

with her new home. She paced off the distance from the stake at the southern edge of their lot to the one at the north. "The front of the house should face in that direction," she said. "We'll be able to look at the river and also get a glimpse of the ships coming across the bay."

She stepped into the place where the house would stand. "Here's the place for the kitchen, with the fireplace over here," she said, pointing things out with her slender fingers, "and some nice comfortable chairs over there." She walked about indicating parts of the house as if she were giving instructions to a group of workmen. Her enthusiasm was contagious.

"Back here will be the garden," Pieter called out from a place two-thirds into the lot. "We'll have trees. And berry bushes. Fruit trees and berry bushes to fill the air with their scents. And it will look as if we'd dyed the earth red with strawberries."

Christiana came toward him, her cheeks flushed and her eyes on fire. "Think of how wonderful it will be for the children! A front yard of pearls and a backyard of berries!"

The thought of children caused Pieter to blush, and he could not speak, but only tighten his grip on her hand.

The darkness came and they returned to the hut beside the fort. They continued to talk about their new home. Christiana decided the house would have many windows and outside each would be a flower box so that when they looked out, their splendid views would be bordered by the most delicate of nature's creations.

They ate a meagre meal on top of a packing crate by the light of a single candle, but thoughts of their beautiful new life canceled out their present surroundings.

The reverie was interrupted when a soldier of the fort's garrison arrived and informed Pieter that Governor Minuit required his presence.

Christiana's happiness and sense of well-being lasted only a few minutes after Pieter left. She looked around the hut; once again it was mean and sordid. She went to the door and looked out. Dark and silent but for sporadic torchlight flares and the occasional sound of men and animals, this land brought little comfort. It was an empty land, wild, hostile; a land of shadows where danger lurked.

Christiana was a gentle person from gentle surroundings. Although she had had a general idea of life in the New World, she had not really been prepared for its ugliness, its emptiness, its *reality*.

But now she realized there would be many times when Pieter would not be at her side and she would be left alone in this strange place.

I will be strong, she thought. *I will stand by myself and not wither before the storms of this wilderness. I will do what I must, because it is the wish of my husband. I will be strong for myself and I will be strong for him.*

A warmth crept back into her body and spirit at the thought of Pieter. He was handsome and kind, strong and loving. He would overcome the perils of this New World, and his love would help her do the same.

She was going to be brave. It would not be easy, but she was going to do it. At the core of this resolve was the knowledge she had no other choice. She *had* to do it.

And with this thought her fear returned.

Minuit's office was a large, comfortable room at one end of the barracks within the fort. Inside, a second door opened into the governor's bedroom. These two rooms comprised the governor's official "palace."

The governor and three other men were in the office when Pieter appeared.

The governor stood by the window, gazing out at the night, surveying his new domain. He seemed pleased that finally, after so many years, his goal of establishing a real colony was beginning.

The other three were a diverse lot.

Keyn Frederijke, a large, florid-faced man of forty, was an engineer known for building some of the finest docks in Amsterdam. He had recently lost his wife, triggering his decision to settle in the New World. The thought of staying in Amsterdam in the same house where he had lived with the woman he had loved depressed him.

Abraham de Witt was a sparse man, wiry and full of spunk. At twenty-five years of age, he was young to have been named Provincial secretary by the company. His main function was to protect its financial interest in the colony, but he had been known to say that the well-being of the colonists was truly his primary job.

The third man was Michael de Pauw, a man Pieter had grown to distrust during the two-month voyage they had spent together. Handsome and arrogant, he had been a reasonably prosperous merchant at home, but who, at thirty, had abandoned it all because he was restless and anxious to see how far the New World would allow a free spirit to go. De Pauw, Pieter felt, played at life as if it was a game; the higher the stakes, the better.

The governor's servant brought a tray with mugs of cold beer. The governor took a mug. "Before we begin, gentlemen, let us toast to the success of our new town."

The others took their mugs.

"To New Amsterdam!" the governor said.

"To New Amsterdam!" the others echoed, and they all raised the mugs to their lips. The frothy amber liquid felt cold and good.

When the men had finished their beer, they sat at a long table that ran down the middle of the room. The governor sat at one end and got down to business: "There's much to be done. A town must be more than a collection of farms. To accomplish the many tasks facing us, I turn to the men in this room."

The four tried to appear unmoved by this praise, but failed, each man pleased to have been singled out in such a manner by the governor.

Minuit placed some papers on the table. "I've taken it upon myself to make some initial assignments. I trust you'll all agree with my judgment."

He turned to the engineer. "Keyn Frederijke, I ask you to repair the fort. Build us a strong defense so that we may sleep nights. I also charge you with the construction of a quay, and proper docks and wharves so ships may tie up to facilitate their loading and unloading."

"Do the docks come before the fort?" Frederijke asked.

"Both at the same time," the governor replied. He looked at the others. "Until we have a proper town all of us will be asked to do the work of at least two men."

The men nodded their acceptance of the burden, and the governor continued. "Local ordinances must be created and a body of laws written. These will be my tasks

in addition to the ones I already have as governor of the
colony and commander of its military forces."

The others again nodded their approval. They liked
the way the new governor was going about his job. Although the charter from the States-General gave the governor the powers of a total autocrat, it would never do to
act in such a manner, Dutch pride and love of indepen-
dence being what they were.

The governor then addressed the provincial secretary.
"De Witt, in addition to watching the coffers of the company, you will erect a warehouse and take charge of issu-
ing stores to the farmers. It's a great deal of extra work,
I'm afraid, but the job needs a man like you."

De Witt accepted the burden without a word. He shook
the stem of his pipe in agreement.

The governor turned to Pieter. "The company has been
good enough to supply us with a complete set of plans for
the building of New Amsterdam." He reached into a canvas sack and drew out a packet of drawings and maps.
"However," he said as he tossed them on the table,
"they're completely useless. Pieter, I want a new survey
of this island and all the lands around it. I also want your
recommendations for a commercial district, a common
area, and a layout for streets."

The prospect of so vast an undertaking awed Pieter.
And it pleased him. He was to have the honor of mapping
the future of the colony. His modesty forced him to enter
a minor protest. "I'll be happy to do this, but I warn you
I have no experience at this sort of thing."

The governor shrugged. "And I've never been the governor of a colony. There is work to be done and we must
learn to do it."

Pieter bowed his head. "I'll do my best," he said quietly, forcing himself to contain his joy.

The governor turned to Michael de Pauw. "We need a
windmill as soon as possible. When the farmers begin
bringing their wheat we must be ready to turn it into
grain. We also need lumber if we're to build houses.
Therefore, I ask you also to build a sawmill. I leave the
sites of these two places up to you."

De Pauw smiled, but inwardly he seethed. The idea of
spending his days on the construction of a windmill and a
sawmill did not appeal to him in the slightest. This was

not the reason he had come to the New World. He had
come for adventure, excitement, and quick and easy
wealth. He had a sudden inspiration. "My dear Governor," he said smoothly, "I'll willingly apply myself to any
task you desire, but for the sake of New Amsterdam I
think each task should be done by the man with the best
qualifications, don't you agree?"

A puzzled look came over the governor's face. "Yes, I
must agree with that." He waited for de Pauw to continue.

"You assign me two important construction jobs, but I
know nothing of such work. I'm a trained surveyor. You
assign our friend, de Kuyper, to the surveying job, but by
his own admission he knows nothing of this task. He is an
ironworker and carpenter. It appears you have given de
Kuyper's natural task to me, and mine to de Kuyper."

Pieter could barely conceal his anger. He wanted with
all his heart to conduct the land survey, and now this
damned de Pauw was trying to take the job away from
him! "I have no doubts that I could successfully survey
our new lands."

"Nor do I," de Pauw said. "But surely these first tasks,
because they're so vital to the colony, should be done by
those best qualified. I hate to think of the farmers having
to wait a year while I fumble my way through the building of a windmill." He was smiling and looking at Pieter,
but his words were for Minuit.

The governor was pensive. "I hadn't known you were
a surveyor as well as a merchant, de Pauw. What do you
say, Pieter? Will you exchange tasks with de Pauw?" And
while Pieter remained dumbstruck, he added, "It's for the
good of the colony."

"Of course," Pieter said in a voice choked with emotion. He looked at de Pauw. The man had a smile of
triumph on his lips.

Pieter left the meeting in a rage. He returned to his
hut and released his anger. "That damned de Pauw!" he
shouted, and Christiana shrank back. Pieter had always
been in control of his temper; this was a side of him she
had never seen.

"The son of a bitch!" Pieter seethed. "I'd be willing to
bet he knows no more about surveying than I do, yet he
pretends to be a master builder! What could I say? Every-

one knows I'm a carpenter and ironworker. They know
I can build their damn mills!"

He held his head in his hands. "The governor gave me
the surveying job and then I let that smooth-talking son
of a bitch de Pauw take it away!" He sat down dejectedly
on a packing crate.

Christiana felt her husband's frustration and loss. Her
own cares and worries were instantly forgotten: Pieter
needed her. She walked around behind the packing crate
and began to stroke the back of his neck, the way she
had done every night aboard the ship. His muscles were
hard, bunched and knotted, and she pressed her fingers
down and moved them in a circular motion, kneading the
flesh, softening it.

When she could feel he was relaxed, she knelt down
and placed her lips against his ear, nipping at it, kissing
it, murmuring in a soft voice. It was a trick she had
learned on the voyage. At night the two of them had lain
together on the tiny shelf that was their bed. There were
eight similar shelves in the cabin—and the people on the
shelves were the lucky ones, because the others slept either in hammocks made of fish netting or on the deck.

The winds of the storms would howl through the rigging and find their way through a hundred cracks and
crevices into the cabin buried in the hull. Christiana
would begin murmuring endearments in Pieter's ear, exciting him. He would lie still for a time and then begin to
stroke her face gently, his fingers starting on the forehead
and following the line of her cheek down to her lips. The
softness of his touch would set her skin to tingling, and
they would both forget about the storm.

The murmuring now was having the effect it always
did. Thoughts of Michael de Pauw were quickly forgotten as Pieter began to want his wife. He took her down
onto his lap, his hands tracing the lines of her body. She
seemed as light and delicate as a bird of the air. He felt
through the thickness of her clothes and his hand
moved over the round hip, marveling at its smoothness
and the miraculous way it flowed into the soft flesh of
her stomach. His hunger grew and he began to kiss her.
Her murmuring became more insistent and their need
for each other built.

There was no bed in the dwelling, no mattress of soft

feathers, only a pile of straw in the corner with a few salt-encrusted blankets thrown on top, but it didn't matter. Without a word they fell onto the pile and their hands moved over each other, touching, loving, desiring, peeling away the clothing that kept their flesh from melding.

Christiana had been raised in the same manner as thousands of other Dutch girls of her time. There had been no talk of sexual matters, only a vague instruction that it was the duty of every wife to submit to her husband and bear his children. The stern Protestantism that ruled their lives dictated that the sex act was not to be looked upon as pleasurable. Our flesh is a penance, said the dominies; it is our burden to carry, our test in the eyes of God. The joining of man and woman is necessary for the continuation of the human race, nothing more.

But from the beginning she knew it was a pleasurable act. It was impossible for her not to enjoy it. The touch of Pieter's hands made her feel hot. When he entered her body she lost all control of herself, wiggling and squirming, pulling him in as far as possible as if she wanted to devour him. Animal noises came from her throat.

The first few times they made love she had been ashamed of her passion, and had cried. Her upbringing told her it was wrong. She wasn't supposed to feel like this. Surely it was the Devil who was urging her on, causing her to act so wantonly.

But as she thought about it, she began to change her mind. She and Pieter had been joined in the eyes of God. If He was allowing this to happen, then He must approve. The sense of shame and wrongdoing left her, and she gave herself to Pieter with abandon.

They took each other on the blankets and straw, and it was as if they were trying to blot out the angers and fears they felt over this new land. *OhmyGod, OhmyGod,* sounded in Christiana's mind, and her ecstasy was so great she felt carried to another world. Her fingernails dug into Pieter's back and drew blood, but she barely heard his cry of pain. The fire in her body built until it could be controlled no longer, and it burst in a climactic violence. Her teeth bit into his shoulder and she clung to his body, afraid that if she let go she would slip down, down into an abyss.

And now it was her turn to bring him to the heights,

to hold him there as long as possible, to keep him teetering between expectation and fruition, to prolong that almost unbearable ecstasy.

And I am yours and you are mine, she thought, and let her hands slide up and down his muscled body, stroking and touching, firing his passion, feeding it, drawing it out, draining him of all thought, of everything except the completion of this singular act.

To be together at this moment. To make this moment last forever. To make this moment the meaning of life.

"Christiana!" he cried in a hoarse voice; and then his head was buried in the straw -beside her and his voice tried to call her name again but came out only as a whimper. And she pulled him closer with a fierceness that seemed impossible in that slender body.

They held each other for a long time, not talking, not thinking. They lay there, in the light of the guttering candle, drenched in their own sweat, their bodies tangled together. When their strength had returned, slowly, ever so slowly, he stretched forth his left hand and took hold of her right, resting above her head. They lay like this for what seemed a long time, finger to finger, breath returning to normal and the shape of the room coming once again into focus.

Finally he found the strength to get up and go over to the pile that represented all their earthly possessions. He rummaged until he found what he was looking for—a bottle of wine they had hoarded all the way across the ocean.

They drank most of it and fell asleep in each other's arms. For this night, at least, there were no bad dreams and no fears and no discontent. For this night, having each other was enough.

The new dawn washed away Pieter's cares of the previous day. He accepted that he was not going to do the survey and threw himself into his other tasks with fervor. The most pressing need was for lumber, so he put the construction of the sawmill before the windmill. He spent the better part of a week scouting for the best location, and after considerable thought he recommended the sawmill be built on Nutten Island.

"But why there?" the governor objected. "Surely it would be more convenient if it were on Manhatan?"

Pieter had thought it out. "Nutten Island is convenient enough. Once Frederijke builds a quay we'll use a flat-topped barge to haul the lumber. Nutten Island has the greatest concentration of trees. It's the best place."

Pieter had other arguments to back his choice. As well as thick groves of pine, Nutten Island had many oak trees soaring sixty and seventy feet into the air—and oak was the wood they wanted most. Also, the sawmill would be a noisy and dirty place, with chips of wood flying and dust swirling in the air. To breathe in such a place a worker would be forced to wear a wet cloth over his mouth and nose. "It would be better for the health of the people if the sawmill was not located in their midst," Pieter said. "After all, by next year we expect to number over three hundred souls."

The governor finally agreed, and construction of the sawmill began on Nutten Island. The first building to go up had many openings in the walls to allow the dust to escape. It seemed flimsy, but Pieter had erected stout posts in the corners to keep it from being torn down during a storm. The precious saws, smeared with grease and covered with heavy canvas to protect them during the ocean voyage, were brought to the island, cleaned, and tested.

On the day the mill began to operate Pieter turned the project over to David Krieberk, the newly appointed foreman. The two of them watched as the first log was brought in by a crude block and tackle. It was placed in a vise. The vise moved forward down the track and the whirling teeth of the saw bit into the wood, spewing dust in the air, screaming until a man thought his eardrums would burst. But the teeth kept biting and slicing through the wood until the length of the log had passed under them. Pieter went to the end of the track and inspected the piece of lumber that had been cut from the log. It was ten inches wide and two inches thick. After it had been planed it would be ready to become part of the side of a house.

The sawmill was in business.

Two months had elapsed since their arrival, and Pieter was being hailed as a hero, because every one of the cattle had survived.

An area a mile to the north of the fort was selected as grazing land, and the cattle were sent there under the protection of two cowherds. There was a large, swampy marshland next to the pasture, and at first the settlers were concerned for the safety of the animals. But none of the cattle ever became mired in the swamp, and they seemed to thrive even when they ate the tall swamp grass.

The governor received many petitions from farmers who wanted a milking cow of their own, but he refused to split the herd until the spring calves had been born. At that time, he said, he would entertain the thought of selling cows to individual farmers. This caused little protest, because the husbandmen had their hands quite full with the many chores of starting a farm from scratch in the hostile wilderness of Manhatan.

The cat waited patiently behind a tuft of wild grass. He was a young tabby, filled with the strength of his new cathood and sure of himself. His eyes did not blink as he watched the feeding sparrows. They perched on the branches of the trees and cocked their heads, peering in all directions. Finally deciding there was no danger, they flew to the ground, walking around on their spindly legs, pecking at the earth for loose seeds. They came closer and closer to the patch of grass, unaware of the predator waiting for them to come within reach of his sharp claws.

Christiana was on her way to the stream with a water bucket. She was nearby when one bird came too close to the tuft of grass and the cat sprang. She saw the bird make a desperate try for safety, but the cat was too quick and his paw slammed the squawking creature to the ground.

Christiana screamed, dropped her bucket and then ran toward the unfolding tragedy. Startled by the woman, the cat remained frozen for a moment and then realized she was out to rob him of his catch. He clamped his jaws about the quivering bird, turned, and started to run away.

"Come back! Come back, you nasty cat!" Christiana shouted as she sped after the fleeing animal.

Several men nearby were digging the cellars for new buildings; they paused and leaned on their shovels, grateful for any amusement that would give them a moment's respite from their labors. The cat sped toward them, and as a lark they hooted and shouted at him, waving their arms and chasing him off in the direction of the fort.

Governor Minuit was coming from the fort, saw what was happening, and became part of the commotion. He waved his arms and, to avoid him, the cat turned back —toward Christiana. The tabby saw no escape except through the open door of a small shed where the workmen stored their tools at night. But the door was the only opening and the cat was trapped inside.

"You naughty animal," Christiana said as she spied the cat trying to hide behind some shovels and picks at the rear of the shed. She advanced and the cat attempted to charge past her. Several shovels clattered to the ground, but Christiana managed to grab the dashing tabby and hold on.

"Wicked beast," she said. "Wicked, wicked beast!"

The cat was quite unwilling to give up his captive. Christiana held him flat on the ground and, after a struggle, managed to pry open his jaws wide enough to allow the bird to drop to the ground, where it fell motionless. She snatched the bird up before the cat could grab it again. It was alive, but it couldn't move. The woman held it gently in both hands and went back outside into the open air.

Governor Minuit was waiting. He saw that Christiana was crying. "Let me have him," he said.

Christiana handed him the bird and then started wiping away her tears.

"He's just scared out of his wits," the governor said. "He'll be all right in a few minutes." He walked over to a tree and carefully placed the bird on a spot where two twigs formed a perch. The bird's eyes were blinking, but he was still too frightened to fly.

The cat had followed Christiana outside, grumbling and glaring at her and greedily eyeing the bird in the tree.

"Scat!" Christiana said and stepped toward him. The cat wisely retreated and then sat to watch the woman and the bird.

"That cat is too big to climb out on that thin branch," the governor said.

"I'm not leaving until he flies away," she said. "I'll stay all day if I must."

She was so determined it was difficult for Minuit to suppress a smile. "Just a few minutes should do it," he said.

"We'll see," Christiana said, giving the cat another dirty look.

They waited about five minutes. The governor reached up and touched one of the bird's wings. The bird instantly flapped both wings and flew away.

The governor accompanied Christiana as she went to retrieve her water bucket. "You shouldn't let it upset you so much. Cats have been chasing birds for thousands of years."

"I hate to see one creature hurt another," she said. "Why should there be such cruelty?"

"It is cruel," the governor admitted. "But we must learn to accept life on its own terms."

She said nothing, but it was obvious from the set of her jaw that she wasn't convinced. She picked up the bucket and continued on her way to the spring. As the governor watched her go, he worried about her. She was such a sensitive soul, and New Amsterdam was not the most gentle of places. We are all birds and cats in this world, he thought, and there is always some other creature to fear. He hoped that Christiana de Kuyper would develop a certain toughness. If she couldn't, things would not go well for her.

The cat watched them go through narrow slits of eyes. He casually turned his head and licked the fur on his shoulder. Then he walked away and, just in case anyone was looking at him, assumed an attitude that clearly indicated he had won.

The great day of the purchase of the island arrived. The sachem of the Canarsie Indians had agreed to meet with Governor Minuit about the sale. The governor, dressed in his finest coat and accompanied by a dozen of the leading citizens, including Pieter, met the Indians beneath a large tree on top of a knoll that afforded a fine view of the land they were buying. To the south were the fort and the buildings of the settlement; to the east the waters of the Hellegat, to the west the North River and the distant palisades of its far shore; and to the north the island extended as far as the eye could see, the green turning to gray until it was lost in the haze.

The governor opened several chests of trinkets, beads,

rolls of cloth, bars of lead, tins of candies, and coats made of coarse duffel.

The great assortment pleased the Indians, and the sachem solemnly made his mark on the various papers given him by Minuit. The governor then signed each document with a flourish. He and the sachem spoke to each other in a combination of sign language and certain words that had become a lingua franca between the races.

A hatchet was buried; a peace pipe smoked. Finally the sachem and his people gathered up their new possessions and disappeared silently into the woods.

The irony of this transaction was that Manhatan had not really belonged to the Canarsie Indians. The island was the ancestral home of other tribes as well as theirs, and all could lay claim to various sections of the land. At this time, however, the Indians did not attach much value to pieces of paper, nor did they understand the nature and intentions of the white man. When the Dutch said they "owned" Manhatan, it meant as much to the Canarsies as if Senadondo, chief of the Wickquaskeeks, had said he "owned" it. It was a concept that had no meaning to them. As far as they were concerned, Manhatan was a big island and there had always been enough of it for everyone. Why should the coming of the white man make any difference?

"And now the island is truly ours," the governor said to Pieter as they walked back to the settlement.

"I don't see how a piece of paper makes much of a difference," Pieter said. "The Indians accept that we're here. They need no paper to prove it."

"The paper has nothing to do with the Indians," the governor said. "France, Spain, Portugal, the damned English—they're the ones I worry about. Any of them could get the idea of settling here. But now that we have a legal bill of sale it makes it more difficult for them." He touched the papers under his arm and smiled. "And quite a bargain it was."

"What was the value of the goods you gave the Indians?"

"About sixty guilders. Think of it! Twenty-five thousand acres of rich land for sixty guilders! That should please the company."

Pieter shook his head. "Nothing will please the company. Give them one hundred percent profit this year and they'll want two hundred the next."

Minuit was glum, but only for a moment. "You're quite right, of course, but that doesn't change the fact that this is a great day for New Amsterdam."

Pieter became thoughtful. "The burghers back home really don't understand what we're doing here. They look at the New World as a place of quick riches. But it's much more than that. A new way of life exists here. Look around at the vastness of the land, the wide waters. Smell the freshness and cleanness of the air. Look at the emptiness of the place." He shook his head in sadness. "Men who spend their days in musty countinghouses can never understand what this land is all about."

The governor looked at Pieter, and his admiration, always great, increased even more. Pieter de Kuyper was becoming the first of a new breed of man.

The man of the New World.

Christiana had managed to make the hut livable. A sturdy bed stood in one corner of the single room. It was covered by a soft down quilt, brought from home and one of the few in New Amsterdam, a treasure that was the envy of the other women. Pieter had contrived to get an old stove, and on this primitive appliance she produced delicious meals.

She had arranged cloth curtains along the top frame of the door, and there was a cheeriness to the place even when the floor was flooded with an inch or two of rainwater. She hung on the dappled and peeling walls the pictures given to her by her mother, and when she looked in their direction, she pretended only the pictures existed and not the walls.

It was midday, and she was at the small table preparing a dinner of hare and vegetables when she felt faint. She almost fell against the table, but saved herself by placing a hand against the wall. She felt light-headed and sick to her stomach.

A sudden panic overcame her. Was she the victim of some unknown New World disease?

She managed to make her way to the door, using the wall as a support. She stopped at the opening and took deep breaths of the fresh air. After a few moments she gathered all her strength and managed to climb over the step and reach the outside. She stood with her back to the wall of the hut, her breath coming in short, difficult gasps, her face ashen.

Geertie Smit, the wife of a ship's chandler, a middle-aged woman who had left grown children behind in Holland to follow her husband, was walking past the hut. She saw the stricken girl.

"Child, child! What's the matter!"

Christiana shook her head. It was difficult enough to breathe, much less talk. Geertie put her arm around the girl, then reached down and felt her hand. It was cold and clammy. She touched Christiana's forehead. It too was cold and covered with great beads of perspiration.

The older woman held the girl for several minutes, and gradually the clamminess passed and her complexion returned to its natural color.

As Christiana regained her composure, she found her voice. "I don't . . . don't know what could . . . I've never had . . ."

On a sudden impulse Geertie Smit's hand reached down and felt the girl's belly. It was firm, but the beginnings of a bulge could be felt through the several layers of petticoats. Geertie took her hand away and smiled. "There's nothing wrong with you, child, nothing at all. You've been blessed by God."

Christiana did not understand for a moment, and then, as comprehension came, her head spun and her eyes widened.

"Yes, yes, dearie," Geertie said. "You're with child."

The idea became crystal clear, and Christiana's mind filled with happiness and wonder.

When Pieter returned home that evening, she told him the news. He picked her up and whirled her around until a realization struck him. He stopped and put her gently back on her feet.

"There must be no more of that," he said. "After all, we can't take any chances on hurting my son."

Christiana wanted to ask him how he knew it was going to be a son, but she kept the question to herself. Pieter's joy was so great she wanted nothing to spoil it.

She knew Pieter would love the child as much if it were a girl.

"Our son will be born in the New World," he said proudly. "One of the first."

Christiana decided her baby was to have the finest cradle in the New World. It was to be constructed from materials that had been brought from Europe.

"I'll build it," Pieter offered, but she would have none of this. The cradle was to be made only by an accomplished joiner, a master craftsman in the art of carving.

She inquired about and soon learned that there was only one such man living in New Amsterdam. His name was Hendrick de Thuyn, and he had been sent over by the West India Company as a shipwright. A more talented woodworker could not be found in America, she heard, and probably few in Europe were any better. Hendrick de Thuyn had been hired by noble families in several European countries and, it was rumored, had carved a royal chair for a reigning monarch. This was all Christiana needed to know, and she proceeded to the ramshackle building next to the fort where de Thuyn lived and worked.

Hendrick de Thuyn was everything people said of him, and more. He was one of the meanest, most irascible men God had put on this earth; his consumption of spirits was monumental even by the standards of the hard-drinking settlers. He worked when he wanted, and drank when he pleased—which, unfortunately for his employers, was most of the time. He had a long-term contract with the company, and after the burghers had despaired of him, they sent him off to the New World in the mistaken belief that if he was out of their sight the dent he made in their coffers would not seem so painful.

"Don't waste your time with that one," Geertie Smit advised.

"Hendrick de Thuyn?" Pieter said in surprise. "Like visiting a lion in his den." He shook his head when she stubbornly refused to listen.

In this instance they all underestimated Christiana. The cradle wasn't simply a cradle to her. It was a vital symbol of civilization. It was, to her mind, something the child *must* have. If de Thuyn turned out to be a lion, very well, but he was going to have to deal with a tigress.

Christiana appeared before this bleary-eyed man and told him of her desire for the most exquisite cradle in the colony. It was to be special, she said, because her child would be special, one of the first born in America and therefore deserving of unusual recognition. De Thuyn listened quietly, sipping now and then from a bottle at his side, waiting for this babbling woman to be done.

"A cradle you want, eh?" he said when Christiana finally stopped. "I don't build cradles; get out."

He turned his back and went over to the long shelf on which he slept. He sat down and was about to lean back to enjoy a nap when he realized the woman had followed him and was standing next to the shelf. "I told you to get out!" he shouted in his crankiest voice, a voice that had caused even lords and barons to back down. Being known as a genius at one's craft had its compensations.

"I don't intend to get out and would you please lower your voice," she said quite reasonably.

Hendrick de Thuyn was not accustomed to argument, and he blinked his eyes like an owl. He looked closely at this girl who acted more like a queen or empress than like one of these grubby women who had followed their men to live in the primitive conditions of New Amsterdam.

"What do you want of me?" he asked, hoping to buy some time to allow his sodden brain to think.

"I told you," she said.

"Why should I build a cradle for your brat?"

"Everyone says you're the best joiner in New Amsterdam."

"Carver! Not a damned joiner! Those sots are good enough to slice a slab of wood, but to be a true carver . . . ah . . ."

"Very well; carver. You are the best, aren't you?"

"Of course I am!"

"Very well," she said, smiling sweetly, "that's why I've come to you. Because you're the best."

The praise mollified him somewhat, and he put the bottle to his lips and took a long swallow. "But I'm still not building any cradle," he said.

Christiana eyed him closely and decided to gamble. De Thuyn was obviously a difficult man, and her hopes for a beautiful cradle were dwindling. The only way to get him to undertake the task would be to trick him into it. She

started toward the door, and sighed. "And I had so wished
the rumors were untrue."

"What rumors, dammit! Tell me what they're accusing
me of now!"

At the door, she turned and spoke sadly, but matter-of-
factly: "Why Mister de Thuyn, don't you know that
everyone says your great days are behind you? That's
why the company sent you here? To get rid of you? To
make way for someone else who could do a proper job."

She stepped through the narrow doorway and walked
three or four feet, listening intently for activity from inside the building. She was rewarded by the sounds of
cursing and the heavy thuds of a man running unsteadily
across the room.

He arrived at the doorway and braced himself against
the jamb, panting from exertion. "You, wait a minute,
you!"

"Yes, Mister de Thuyn?"

"Them's lies you heard. Nobody got rid of me. And
there's nobody can do what I can do."

Christiana smiled again. "Of course, Mister de Thuyn,
whatever you say." She kept walking and held her breath,
hoping her bluff would hold.

"Wait a minute, dammit," de Thuyn said in a thick,
whiskey voice. "I'll build your cradle, I'll show them
who's spreading rumors about me."

She turned and looked at him, carefully suppressing
any semblance of triumph. "Talking about building a cradle is one thing, doing it another."

"Come back here," he said gruffly. "Let's see what you
want."

Christiana managed to retain her skeptical look as they
discussed the design of the cradle. As he talked, de Thuyn
kept glancing at her for approval. When none was forth-
coming, he kept changing his design, modifying it, making
it more pure and beautifully simple. He finally dropped
the sketch pen and smoothed his hand over the rough
tracings. "Take my word for it, it'll be the most beautifully carved piece of wood you've ever seen."

"I'm sure it will, Mister de Thuyn," Christiana said
carefully. "How soon do you think it will be finished?"

De Thuyn was about to take a drink while debating
with himself about the length of the job when he suddenly

realized she was staring pointedly at the bottle in his hand.

"Listen, my drinking has nothing to do with my leaving Europe," he said with a show of bravado.

She smiled and said nothing.

"I guess I could be finished in, oh, maybe three months."

"Three?"

"Well, I've got other work to do, you know, the company has some claim on my time."

She looked again at the bottle in his hand. He put it down on the table. "All right, two months. In two months you'll have your damned cradle. And now if it's all right with you, might I have a drink on it, to seal our bargain so to speak?"

She nodded, and he took a deep, long draft. He sighed and placed the bottle back on the table. "Two months and it'll be yours."

"And the cost?"

He looked at her as if trying to measure how high he could go without scaring her off. "This sort of job is expensive, and a bargain at whatever the price. You know that, don't you?"

"Yes," she said. "And whatever it is you ask, we'll pay. My husband and I don't have much money, so we may not be able to pay it all right away. But we'll pay what you ask."

"You're Pieter de Kuyper's wife, aren't you?"

"Yes."

"A good man," de Thuyn said. "I'll let you know about the price when she's finished."

Christiana left, but once a week thereafter she stopped by the wood-carver's house. She never tried to hurry him. Several times she found him drunk; and Hendrick de Thuyn wouldn't admit it, but he hated to have her see him when he was in his cups. The unspoken reproach and the hurt look in her eyes were too much for him. He stopped drinking and finished the cradle in six weeks. It was a work of art. The fittings were precise, and the little angels carved on the side were designs of simplicity and beauty.

"And the cost?" she asked.

"Nothing."

"That wouldn't be fair."

He looked at the cradle and patted it with his hand. "You've already paid me." She looked quizzically at him, and he explained. "I know you tricked me into doing this. I know you played up to my vanity. And it worked. The truth is I hadn't tried anything so good in quite a while and wasn't sure I could still do it. Those rumors you heard about me—"

"I made that up."

"Well, whatever it was, it worked. And I thank you for it. So the cost is nothing. As I said, I've already been paid."

Pieter admired the cradle when it was brought to the house, but he couldn't understand why his wife had so deeply wanted such a thing. Since his life was filled with work, sixteen to twenty hours a day, he promptly dismissed the matter from his mind.

Not Christiana. She would look at the cradle many times each day and know exactly why she had wanted it. Everything else in her life was stark and raw, as rough and wild as this country itself. It pleased her to have a thing of beauty, an emblem of civilization, near at hand, especially since it was destined to belong to her child. At least the baby would have a touch of refinement for the first months of his life. After that he would begin noticing the world beyond his cradle, but in the very beginning he would not know of the harsh conditions that defined his life.

Christiana wanted nothing less for her firstborn.

The settlers were worried by an ugly event that occurred during the summer.

Michael de Pauw's surveying party had a skirmish with a band of Indians. The natives had tried to steal one of the surveyor's longboats, and in the ensuing fight a white man was struck in the shoulder with an arrow and two Indians were killed by musket fire.

There were rumors of war with the Indians and the two hitherto peaceful groups knew the first hostility between them. For a week or so, the settlers went about armed and the number of Indians bringing furs to trade dwindled.

Affairs returned to normal when it was learned the

Indian raiders belonged to a tribe dwelling on the other side of the North River. The local Indians resented their presence more than that of the white men. When this became known, the governor sent presents to the local chiefs, and the chiefs in turn ordered that normal trading activities be resumed. Once again furs and pelts began to pour into New Amsterdam.

It was over, but a dangerous precedent had been set, and the naïveté that equated New Amsterdam with the Garden of Eden was replaced by a new constraint.

It would never again be the same.

In the late fall, something happened that would change the course of Christiana's life.

It was unseasonably hot and muggy, and her clothes stuck to her skin. As she walked to Geertie Smit's house at the side of the fort, she carefully avoided stepping in the muddy puddles left by the previous night's rain. She was taking no chances with the growing infant in her body. The safety of that new life was constantly on her mind.

There was one other thing always on her mind: Indians. They were evil and treacherous; she was convinced of it. She had been terrified from the first time she had seen one—a tall, vicious-looking brave with a tomahawk hanging from his deerhide belt. He had watched her with an unblinking stare, and she had feared for her life.

Everyone, including Pieter, had scoffed at her fears. But the recent troubles proved those fears had not been groundless. The red men were murderers, all of them, she thought, and the settlers were fools to let them wander freely about the town.

She was passing a stand of oak trees that grew a short distance from the Smit house. As she admired their stately strength, she heard a thump on the path behind her. She turned and froze in fear when she saw that an Indian had jumped out from behind the trees. He was hunched over, his arms dangling at his sides, his eyes greedily focused on her. He started to come forward, but stumbled and almost fell to the ground. He seemed very drunk.

She looked around wildly, but there was no one else in sight. She backed up a few steps and then turned and fled toward the Smit house. The Indian gave a whoop and started after her.

No longer was Christiana concerned with taking dainty steps or worrying about muddy puddles. She ran as fast as possible toward the door of the Smit house. The lower part was closed, but the upper half, in typical Dutch fashion, was open to let in fresh air. She turned the latch handle, moved inside, shut the bottom half, and was about to do the same with the top when the Indian's hand smashed into it and forced it back. Christiana didn't have the strength to stop him. She stumbled backward as the brave vaulted over the closed part of the door and drunkenly crashed to the floor at her feet.

For a moment the man held his head and groaned. If Christiana had had her wits about her, she would have fled past him and been back outside before he knew what had happened. But she was so terrified she could do nothing but shrink away from the man, trapping herself in the room.

The Indian gave his head a final shake and looked again at the frightened woman. He got to his feet and stumbled, but managed to grab the back of a rickety chair. Then he started toward her, a leering grin on his face.

Christiana moved back until she was stopped by the wall. Now there was no more room for retreat, no chance for escape. She watched dazedly as the leering face came closer and closer, the eyes riveted on her. *They don't blink*, she thought, *they really don't blink*. And then he was next to her, towering over her, looking straight down into her whitened face, his fetid, alcoholic breath enveloping her, the stink of the bear oil on his hair making her sick to her stomach.

She waited for the blow from the flashing tomahawk, the blow that would put her out of her misery. Death was here in the room with her, and she would be killed because a settler had given an Indian whiskey for his furs . . . and the child in her belly would die even before he was born and what difference did it make because the Indians were going to kill all the white people, all of them were going to die. . . .

And then she realized the Indian wasn't planning on

killing her. One hand was forcing her to the floor while the other was trying to tear the dress from her body.

"No . . . please . . . the baby, the baby," she protested even as the Indian tore away her dress, revealing her breasts and then her naked legs and buttocks. In the style of the day, Christiana wore nothing under the heavy folds of her outer clothing. She tried to push him back, but he was far too strong and she felt her legs being pushed apart as he lowered his body between them. She started to cry, but the Indian paid no attention. He dropped his breechcloth and his manhood was exposed. He took it in one hand and guided it toward her. The man was quite drunk and he wasn't very erect, but he was determined to get into the woman's body.

"You'll kill my baby," she said in a strong voice that startled her. She had her voice! *Scream, you idiot, scream!* she told herself.

She got out several loud shrieks, but then the Indian covered her face with the palm of his huge hand, cutting off both her screams and her air supply. He went back to his struggle to enter her. His flaccid member kept bending and refused to go in. Christiana was close to fainting from lack of air, and her eyes rolled upward in their sockets, exposing the whites. The brave shifted his hand on her face, giving her the opportunity to close her teeth around one of his fingers. She bit down as hard as she could.

He screamed and snatched his hand away from her face. Christiana began screeching again as he sucked his bloody finger and paid no attention to her.

She got a good look at the man's dark penis, and she was frightened enough at the sight to conjure up strength from some inner well. She started to crawl away, but the Indian caught her movement and stopped worrying about his finger. Grabbing her, he dropped his full weight back on top of her, cuffed her on the side of the head, and returned to his grotesque attempt to enter her.

Crack!

The Indian howled, and Christiana felt his body press harder on top of her.

Crack!

Geertie Smit stood over the red man with a heavy stick. He put his hands over his head to protect himself, and she began whacking his knuckles. "Get out! Get out!" the stout Dutchwoman was shouting, and the Indian went as fast as he could, lurching and stumbling but moving as if he had stepped on a wasp's nest. Geertie chased him out the door, and the Indian didn't look back; he rapidly weaved his way down the road.

Geertie turned to Christiana. "Dear, dear child . . ."

"My baby!" Christiana yelled in a shrill voice. "He killed my baby!"

"Hush! Nothing's happened to your baby," Geertie said as she went to the girl's side.

"He was trying to . . . trying to . . ." Christiana said between sobs.

Geertie helped her to a chair and put a blanket over her lap to cover her nakedness. She poured brandy into a cup and brought it to Christiana's mouth. "What's happened has happened. The best thing is to forget it."

"Forget it?" Christiana said after taking a sip of the fiery liquid. "The savages are going to rape and kill us all and you want me to forget it!" Her sobbing redoubled.

Geertie tried to reason with her and comfort her. "He was drunk," she said. "That's what's causing all the trouble. Maybe now we'll learn not to sell them whiskey. You just rest now and put it out of your mind."

"They want to kill my baby!" Christiana said, and there was a wild look in her eyes. "Don't you understand, they want to kill my baby."

It took a long time, but Geertie managed to calm her. She gave Christiana a dress to wear and took her home. When Pieter heard what had happened, he threatened to kill the Indian. But no one knew the identity of the man, and a drunken Indian was no oddity.

After Geertie left, Pieter spent hours talking to Christiana, trying to reassure her, trying to convince her it had been a freak occurrence, that it could never happen again. He stroked the smooth skin of the belly holding their child and gently kissed each of her fingers.

She finally told him she understood what he was saying, but not for a moment did she believe her own words, or his. There was a new hollowness in her eyes, and a new nervousness to her movements. And there was a new, deep-rooted fear that could not be appeased by gentle fondling or reassuring words. It was a fear that would

make her jump at every sudden noise and gasp whenever
she heard the door opened or shut.

When, at the end of that first summer, *The Arms of
Amsterdam* had set sail ·for Holland as the first ship to
depart from the legally established colony, its cargo consisted of:

    7,246 beaver skins
    853 1/2 otter skins
    81 mink skins
    36 wild cat skins
    34 rat skins
    many logs of oak and nut wood

It was not the wealth of the Indies, nor would it bring
riotous joy to the burghers. But it was a substantial cargo
that would yield a good profit.

New Amsterdam was beginning to show it could be a
good investment if given enough time.

After completing the sawmill, Pieter turned his attention to the construction of a windmill. For the site of the
mill he chose Battery Place, a point west of the fort and
slightly to the north. It was an ideal location. The farmers
found it convenient. It was close to the ships anchored in
the harbor. It stood protected by the fort. And, most
important of all, this site made it possible for the four
large sails of the mill to catch every breath of wind that
came down the North River, or up from the bay.

The building of the windmill took longer and was
more involved than that of the sawmill. For two months
Pieter and his men worked sixteen hours a day, taking
time out only to eat and sleep. They worked harder as the
air turned colder, and there were many days when their
breath came out in great steam clouds.

Finally the job was almost finished. The men were in-
stalling the main shaft, which would be turned by the wind
vanes. It then would turn the vertical shaft that would
turn the millstone. The main shaft had been hewn from
the trunk of an oak. It was twenty-two feet long and
weighed several thousand pounds. To install it, a team of
stout horses pulled on thick ropes attached to a pulley

that was fastened to the main beam, which spanned the diameter of the mill beneath the roof.

Pieter stood on a small rafter above the main beam and called his instructions down to the men working the horses. Other men held guide-ropes in their hands, attached at either end of the shaft. When the team of horses lifted the shaft, the men with the guide-ropes would swing it into place.

Claes Vincent stood on the main beam with a guide rope in his hand. His task was to feed the shaft through the opening at the front of the mill. It was a tricky job, because the oak shaft was only slightly smaller than the opening and the movement had to be precise. It was also important to feed exactly four feet of shaft through the opening, since this was the length needed for the attachment of the large, oblique sails that would catch the wind and drive the shaft.

Everything was going according to plan when one of the back pulleys pulled loose from the beam. The weight of the shaft shifted and its thousands of pounds lifted at the front in a short, vicious arc.

Claes Vincent had knelt down on the beam, and his hand was beneath the wooden support; he had no time to withdraw it. There was a solid *crunch* as the shaft smashed into his hand, crushing it against the bottom of the beam. The shaft began its swing in the other direction, and it was then that Vincent found his voice and screamed. He brought up his hand and stared in disbelief at the mass of pulped, bleeding flesh. His face went white and he began to lose consciousness.

Claes Vincent would almost certainly have fallen to the ground and been killed had it not been for Pieter. Without a moment's hesitation he leaped from the rafter to the main beam six feet below. He teetered for a moment, and the men looking up gasped, thinking he was about to plummet to the earth. But Pieter managed to balance himself and, in almost the same action, grab hold of Vincent's coat. The other man blacked out and Pieter was left with the dead weight in his hand. He crouched down on the beam and realized the moving shaft was a threat to himself and the unconscious man. It would have to be set in place before he could move to safety.

"Hold the shaft steady!" he cried out, and the men below dug their heels into the dirt and strained until the swinging shaft stopped its violent rocking, slowed, and finally became still. Pieter pulled the rope at the head of the shaft until it snapped taut.

"Move it forward!" he commanded, and once again the team of horses tugged on their ropes and the shaft moved slowly toward the opening at the front of the mill. "Stop!" Pieter cried. "Now raise the back of the shaft!"

The men worked the pulleys until the shaft was again on a line with the opening. They slowly raised the back until it was higher than the front. Now they guided it over until it was above the slot at the back of the main beam. Pieter lowered his hand and the men slowly dropped the back of the shaft until it rested in place in the slot.

"Forward . . . slowly . . . slowly . . ." Pieter said, and the men moved the shaft forward an inch at a time. Then Pieter used the guide-rope to fit the shaft through the groove of the opening.

When the shaft was through, Pieter raised his hand. The shaft could be fitted in its proper position later. For the moment it was secure enough.

Several men scampered up the rickety ladders. They fastened ropes about the unconscious Claes Vincent and lowered him to the ground.

Pieter climbed down the ladder, and only when he had reached the ground did he realize that the muscles in his arms and shoulders were knots of pain.

His left hand had struck the main beam when he had jumped to save Vincent. It was bleeding and prickled with splinters. It was the first he was aware of it. A man bound the bleeding hand with a piece of cloth, and Pieter grimaced with pain as the bandage drove several of the splinters deeper into his flesh.

"Tomorrow we install the vertical shaft and the millstone," he said. "The next day we install the sails and then the job is finished." He walked away and went to his hut by the fort.

Christiana fretted and fussed as she pulled the splinters from his hand. She scolded him for being careless. He didn't tell her how he had gotten the splinters, or that he had saved another man's life.

The next day he went to see Claes Vincent at the fort's crude infirmary. There was no proper doctor in the col-

ony, and no one with enough skill to repair a smashed
hand. They could do only what their limited knowledge
permitted. They had amputated Vincent's hand at the
wrist, cauterized the stump and bandaged it. Despite the
ordeal, Vincent managed to smile when he saw his visitor.

"I understand you saved my life."

"You would have done the same for me."

"Yes, but not so smartly. They tell me you moved as
quick as a cat. Thanks. If you ever need a favor, anything, anything at all, Claes Vincent's your man."

They talked for almost an hour, and when Pieter left,
he knew he had a friend for life.

The mill was finished and the first grain made into
flour. The governor came and made a speech. He
awarded Pieter a five-percent share in the profits of the
mill for five years. Pieter immediately gave half of this to
be divided among the men who had worked for him on
the project.

The governor also offered Claes Vincent a permanent
job at the mill. He was to be in charge of the weighing sta-
tion, a job which a man with only one hand could do as
well as any other. Vincent gratefully accepted, and while
it did not repay him completely for his misfortune, it assured him of a decent livelihood.

Pieter now turned his full attention to the house on
Pearl Street. The governor had ordered the soldiers to construct the frame while Pieter was working on the mill, so
he did not have to begin from scratch. A pile of planks
from Nutten Island's sawmill had been stacked next to
the frame, and Pieter began to use these to erect the walls.
Because Christiana was pregnant, he drove himself even
harder than when he had been building the windmill. He
worked in the frigid November air until his hands would
almost freeze. He drove himself as if there were a devil
at his heels. He did not want his first child to be born in a
miserable hut; but, perhaps, it was already too late to
get the house ready for occupation before the first snows
fell.

Claes Vincent, the stump of his arm healing well,
stopped by the de Kuyper hut to pay his respects. Pieter
was working on the house by the river, and Christiana

told Vincent how her husband was driving himself. "He'll either get the house built, or he'll kill himself," she said.

An hour later Pieter was on top of the house, laying part of the roof, when a dozen men led by Claes Vincent arrived.

"Hello, Pieter."

"Hello, Claes. What can I do for you?"

"Can you use some men to help with the house?"

It took a few seconds for Pieter to understand. His mind was almost as exhausted as his body. Then he grinned. "Make yourselves at home."

The men went to work. Two saws began to cut through wood. A half-dozen hammers began banging away. Other men took on the task of windows and doors. The construction site on Pearl Street looked like a beehive at swarming time.

Pieter came down from the roof and stood beside Claes Vincent. "Thank you."

Vincent shook his head. "I told you I was your man. Hell, it isn't even a bother for these fellows. With winter here they don't have that much to do."

Pieter knew this was far from the truth, but he let it pass. Most of the men, he noticed, had worked with him on the windmill.

It took them only four days to complete the house, the last two as the first powdery snows of the season drifted to the ground, hushing the sounds of hammer and saw, creating a fairyland of white.

Pieter and Christiana moved into the house. The snows were heavy that winter, and Pieter worked away on the interior while Christiana's belly continued to swell. Her time finally came, at the beginning of March. As her contractions came closer and closer together, Geertie Smit and Tryntje Vincent took over the household.

"Just keep boiling more water," Geertie said to Pieter, mostly to give him something to do and keep him from getting underfoot.

Pieter found himself drawn to his wife's side the way a piece of iron is attracted to a magnet. "Are you all right?" he would ask in a voice barely above a whisper.

"It hurts," Christiana admitted, but she forced a brave smile anyway. She looked, to Pieter's eyes, so helpless as she lay on the heavy bed he had made.

"Now you get out of here," Geertie said, grabbing his arm and pushing him toward the door. "We'll handle things in here."

With Pieter gone, the two women approached the bed in a businesslike fashion.

"Now we'll have to prop your legs up," Geertie said as she began to uncover the girl.

"An infant needs help to enter the world," Tryntje said, smiling. She reached out and touched the naked skin of Christiana's belly.

The two older women exchanged glances as another spasm gripped the girl. She gritted her teeth but could not hold back the shriek of pain. Geertie nodded, and she and Tryntje began to get Christiana into a more comfortable position as her labor began.

Pieter sat by the stove, watching the water boil itself away, feeling useless and unneeded. His hands trembled, and he would jump in his chair every time Christiana cried out. Then came a screech so anguished and drawn-out that he could sit no more. He ran to the bedroom, threw open the door and was immediately confronted with an angry Geertie Smit.

"Get out! Get out! Everything's going as it should!"

"Christiana needs me!"

Christiana cried out again, and Pieter would have rushed to her side except Geertie grabbed his arm. "She needs *me*. And she can't have me if I'm to stand here and argue with you."

Pieter surrendered.

"I've delivered scores of babies," Geertie said reassuringly. "So has Tryntje."

"But she's in pain," Pieter said in a feeble voice.

"There's always pain," Geertie said sharply. "It's the price women pay to God for the miracle of birth."

She closed the door in his face. He paced back and forth through the house, working himself into a fearful state as he listened to the noises and moans coming from the bedroom. Finally, there was a long period of silence— and then the sound of a baby's cry.

He was at the door when Geertie opened it. "You can come in now," she said, all smiles.

Pieter walked slowly into the darkened room. He went to the bed and looked down at the now-serene face of his wife. At her side, wrapped in a soft, warm blanket, was a new member of the de Kuyper family.

Pieter looked in wonder at the infant. He looked back at Christiana.

"You have a son," she said in a whispery voice.

Pieter slipped down on his knees, and tears came to his eyes as he looked upon the faces of his wife and son. "A son . . ." he finally murmured. "Christiana . . . it was you I was worried about . . . you—"

"I'm all right. And you have a son," she said again and covered Pieter's hand with hers.

"And a fine, healthy son he is," Tryntje announced from the far side of the room.

"Shall we name him after my own father? Adam?" Pieter asked.

Christiana slowly shook her head. "He'll be named after you, Pieter. Young Pieter. No other name would be right."

"Young Pieter," he said almost inaudibly.

Christiana smiled. "Young Pieter. And he'll be a gentleman," she said softly. And then her eyelids closed and she drifted off to sleep.

A few hours later the governor called to greet the infant citizen. The amenities over, Minuit and Pieter sat by the fire in the kitchen, drinking mugs of the delicious coffee brought the past summer by a Dutch ship that had come from Brazil.

"Have you made any plans for the spring?" the governor asked casually.

"Yes. I want to build a forge on a scale not yet seen in the New World. A great ironworks equal to anything in Europe. Then we'd no longer be dependent on their whims, but could create what we need for ourselves."

"Yes, we could use a forge like that," the governor said in a way that told Pieter that was not what he wanted to hear.

"I take it you have something else in mind?"

"Yes."

"Well, what is it?"

"Road construction. We need streets if people are to get around."

"I thought that was de Pauw's job," Pieter said, unable to keep the resentment out of his voice.

"Surveying is one thing, building another. We need roads, Pieter. We need you. Will you do it?"

Pieter looked out the window at the falling snow. Each flake seemed another weight falling on his back. Was he so invaluable that he must continue to work for the colony and not be allowed to work for himself? But he could find no answer that satisfied him.

"Yes," he said.

And the matter was settled.

Pieter got little sleep that night. He stayed by the fire in the keeping room, a large room that served as kitchen, pantry, dining room, and general gathering place. He jumped every time he heard a sound from the bedroom. From time to time he would peek in on his wife and newborn son. Christiana was usually asleep, but once he found himself peering into her open eyes.

"I love you," he said, and then he looked at the infant. "And our wonderful son."

"Don't wake him," Christiana warned softly.

"He'll have the best this world has to offer," Pieter vowed in a husky whisper.

"I hope so," she said, and then added, as if it were something she'd just remembered, "even here in America."

Pieter looked sharply at her, but this was no time for a discussion. He went back to the keeping room and finally drifted off to sleep.

A few hours later, at dawn's light, a hungry Young Pieter de Kuyper cried a greeting to his first full day in this world.

Winter passed. The frigid polar winds that cut through clothing and skin to the bone, the iron frosts, the frozen lakes and the glacial streams, all softened before the warm smile of spring. New life abounded. It could be seen in the green of the forest, the colored buds sprung from stillness, the unsteady flight of tiny birds discovering their wings, the awkward scamperings of a new generation of deer, rabbits, mice, squirrels; and in the gurglings and hesitant movements of Young Pieter de Kuyper.

Christiana lavished her love on the baby and spent

most of her time with him and the few books she had brought from Europe. The books were a salvation: if she could not actually be in the Netherlands, she could read about her homeland and look at pictures of it in the precious volumes.

Several new books arrived, along with a letter from her mother. The letter had been written by the dominie, since her mother had never been taught to read or write. The books, said her mother, were gifts from the family, because they all knew how she treasured them. She reread one portion of the letter over and over, and it brought tears to her eyes.

> . . . and I know your father forgives you although he will never come right out and say it. But many times I find him in your room, staring at the sleeping alcove. You are his favorite child and he cherishes you more than anyone else. He misses you very much. I think if it were possible he would like to move to New Amsterdam to be near you. But that is impossible and so he must be content to look at the place where you once slept. . . .

She hugged the letter to her chest. She would have given much to see her father again, but that was not to be—at least not for some time, she told herself. For now, she was very thankful for the comfort of the books.

She asked other women about their books and was disappointed to learn that not only did most of them not have books, they couldn't even read. In the beginning she tried to interest them in books, even offering to teach them to read.

"Why would I want to read?" Geertie Smit asked. "The only book worth reading is the Bible."

"Well, you could read the Bible," Christiana said hopefully.

"The dominie explains it well enough for me, thank you," Geertie replied. "No sense confusing my mind trying to understand the word of God by myself."

Christiana fared no better with those who could read. Most of them spent so many hours caring for their children and tending their houses that they hadn't the strength left for such exotica as reading. And even if

they had, it was doubtful they would bother. Most of
their husbands didn't read; why should they? They began
to look oddly at this young woman with the strange ideas.
They didn't actually snub her—if they passed her in the
village they would nod—but none of them went out of
their way to be her friend.

Christiana wished to spend more time with her husband, but Pieter was either at work at some task for the
governor, or discovering the joys of a newfound love—
small boats. Although he had grown up in a port, and
loved the sea, he never had had the time or opportunity
to discover the delights of a small boat heeling over as
it sliced into the wind. But then he had spent a week
helping another man on his fishing boat, and this gave
him a new goal. He had managed to save enough money
to order construction of a small boat, and now spent as
much time as possible on the water reaping the harvest
of the sea. He became quite proficient, and his catches
were bringing in handsome sums of money. His dream
of owning a forge was replaced by thoughts of a fishing
boat, one large enough to permit the hunting of those
monarchs of the sea, the whales.

It seemed that the only person Christiana could count
on to need her was Young Pieter.

By now his world was no longer bounded by the beautifully carved cradle; no more was he protected from the
roughness of this wild place. But the child didn't seem to
notice. He crawled around on the wooden floorboards as
if they were the marble halls of a palace. He delighted in
being bounced on the rough-trousered knees of his father,
and he never wrinkled his nose at the fishy smells the
way his mother did when Pieter returned from a long day
on his little boat.

My son will grow up to be a savage like the others,
she thought. Frantic to save him from such a fate, she
would teach him to read, teach him of Europe, instruct
him in the manners of a gentleman so that when they
returned home . . .

Home. In her deepest thoughts she was a stranger in
this land, a sojourner with no desire to spend the rest of
her life here. And if she didn't plan on staying, surely her
son could not stay either. He would be a good son and go
with his mother.

Christiana looked at the infant as he tried to bite a piece of wampum he had found on the floor. She let out a yelp and took the offensive thing away. Young Pieter immediately began to cry and hold out his pudgy hand for the delightful toy, but even his tears were not enough to convince her to give back the Indian money. He would learn of Indians soon enough, but she planned to delay that day as long as possible. She found a red ribbon in her sewing basket and dangled it in front of the child. His tears stopped and he forgot the wampum. She gave him the ribbon, and he immediately brought it to his mouth. She sighed and resigned herself to letting him chew on it with his toothless gums. Anything was better than something that smelled of Indian.

Hendrick de Thuyn paid a visit one day and announced he was returning to Amsterdam. "The burghers have decided they're wasting their money by keeping me here," he said. "They're building new rooms at the West India House and I'm to carve the wainscotings."

"I'm happy for you," Christiana said, biting her lip and trying to contain the jealousy she felt.

"I have you to thank." He waved his hand toward the cradle that stood near the hearth. "And that piece of wood you wheedled me into making."

She looked blankly at him, and he nodded his head and smiled. "Yes, it's the truth. When I was a very young man I could drink as much as I wanted and still do first-rate work. But these last few years," he said with a sigh, "I can only do my best work when I don't drink." He shook his head sadly; time had cheated him by taking away one of his greatest pleasures.

De Thuyn went to the cradle and ran his hand over the sleek wood. "After I carved this I realized I enjoyed work more than grog. I cut down on drinking and began to work as I did in the old days. It didn't escape the notice of the burghers and they're bringing me home."

Christiana tried to hold back the tears, but failed.

"My dear child," de Thuyn said. "What's the matter? Is it something I said?"

"I want to go home too," she blurted out, and then, because he was compassionate and a countryman, she threw her arms around his neck and sobbed on his chest until his heavy vest was wet with her tears.

"I know how you feel," he said. "It's been hell for me
to be here. Not one night goes by that I don't dream of
Amsterdam—hearing the bells, smelling the odors of the
wharfs, seeing throngs of people on market day, when a
man could stroll down the streets and take his pick of the
best Europe had to offer."

"I want to see all that again," she said.

"You will, child, you will," he said stoutly, but Christiana did not see that his face lacked conviction and was,
in fact, masked in sorrow.

He comforted her for a few minutes, until he saw it
was doing no good. Finally he made his farewells and left
for the pier, and the longboat that would take him to the
ship that was to carry him across the ocean.

Christiana cried for over an hour. And then she dried
her eyes and promised herself that soon she too would be
going down to that pier. She would be getting on a ship.
She would be sailing for Europe. And Young Pieter would
be going with her. Soon, very soon, she would be back
where she belonged.

And the spring turned into summer and the pestilential
heat fell on the settlement and the flies swarmed and the
men cursed as they worked and sweated and the women
went about their chores as before.

Fall returned with its delights. The leaves exploded into
color, a thousand different hues, as cool breezes wiped
the sweat from the brows of the colonists who celebrated
another year's harvest. They looked about their town, saw
the progress they had made, and congratulated themselves.

Christiana's heart was a stone. Pieter could not help
but notice her unhappiness, and he tried to console and
cheer her. He bought her lovely trinkets and bolts of fine
cloth. He tried to please her, and because he wanted her
to be happy, he deceived himself into thinking she was.
Christiana loved him with all her heart, and for his sake
pretended to be happy whenever he was around.

But another year went by and then another and then
still another. And then she found herself pregnant once
again. She managed to smile when Pieter danced a jig on
learning he was to be a father again. She didn't have the
heart to spoil his pleasure.

Now she was trapped. She finally accepted it. She was

never going to return to Amsterdam. She would have the second baby—and the third, and then a fourth and a fifth and . . .

She was *here,* and here she was going to stay. Accepting her fate had very little to do with being pleased with it, but her act of acceptance had one benefit. She resolved to look for the good side of everything in this New World, and to find ways of occupying her mind. She hadn't the slightest idea of how to go about doing these things, but Christiana's simple promise to herself of better days to come gave her a sort of satisfaction.

To this extent one could say Christiana de Kuyper was content with her present life.

3

Whales and Thieves
1633 - 1637

A NEW GOVERNOR, WOUTER VAN TWILLER, arrived in New Amsterdam. The official welcoming committee, headed by Pieter de Kuyper, greeted him as he stepped from the longboat and accompanied him to his newly built house within the walls of the fort. A fresh cask of wine was tapped, and the toasts were brave and numerous. Van Twiller promised prosperity and happiness; he claimed all the colonists would live long and well. The colonists told him he would be a wonderful governor.

He introduced two of the men who had accompanied him on the voyage from Holland: Dominie Everardus Bogardus, new pastor of the Reformed Church, and Carl Roelantsen, a schoolmaster who would begin the education of the colony's children.

The tall, stately dominie had dark, penetrating eyes that seemed to stare past flesh and bone straight into one's soul. He also had a mind of his own and a sharp tongue. He had not been on the island more than an hour when he announced that construction of a proper church must begin. "It is not fit," he said, "for the services of the Lord to be conducted in a windmill." The people nodded their heads in solemn agreement, but most had their doubts. If the windmill had been good enough for Pastor Michaëlius, why wasn't it good enough for this one?

"Bringing his snooty ways over from Holland," was the way Abraham de Witt expressed it. Other men mumbled their agreement, but quietly so as not to be overheard by the intimidating dominie. Their shared experiences

73

on Manhatan had brought them together in a suspicion
of the ways of their former homeland. Europe had become a foreign place, almost as far removed from the routine of their lives as was the moon in the sky.

The schoolmaster, Roelantsen, was the source of quite
another form of dismay among the colonists. A jovial
young man with a round, cherubic face, he laughed a great
deal and drank even more. The stoical settlers, who spent
their days grappling with the hostile elements as they
tried to build an entire world from the ground up, did not
feel at ease in the presence of a man who did not seem
serious about life.

Pieter returned to his comfortable home on Pearl
Street, now one of the finest houses on the island. He informed Christiana he was quite unimpressed with the
new governor.

"Van Twiller is as fat as a hog," he said disgustedly.
"And well he might be, having spent his life as a clerk.
Imagine! He takes two voyages as a supercargo and they
make him inspector-general and governor. A man who
counts things and weighs things and then scribbles the
amount down in his notebook! Now he's the governor!"

He slumped into a chair by the window and looked toward the river. A profusion of spring flowers and bloom-
ing trees grew in the garden, fulfilling the promise he
made seven years before when his land had been only a
weed-strewn mud-hole.

"But he must have some qualifications," Christiana
protested.

"Oh yes, yes indeed," Pieter said with a mirthless
laugh. "His wife is the niece of Kiliaen Van Rensselaer.
The old thief probably bribed half the company officers
and half the States-General to get his nephew-in-law this
appointment."

The moment Christiana heard the name Van Rensselaer, she wanted to hear no more. The very name made
Pieter angry. His face would turn red and in no time he
would be shouting. "I must tend to the food," she said,
walking toward the other end of the room. The room
went from the front of the house to the back—the front
part serving as parlor, the rear as kitchen. Christiana
started helping the slave girl, Zilla, with the preparations
for dinner.

Pieter continued to look out the window. He smiled as he realized the reason for his wife's hasty departure. She was right. The subject of Van Rensselaer made him unreasonable.

His hostility was born in 1628, when the trickle of settlers coming from the Netherlands almost stopped. Word had gotten back to the homeland that the New World offered a meagre existence, with no rest from strenuous labor, poor food, and the constant danger of murder by the local savages. There was some truth in all this, of course, but it had been greatly exaggerated and distorted. In any case the tale succeeded in dampening the enthusiasm of many who might have been tempted to try their luck in America. The colony was being denied desperately needed settlers.

The burghers in the company building on the Brower's Graft Canal in Amsterdam devised an unusual plan to encourage the growth of the colony. If any man would land fifty settlers in the colony, they said, he would be made a patroon and receive a reward of a tract of land extending for sixteen miles along a waterway and as far inland as he wanted. The alternative was to take eight miles along *both* sides of a waterway.

The first man to take advantage of this magnanimous offer had been Kiliaen Van Rensselaer. He took his tract of land on both sides of the North River a few miles south of Fort Orange. True to the terms of the agreement, he landed fifty settlers, each receiving the promised cash bonus. This was all well and good—unless you happened to be one of the settlers and found yourself in a vast empty land with no opportunity to take advantage of it because you were tied to one man as an indentured servant. The whole system had a medieval air to it, completely out of place in the Americas, but it seemed at the time to be a solution to the lack of new settlers.

The basic problem, as Pieter saw it, was that the patroon Van Rensselaer had never once set foot in his own domain. He remained in his Amsterdam counting-house, an absentee landlord profiting from his estate as if he were a prince. This high-handedness incensed Pieter. Van Rensselaer was not the sort of man New Netherland needed. The colony depended on strong, able men who would make it their home, whose toil would increase the prosperity of all.

But instead the colony was given Kiliaen Van Rensselaer and the other patroons—Johannes de Laet, David Pietrszoon de Vries, Samuel Godyn, and Samuel Blommaert. Michael de Pauw became a patroon, but at least he lived in the colony. The others, aside from de Vries, never bothered to inconvenience themselves in this way.

To a great extent, de Pauw was the man who promoted the scheme in the colony. When he surveyed the land, he designated many choice sections to be used for his own purposes. The moment the burghers created the patroon system, de Pauw laid claim to an entire island as his private fief—Staten Island, he named it, in honor of the States-General. To make matters worse, from Pieter de Kuyper's point of view, de Pauw settled the land not only with good Dutch farmers but also with Englishmen who preferred to live with their families under the Dutch flag rather than suffer religious persecution as dissenters under the British Crown.

Pieter brooded until Christiana called him to dinner. He took his place at the head of the table, and his black mood dissolved when he looked at his children. Young Pieter, seven years old, was anxiously eyeing the food, although he was well aware he couldn't touch it until grace had been said. Anne, who had turned two a month ago, had no such inhibitions and was already attacking her bowl of mush with a spoon. She managed to get at least half of it into her tiny mouth, allotting the other half equally to her lap and the floor.

Young Pieter watched his sister and wished in vain he could once again be young enough to defy the rules of the house. He couldn't stand it anymore. "You're supposed to wait until we say grace."

Anne smiled at him. "Grace," she chirped. She turned to her father. "Grace?"

Pieter reached out and placed a gently restraining hand on her tiny arm. "Your brother is right. We say grace before we eat."

Young Pieter had a triumphant look on his face, but it vanished when Anne said, "Don' wanna," and pulled her arm away from her father to reattack the mush.

Pieter smiled. "So you have a mind of your own, do you, young lady?"

Anne paid no attention. She spooned up a large dollop and brought it toward her mouth. The little hand turned the wrong way and the mush fell on her lap. "Bad, bad, bad," she said to the inert pile of food. She pushed it off her lap and it fell to the floor with a splat.

Pieter couldn't help but laugh, and Christiana turned to see what was going on.

"Pieter!" she scolded. "Don't let her do that! Zilla just cleaned the floor!"

Pieter used a knife to scrape the mush onto a small plate. As he was leaning over, his son reached out, snatched several berries, and popped them into his mouth. Pieter happened to look up, and Young Pieter, caught in the act, turned red.

Pieter tried to put a stern look on his face, but failed. "Christiana, will you get the food on the table? We're all starving to death," he said and winked at his son.

Christiana and Zilla brought the plates of steaming food to the table—baked ham, a dish of turkey wheat mixed with small beans, heavy pork sausages bursting through their skins, potatoes, fluffy rolls of buckwheat— all washed down with the good beer now being brewed in the town. For dessert there were large bowls of strawberries and raspberries. The tables set by the settlers had improved a great deal over the past few years. The average farm wife might still dress primitively in a single garment that reached from her neck to her ankle, but her dinner table groaned under the weight of boiled and roasted meats and baked fish, all usually drowning in a thick gravy. And the good farmer himself was changing. He still worked six days a week in his fields dressed in a coat-shirt and wooden shoes, but on Sunday he put on a three-quarter-length coat, a broad-brimmed hat sporting a feather, and leather boots or shoes as he proudly took his family to church. His wife's Sunday dress was the same sort as she wore on other days, but usually it was of better material, and her bonnet boasted lace trim and ribbon ties. Most of the settlers walked to Sunday services, but there were those who arrived in a wooden cart pulled by a horse and each year more families boasted such a luxury. The carts themselves were becoming fancier. The first ones had seen double duty as farm vehicles, but now some were being built simply for transportation. The carts were becoming carriages.

When they had finished their dinner, Pieter took out his pipe and filled it with the tobacco now being grown on farms in the northern part of the island. Using tongs, he took an ember from the fire and held it against the tobacco until a cloud of satisfying blue smoke billowed about his head.

"You're sailing tomorrow?" Christiana asked.

"The *Bright Hope* leaves on the morning tide," Pieter said, referring to the two-masted carrick he had bought several years earlier when he had decided to go into the whaling trade. The waters of the New World were fairly swarming with the great beasts, and he was becoming prosperous with his venture.

Christiana said nothing more. Pieter's whaling trips generally lasted several weeks. The whalers stayed at sea until the holds of their ships bulged to overflowing with the pungent blubber. They returned then, and not before.

She often thought how different it would have been if Pieter had started the forge he had always talked about. A man who owned a forge stayed in town and was home for his supper every night. But apparently this was not to be. While Pieter had been building roads for Governor Minuit, another man, David de Hatten, had started a forge. Pieter realized the tiny town had no need for two forges, and so he became a whaling man.

"We have a schoolmaster," Pieter said.

"Good," Christiana said. "It's time Young Pieter began his book studies."

"From the looks of the schoolmaster, I doubt if Young Pieter will learn very much. The man's not our sort at all."

"A man doesn't have to be our sort to be good at book learning. He'll teach Young Pieter to read and do sums."

"I'm already teaching my son to read," Pieter said with annoyance. "As for sums, he'll learn what he must. Too much work with sums turns a man into a . . . a Van Twiller!"

Christiana loved her husband and knew him very well. She stood behind him and put her fingers on his neck. "You miss Governor Minuit a great deal, don't you?"

"Of course I do! Minuit understood this place. He knew what was needed. The reasons given for his recall two years ago are a lot of rubbish. Minuit worked for the good of New Amsterdam. That's more than you can say for those overstuffed burghers in Europe. Or the likes of thieves like Michael de Pauw who take what they want for themselves and to hell with everyone else!"

"Perhaps Governor Minuit will return," Christiana said, trying to soothe her husband's anger.

"No, he will not return. He went to Amsterdam and made his peace with the burghers. He'll not be back. Van Twiller's our new man and we must learn to live with him," Pieter said with a touch of sadness. And then he smiled. "Anyway, he'll no doubt be better than Krol and his damned doughnuts."

Even though Christiana was upset by Pieter's unhappiness, she smiled with him in recollection of the temporary governor who had replaced Minuit.

Bastiaen Krol was a harmless fellow who hadn't wanted to be governor. His very harmlessness was the reason the burghers had installed him in the governor's chair in the interim between real appointees.

Krol had a passion for round balls of sweetened dough fried in hog's fat. The custom was to leave a hole in the middle of the dough so they could be dried on a stick. These confections were known as *olykoecks,* or doughnuts. Krol's love for doughnuts—he would eat them during council meetings and at Sunday services—became a local joke, and people began calling them *krol-ers,* or *crullers.* Although Krol's accomplishments were modest, to say the least, a new word was added to the language because of his preferred food.

The thought of Krol lightened Pieter's mood, and he went to bed early, his mind already on board the *Bright Hope.*

After the dishes had been cleaned, the pots scrubbed, the children put to bed, and the last chores of the day finished, the slave girl Zilla left the de Kuyper house and went north to the building that housed the company's slaves. It was a two-story structure, new and solidly built. There were no locks or guards, no fences or gates to set it apart from any of the other nearby houses. Within its walls lived twenty-three souls, men and women, all slaves and all black. Zilla had lived here when she first arrived in New Amsterdam and cooked meals for the soldiers of the garrison. But Governor Minuit sold her to Pieter de Kuyper, and she had moved into the house on Pearl Street, where she had her own room. It was cramped under the sharply slanting roof, making it difficult to stand erect except in the very center, but it was her own room, and it had a door. Zilla knew the blessing of privacy for the first time in her seventeen years.

"Manuel?" she called softly as she stepped inside the shadowy darkness of the slave house.

"Zilla?"

"Yes," she said, and moved toward the sound of her brother's voice. She found him on the floor, seated on his bed of rags. He stood up, and the two of them went quietly past the canvas that divided the room in half and into the kitchen in the back part of the room. Manuel lit a candle from an ember in the smoldering fireplace, and they sat down at the rough table. Besides the table there were half a dozen chairs and a large cooking pot. There were no decorations on the walls and no curtains on the windows; there was no other furniture, and no food. An earthenware jug and a wooden cup were on the table. Manuel filled the cup with water. Zilla declined when he held it out to her.

"How is Master Pieter?" he asked.

Zilla nodded her head. "He is a good man. And the mistress as well."

Manuel agreed. "This is a good place for us. The work at the fort is hard, because we are facing it with stone. But there is plenty of food and there are no overseers with whips. The engineer, Master Keyn, is kind." His features broke into a smile. "Every day he gets drunk at lunch and falls asleep. Not much work gets done in the afternoon."

"Then you are content?"

Manuel's mouth tightened. Even in the semidarkness Zilla could see the pain on her brother's face. "A slave must always be content," he said. "He has little choice. He can run away, but where does one run in this land? If the Indians catch him he dies. And if his masters catch him he dies. So, yes, I am content. As much as I can be without being free or without—"

His voice broke off. Even today, four years later, he could not bring himself to say the name of his wife, who had been beaten to death by a Portuguese overseer during the time the Dutch were being hounded from their homes in Brazil.

Manuel and his wife and younger sister had been slaves of the Dutch when war broke out in Europe between Holland and Portugal. Eventually the war reached the New World and the superior forces of the Portuguese attacked the Dutch, with the result a foregone conclusion. The Portuguese, in an uncharacteristically humane gesture, allowed the remaining Dutchmen to flee with their lives. The Portuguese commander even allowed the Dutch to take their slaves. This was perhaps less a display of generosity than an admission that given the presence of the Africans and the local natives, there were more than enough slaves for everyone. Both nations had been bringing the blacks from Africa for over a century. Some of the slaves, Manuel and Zilla included, were of the third generation of their families in the New World.

Dutch ships were allowed to transport the refugees. They dispersed about the globe, some returning to Holland, others to the faraway Dutch East Indies, which gave Europe nutmeg, cloves, cinnamon, and ginger and always welcomed new planters and traders with slaves. Still other refugees boarded ships that made their way to the colony of New Netherland.

While the ships were being loaded with the Dutch and their slaves, one of the Portuguese overseers took a liking to Manuel's comely wife. She resisted and, in the struggle, managed to bite the guard's hand. In his rage he beat her to death with the butt of his musket. Manuel would have attacked the guard, but a Dutch planter, realizing the consequences of such folly, cracked a belaying pin against Manuel's skull; he was unconscious when the ship raised anchor and departed from the hated coast.

Manuel had his chance for revenge when the Dutch ship was attacked on the high seas by a Portuguese raider. The fighting was fierce, with no quarter given by either side. The ships were drawn together by grappling hooks, and the decks of both were aswarm with fighting men. Muskets and pistols boomed, dirks were thrown, and cutlasses whistled through the air. Manuel fought like a wounded tiger. He killed two men with his sharp blade, and when it broke as it sliced down through the skull of a third man, the slave fought with his bare hands, tearing each man apart as if he had been the devil who had taken away his wife.

When it was over, the decks of the ships were strewn with bodies and awash with blood. They threw the corpses over the sides for the sharks. The Portuguese ship was scuttled with ten wounded and dying men still aboard. As the Dutch ship moved away from the sinking wreck, the cries of agony and tortured appeals for mercy coming from the doomed Portuguese sailors sounded sweet to Manuel's ears.

The Dutch ship arrived in New Amsterdam without further adventure. The West India Company appropriated the slaves and put them to work on streets and roads and on the rebuilding of the fort, which had crumbled almost to bits. Several slaves, Zilla among them, had been sold to individuals at a nominal price as a reward for various services to the colony

The lot of the slaves was infinitely better than it had been on the plantations of Brazil, where the work had been exhausting under the broiling tropical sun and the overseers sadistic brutes who knew only the law of club and whip. But slaves they remained, even in New Amsterdam, occupying a place in the world plan somewhere between the white man and the dumb cattle who grazed in the fields until the day they went beneath the butcher's knife.

"Master Pieter sails again tomorrow," Zilla said

"On the *Bright Hope?*"

"Yes. For whales."

"Whales!" Manuel said, his eyes brightening and his voice betraying his suppressed excitement. "Remember the time we saw them in the ocean when we came here? Remember? Whales! Ahhhh, I'd like to hunt the whale . . . there's a life for a man!"

"Remember who you are!" Zilla chided. "Your work is building the fort. Forget about whales."

"I'll build their fort. But I'll dream of whales as I work. Someday, Zilla, I will hunt the whale."

"Foolishness," Zilla said as she stood up. "I must get back to the house." She handed him a small package.

"Food?"

She nodded. "Some pieces of good, fresh-cooked ham."

"You didn't steal it?" he asked suspiciously.

She smiled. "The de Kuypers treat me as their own. I talk to the mistress all the time—even about you. She said I could give you some of Master Pieter's old clothes, but they wouldn't fit. You're so big they'd split apart if you put them on."

With the package of food in his hand, Manuel walked at his sister's side until they were outside the house. Zilla was of normal size but appeared tiny beside the man. He stood six and a half feet tall and weighed over two hundred and fifty pounds, all hardened muscle that bunched and rippled as he moved. Brother and sister touched hands in farewell and parted.

Manuel stood in the doorway and watched until Zilla disappeared down the road. He continued to stare into the darkness long after she had gone. His thoughts were of a ship at sea and a mighty whale breaking through the waves, the great head emerging above the water and then plunging down as the beast sounded, a titanic force on its way to the floor of the sea.

Manuel knew he was a slave. Yes, a slave, he thought; but what if a man hunted the whale? What sort of a man was that? A slave? No, not a slave. Such a man could never be a slave . . . no matter what other men called him. Such a man was a master . . . such a man was free.

Manuel did not often admit it, even to himself, but he desperately wanted to be free.

After Zilla had left the house and Pieter had gone to bed, Christiana sat down in front of the fire and stared at the flames. The stirring of the wind caused the quiet house to creak and groan, the soft moanings taking on ominous meanings. Each noise caused her to look up nervously, expecting trouble, her eyes darting about the room, checking to see that nothing was amiss. She knew she was being foolish, but couldn't help herself. Nervousness had become her constant companion.

It had been aggravated by the birth of Young Pieter. For the first week she had been certain he was not going to live. While the infant slept she kept going to the cradle, placing her ear against his tiny chest, assuring herself his heart was still beating. She would do this five or six times an hour, hardly sleeping until, finally, at the end of a week and a half, she collapsed from exhaustion. Geertie Smit was brought in to run the household and care for the helpless girl and her baby. Within a few days the young mother had recovered most of her physical strength.

But Christiana was afraid of the outside world. Even the short walk from her house to the fort made her unhappy. The faces she saw appeared hostile, and every gesture seemed to mask a threat. She imagined she was being watched, followed by blazing eyes belonging to people who meant her harm. But worst of all were the Indians. The sight of one of these savages caused her hands to shake and her heart to beat faster. The red men, with their tomahawks and knives, seemed always on the brink of a fitful rage that would throw them at the throats of the white settlers.

Her fears caused her to spend most of her time in the house, worrying about her husband when he was not home, despairing for her son every time he ventured out, if only to play in the garden at the back of the house. She realized these were unnatural fears and tried to conceal them from others. She did not want them to make fun of her. By themselves the fears were bad enough, but the effort to conceal them took an even greater toll. Since she couldn't talk about her problems with anyone, she began to talk to herself, sometimes aloud but mostly in silence lest someone overhear.

The result was that, gradually and intermittently, Christiana slipped into a fantasy world. She pretended she was living back in the Netherlands, surrounded by the good farmers and burghers of her childhood memories. She told herself the world outside her house was one of prosperous fields with a sprinkling of neat, well-scrubbed houses with cheery hearths. There was no wilderness; there were no vast stretches of unexplored land, no untamed rivers that bore no names, no vistas of treetops stretching to the horizon. *And there were no Indians.* Not a single one. They did not exist. Their painted bodies, their beads of wampum and their tomahawks, these and the evil they planned for the settlers were only remnants of a long-gone nightmare that was receding behind the outer edge of memory.

At first she knew she was weaving fantasies and was scrupulously careful to conceal her thoughts from Pieter. But in time, as the real world blurred before her eyes, she began to make occasional mistakes.

"Aunt Mitje baked the most delicious jam tarts for dinner yesterday," she said happily to Pieter as he sat by the fire waiting for his dinner to be served.

He looked at her in confusion. "Aunt Mitje? But Aunt Mitje is back in the Netherlands."

She turned crimson and busied herself at the far end of the room. "Oh yes . . . well, what I meant was . . . Aunt Mitje always bakes jam tarts at this time of year."

That answer satisfied Pieter, but there were other incidents that made him begin to realize something strange was happening to his wife. It caused him concern, but his days were filled with work and its many problems, so he relegated this one to the back of his mind. Christiana was ordinarily very practical-minded, so he was reasonably hopeful she would manage to get over whatever it was that sometimes bothered her and made her behave unlike her usual self.

Her descents into fantasy had an effect on young Pieter. Christiana felt an abnormal protectiveness toward her son. She wanted to bring him into her private world where there were no problems and everyone was safe. She wanted to convince him, as she had herself, that they were living back in the Netherlands. Having little in the way of a frame of reference, the boy flitted back and forth between what seemed to be the real world, and the world as interpreted by his mother. This, of course, caused trouble between the boy and his father. Pieter could not understand why his son seemed "different" from the other boys of the same age. He had little patience with his son's excessive timidity and his curiosity over useless details. He was curt with him, and he closed his mind to the fact that the boy's problems had their source in his mother. The boy, quite naturally, feared and distrusted his father. He did his best to avoid him and spent most of his time with his tolerant and understanding mother.

But now the house was quiet.

Christiana sat by the fire, and the flames were the

same flames that had danced in the hearth of the snug house where she had been a child. The flames calmed and reassured her. Her father was in his chair, and she imagined she heard his strong, regular breathing. In a little while her mother would take her to bed. There would be a quiet little song and then the heavy coverlet would be tucked around her shoulders and under her chin. She would become toasty-warm and drift peacefully into sleep. A smile came to her lips at the delicious thought. The fire burned on, its warmth seeping into her flesh and bones.

She fell asleep, smiling in contentment.

Several hours later Pieter awoke and missed her. He went to the keeping room and found her in front of the embers. Her peaceful demeanor made him happy. It wasn't often she looked as contented as this.

He took her hand and rubbed it as he kissed her eyes and nose. She finally stirred and looked at him. She smiled.

"You should come to bed now," he whispered.

She nodded and stood up. "The fire was so nice, I guess I just dozed off."

They went to the bedroom and soon were snuggled side by side under the covers. After many minutes, she noticed in the moonlight that Pieter was staring at the ceiling. She knew what was on his mind. Lovemaking.

Once their lovemaking had been a series of wild, passionate bouts, but over the past few years it had lost its intensity and fire—and, alas, its frequency. She knew it bothered him more than he would admit.

I am hurting this man, she thought, causing him pain, and he hasn't done anything to deserve it.

She wanted to please him. She snuggled up against him and kissed his cheek. She saw his look of surprise and felt ashamed. *And have I become so bad a wife that my husband looks at me with surprise when I become affectionate?*

"Pieter . . ."

"Yes."

"Do I make you happy?"

It was the voice of a little girl, and it touched him. "How can you even ask such a question?"

"I'm not always sure I do."

He squeezed her hand.

"I try, I really try," she said, and there was a note of desperation in her voice.

Pieter understood she was appealing to him from the depths of her heart. His mouth was dry and his voice filled with emotion. "I'm sorry if I haven't made the perfect life for you."

Oh dear God, she thought, and now he's blaming himself and it's all my fault. "No, really, you mustn't—"

"I try, too . . ."

"Pieter, dear Pieter . . ." she murmured over and over. "You know I'll do anything for you—"

"Stop talking," she said fiercely, suddenly determined to please him. Her hand moved under the cover and began to touch his flesh, gliding slowly and gently until she could feel him quiver with anticipation. And now, for the first time in many months, she began licking his ear and murmuring into it.

Their surroundings faded and time dissolved. They were back on the ship, two people discovering the joys of each other, lòvers, sensualists, *savages* with skin to explore.

Christiana's mind was reeling: *I am his. He is mine. And we are one.*

His body slid on top of hers and their heat fused and his voice was anguished as he cried, "God, God, God, I love you."

She was waiting for him, eager for him, wanting him so badly she could cry. But then, at the last moment, just as she was about to be swept away in the throes of passion, an image of the Indian who had tried to rape her flashed into her mind and all her lust and desire vanished and left fear in their place. Unreasoning fear, mindless fear. She knew this was Pieter with her, Pieter, dear tender Pieter, *her* Pieter, but it did no good. No matter what she told herself, no matter what her eyes told her, it was the Indian, the Indian, the Indian. . . .

She fought with herself. She pretended to enjoy herself, pretended she was in a state of rapture, but it was all a sham and her body stiffened and her bones froze with fear.

Pieter could feel her tightened muscles and see her jaw set in fear. It destroyed his passion, made the act of love joyless and empty. He tried to fathom what

88 FROM DISTANT SHORES

was happening, but could not. It was over. They lay side by side, and Pieter kissed her fingertips with a gentleness and tenderness that left Christiana even more unhappy.

He is so good, so kind, she thought, he does not deserve this. She tried her best, but it wasn't good enough. Every time they made love the Indian reappeared, causing her to freeze, draining away all her desire, robbing her of any pleasure, and, of course, ruining the moment for her husband. Would it never stop? Would it be this way for the rest of their lives?

Tears streamed from her eyes. She said nothing, only stared straight up at the ceiling. The pain of what was happening was more than she could bear.

Michael de Pauw had finished supper in his large house in the new settlement of Staten Island, and was now seated at the table poring over maps. He was marking likely places for future settlements in his domain.

The door opened and Dirk Stratling entered. "Evenin', Guvnor, a word with you, if't please you."

De Pauw nodded. "Help yourself to a drink," he said, pointing toward a large sideboard.

"Don't mind if I do," Stratling replied, moving to the sideboard and filling a silver goblet halfway to the top with brandy.

Dirk Stratling was an Englishman who had settled in New Amsterdam. There were thirty or forty of his countrymen in the colony, mostly religious dissenters who settled here because the Dutch cared less about a man's beliefs in God than they did about his belief in hard work. But Stratling was hardly a dissenter. His reason for preferring Dutch soil was much simpler: he was a convicted murderer who had managed to escape from an English jail.

"Have you met Van Twiller?" he asked.

"Yes," de Pauw said. "A stupid sort of person, but he'll prove harmless. I told him how much the colony needs Staten Island, and he told me he'd help us with settlers and money. I think Van Twiller will be a gold mine for me."

"Good enough I be sayin', but did talk turn to whales?"

"No. But I'll get to it."

Stratling was annoyed. He was captain of a whaling

ship that belonged to de Pauw. He received a ten-percent
share of the profits, and since whaling was proving to be a
very profitable business, Stratling was beginning to imagine himself becoming a rich man. But he thought of
competition as nothing more than a means other men
used to pick his own pockets. One of the most successful
competitors was Pieter de Kuyper, who had begun to
work the areas down the coast from the Lower Bay, all
the way to the South Bay, waters that Stratling had decided were his own private preserve.

"But, Burgomaster," Stratling protested obsequiously.
"Waters of the South Bay be ours! These other beggars
are comin' and 'tis not right!"

Michael de Pauw smiled. Stratling was a ruthless and
vicious man, but he lacked cunning and shrewdness.

"I take it Pieter de Kuyper has been catching more
whales than you."

"That poxed scum!"

"There are enough whales for everyone," de Pauw
said. "What's wrong with de Kuyper getting his share?"

"You're not understandin'. If a ship be forced to whale
in open ocean it be two months afore she load on't a full
cargo. But if she stay in t'bays she can load a cargo in
two-three weeks. Think of how many more trips a
ship makes if voyages last weeks, na' months!"

"And, of course, the more voyages the more money
the captain makes, isn't that it?"

"You be makin' more from your share than rest of us
together," Stratling said in a sullen voice, his brows coming together until they almost touched one another.

Michael de Pauw was amused. He enjoyed taunting
Stratling; the contest was always so one-sided. Still and
all, the vicious man had his uses, so he decided to appease
him. "Maybe you're right after all, Stratling. I'll speak to
the governor. But first I must find out what it is that he
wants, do you understand? You can't approach a man
with what *you* want. First you must find out what *he*
wants. Give a man what he wants and you own him."

Stratling's ugly mouth twisted itself into a mockery of a
smile. "Ah, Burgomaster, clever, clever!"

"Your friend de Kuyper was at the reception for the
governor. He mentioned he was sailing tomorrow."

"Bleedin' scum!"

"What good are ugly names? Instead of talking why don't you do something?"

"Do somethin'?" the Englishman said.

"Take your ship to the waters where de Kuyper is going. Cause some trouble."

"Trouble?"

Michael de Pauw could never get over the Englishman's thickheadedness. "Yes, trouble. Get into an argument over a whale, or something like that. Anything but a real fight. I want none of that. Give me some trouble and I'll make a legal case out of it. If I can put the governor in my pocket—and I think I can—who do you think will win any case brought into a court of law?"

It took Stratling a few moments to make sense out of de Pauw's argument, but when he understood his face glowed with admiration. "Ay, sharp and bright, Burgomaster, sharp and bright indeed!"

"Now be off, and get the *Pavonia* ready for the morning tide," de Pauw said, waving his hand in dismissal. When the man had gone, his thoughts turned to Governor Van Twiller. The clod should be easy to get to, and there had to be ways of insuring his cooperation. He thought about Van Twiller's being related to Kiliaen Van Rensselaer. Now *there* was a man who knew the value of making friendships based on mutual help. Yes, perhaps the ultimate key to the governor was his uncle back in Amsterdam.

He immediately composed a long letter to Van Rensselaer that would be sent back to Holland on the next ship. In the meantime he planned on seeing the governor and nurturing their friendship. The man would want something, he thought; every man wanted something.

Michael de Pauw was determined that he would be the man to get Van Twiller what he wanted—whatever that was.

The faintest hint of the new day rising in the east softened the black of the June sky as Pieter made his way down to the fort, where the *Bright Hope* rode at anchor.

As he walked down the road through the silent town, he looked around and realized how much had been accomplished in the past seven years. Despite the fact

that the growth had not been as great as expected, there
was much to be proud of. From a few huts with a handful
of men, New Amsterdam had grown until now almost
four hundred people called it home. And quite a collection
it was: Dutch, English, some French, Germans, Negroes,
even a few Spaniards and Portuguese who were willing to
accept the rule of the burghers in exchange for the free-
doms they granted. The result was a polyglot of population speaking a half-dozen languages in the streets—
especially near the fort, where an increasing number of
ships rode at anchor. Most of the ships were anchored,
because the single quay was used only for loading or unloading. It was obvious the settlers needed more wharfs
and docks, but there had been so many other tasks that
the building of new docks was always being put off to
another day.

Pieter passed the fort as the slaves were arriving to
begin their day's work. The black men were working six
days a week, on the fort and on the new governor's
house. He came to the pebbly beach at the foot of the
fort and spotted the longboat from the *Bright Hope*. Several of the carrick's sailors stood near the boat warming
their hands over a nut-wood fire. Green or dry, the nut
wood had a peculiar sap that helped keep the flames
dancing.

The first man to see Pieter was Claes Vincent, now the
Bright Hope's bosun. Where his left hand had been he
now wore an iron hook. "Mornin', Cap'n," he said, raising
the hook in his version of a salute.

"Does the tide hold?" Pieter asked.

The bosun nodded. "It will be running within the
hour." He called the sailors, who left the warmth of the
fire and took their positions alongside the longboat as
Pieter and Claes Vincent climbed aboard. "We'll make
good time with this wind," Pieter observed.

The longboat was launched, and the sailors manned
the oars. It soon pulled alongside the hulking shape of the
Bright Hope. The carrick was a rather ugly, squat ship,
higher at both ends than in the middle. Broad-beamed
and round-bottomed, it would wallow in high seas. It
would be a dreadful ship to take across the ocean, but it
had never been built with that in mind. The foremast was
square-rigged and the mizzen was rigged fore and aft,

which made the *Bright Hope* easier to handle in the
erratic winds along the coast, whose waters she was meant
to ply as a heavy-duty work boat.

The men prepared the ship while they waited for the
tide to become favorable. Pieter made his rounds, checking sails and rigging, satisfying himself there were enough
barrels to store the quantity of blubber he hoped to bring
back to the town. Neither the *Bright Hope* nor any other
ship had on-board facilities for the extraction of the precious oil, so the blubber would be flensed and stored in
barrels until it could be gotten ashore to the huge stoves
that were necessary to process it into oil. For the most
part, the whale meat was simply left in the sea and de-
voured by the denizens of the waters. Some ships tried to
salt it and bring it back to shore, but they soon found it
took up too much space and was more trouble than it was
worth.

Pieter came across his first harpooner, Santiago
Equirra, a giant of a man from the Basque country who,
according to the stories, had killed his first whale when
he was ten years old.

"Look at this, Captain," he said when Pieter approached. He held up a lance whose head was fixed with
long razor-sharp knives. "New," he said proudly.

Pieter hefted the harpoon. It was heavy; but if he
moved his hand an inch or two from the fulcrum, the
other end would begin to dip, so precisely balanced was
the terrible weapon.

"Many whales," Pieter said, and the first harpooner
smiled in appreciation of one whaling man's salutation to
another.

And now the tide began to run and the *Bright Hope*
shipped her anchor and headed across the Upper Bay
toward the Narrows, the mouth of the Lower Bay—and
the open sea.

"A fair wind, sir," the bosun said, standing beside
Pieter on the quarterdeck.

Pieter looked at the green hills of the Narrows as they
passed through. "And a fair land," he replied. The Narrows could easily be seen from Manhatan, but the distance made them appear gray. It was only up close that a
man could appreciate their richness and beauty.

They passed into the open sea and hugged the coast

as the *Bright Hope* wallowed in the waves that rolled relentlessly in from the center of the ocean. Even the strong-stomached sailors began to feel queasy and cursed the round bottom of the carrick.

They sailed for hours.

At one point Pieter tapped Vincent on the arm and pointed at a cachalot that was moving northward on their port beam. It was a huge beast, its head comprising at least a third of its vastness. The great bulk moved through the water, first thrusting upward and then dropping back until it almost disappeared. Its blowhole sent a spray thirty feet into the air. Bosun Vincent estimated its length at eighty feet. There was no possible way to estimate its weight, but the whale was so great it sent waves rippling out in its wake and they slapped and bounced against the *Bright Hope*'s hull.

There was a playfulness in Pieter's voice as he said, "Shall we try the cachalot, Mister Vincent?"

Bosun Vincent, who had nothing remotely resembling a sense of humor, looked aghast. "A sperm? Are you serious? Why, that monster could as easily wreck the *Bright Hope* as I could spit over the side!"

"We could do it."

"No man in his right mind takes on a sperm."

"Think of all the oil," Pieter said, enjoying the game.

"What good is oil if we end at the bottom of the sea?"

Pieter gave a mock sigh. "Very well. We'll let him live."

Bosun Vincent walked away, shaking his head and worrying about Pieter's sanity. Pieter managed not to smile.

He watched the retreating back of the whale as it continued its northward journey at a speed that was easily twice that of the swiftest sailing boat in the world. Pieter would have enjoyed the adventure of tackling a sperm. As far as he knew it had never been done. Someday, he thought, we will have ships and weapons equal to the sperm, and then we shall have whale hunts the likes of which have never been seen on this earth.

They sailed all day and all night to reach the whale-rich waters of the South Bay, which had vaguely been claimed for England by Lord De La Warr of Virginia, a claim which had never reached the ears of the men of New Amsterdam. The sun came up on the second day, and the tension and excitement mounted as the men knew they were near their destination.

It was several hours before noon when the *Bright Hope* nosed around the long sand dune that extended far into the water, forming the north edge of South Bay. The ship entered the calmer waters, and as it stopped its wallowing the sailors' faces lost their greenish hue. They sailed smoothly across the bay for half an hour, and then the lookout, stationed two-thirds of the way up the foremast, gave the universal cry:

"Thar she blows!"

Pieter was instantly at the rail with his spyglass. He scanned the waters, and . . . there they were, a pod of a dozen right whales taking their rest in the calm waters of the bay, sleeping or lazing about before they continued their trip to the frigid waters of the north.

"Our luck holds," Bosun Vincent said to Pieter.

Pieter nodded. "I was hoping for more sperm," he said, glancing out of the corner of his eye to see the other man's reaction. "But these appear to be right whales."

The bosun again looked at Pieter as if he were daft. "Aye, they're right whales, and that means they're the right whales for us."

The bosun, without even knowing it, gave the reason for this whale's common name. The early whalers knew only that it gave a good quantity of oil and yet did not have the awesome size and ferocious power of the sperm. They called it the right whale because, for them, it was the right whale to hunt.

At the rallying cry the crew sprang into action. The two longboats were swung out on davits and lowered into the water. Seven men climbed into each—the officer in charge, the harpooner, a coxswain, and four oarsmen. Bosun Vincent commanded one longboat; Pieter was in charge of the second. The remaining sailors dropped most of the *Bright Hope*'s sails and allowed her to drift slowly, carefully avoiding the whales so as not to frighten them.

The oars of the longboats slipped quietly through the water. The oarlocks were heavily greased to keep them from making noise. The great whales, for all their size, could be very timid. Sometimes they would panic upon hearing a strange noise. If they did, there was no way a longboat rowed by four men had the slightest chance of catching up with them.

The arrangement of the oars was odd—two fifteen-foot oars on one side, and three shorter oars on the other. The harpooner manned the third short oar. The idea was to bring the short-oared side of the longboat alongside the whale. Because of their size the oars could be used almost to the last minute without any danger of hitting the whale and frightening it. With the boat right next to the whale, the harpooner put down his oar, picked up the weapon, and had a clean shot from a very short distance. This was the theory. However, in practice things were often far more difficult, because the swells in the water would rock the boat and affect the harpooner's aim.

If the whale was only grazed, a quick movement by the beast could smash the boat to kindling and throw the men into the water, often maiming or killing one or more of them.

Pieter studied the whales. He decided on the one at the extreme left edge of the group. The bosun saw Pieter's signal and started his boat toward the whales on the other side of the pod.

Pieter's boat headed for its intended victim.

If the whales were aware of the boats, they gave no indication. They continued to lie still in the water, their only movement caused by the continuous expansion and contraction of their great lungs. The water flooded off their backs as they rose, and came back again as they settled.

Pieter's longboat came closer and closer, and the coxswain turned the tiller so the boat pulled alongside the monster.

Pieter nodded at Santiago Equirra, and the Basque harpooner placed his oar in the bottom of the boat and took up his weapon. He checked the line attached to the end of the harpoon, looking down into the basket to see that the remainder was properly coiled. He knelt on the gunwale, raised the weapon over his head, and drove it with all his might toward a spot near the whale's left eye. The sharp blades sliced through the tough skin and penetrated the blubber, and the weapon gouged its way into the warm flesh of the animal.

Instantly it was as if a bomb had exploded. The whale's

enormous body rose straight up in the water and then
crashed down more than thirty feet away, the head bur-
rowing beneath the water as the great sea creature dove
toward the bottom of the bay. The moment the harpoon
had hit the whale, Santiago Equirra had thrown the rope
around a sturdy post in the bow of the longboat. Now the
line fed out of the basket. As the whale took it with him
on his dive, the rope spun madly around the post. Equirra
played the line while a sailor poured water on it. The
enormous heat generated by the friction would have set
the rope afire if it had not been kept wet.

The whale reached the bottom of his dive, twisted his
body around, and raced back toward the surface. The
rope stopped spinning around the post. Equirra quickly
made several half-hitches on the rope, holding it fast to
the post.

The beast splashed through the surface of the water a
hundred feet from the longboat, the great body stretching
out as it began to swim furiously on the surface. The
harpoon held fast, the rope snapped taut, and the bow of
the longboat lifted in the air and the craft was pulled
through the water at a speed of fifteen knots.

It was wild, exciting, bizarre; a ride that could be provided by nothing else in the world. The enraged cetacean
dashed madly through the water, his flukes pumping
wildly, the longboat following as white water whirled
and splashed, soaking the men, blinding them with salt
spray, filling their mouths and nostrils with wind and water. And the Basque harpooner began the dangerous
journey to the stern of the boat while Pieter, a sharp lance
held in one hand, went from stern to bow, the two passing
each other in the middle of the boat. One slip and a man
would fall overboard. One false move by Pieter and he
could impale one of the crew. This exchange of places by
the two men was a tradition whose beginnings were lost
in the memories of the first whalers. The officer of the
longboat always performed the coup de grace with the
lance. Pieter thought it a silly superstition, but Equirra
refused to do it any other way. It was the way they had
done it on the Bay of Biscay, the way it had been done by
his father and his father's father and his father's father's
father, and it was the way he was going to do it.

Pieter managed to reach the bow without falling out of

the boat. He held tightly to the gunwale, and for over ten minutes he waited.

Finally the whale weakened and the mad rush slowed. The exertion of towing the boat and the loss of blood had begun to take its toll. The whale slowed and then stopped, its body heaving as the great lungs gasped for air. The sailors immediately manned the oars and pulled alongside the exhausted and quivering giant. Pieter raised the six-foot lance. Its head contained five razor-sharp blades. He drove it directly into the whale's eye. So sharp were the blades that the shaft went three feet into the whale. Pieter held onto the shaft and twisted and turned it, tearing at flesh and membrane, hastening the now-certain death.

In a last burst of fight the whale struck the longboat with his tail, but most of his strength was gone and the thump against the gunwale was a mockery of its former power. No damage was done.

The whale died. A cheer went up from the men in the longboat! "Flurry! Flurry!" they shouted, in the tradition of whaling men who knew they had made a kill.

But there was no time to lose. Lines were drawn around the carcass, and the sailors put their back into the oars as they towed their prize back to the mother ship.

Claes Vincent's longboat had not had the same good fortune. At the moment of his harpooner's thrust the boat was rocked by a wave. The blade merely grazed the head of the whale and slid into the sea. However, it had been enough of a disturbance to disturb the cetacean's dreams. He flicked his tail, dove immediately, and was lost to view. The two other nearby whales, both cows, were upset by his movement, and they too sounded to the bottom of the bay.

Vincent urged his men on as they rowed toward another whale a quarter-mile away.

By this time Pieter's crew was pulling their whale toward the *Bright Hope*. The sailors saw the longboat coming with its prize, and they prepared to accept it.

Ropes were worked about the whale, holding it close to the side of the ship. Pieter shouted orders, and men jumped from the ship onto the whale's back. Using their razor-sharp knives, they flensed great strips of blubber from the carcass. Other men passed down lines with hooks attached to them. The blubber was fixed on the hooks, pulled aboard, and quickly packed into waiting barrels. As soon as a barrel was filled it was whisked away to the hold.

The sea was red with whale's blood, attracting all the sharks in the vicinity. They came, these flesh eaters, wild-eyed and open-mouthed, their nostrils filled with the smell of blood, their tiny brains attuned only to the kill. The sailors standing on top of the whale, working only a few feet away from rows of murderous teeth, were glared at by dozens of shark eyes as they hacked away at the slippery blubber.

Pieter jumped aross the small open space between longboat and carcass. He watched as the blubber was taken from one side of the whale. Now the ropes slowly turned the carcass so the blubber could be stripped from the other side.

"The ropes!" Pieter shouted to a sailor who almost lost his footing. "Hold onto the ropes!"

The carcass was turned and the men quickly went back to work. The waters turned a deeper and deeper red.

"Avast!" Pieter cried. "Here they come!"

The smell of blood had become too much for the sharks, and they threw themselves at the carcass, the teeth of their distended jaws sinking into the meat, their heads whipping back and forth in fury until a chunk was torn away. As each killer attempted to escape with his prize, other sharks tried to take it away from him. The sharks were driven to ever-greater frenzy, and the activity at the side of the ship resembled a scene from Dante's *Inferno*. The waters boiled and bubbled with blood and slashing sharks fighting among themselves.

Pieter watched in awe as one shark thrashed out of the water, a gaping wound in his side. As he splashed back down he was hit from all sides and ripped to shreds. A fine mist of blood spread through the air, settling on the carcass, the ship, and the men.

And through all this the men on the carcass continued to work, cutting and pulling at the blubber, seemingly calm but fully aware that a single misstep would plunge them to a horrible death. The blood continued to run. The blubber went aboard. And the sharks went beyond the bounds of rage and began biting everything in sight including the hull of the ship.

Finally all the blubber was aboard and Pieter ordered the remainder of the whale cut loose. As the *Bright Hope* and the longboat drifted away, the men relaxed. The furious sharks no longer fought and crashed at their feet, but moved away with the drifting carcass. A few sailors joked to release the nervous tension.

It was Pieter who first noticed a new drama unfolding. A carrick, driven smartly by the brisk winds, moved across the bay in the direction of Claes Vincent's longboat. The carrick passed between the longboat and the whale it was pursuing, and then changed course to bear down directly on the longboat.

Claes Vincent saw the carrick coming but assumed it would bear off when it noticed his longboat. Soon, however, the carrick was within hailing distance and still its bow drove steadily toward the smaller craft. At the last moment Vincent turned his boat to avoid the carrick. This desperate move saved the boat, but the carrick passed so close by that it sheared off the fifteen-foot oars, leaving Vincent's longboat helpless in the water.

"You bloody bastard!" Vincent screamed at the carrick as it drove past, leaving him in its wash. At the stern he saw the name of the offending ship. It was the *Pavonia.*

Pieter watched in disbelief as the carrick sheared off the longboat's oars. He was choked with anger as he hastened up the rope ladder to the *Bright Hope*'s deck. He wanted to get his glass to have a better look at the other ship. To his surprise the carrick turned and headed straight toward him.

As the carrick approached, the men on the *Bright Hope* armed themselves and waited grimly. Surely the other must be a pirate.

But the carrick came around the *Bright Hope*, pulled into the wind, and came to a stop, its sails acting as brakes. Two ships rocked gently in the water within hailing distance.

"What the hell do you think you're doing?" Pieter shouted across the water. "And just who are you?"

"Beggin' your pardon, Cap'n de Kuyper. Dirk Stratling 'ere, on board carrick *Pavonia.* My 'pologies for smashin' oars o' your longboat. I was na' seein' 'er and that be truth."

"You're a goddamn liar!"

"As you wish, Cap'n, but I claims not to see 'er. That be my story if't comes to court of law."

"It *will* come to a court of law, you son of a bitch! I'll have your head on a plate!"

Stratling remained unruffled. "We be seein' t'all that soon enough, but meantime there be t'other matter to speak of."

"And what's that, you nameless son of a whore!" Pieter shouted, his rage almost choking the words in his throat.

"These be the waters of Michael de Pauw. Be unlegal for you t'be 'ere. These whales be de Pauw's whales. Best ye find t'other waters."

Pieter's rage turned to astonishment. "What are you talking about? These waters belong to New Netherland. And so do the whales."

"That be your side of the story. Methinks there be t'other side. Best be off."

"Try another trick like the one you just pulled and I'll blow you out of the water."

"And 'ow you be doin' that, Cap'n?"

Pieter turned and issued an order; the crew sprang to life. A large crate on the deck was opened and an ominous eight-pounder was rolled across the deck until its muzzle stuck over the railing and pointed directly at the quarterdeck of the *Pavonia*.

This was more than Dirk Stratling had expected. There was nothing on board his ship that could match an eight-pounder. His attitude changed instantly. "See 'ere, Cap'n, there be no need for that. I be tellin' you it were poor seamanship took oars off your longboat."

"Liar! It was no accident!"

"I be off now, Cap'n," Stratling said. "P'rhaps it be best this matter be settled 'tween you and Michael de Pauw in court of law."

The *Pavonia*'s bow veered off and the wind settled into her sails, filling them, taking the ship away from the *Bright Hope*. Pieter looked longingly at the eight-pounder. *Pavonia* was still well within range, and it would have been simple to drop a few shots on her decks. He resisted the temptation. He knew that Stratling would continue to claim he had been guilty of sloppy seamanship: hardly cause for Pieter to blast him with a cannon.

And anyway the quarrel wasn't with Stratling. The Englishman was only a hired hand. The real antagonist was Michael de Pauw.

He ordered the sails hoisted, and they set out to rescue the other longboat. The bosun came to the quarterdeck.

"Return to port," Pieter said.

"Aye!" Bosun Vincent said, trembling with anger over the recent injustice. "We have a score to settle with that scum!"

"This time Michael de Pauw has gone too far," Pieter said. But he wondered . . . Michael de Pauw must have known what would happen after his man sheared off the oars. What did he have in mind?

The council met in the wooden building next to the fine brick house that was being constructed for the governor. The work was being done by company slaves, which meant that the fort would not be finished quickly. But no matter, said the governor, anxious to have a house he deemed worthy of him.

Pieter sat in the front row of benches before the governor's desk. He looked down the row and saw de Pauw seated, calm and smiling, at the end. At his side sat Dirk Stratling, also looking quite unperturbed.

The governor arrived, wheezing as he dropped his bulk into the large chair behind the desk. The others had risen at his entrance. "Sit down, sit down," he said impatiently. "Now what's so important that we're forced to call a special council meeting? What's this all about?"

Pieter rose. He recounted the incidents of the South Bay. He repeated Stratling's claims, and then concluded by telling the assembly, "Not only are these claims untrue, but they indicate to what lengths certain men will be driven by their avarice. If we are to remain a colony of free men, then we must not allow the fisheries to be restricted. When some rights are denied to all but a few, then it is only a matter of time until all rights are denied to all but a few."

Before Michael de Pauw could give his side of the argument, the distinguished Dominie Bogardus came to his feet. "May I be permitted to speak?" he asked the governor.

Van Twiller nodded, and the dominie wasted no time. "Let's get to the heart of the matter. Michael de Pauw has filed a claim for the lands of the community of Swanendael, that unfortunate village in the South Bay area whose inhabitants were massacred by the heathen Indians two years ago. On the basis of his claim for the lands he has recently filed a claim to the exclusive rights of the waters."

The dominie drew himself up to his full height and stared straight into de Pauw's eyes. "This is a disgrace. It is an outright attempt by one man to rob the colony of its wealth. The Swanendael community itself never had exclusive rights to the waters. Your claim, sir, is spurious and false."

The dominie turned to the governor. "And so I must ask you, Your Excellency, why are we indulging in this farce? Must we sit here and discuss Michael de Pauw's claim to fishing rights that don't exist? Why do we subject ourselves to nonsense?"

He sat down, and Governor Van Twiller glanced nervously about the room. Both de Pauw and de Kuyper were important men, and he had no desire to antagonize either of them. His own wish would have been to let the two of them settle their dispute between themselves. However, that recourse had just been denied him by the intervention of Dominie Bogardus. The governor was intimidated by the dominie; he knew the clergyman was one of the few men who could care less that he bore the title Governor. The long ocean voyage had acquainted him with the pastor's acid tongue. Therefore he had no choice but to turn to Michael de Pauw and ask:

"Is it true that you've applied for the fishing rights formerly belonging to the Swanendael community?"

"It is true, Your Excellency."

"But that charter makes no mention of exclusive fishing rights. Surely you're aware of this."

"No sir, I was not aware of this," de Pauw lied smoothly. In his long-range plans to obtain concessions from the governor, the exclusive fishing rights played an insignificant role, and his immediate goal was to make friends with the man. Therefore he spoke politely. "But now that Your Excellency has been so good as to point this out, I immediately withdraw my claim to the fishing grounds of the South Bay, now and forever in the future."

Stratling looked at de Pauw as if he had just been stabbed in the back. "I'll make it up to you," de Pauw whispered in a low tone. "With some land." The Englishman recovered quickly. He nodded and smiled. Very well, if he couldn't become a rich whaling man, he would become a rich landowner.

The governor looked relieved. There weren't going to be any long, tedious arguments. The matter was settled. "Very well. In that case, there being no further disputations to be resolved—"

"One moment, sir," Pieter de Kuyper said, leaping to his feet. "There is the matter of the *Pavonia*'s attempt to scuttle one of my longboats. I call this an act of piracy!"

Unhappiness returned to the governor's face. He turned back to de Pauw. "And what do you say to this charge?"

"Captain Stratling has already explained this accident to me," de Pauw said. "It was unfortunate and we are deeply sorry. However, it was merely an accident and hardly an act of piracy."

"An accident?" the governor said. "Captain Stratling, is that all it was?"

"Aye. 'Twere a busy time and I 'ad my mind on other matters. Sloppy seamanship it were, sor, and for that I makes my 'pologies."

"And, of course," de Pauw said quickly, "we'll replace the oars that Captain Stratling tells me were broken in the accident. They will be delivered today to the *Bright Hope*."

The governor had finally had enough. "It seems to me, de Kuyper," he said in a chiding voice, "that we're all wasting our time here. Now do you have any further concerns over such petty matters?"

Pieter was seething with rage, but he knew he had been beaten. "No, sir, I believe we've settled all the particulars."

"Good!" the governor said as he stood up. "This council is now adjourned."

Claes Vincent stood beside Pieter. "The dirty bastards were lying through their teeth," he said in a low voice.

"I know, but there will be another time."

Michael de Pauw made his way across the room to the governor's side. "There are some matters I would like to talk to Your Excellency about in private."

The governor was hardly cordial. "I'm very busy. Can't they wait?"

Michael de Pauw smiled. "These are matters that concern Rensselaerswyck. I thought perhaps you might be interested."

The affairs of Kiliaen Van Rensselaer were of the utmost importance to Van Twiller. He looked more closely at de Pauw. "And what is your connection with Rensselaerswyck?"

"I'm a friend of your uncle's. We are careful to look out for one another's interests."

The governor's manner changed. "Well, in that case, let's have a chat. Come to my quarters. I have several bottles of the finest French brandy to be found on this side of the ocean."

The two men disappeared through the door leading to the governor's private quarters.

Pieter watched, and a frown came to his face. He did not like to see the governor becoming friends with Michael de Pauw. The governor was a soft-minded fool. If he fell under the influence of a man like de Pauw, it could mean trouble for the general well-being of the colony. He turned and walked out of the room, with Claes Vincent at his elbow.

He noticed Dirk Stratling watching him, a smile of triumph on his ugly face. Pieter was a peaceful man, not given to brawling and revenge, but he had a healthy temper and a powerful body. The sight of the gloating Englishman did something to him. He vowed he would take the smirk off the man's face. And soon.

Smile, Dirk Stratling, smile while you can. Because when I get through with you, you will never smile again. A chill ran up Pieter's spine as he became aware of the fury he harbored.

As Pieter made his way from the fort toward his home on Pearl Street, he passed a small shed and a fenced-in lot that held a dozen goats. Christiana was there with Geertie Smit and two other women. Christiana looked up from the goat, on whose sore forefoot she was applying a salve, and saw her husband. She motioned for Geertie to complete the task and went to the fence where Pieter stood.

"What happened?" she asked, noticing the scowl on his face. "Did something go wrong?"

"You're determined to go ahead with this foolish goat idea, are you?" he said, ignoring her question and directing his scowl toward the other women and the goats.

She was puzzled. "Just the other day you agreed it was a good idea," she said. "Soon it will pay for itself, you'll see."

"It's an unnatural idea," Pieter said. "The other men think as little of it as I do."

"That may be because the other men didn't think of it," Christiana said spiritedly. "I did. And the women seem in favor of it."

"A waste of money!" Pieter said.

"You're not being fair," Christiana said stubbornly. "You have to give it a full season to know whether or not it's a waste of money."

She looked at the goats with pride. It *was* something of an unnatural idea, even a daring one. And it had been all hers.

After she had despaired of interesting the other women in books, she had searched for some project that they might undertake in common. She did it mostly because she tried to keep as busy as possible. When she was occupied, her mind didn't have time to dwell on Indians or other hateful aspects of this place that made her life miserable. She had come up with the goat idea one day when she saw Geertie Smit milking her animal.

"Wouldn't it be a good idea," she said to Geertie, "if several of us women got together and tended our own goat herd? We could divide the work among us. Some of us would milk, others would clean up and care for the animals."

"You mean we'd all own the goats together?" Geertie said, her features reflecting her puzzlement over this novel idea.

"Yes."

"I don't know if Jan would like—"

"The men would have nothing to do with it," Christiana interrupted. "The goats would belong to the women."

This heresy caused Geertie to step back. Own property alone? Without her husband? She knew Jan would hate that idea. "Where would we get the money to buy the goats?" she asked, aware that Christiana was probably in the same straits as every other woman in the settlement, totally dependent on her husband for every penny of hard cash.

"We'll borrow it from our husbands."

Geertie shook her head at this, but Christiana now had the bit in her mouth and refused to slow down. Here was a project that made sense, because it fitted into the daily lives of the women. They may not have been interested in reading, but how could they not be interested in goats? "We'll have milk and cheese, and we'll sell it and use the profits to care for the goats and buy more of them," she said, thinking out the plan even as she spoke.

When she proposed the plan to Pieter, he didn't know what to make of it. But he was aware of his wife's general unhappiness and decided that if it would give her pleasure, it would be worth trying. The money he gave her settled the issue in Christiana's favor. When the other wives saw how generous Pieter de Kuyper could be, they hounded and badgered their own husbands into giving them a like sum. It became a point of honor for each woman to prove that her husband was as generous as anyone else's.

The goats were bought from the West India Company and a large lot was rented from the same source. The first cooperative on Manhatan Island was in business and it was run by a group of women. Most of them had had a goat or two at home, but this was different. Let the men spend their time whaling or farming or running breweries and bakeries, the women said, we'll show them we can do as well in business, or better. With the growing number of ships anchoring off the island, there was always a demand for cheese. Surely this goat "factory" would prosper if it catered to the crews of the sailing vessels.

So far, however, the venture had yet to turn a profit. They milked the goats and made cheese and sold it, but by the time they subtracted their costs, there was hardly any money left over. Christiana argued that their profit was so small only because they were still paying for the livestock, a situation that would end next year, and because they had had to pay cash for lumber to build the shed and fencing, again a one-time cost. But the truth of this did not deter the women's husbands from deriding the entire affair.

Pieter had been tolerant of the enterprise because he was glad to see Christiana busily tending the goats and keeping the ledgers instead of nervously peering out through the windows as if she expected trouble at any moment. So his reaction this day was unusual. He was really angry with de Pauw and Stratling, but he was only human, and he vented his frustration on Christiana.

"I think it would be best if you sold the goats and took the loss," he said. "It's stupid to keep paying for the upkeep of these creatures."

Christiana recognized the injustice of the statement. Pieter had originally put up the money; that much was true. But he had never been asked for a single penny since that day. Once the other debts were settled, Christiana would pay back the money she had borrowed from Pieter. All the women had agreed to this plan.

Christiana was aware now that something apart from her venture was troubling her husband. "You brought me to this godforsaken place," she said. "When I mope around the house you tell me to find something to do. Now that I've found it, you're telling me to go back to the house. Is that what you want?"

It was the last thing Pieter wanted, and she knew it. For a few moments he could think of no response. Finally, gruffly, with as much grace as he was able to muster, he said, "Very well, we'll give it a full season."

"Thank you."

"But if it keeps losing money, next year you'll have to stop."

"Naturally," she said coolly, pretending to be hurt. "If you have no faith in me—"

"Dammit, woman," he exploded, "I have faith in you. It's just that . . ." and he could speak no more, because the thought of de Pauw and Stratling choked him with rage.

"If you've nothing more to say to me, I'll be about my work," Christiana said. There was no sense in talking to Pieter when he got into one of these black moods. The best thing, she had learned, was to leave him alone. Eventually he would calm down and talk about it.

"Is my son at home?" he asked.

"Yes."

"I'll go see what he's doing," Pieter said and walked off toward the house on Pearl Street.

Christiana shuddered and hoped, for Young Pieter's sake, that he was engaged in an activity that would meet with his father's approval.

She turned back to the pen and admired her goats. They were white, of Alpine stock, and the larger ones would grow to a weight of one hundred and fifty pounds. A goat like that would yield a thousand pints of milk a year and bring forth two or three healthy kids. If things went according to plan, the women would have a thriving enterprise within two years.

A woman approached her and timidly asked if she was in charge of the goats.

"Yes," Christiana said.

"My name is Maria de Peyster. We've only just arrived from Holland, and I heard about this," the woman said, looking about at the herd. "I think it's wonderful."

"Would you like to join us?"

"Yes, but . . ." she said, swallowing, and forcing out the next words. "How much does it cost?"

"Each woman puts in fifteen guilders, or the equivalent in silver," Christiana replied.

The other woman's face fell. "Oh."

Christiana realized the de Peyster woman didn't have this much money, or more likely, couldn't get it from her husband. She placed her hand on the other's arm. "But if you're really interested I'm sure we can work something out."

"Could you?" A ray of hope crossed the other's face.

"Of course," Christiana said, taking her by the arm and leading her toward the herd. "Nothing could be easier."

It wouldn't be easy, of course, but the woman had looked so crestfallen Christiana didn't have the heart to send her away.

But how would she raise the money? It would be unfair to ask the other women to share this extra cost. After all, it had been Christiana's idea; so this was her problem to solve. Somehow or other she'd have to get the money from Pieter. She sighed. It *wouldn't* be easy, especially after his latest comments.

The look on Maria de Peyster's face as she petted the kid gave Christiana more resolve. It was wonderful to be able to bring happiness to the women of the colony. And an equal pleasure to be accepted by them. In the earlier years, when she had tried to interest the women in books, they had remained aloof from her. But now many of them were becoming her friends.

It also pleased her to be working with the goats. She had always loved gentle animals; they seemed so helpless and dependent on people. She cherished the idea that she was responsible for their care and well-being. And then she thought she saw one of her charges limping, and rushed to see if there was any problem.

And while Christiana kept busy, worrying about people like Maria de Peyster, and taking care of the goats, she didn't even realize she forgot to worry so much about herself.

"A good brandy, quite excellent," Michael de Pauw said as he looked at the dark liquid in the crystal goblet, a kind of drinking vessel that was exceedingly rare in the New World. "As you said, the finest to be found on this side of the ocean."

The two men were seated in the room that served as the governor's parlor. A black slave brought in a platter covered with wedges of cheese, hunks of bread, and several kinds of cold sliced meats. He placed the platter on the low table in front of the men and left the room.

"Damn nasty business, de Pauw," the governor said through a mouthful of cheese, "claiming exclusive fishing rights when they don't exist."

"My apologies, Your Excellency. It will not happen again."

"See that it doesn't. And now, tell me of the matter concerning Rensselaerswyck."

"Poachers are trading directly with the Indians. All trades are supposed to be made through the patroon."

"Ah yes, these damned poachers . . . no respect for a man's property. Well, what of it?"

"If such men are caught they will be tried and punished?"

"Of course."

"And their furs returned to the patroon?"

"Yes, yes."

"Good. The patroon will be happy to hear."

The governor stopped eating and stared at de Pauw. "This is the matter you desired to talk about in private? See here, de Pauw, what's your game?"

"My lord has seen through my not-too-clever ruse," de Pauw said, playing to the other's vanity. "Actually you're quite correct, there is another matter I wish to speak with you about."

"I thought so," Van Twiller said smugly, pleased he had successfully demonstrated his astuteness.

"And it has nothing to do with Rensselaerswyck."

"I guessed that, too. Well, what's on your mind?"

"When this colony was founded I was commissioned to survey the land. In all modesty I can say that I know more about our lands than any other man in the colony."

The governor was again perplexed, but he pretended otherwise. "I know that. But come, man, get to your point."

"We stand at the beginning of a new era," de Pauw said, rising to his feet and walking around, forcing Van Twiller to follow him with his eyes. "And the key to this new era is land. I already own a great deal of land—on Manhatan, on Staten Island, even some near Fort Orange, thanks to our mutual friend, Kiliaen Van Rensselaer."

The last remark brought a look of filial piety to the governor's face, which was the very reason de Pauw made it. He was using every bit of ammunition he had.

He continued. "In a few years the land I own will be worth much more than it is at present—three times, four times, maybe ten times as much. There is no limit. Even what I own is only a pittance, the tiniest bit compared to the abundance of land about us. However, it is wild land and needs to be developed. Only then will the value increase. But it *will* be developed, because with every passing year our colony grows as new settlers arrive. And what is it that brings these men to our colony? It is land, sir. Land, land, and more land. The man who controls the land today, controls the fortunes of tomorrow. The man who buys land today will *own* the fortunes of tomorrow!"

The governor was most interested, de Pauw decided; now it was time to appeal to his self-interest.

"But it's not as simple as just buying land. The key is to buy the *right* land. And that's where I have the edge on the others. I know which are the right lands to buy, which ones will increase the most in value. I want to buy these lands and develop them for settlement. With the approval of Your Excellency, the company could grant me the right to buy these lands. Since we would be entering into this agreement in a sense of partnership, I was wondering if Your Excellency might not be interested in sharing in some of my ventures."

"I cannot use my office for private gain," Van Twiller said self-righteously.

"Of course not," de Pauw said smoothly, "nor would I even dream of asking such a thing. But doesn't the governor have the same rights as every other citizen? Is it fair to make the governor stand idly by and watch others make fortunes? No, that isn't fair at all."

"I must agree with that," Van Twiller said eagerly, hoping de Pauw could figure out a way for him to get land without compromising his office. He was not to be disappointed.

"Good!" de Pauw said. "I'm glad Your Excellency thinks the way I do. My proposal? I will apply to buy several tracts of land, some on Manhatan, others on the shores of the other side of the North River. Your role in our partnership will be to obtain the company's approval. For this invaluable service I will give you title for certain of the lands on Manhatan. By this means your name will never be submitted to the company as the initial buyer of the lands. But believe me, Your Excellency, we'll be doing this for the good of the future development of New Netherland," de Pauw said, giving Van Twiller yet another crutch to support the morality of the scheme.

But the governor was already beyond the need for crutches. "Where would my lands be?" he asked.

De Pauw went to the wall, which held a map of the colony. "I think Nutten Island would be of interest to Your Excellency."

When they parted several hours later, Michael de

Pauw had the governor's promise to support his bids on various lands. He also had a commission to start a settlement at Pavonia, a place on the mainland west of Staten Island. In addition he had put down a sum of money for the purchase of Nutten Island, whose title would be passed to Governor Van Twiller.

Both men were pleased with the business of the day.

Young Pieter sat on a bench at the rear of the house, savoring the treasure given him by his mother: a most wonderful book with many drawings of Amsterdam. How she had come by this prize was a mystery, but the book was in his hands and he sat marveling at the magical drawings that filled it.

The buildings were so tall he feared they would topple over into the street. And the churches! The height of the spires! The tall steeples towering over the vast roofs! Did such things exist? Why, one church looked big enough to cover the entire settlement on Manhatan. It was the most wonderful building in the world. Wouldn't that be something to see! He imagined himself entering through the huge doors and staring up at the ceiling. He would have to be careful not to topple back onto the floor. The drawing made the ceiling so high it seemed to reach to the sky. It was incredible. Still, it must be so; here it was in a book. Even more astounding, under this vast roof were gathered a thousand people, all facing the altar and saying their prayers. A thousand people! More than lived on the entire island of Manhatan!

Since he had only recently begun to read, he could not understand most of the words in the book, but that didn't matter. The drawings were the important things. They brought to life the stories told to him by his mother—stories of paved streets and broad avenues; stories of houses with five and six levels, busy houses of government and commerce where men of importance decided the fate of cities and colonies around the world. To such men the settlement on Manhatan was only an entry in their books, simply another port of call and probably not a very important one at that.

Young Pieter closed his eyes and imagined himself as a young man, elegantly dressed and assured, casually entering one of these tall guild halls. People nodded in friendly fashion, acknowledging that he was no stranger to these grand chambers. Liveried servants with silver buttons on their tunics bowed their heads in deference, aware this young man was a lordly person accustomed to such courtesies. He climbed wide staircases, walked down broad, carpeted halls, and entered magnificent rooms where tall windows were flooded with sunshine. The rooms had high bookcases crammed with volumes whose gold lettering on the spines reflected the bright light. Chandeliers hung from the ceiling, huge devices of ponderous weight supporting hundreds of bits of crystal. The young man entered this glorious room. Wise and important men turned to greet him. They welcomed him; a young lord at home in the den of the graybeards.

It was a wonderful dream. It lifted him into a sphere of joy. He savored it to the fullest and then decided it was time to look at another drawing and imagine himself in this new setting.

He opened his eyes.

His father was standing in front of him, an annoyed look on his face. The young lord vanished and left a nervous little boy in his place. The Netherlands became Manhatan.

"What sort of book is that?" Pieter asked.

"A book of pictures," the boy managed to say.

"Pictures? Pictures of what?"

Young Pieter knew his father did not approve of books about Europe. He wanted to run and hide, but knew it was too late for that. "Pictures of Amsterdam," he said.

Pieter took the book from his son's hands and skimmed through it. "Amsterdam, eh? They always make it out to be grander than it is." He shook his head. "There are better things to do with your time than fill your head with lies."

The boy said nothing.

"Why do you read such nonsense?"

Young Pieter wanted to say he liked to look at the pictures even if they were nonsense. He wanted to say he liked beautiful buildings and grand churches. He wanted to say many things, but as usual he said nothing. His head drooped and he stared at the ground.

"None of that," Pieter said sternly. "Look at me."

The boy's head came up slowly, and he fought back the tears as he looked at his father.

"The pictures are lies. Do you understand?"

"Yes, Father," he said almost inaudibly.

"I want you to give that book back to your mother."

"Yes, Father."

"I'd do it myself, but I want you to do it. Do you know why?"

"No, Father," he admitted miserably.

"Because I'm putting you on your honor to do it. It's important that a man have a sense of honor."

"Yes, Father."

Having made his point, Pieter relaxed and became more amiable. "Good lad. You'll learn that you must be a man."

"Yes, Father, I must be a man," the boy said, attempting to use the strongest and bravest voice he possessed. But he was very upset and his voice cracked.

Pieter patted his son on the shoulder, placed the book beside him, and walked into the house.

Yes, and I must be a man, Young Pieter thought. And a man does not dream silly thoughts. He does not waste his time on useless books. He is strong and able to take care of himself. He is not a little boy or a silly girl or a weak woman. He is like my father. Yes, that is a man, someone like my father.

Young Pieter glanced at the book at his side. He no longer had any interest in it. All its golden hopes, all its dreams and magic had been taken away by his father. It no longer was the door to a fabled land, simply a dusty old book that belonged on a shelf along with his dreams. Words, pictures, nothing.

Yes, and I must be a man, Young Pieter thought. And he wondered why.

It was Maria de Peyster who warned Christiana about the trouble brewing between Pieter and Dirk Stratling. They were at the goat pens, and Christiana was happily tending a newborn ewe.

Maria explained what had happened with Stratling and the *Pavonia*. "Your husband seems to have taken it personally," she said. "It's common talk among the men that there'll be a fight."

This revelation màde Christiana realize why Pieter had been so cranky lately, why he had been moody and sullen.

"But what can I do?" she asked.

"Maybe if you went to the governor and explained, he might do something about it."

Christiana thought it over. She hardly knew the governor, a heavyset, formidable figure. What could she say to him? What could she ask him to do?

"It's worth trying," Maria said.

Christiana became resolved. Maria was right. She had to do something to help Pieter.

"I'll go with you if you want," Maria said.

"Why would you do that?"

Maria shrugged. "You were a friend when I needed one. Now I want to be yours."

Christiana was touched. She reached out and squeezed the other's hand. "Thank you, but this is something I must do by myself."

She went home, put on a clean dress, combed her hair, gathered her courage, and went to the governor's office. He kept her waiting in an anteroom for over an hour before admitting her to his presence.

He was gruff and distant. It had been a busy day, and he had no time to waste on de Kuyper's wife. He told her to be seated and dropped his own considerable girth into a chair, whose frame squeaked in protest at the weight.

"I've heard there will be trouble between my husband and a man named Stratling," she said, coming directly to the point.

The governor said nothing.

"You must do something to prevent it," Christiana said.

The woman's tone of voice annoyed him. Who did she think she was to give him orders? "Must?"

"Yes," she replied, a little less firmly as she weakened under the governor's baleful stare.

Van Twiller had heard several rumors about this affair. Tricky business it was. On one hand, Pieter de Kuyper was well liked and a man of some influence. It would be a simple thing to take his side, especially against an Englishman.

On the other hand, this particular Englishman worked

for Michael de Pauw, and the governor certainly didn't want to offend that estimable gentleman. There seemed only one course to take.

"I don't see that I can do anything," he said.

"But you . . . you're the governor."

"That I am."

Christiana had expected the man to be more understanding, more sympathetic. "This man, Stratling, he isn't Dutch."

"Quite so."

"He's an Englishman—a foreigner," she said, as if this would make the situation clear to this blockheaded man.

"What does that have to do with it?"

"Expel him! Throw him out of the colony," she said, beginning to lose control of herself.

"But, my dear woman," the governor said in his most reasonable tones, "the man's committed no crime."

"Trying to hurt another man is no crime?"

"Who's been hurt?"

"How can you sit there and take the part of a foreigner against one of your own countrymen?" she asked angrily. As usual, Christiana was thinking more with her heart than her head. Also, the man's indifference was upsetting her and muddying her logic.

"See here, madam," Van Twiller said, his own anger rising, "how dare you accuse me of that?"

"You're taking sides!"

"Taking sides? Taking sides over what? Nothing's happened."

"But it *will!*" she said shrilly, all semblance of calm departed.

The governor glared at her. This was the woman who had stirred up trouble between some of the men and their wives. Over a herd of goats, no less. Why, it had even caused an argument between himself and his own wife! She had wanted to join the women in their stupid goat venture and had been dissuaded only when he pointed out it was improper behavior for the wife of the governor. And now this same troublemaker was in his office, shouting at him. What effrontery!

"If you're so worried about your husband," he said nastily, "I suggest you talk to *him*. He seems to be the one causing trouble."

Christiana tried to reply, but tears came to her eyes and she forgot what she was going to say. She wasn't even sure Van Twiller wasn't speaking the truth.

She put her face into her hands and began to sob.

"Now, now, none of that," the governor said, coming around the desk.

Christiana cried and the governor fretted about, trying to calm her and not succeeding. After a minute she dried her eyes and left the office without another word. The governor sighed, wiped the sweat from his brow, and vowed never again to admit a woman into his office.

Christiana went home and pretended nothing was wrong. Every time she looked at Pieter she wanted to cry. She had tried her best and it hadn't been good enough. She felt inept and useless.

A week passed, and then another. Finally the situation resolved itself.

Pieter was seated at a table in Frans Kock's new tavern at 1 Broad Way. With him were Claes Vincent, David de Hatten, who owned the forge, and Captain Arne Swensen, a Swede who worked for the West India Company as master of a cargo ship that regularly plied the Atlantic with supplies for the colony.

Most of the tavern's other patrons were Dutch seamen, although there was a sprinkling of foreign sailors. At one table was a group of farmers, and a few other tables were occupied by merchants. Kock's Tavern had been a favorite of the men since the day its doors opened. The drinks were strong and of a generous size; the food excellent as it came steaming forth from the kitchen on huge platters. And the conversation was good, since Frans Kock was one of the greatest liars in the colony. His hair-raising stories of adventures among the Indians were cut from whole cloth, as anyone who had ever dealt with the savages knew. But the stories were told with such mirth and verve that no one saw any need to challenge the tavernkeeper, and everyone had a good evening's entertainment.

Dirk Stratling and two other Englishmen came into the tavern. They took a table and ordered drinks. Pieter saw Stratling the moment he entered, but ignored him. After the Englishman had a few drinks, Pieter decided it was time.

"Frans," he called to the owner, who was standing behind the bar next to a barrel of beer, "you should hear the story Captain Swensen's been telling me."

Kock was interested, but there was a look of bewilderment on the Swedish captain's face, for he had been telling no story. Pieter winked, and the Swede understood. "Yes, quite a tale," he said in his deep, booming voice.

"The story is about the seamanship of men of different countries," Pieter said. "The captain, naturally, maintains that Swedes are the best sailors in the world. But he admits the Dutch are a close second, far better than, for example, the French."

There was scattered laughter among the sailors. They all looked to a table near the door where the captain of a French caravel was seated. The Frenchman managed a weak smile. "There are other things—more important things, such as wine and women—at which we excel," he said, joining in the laughter that met his acceptable retort.

Pieter laughed, bowed at the rebuke, and said, "Ah, compared to some, the French sail as if they were inspired by the Almighty Himself. These others are men who should not be allowed even to clean bilges, much less set their filthy feet upon a quarterdeck."

Claes Vincent took his cue. "Yes, I've heard of these people, Captain. Are they not those who can't see where they're going and so bump into everything in sight?"

"The very same. The way they find the New World, or at least so I am told, is they are towed from port and pointed in the right direction. Since there is nothing in the ocean to hit, they sail on until they finally bump into the land on this side of the Atlantic."

"I've forgotten the name of . . . this breed. Forgive me, I almost called them sailors, but that is certainly a mistake," Claes Vincent said

"A terrible mistake," Pieter agreed.

"By what name do we know these people?" Frans Kock asked, thoroughly enjoying the sport.

Pieter hung his head as if in shame. "I find it a most distasteful word to say."

"But you must say it," Kock argued, wondering who

was to be the butt of this fine joke. "It isn't fair if you don't tell us."

Pieter was smiling as he looked directly at Dirk Stratling. "Very well, if I must I must. . . . They are known as . . . the word stumbles on my tongue . . . the English," he said, immediately grabbing his beer and taking a long draft as if to clear his mouth of the filthy word.

Someone laughed, but most of the men turned in their seats and looked at the three Englishmen. Stratling had a murderous look in his eyes, and his hands were clasped so tightly together that the knuckles were white. But he remained in his seat and said nothing.

Pieter realized he would have to go further. "But there's more to the story," he said in the quiet of the tavern. "Even among the English there's a class of sailor considered the lowest of the low."

"Lower than the English?" Claes Vincent said in a mock whisper that implied such foulness could not actually exist.

"Yes, even lower than the English. But I dare not say the name. It's so vile it isn't even human."

"Come, de Kuyper," Frans Kock said. "We're all strong men in this room. Speak the name of the creature!"

"Yes," a Dutch sailor cried, "tell us what is lower than an Englishman."

"Stratlings."

The silence was now deafening, and Pieter spoke again. "Stratlings. Named after the lowest scum who ever sailed these waters." His voice was low and his eyes were fastened on the face of the Englishman.

Dirk Stratling leaped to his feet, his chair falling to the floor. His companions remained seated, nervously looking about, realizing that if they were to defend their companion's honor, it would be against fearful odds.

"You filthy Dutch pig!" Stratling hissed.

Pieter remained seated. He looked around as if he did not see Stratling. "Did someone speak," he asked calmly, "or was that merely the sound of a sow farting?"

Stratling's anger overcame his common sense. He charged across the room and threw himself at the Dutchman. Pieter had been waiting for this, and he moved aside as Stratling crashed heavily into the chair and fell to the floor. He scrambled to his feet, a wild look in his eyes, and a knife suddenly appeared in his hand.

"No knives, no knives!" Frans Kock shouted, but his alarm was unnecessary, as Claes Vincent's hook slashed out and penetrated the Englishman's wrist. Stratling screamed in pain and the knife clattered to the floor. Vincent wrenched the hook loose with a flip of his forearm.

Stratling barely looked at his wounded wrist before he leaped again at Pieter, who was now standing in the middle of the open space between the tables.

Pieter did not duck this charge. He met it head on, smashing his fist into the other man's face. There was a loud *splat!* as Stratling's nose was mashed into his face; the bone broke and a spout of blood reddened his cheeks and drained down his chin.

The Englishman attempted to get his arms around Pieter's neck, but the canny Dutchman simply dropped down and slipped away from him. In the same motion Pieter got behind his opponent and pinned both his arms in the air, holding the back of the man's head in front of his own hands. In this position he shoved him across the floor, picking up speed as he pushed, until Stratling's head crashed into a stout post that went from the floor to the roof.

Pieter released his hold. The dazed Englishman stumbled, but remained on his feet, his eyes glazing as he turned to face his torturer. Pieter cocked his fist and delivered a blow with all the might of his body behind it. Stratling's mouth took the full force of the fist, and he went down as if he had been hit by a cannonball, his broken teeth cutting through gums and cheek, his jaw broken in three places, his brain gratefully giving way to unconsciousness.

The other two Englishmen had not moved from their places at the table. They suddenly became very interested in their beers. They did not look at Stratling.

"Remind me never to get into a fight with you, lad," Captain Swenson said as Pieter returned to the table and finished his beer.

Governor Van Twiller was annoyed when he heard about the fight. He wanted no trouble between de Pauw and de Kuyper. Deciding to get Pieter out of the way for a time, he commissioned him to make a tour of the colony and submit a report on its present status.

The governor thought that the best way to keep the peace was to keep Pieter away from de Pauw. The commission was issued as an official government order, which made it impossible to refuse.

So Pieter went out to do his survey, angry at first but more and more pleased as he gained a firsthand understanding of what was happening to this colony he had helped found.

For truly, these were years of great expansion and activity for the people of New Netherland.

Pieter began by inspecting the bouweries of the hardy farmers on the outskirts of the tiny town, and then followed the signs of civilization as they moved farther up the island, up to the shining lakes in the middle, and beyond to what soon would be called the new settlement of Harlem.

He spent weeks tracing the wanderings of the farmers: west across the North River to the farms at New Korshem, Hackensack, Hoboken, and Pavonia; north up the river past Manhatan to the wildernesses of Schenectady, Schoharies, Kinderhook, Pooghkeepsie; east across the turbulence of the Hellegat to the farms of the BruijkleenVeer that were beginning to sprout into the settlements of Midwout, Amersfort, Utrecht, Bushwick, and Breuckelen. The farmers had spread to the south as well, to Staten Island, and this was as far as Pieter went, although the settlements extended down to the palisades near Fort Nassau on the South River and the South Bay.

Pieter marveled at the growing complexity of his colony. He compared what he saw to the original bouweries in New Amsterdam which were simple affairs, a few fields and a single structure, one end of which was the house, the other the barn. But now the farmers were prospering and their houses becoming larger and more elaborate. Even as they grew in size, however, the houses remained plain dwellings, reflecting the character of these people who wrested a living from the virgin earth. They retained their humility when the harsh scramble of the first years was only a memory.

Pieter called on many farmers. They proudly showed

him the great strides they had made in creating a comfortable life for themselves and their families.

"First winter about all we had to eat was a peck of moldy corn," one farmer said. "Almost starved. Snow was so deep we couldn't go anywhere."

But now the farmers planted wheat, rye, barley, and oats; buckwheat, canary seed, small beans, and flax flourished; the land grew heavy with cranberries, blackberries, raspberries, and strawberries.

The farmers took Pieter into their homes and smiled at his astonishment at the bounty and variety he saw. Their tables were blessed with lobsters, oysters, clams, crayfish, and dozens of other gifts from the abundant waters; from the Indians they had learned of potatoes, cabbage, parsnips, carrots and beets; they enjoyed the pungent spices of rosemary, hyssop, thyme, sage, marjoram, balm, wormwood, chives, and tarragon, which they called dragon's wort; their hogs grew fat, the horses thrived, goats wandered about, and the large-boned Dutch cattle grazed on the lush grasses. The settlers were learning that the smaller cattle found in New England were hardier and had more resistance to the harsh winters; subsequently they began to buy these smaller animals from the English, who were spreading down from their original settlements in Plymouth and Salem, moving to fields on the Connecticut River and on Long Island.

These contacts between the Dutch and the English were the cause of growing problems. Governor Van Twiller was alarmed when Charles of England granted Long Island to Alexander, Lord Stirling. The governor immediately sent word to Pieter to interrupt his survey and go to Plymouth, Massachusetts, in a fast packet to confer with William Bradford, the English governor.

"But my dear sir," the Englishman said blandly, "this is a vast country with more than enough room for all of us."

"The grant to your Lord Stirling includes lands already settled by the Dutch," Pieter pointed out with a certain amount of sarcasm. "Although we agree there is room for everyone, it is not wise for both of us to occupy the same space."

"Of course, of course," Bradford agreed. "I will instruct our people they are to avoid the western end of the land."

"For how long?" Pieter said softly, but the English governor pretended not to hear his remark.

An uneasy peace was established, but Pieter spent a few days among these English settlers and noted the grimness with which they attacked their lives, the extra sternness of the religion they inflicted on themselves, their desire to carve a place in this wilderness that would be theirs and theirs alone. It would not be easy to live side by side with these people, and he quietly predicted that one day there would be trouble.

"In the near future?" Van Twiller asked nervously when he received the report from his emissary.

"It will take time. Ten, twenty, even thirty years. But there will be trouble," Pieter answered. The governor dismissed the matter from his mind. He had no intention of being here ten, twenty or, God help him! thirty years from now. That would be a problem for someone else to worry about.

Pieter concluded his survey by recording happily that the first attempt at growing tobacco on Manhatan was a success. The company's farm was halfway up the island, in a remote wilderness.

Pieter's report included the fact that that Fort Amsterdam was finally completed. It was 300 feet long and 250 feet wide, quadrangular in shape. There was a battlement at each corner, and the northwest face bore a coat of stone. A new barracks had been built within the walls, and a new guardhouse. There was a small windmill and, of course, a splendid house for the governor. Dominie Bogardus's new wooden church stood immediately outside the walls, and nearby was the town's first burial ground.

The report noted there was a good commerce on the North River as the tiny *vliebooten,* or flyboats, plied their way up and down carrying traders and merchants; the former looked for Indians with furs, the latter for farmer's wives who would buy the pots, pans, bolts of cloth, knives, axes, latches, nails, and other necessities of life.

Pieter compiled statistics that gave a good picture of life in the colony. But behind the statistics there was the harsh face of reality. One day a slow, somber procession was wending its way toward the burial ground, and he joined it. At the edge of the open pit, he remarked on its small size. The man at his side nodded his head. "A child," he said.

"How old?"

"Seven months."

Seven months, Pieter thought; seven months in the New World, seven months and it was all over, over before the child knew who he was or where he was, or why he was. Seven months and the bell tolled and the small bit of humanity was lowered into the earth while prayers were mumbled. And then the mourners went to their homes and there was only a memory, and a short one at that, of a tiny being who had lived all the life it had been allowed.

And such a death was not an unusual occurrence; infant mortality was extremely high. The death rate among adults was also extraordinary. Few partners in marriage reached the age of forty together. There was a high proportion of widows and widowers in the colony, and a large number of second, third, and even fourth marriages.

Laws and civil codes were being compiled—most of them from expediency, such as the one forbidding "late-night carousing," passed after a Danish seaman had been stabbed in a drunken brawl outside Frans Kock's tavern. This came very soon after Pieter de Kuyper had smashed up Dirk Stratling, and Governor Van Twiller was determined to keep the peace.

But most of the laws, Pieter observed, were codes that had to do with trade and land boundaries. In these days land was the most abundant commodity in the New World, but even so there were men who understood the future wealth represented by this land. It was the truest measure of wealth—farmers could be killed by Indians; crops could be burned or wiped out by natural disasters; houses could be destroyed or crumble into rubble; but after everything else had been ruined or destroyed, there would still be the land, millions and millions of acres of it, a vast empire beginning where the weeping waves of the Atlantic dashed out their lives on the rocky coast, and extending across a continent for thousands of miles; there was an entire *continent* at their feet, and those with foresight knew the land itself was the greatest and richest and most permanent gift of their new home.

Pieter at first had been annoyed with the task of surveying the colony, but now that it was done he was glad he had been the one to do it. It gave him a new perspective and made him more certain than ever of the coming greatness of New Netherland.

"It is completed," he said when he placed the thick folio of papers on the governor's desk.

"Mmm," the governor said as he cursorily leafed through the stack, scarcely reading a sentence. "Think you've learned to stay out of trouble?"

"Hopefully we all learn that in time," Pieter replied mildly.

"And what exactly do you mean by that, sir?" the governor demanded, his eyes closing to slits.

"I mean that we'll all be better off if we stick to our jobs. Mine for the moment is catching whales, and yours is the dispensation of justice."

The governor said nothing further, but watched Pieter carefully as he left the office. There had been some nasty gibe in his last remark, but the governor was unable to determine exactly what it was. "A troublemaker," he mumbled beneath his breath, and the last thing Van Twiller wanted was trouble. He wanted everything to be peaceful while he amassed his fortune. After I'm gone, he thought, they can make all the trouble they want. He made a silent prayer to the Almighty that He would spare him any trouble.

The Almighty, it seems, was not listening that day.

Pieter, Christiana, and the children were among the congregation attending Dominie Bogardus's Sunday services in the new church. The dominie was, as usual, delivering a lucid sermon, this one on the virtues of sobriety —a frequent exhortation, but it had no effect on the great amount of drinking that went on. The dominie pointed out that drunks were often whipped or put in stocks in the more pious communities of the staid English. The Dutchmen kept solemn looks on their faces as they listened, inwardly rejoicing that they lived in a community too advanced and sophisticated to punish a man for so trivial an offense as public drunkenness. Their work, after all, was very hard, and it did a man good to get sotted after a day's exhausting labor. The sailors among them

had even stronger feelings. After weeks and even months
at sea, what better relaxation could a man find than a
complete and thorough drunk? Besides, no one could take
the dominie very seriously on this subject, since he was as
solid a drinking man as anyone in New Amsterdam. He
had an enormous capacity for spirits; and not a man
could honestly say he had ever seen the pastor drunk.
Why, then, the colonists wondered, all this fuss about
drinking habits?

The services were interrupted when a soldier of the
garrison ran into the church, found Governor Van
Twiller, and whispered in his ear. The governor listened
for a few seconds and jumped to his feet. "There is an
English ship coming up the bay!" he cried with great
alarm.

The congregation came to their feet as the governor
rushed from the church, forgetting the dominie, who had
been cut off in midsentence.

"Take the children and go home," Pieter said to his
wife.

"Is there going to be trouble?" she asked.

"Probably not," he said. "But it isn't every day we see
an English ship. Best to be on the safe side."

This message was being repeated all over the church,
and in minutes it was empty as the women and children
hurried to their homes and the men took their weapons
and walked down to the spit of beach off the fort.

The English ship was the *James,* Captain Jacob Elkins
in command. It lowered sail and dropped anchor. A longboat was lowered into the water and four sailors rowed it
while the captain stood in the stern. The little craft
bobbed its way toward the Dutchmen until its nose
shoved up onto the beach.

Several of the men on shore recognized the English officer, and whispering spread like wildfire. Jacob Elkins
had been an agent of the Dutch at Fort Orange. There
had been some trouble, and he had been dismissed for
dishonesty. He was now obviously in the service of the
English; and God alone knew how much trouble that
could cause, since the man knew a great deal about the
land and the various settlements.

Elkins stepped ashore, his eyes scanning the group of
men. Van Twiller came forward, and the Englishman

moved to meet him. "I take it, sir, that you are Governor Van Twiller?"

"I am Van Twiller. What is it you want here, sir?"

"We are a peaceful vessel on a trading mission for His Majesty, Charles of England. I am Captain Jacob Elkins with a Royal commission to begin trading with the Indians along the reaches of this river."

Van Twiller was annoyed, but also confused. The man spoke with great authority, and yet he had no right to be here. "Trading, eh?" was the only thing he could find to say.

"With your permission we'll proceed upriver at once, sir," Elkins said.

Abraham de Witt was standing at the governor's shoulder, and he whispered, "Ask to see his commission."

The governor managed a nervous smile. "I would like to see your commission, if you please."

A dark look replaced the smile on Elkins' face. "But my dear governor," he said with a patently false friendliness, "you forget my ship flies the flag of England. I'm not under your jurisdiction. I stopped merely because I didn't want you to be alarmed by my presence."

"This is Dutch territory," Pieter de Kuyper said as he stopped forward. "Even if you do have a commission from the King of England, it's worthless here."

Elkins smiled again. "There are those who would disagree with you, sir."

"Get out of our waters!" the governor said with uncharacteristic bravery.

"I've come to buy furs on Henry Hudson's river," Elkins said mildly. The threat was clear. Henry Hudson had been an Englishman; Elkins was implying other Englishmen therefore had the right to use the river as their own.

"Don't talk to us of Henry Hudson's river! It's the River Mauritius," Pieter said angrily. But even as he said the word Mauritius, it sounded as false to him as Hudson. The North River was the North River.

"By your leave, sir," Elkins said, saluting the governor. He stepped into his longboat, and the sailors began to push it off the beach. "I've informed you of my intentions," Elkins called out. "More than that I will not do."

In minutes the longboat was aboard the *James*, the sails

were raised, and the anchor was brought aboard. Wind filled the sails and the *James* headed up the North River.

The governor seemed at a loss for what to do. Abraham de Witt pointed to the guns in the fort. "We could blow him out of the water."

The governor could not find his voice.

"We have five twelve-pounders," de Witt suggested.

"No, no, no," the governor complained, shaking his head. "That's not the way to handle this. God knows we don't want trouble with the English king."

"But the man is defying your authority," Pieter de Kuyper said. "That ship has no right to be in these waters!"

"Yes, yes, that's true enough, but we must find a peaceful way to settle this," the governor said, and then he grasped for any straw of logic. "Didn't the man say he was on a peaceful mission? How would it look if we fired upon him?"

Pieter could barely contain his anger. "Peaceful mission? They invade our lands and you call it peaceful?"

"But you don't—" the governor began, but he was cut off by an enraged Abraham de Witt.

"If you let that bastard go we'll wind up being drowned by the English scum! Van Twiller, goddamn you, act like a man!"

There was a hush among the men. Although most of them agreed with de Witt, Van Twiller was still the governor and deserved a certain amount of respect. But if de Witt was supposed to feel chastised, he did not show it. He stuck his jaw into the governor's face. "Well?"

Van Twiller turned and walked back toward his new brick house within the walls of the fort. He was joined by several men, mostly his friends—Keyn Frederijke, Michael de Pauw, and, for some unknown reason, since he was hardly a friend of the governor, the schoolmaster, Carl Roelantsen. The governor ordered a fresh cask of wine, and the men attacked it vigorously.

Pieter talked for a few moments with Abraham de Witt, and the two men found their common battle with Van Twiller bringing them closer to one another.

Hardly a man in New Amsterdam slept soundly that night. Something had to be done, and quickly—but while the settlers lay awake in their beds, their governor slept soundly in the deepest of alcoholic hazes.

At home that same evening Pieter loudly predicted disaster for the colony if the English were allowed to come and go as they pleased. He pounded the table so hard it woke Baby Anne.

The black girl, Zilla, sat in the room listening to her master, and she became concerned. Her imagination began to get away from her. She could see long lines of Englishmen creeping through the night, sneaking into the house, pouncing on them and cutting their throats as they slept. She resolved not to sleep a wink that night.

And she did one other thing. She excused herself and went to the slave house and brought back her brother, Manuel. She hid him in the shed at the back of the house and made him promise that he would not sleep. This made her feel better, because if there was any trouble, one couldn't ask for a better man than Manuel.

"A coward! That's all he is, an overstuffed coward!" Pieter was saying as he poured himself more beer from the small keg. "He backed down without an argument!"

Christiana was almost as upset as her husband, but she hid her fears and tried to calm him. "Perhaps it means nothing. After all, the Englishman did say he was on a peaceful mission."

"Peaceful now, but as soon as they realize the riches to be gained, then they'll come in greater numbers, and who will stop them? Van Twiller? God Almighty, we need a governor with guts, someone like Peter Minuit. Damn it all! How I wish he were back. Minuit would never have knuckled under like Van Twiller. No, he would've told that arrogant swine to get the hell out of Dutch waters—and if he'd been slow about it, Peter would have blown the pox-ridden ship out of the water."

On and on he went until Christiana couldn't take it anymore and went to bed. In a few minutes Pieter joined her. As he rested in his bed, another man was making plans for him.

Dirk Stratling, the front of his mouth empty of teeth and his jaw permanently misshapen, was speaking with difficulty. He would never again speak clearly, but he was able to make himself understood by the two men who

sat with him at a corner table in Kock's Tavern. They
were the same two who had been with him on the night
of the fight with de Kuyper. Like Stratling, they were
Englishmen who preferred life in a Dutch colony to a
broken neck at the end of a rope on English soil.

Their names were James Rose and Aaron Bucknell.
They had escaped from a prison in Virginia, making their
way north until they arrived on Staten Island. They had
approached Stratling and asked his help as a fellow Englishman. Stratling brought them to Michael de Pauw, who
gave them berths aboard the *Pavonia*. Rose and Bucknell
were the sort of cutthroats who appealed to Stratling, and
he had been generous with them. Now they were being
given a chance to repay their debt.

" 'Twould be best if none else in the house get kilt,"
Stratling said to his two countrymen. "De Kuyper be the
only one I be interested in."

"What if t'others get in the way?" asked Bucknell, a
hulking brute whose hairline came down almost to meet
his eyebrows.

Stratling shrugged. "Be too bad, that's all I be sayin'."

The other men nodded. Pieter de Kuyper was to die.
If it could be done without hurting anyone else, that was
fine and good. If not . . . well, that was fine and good, too.
Stratling did not flinch at killing. The important thing, he
reminded the others, was that "that scum be dead by
dawn."

The three men left Kock's Tavern and melted into the
shadows of the Broad Way, then made their way toward
the strand and Pearl Street. They were hidden by the
clouds that passed over the face of the full moon.

Christiana was alone in the front room of the house,
sipping beer and thinking about what had just happened.
Pieter had come to bed and they had tried to make love,
with the usual effect. She had been filled with desire and
then, just when she ought to have been carried into ecstasy, she had grown frightened; her mind filled with
images of Indians and the pleasures of lovemaking were
gone.

She was certain Pieter was aware each time of what
was happening. Their lovemaking sessions were of shorter
duration and the times between them growing greater.

After achieving simple physical release in these hurried attempts at intimacy, Pieter would roll to his side of the bed and fall asleep without uttering a word.

Tonight had been no different. And, as usual, afterward she couldn't get to sleep. What was she going to do, she wondered. How long could she expect her husband to be content with such a wife?

It wasn't that she wasn't trying. She would pet her body to excite herself. She tried thinking of beautiful things like clouds and the river at sunset. She would pretend Pieter had been away for a year and this was the first time she was able to touch his flesh. All of this worked. It excited her and drove her crazy for the touch of his hands, and she would want him so much she ached. And then, always at the same time, it would all be ruined, and not only for herself, but for Pieter as well.

She sipped her beer, beyond tears because she had learned that tears were no help.

Stratling and his henchmen arrived at the back of the de Kuyper home. Knives crept from sheaths, and they hunched forward as they moved silently to the door. Stratling used his knife to trip the latch, and he opened the door and slipped inside, followed by Rose and Bucknell.

Stratling smiled when he saw the figure on the other side of the room. Whoever it was had not heard them enter and was continuing to look out the window.

His first thought was to rush wildly across the room. The surprise would be complete. A quick thrust of the blade and de Kuyper would be dead. But a troublesome thought occurred to him: what if the figure wasn't de Kuyper?

Besides, even if it was de Kuyper, it would be over too quickly and the Dutchman wouldn't know who killed him. No, Stratling thought, that's no good, this damned Dutch pig must be allowed a few moments of life in order to know why he was dying . . . and at whose hand.

His problem was solved when the figure turned and started back across the room.

It was a woman. She kept coming toward him, unaware, unconcerned. She walked until she almost bumped into him, and then it was too late. Her eyes opened in fright as he grabbed her roughly, clapping one hand over her mouth to keep her from crying out. The beer mug clattered to the floor.

"Now you be quiet else'n I be cuttin' orf your purty little 'ead," Stratling hissed in her ear, and to prove his seriousness he held the knife to her throat.

Christiana's eyes rolled to the side and the hideous face came into view. The man's mouth was curved in an evil smile, and his putrid breath overwhelmed her.

Pieter was asleep in bed, but something troubling entered his mind and he woke up. He heard a sound from downstairs, something dropping to the floor. It didn't alarm him, but he suddenly realized Christiana was not beside him. He got out of bed, left the room, and went to the top of the staircase.

"Christiana?" he called softly, not wanting to wake the children.

Stratling looked at Christiana and smiled. She struggled, but he held her in a grip of iron.

Pieter became concerned when he received no answer. "Christiana," he called a bit more loudly and started down the stairs.

"Greet your bloody 'usband," Stratling said and took his hand away from Christiana's mouth.

"Pieter . . ." she gasped.

Pieter plunged down the stairs but stopped when he saw his wife in the grasp of a man holding a knife at her throat. He strained his eyes but couldn't make out the man's features.

"Who are you? What do you want?"

"It be me, scum—Dirk Stratling, that who it be," he said as he kept a tight grip on the struggling woman. "It be good ole Dirk 'n' your good wife."

Pieter wanted to throw himself at the man, but hesitated because the sharp blade was close to Christiana's white flesh. And then he noticed the shapes of two other men by the back door.

Stratling was delighted with Pieter's dilemma. But he wanted more. He wanted him to become frightened and beg for his life and his wife's. Yes, he thought, that was what he wanted, this Dutch pig on his knees, groveling, begging for his life when his throat was slit. *That* would be a proper death for the man who had ruined Dirk Stratling's face.

"On your knees," he said.

"What?"

Stratling pinched Christiana and she squealed in pain. "Start beggin' for your life, scum," he said.

Pieter was a brave man, and a quick one, but he was also no fool. He realized there was no possible way for him to reach the Englishman before his wife's throat could be slit. If he charged, he would be killing her. Ironically, it was Christiana who gave him an idea.

"Save yourself, Pieter!" she said, sobbing.

Pieter stepped sideways and rested his hand on the top of a wooden chair. "And act like the man who holds you? That's what *he'd* do. Run away and leave a woman to die for him."

"Shut yor piss-mucked mouth!"

"You're very brave with women, Stratling," Pieter said in a mocking tone, glancing at the other two men. "I wonder what your friends think of you right now."

"Shut your face!"

"Just you and me, Stratling, how about it?"

"By God!"

"Afraid?"

Pieter had spoken calmly, but his words infuriated Stratling. "I be bringin' you to your knees, scum," he said, roughly shoving Christiana toward the two men. "Take 'er," he cried and leaped forward to engage Pieter.

Christiana came flying into the arms of Bucknell, but even as he grabbed her and began fondling her breasts, a huge black shape emerged through the door. Two powerful arms reached out, grabbing Rose and Bucknell by the neck of their coats and dragging them backward. Their feet went out from under them and Bucknell released his hold on the woman. Christiana stumbled away and then shrank back in terror at the scene she was witnessing.

The giant was dispatching the two men without the slightest attempt at finesse. He was bashing them against one another—bodies, arms, legs, heads—using brute strength to batter them. The knives fell from their hands and blood began to splatter onto the floor and spray everything within range.

Christiana's attention was diverted by another, even more frightening, sight. Pieter was fighting the man with the knife.

As Stratling charged, Pieter picked up the wooden chair and hurled it at him. One of the heavy legs cracked into the Englishman, knocking the wind out of him, forcing him back a few steps. He caught his breath and charged again. Pieter used the other man's blind rage as an ally. He stood perfectly still as the knife slashed toward him, stepping to the side at the last instant. He grabbed Stratling's wrist with one hand and crashed his other fist into the man's face.

As the sound of the blow exploded in the room, Christiana stood in the middle of the melee, too terrified to move. To her right a giant black was pounding two men to jelly, and to her left the man with the hideous face was slashing at her husband with a knife. Paralyzed, she put her hands to her face to blot out the sight.

Pieter and Stratling were locked together in combat, but Pieter now had the advantage because he was holding both of the other's wrists. Sweat glistened on their faces, and the tremendous exertion was making their arms and legs tremble. Pieter was the stronger of the two, and he slowly twisted Stratling's hand until the sharp point of the knife was directed back toward its owner. Stratling realized what was happening and tried to pull back. It was his undoing.

When Pieter felt the other man pulling away, he pushed forward and their combined weight sent them toppling back onto the floor. The knife was pointed down at Stratling and Pieter fell right on top of it, his weight driving the blade deep into the Englishman's chest. Stratling screamed in agony as the cold metal sliced through his flesh and found his heart. In the last second of his life he glared at Pieter. "Dutch scum," he said, and then he was gone.

Pieter grabbed the knife as he came to his feet, and turned his attention to the other end of the room. An enormous black man was standing over the stilled bodies of the two men who had been with Stratling. Pieter kept his eyes on the giant and held the knife steady before him.

The black man stared back with a puzzled expression on his face, but he made no move.

The tension was broken as Zilla came running down the stairs. "What's going on?" she cried, rushing past

Young Pieter, who was a spellbound observer. In the background Baby Anne began to cry.

Zilla stopped when she saw the bodies on the floor. Then she saw her brother.

"Manuel!"

"It's over, Zilla," the man said.

"Who is he, Zilla?" Pieter asked.

"My brother, Master Pieter. He is here to protect us from the English."

Pieter nodded at the black man. "There was trouble with the English. Only not the sort we might have expected."

A long, agonized wail came from Christiana, and she staggered forth and would have fallen had Pieter not been close enough to catch her in his arms. She stared down in horror at the blood seeping from Stratling's chest, dripping down his side, forming a sticky puddle on the floor.

"Who . . . who . . . ?"

"Calm down, it's over," Pieter said as he eased her into a chair. Zilla came over and tried to stroke the almost hysterical woman's forehead.

Pieter turned to the black man. "Your name is Manuel?"

"Yes."

Pieter held out his hand. "Thank you, Manuel."

The black man took the other's hand. "My sister says you are kind to her. I am your friend."

"And I am yours," Pieter replied.

"Pieter!" Christiana cried and jumped from the chair.

Pieter was startled and then realized she was talking to their son, who was standing at the foot of the staircase. He was amazed by his wife's recovery. A moment ago she had been too weak to stand, but now she rushed across the room and took the boy in her arms, using her body to shield his eyes from the sight of the bodies on the floor.

"You mustn't look," she said.

"I want to see," the boy protested.

"No," she said. "It isn't a fit sight for your eyes."

"Let him look," Pieter said. "He'll be a man and shouldn't be squeamish about such things."

"He will not look," Christiana said in a cold voice. "This damned New World with its blood and savages may be all right for you, but it's not all right for my son!"

Pieter had never seen her this way. Rage seemed to be consuming her. Her eyes glinted with fire as she pointed her finger at him. "Don't argue with me, I won't listen!"

He said nothing and watched as she moved Young Pieter toward the kitchen.

Pieter glanced at the staircase, where Anne stood screaming. He signaled to Zilla and she went to tend the crying child.

Pieter turned to Manuel. He pointed to the bodies at the rear of the room. The black man went over and bent down to listen for their heartbeats. After a few moments he stood up and looked at Pieter.

"Both dead."

Pieter considered the situation. He had three bodies on his hands. He could simply turn them over to the night watch, telling the story as it actually happened. It was self-defense. No one would question his right to defend himself. But it occurred to him that Michael de Pauw was either behind the attack or, at least, aware of it. It would be nice to confuse de Pauw, Pieter thought, and what better way than if the three bodies simply disappeared and no mention was ever made of the attack? De Pauw would probably lose a few nights' sleep, and this prospect appealed to Pieter.

He made his decision. He and Manuel dug a large, deep grave at the back of the garden. They dropped in the three corpses and covered them with dirt, then planted several bushes on top of the fresh earth. It was difficult to identify it as a grave even from a few feet away.

"I must go back to the slave house," Manuel said. It was almost dawn.

"You are my friend," Pieter said.

As Manuel walked down the dirt road, Pieter vowed the black man would know freedom.

Young Pieter was waiting at the door, looking toward the grave site. "You saw everything?" his father asked.

The boy nodded.

"Don't speak of it to your mother. Pretend it never happened. That's the best way."

"Yes, Father."

They went into the kitchen. Zilla gave Pieter a glass of brandy. He drank it in silence while his wife stared at

him. He could see the accusation in her eyes—that whatever had happened was all his fault for bringing her to
this place. He finished the brandy and stood up. "I'm
going to try to get some sleep.

"They could have killed us all," Christiana said.

"It could have happened anywhere."

"But it didn't happen anywhere. It happened here."

"He should get some sleep," Pieter said, pointing at
their son.

"He's staying with me!" she said in a sharp voice that
made him realize it would be useless to argue with her.

He nodded and started up to his bed. The last thing
he saw in the kitchen was Christiana clutching her son to
her breast, holding on as if she meant never to let go.

The next day was one of complete frustration for Pieter.
Governor Van Twiller refused to talk to him or anyone
else about Jacob Elkins and the English ship.

Then he came home and Christiana ignored him. When
he tried to speak to her, she left the room, and when he
tried to play with his daughter she was whisked away from
him. "Dammit, woman, you're treating me as if I had
the plague!" he shouted, but like everything else he said,
his protest was met with a stony silence.

"All right, I'll sleep in the barn!" He took two bottles
of good peach brandy and stomped out of the house,
walked past the privy and came to the small barn at the
back of the property. As he entered, the cow gave him a
mournful look and several chickens scattered out of his
way, squawking and complaining. The barn cat looked
up, yawned, and went back to sleep. Pieter ignored them
all and went to the back where the hay was stacked. He
made himself a comfortable place and let himself down
in the hay with a sigh. He opened the peach brandy and
drank three long drafts straight from the bottle.

He decided the only thing was to get drunk. The
governor was acting like a nitwit and so was his wife.
He conceded that Christiana might have some cause to
be upset after what had happened last night, but that
didn't excuse her behavior the rest of the time. The resentment had been building up in him for a long time. A
man needed a woman, and he had every right to expect
that Christiana would understand that. But no, most of

the time when he touched her she acted like a piece of frozen meat. God knows what had happened to her. He shook his head as he remembered their earlier life together. What a wildcat she had been! As eager to do it as he was—no, most of the time she was more eager. The panting and screaming and contortions, great God in Heaven it had been wonderful!

He was halfway through the first bottle of brandy and feeling very sorry for himself when Zilla came into the barn to give him his supper. "Thank you," he said as she placed the trencher at his side. He held up the bottle. "I think this will be all the supper I need tonight," he said with a slight but discernible slur to his words.

Zilla nodded, and couldn't hold back the smile as she realized he was well on his way to getting drunk. "I'll leave the food just in case," she said.

Pieter felt a need for company. "Sit down next to me," he said.

Zilla was uncomfortable, yet he was her master and she obeyed. She tried not to look at him, but every time she glanced up she could see his eyes boring into her.

"What is my good wife doing?"

"The mistress is exhausted after last night. She went to bed at the same time as the children."

They were sitting very close together, and Pieter was fascinated by the silky smoothness of her ebony skin. He took another swig of brandy and offered her the bottle. She shook her head. He reached out and touched her arm. It felt warm and smooth.

Zilla pulled back slightly and looked questioningly at him. She was a pretty girl and knew that men found her attractive. More than one white man had taken her, because she was only a slave and no one cared very much what happened to a slave.

Deeply frustrated, Pieter reached around her waist and pulled her to his side. It was a slender waist. He ran his hand down along her thighs. They were firm, and yet, in some miraculous way, soft as well. He put his bottle down and fondled her breasts.

"Please . . ." she said in a very small voice.

"God, you feel good . . . a woman . . . a real woman . . ."

"Please."

"I'm a man without a woman and I need a woman," he said as his hands traced the shape of her breasts.

Zilla's lip trembled and she tried to speak, but no words came out.

He pushed her back on the hay and slowly and methodically took off her clothes. She did nothing to help and nothing to hinder him. And then she was totally nude. Pieter, now on his knees, stopped to admire his companion. In the poor light of the oil lamp at the other end of the barn, her splendid, long-limbed ebony body seemed to glisten.

"Jesus Christ," he murmured and started taking off his shirt. His body felt ready to burst with his need. And then he noticed Zilla was crying. There was no sound, but the droplets came from her eyes and snaked their way down her cheeks.

Something about the way she lay there, not moving, not fighting but simply crying, touched him through the alcoholic haze that fed his lust. "Don't cry."

She refused to look at him. "I didn't think you'd be like other masters. I trusted you."

There was a long silence, and then Pieter's desire for her was gone. He dropped down on the hay. "Damn!" Another long pause. "Put on your clothes, Zilla. I'm sorry. It's just that I . . . well, I have needs."

"I understand."

"You're like part of the family. I shouldn't have acted this way."

Zilla quickly dressed. She watched as Pieter tossed off more brandy.

"Go back to the house," he said. "I'll never try that again."

Zilla walked from the barn, her head held high, a curious expression on her face.

Pieter shook his head and drank again from the bottle. God! How good she had looked. That body and that skin! But she had said "I trusted you," and he was an honorable man. What does an honorable man do at a time like this? he asked himself.

"Get drunk and pass out," he said aloud.

The next morning he felt guilty when he saw Zilla, but he remembered the problem of the English ship in the waters of New Amsterdam and hurried down to the fort.

He kept promising himself he would apologize to the black girl.

The *James* lay at anchor not far from a brook that swirled and bubbled its way into the river. Jacob Elkins had concluded his bargaining with the Indians. Piles of furs were loaded into the longboat as the Indians withdrew into the forest with their new treasures. Both sides were content with the trading.

The longboat returned to the *James,* and Elkins went to his cabin while the men stored the furs in the hold. The captain went to the master's table and pored over one of the many maps he had stolen from the Dutch while in their employ. He decided his next trading stop would be at a small inlet about ten miles up the river. An Indian settlement existed there, and he was certain the savages would be happy to exchange furs for guns.

Jacob Elkins was satisfied with his new life. When he had worked for the Dutch he had never felt appreciated or sufficiently rewarded. But his new English masters were most generous. He had absolute freedom to trade as he wished. For his efforts he was to receive a ten-percent share of all profits, with an assurance that if he succeeded there would be more voyages, perhaps with more than one ship. If this came about, he would be in charge of the entire expedition.

Well, if he was being handsomely rewarded by the English monarch, he was worth it. He was giving the English the store of his accumulated knowledge of New Netherland—the places to trade, the whereabouts of the Indians, everything. Without him they would be groping in the darkness. His steady beacon showed the way; no time was wasted on preliminary exploration.

A sailor came to the cabin and announced the ship was ready to sail.

Jacob Elkins went up on deck as the *James* got underway.

For two days Governor Van Twiller refused to discuss the presence of the English ship.

He was finally visited by a group of men—Pieter de Kuyper, Abraham de Witt, Dominie Bogardus, and Samuel de Schuyler—who refused to leave until they were given satisfaction. They entered the governor's quarters and argued with him for two hours before he agreed to send a force after the Englishman. Pieter, as an experienced captain was made commander of the expedition. Samuel de Schuyler, as captain of the garrison, was made second-in-command.

Three ships, including the *Bright Hope,* sailed within the hour. The second ship was the lumbering caravel *Utrecht,* a craft more suited for long ocean voyages than for the sprightly behavior wanted on the inland waterways. But the *Utrecht* had size and was able to accommodate forty soldiers of the garrison. The third ship was a swift schooner-rigged pinnace. It was an ill-matched armada, because each ship traveled at different speed. The pinnace was a greyhound; the *Bright Hope* a steady workhorse; the *Utrecht* a ponderous elephant. But for all their faults, the three ships constituted the mightiest flotilla in these waters, and over one hundred and twenty armed men were aboard as they sailed up the river.

Three days later they caught up with their prey. The *James* was anchored in a small cove. Most of its crew were ashore busily trading with the Indians. The Dutch ships anchored alongside the *James,* and three longboats, bristling with musket-carrying men, went ashore. If any of the Englishmen had been prepared to fight, the numbers of their enemy gave them pause. They were vastly outnumbered, and their ship stood under the guns of the *Utrecht.* Captain Elkins did not quibble when Pieter told him his voyage was at an end.

"As you wish," Elkins said calmly. "But you'll regret this day."

"I doubt it," Pieter replied. He turned to de Schuyler. "Confiscate all the furs here on shore and send men aboard the *James* to empty the holds. Take all the furs, all the guns, and anything else you find."

Elkins was shattered by the prospect of losing his ten-percent share of the rich prizes. "Now just wait a—"

"The spoils of war," Pieter said, cutting him off. "And take this message back to your royal master. Every English ship that attempts to trade in our waters will be given the same treatment. All you're accomplishing is saving us the trouble of doing our own trading with the Indians."

The three Dutch ships, soon loaded with the furs that had belonged to the Englishmen, escorted the *James* to the head of the Narrows. There was nothing Elkins could do except sail away from the *Utrecht*'s menacing eight-pounders. He seethed and swore revenge, but he knew he had been soundly beaten. He set a course for Virginia with the hope of taking on a cargo of tobacco. It would not go well for him if he returned to England with an empty ship.

The Dutch flotilla returned to New Amsterdam, where a hero's welcome awaited the men. The governor came to greet them. He extolled their feat, praised their courage, and acted as if their expedition had been his own idea. Expansively, he ordered half the confiscated cargo to be divided among the men who had participated in the foray. The other half he kept for the company, or so he said. More than one man suspected he would keep it for himself.

A week later four men from the *James* showed up in the town. They had been trading inland at the time of the incident, and when they returned to the cove they were bewildered to find their ship had sailed without them.

Van Twiller didn't know what to do with them. Were they prisoners? Visitors? Guests? The Dutch took pity on them and entertained them in their homes. For two weeks the Englishmen stayed in New Amsterdam, drinking and eating, staying up all night at parties, and generally having a wonderful time.

Finally the governor put them aboard a flyboat and dispatched it to the English settlements in Massachusetts, where the sailors were put on shore. One of them, Alfred Sanborn, had enjoyed his stay so thoroughly, that he later returned and became a permanent resident of the colony. He married a Dutch girl and worked at various odd jobs until he signed aboard Pieter de Kuyper's *Bright Hope* as an able-bodied seaman.

A month had passed since the *James* incident, and everyone had settled down again to business. Pieter came home after an unusually tiring day, and the first thing he saw was Christiana showing her picture books to little Anne, who was pointing to each new page and smiling. He didn't say anything, but the expression on his face said it for him. He got himself a mug of beer and laced it with brandy.

"Why don't you say what's on your mind?" Christiana asked.

"It does no good."

Christiana handed the book to the little girl and told her to take it over by the fire, where Zilla was cooking dinner. Then she turned back to her husband. "I know you've told Young Pieter not to look at my books, but I won't have that with Anne. She's a girl and must learn of nice things."

"There are nice things here."

"I'll raise my daughter the way I wish," she said testily.

"To grow up to be like you?" he asked, taking another swig of his beer-and-brandy.

"What do you mean?"

"You know what I mean," he said angrily.

"No, I don't. Suppose you tell me."

"Will she grow up to be a woman?"

"And what's that supposed to mean?" Christiana said, pressing him. "Don't you think I'm a woman?"

"Not all the time—there are times when a woman is supposed to act like a *wife*."

The moment the words were out of his mouth he regretted having spoken them. The coldness that had developed between them was something they never spoke about; both were too embarrassed. And it wasn't something they could discuss with a third person. But now he had spoken, and his anger kept him from apologizing.

"Don't talk to me about being a wife!" Christiana said angrily. "You're supposed to be a husband, and a husband is someone who spends time around his home. But you, oh no, not you! You're always off on that damned boat of yours!"

Pieter slammed his mug down on the table. "To earn the bread and meat on this table!"

"And the beer? And the rum? And the brandy? Don't forget about them!"

"I'll damn well take a drink if I want to!" he roared. "And get drunk if I want to, do you hear me? I'll get as drunk as I want!"

He walked over to the sideboard and took down a full bottle of brandy. "I'll drink what I want and sleep where I want and to hell with it!" he shouted, storming out of the house and heading for the barn.

Christiana went over to her daughter, hoping the child hadn't understood what had happened. Zilla had kept her busy during the altercation. The black girl looked at Christiana. "He has no cause to act like that," she said.

Christiana sighed. "You don't know the whole story, Zilla—maybe he does at that." She took Anne by the hand and walked toward the staircase.

Deep in thought, Zilla went back to her cooking pot. She had been with the family for several years now, and there was little she didn't know. The de Kuypers were so used to her being around that they sometimes forgot she was there. She tasted the stew and decided it needed more salt.

In the meantime Pieter found a soft spot in the hay at the back of the barn and dropped into it. He raised the brandy bottle to his lips, and the fiery liquid gurgled down his throat. He drank most of the bottle and fell asleep while his family ate their dinner in the house and went to their beds.

It was very late when he woke to feel a smooth hand caressing his chest. He kept his eyes closed for a few moments, enjoying the sensation and wondering what had gotten into Christiana's mind. And then the hand began to move in figure eights, the fingernails gliding around and scratching, then scratching harder; it was a delicious and sensual pain, and it aroused him. This had never happened before. He opened his eyes, and in the moonlight coming through a slat he saw her.

Zilla!

She was naked and kneeling at his side. He reached out and let his hand touch that wonderful skin. Neither of them spoke a word. They continued to touch each other, their hands moving greedily, their breathing becoming quicker. And then his clothes were off and they were joined together. Their bodies moved in a slow rolling motion that grew quicker and quicker. A strange gurgle came from Zilla's throat and she moved her head back and forth, causing her hair to whip through the air. She shuddered when orgasm came, and her body vibrated so much that Pieter joined her. It went on and on until finally Pieter rolled away and lay gasping on the hay.

Zilla was already getting dressed. She looked down at him and smiled. "I have needs, too," she said, and walked out of the barn.

Pieter dragged his protesting muscles to a sitting position. It had been one of the most unexpected and exciting experiences of his life. And it was also quite clear that neither of them would ever speak about it. They would continue with their lives as if it had never happened.

There was one other thing he knew. It would happen again.

In the year 1635, Michael de Pauw pulled off a great coup when he sold Staten Island back to the West India Company. Since he had paid almost nothing for it under a patroonship grant, his profits were enormous. He used much of this money to buy more lands on the north of Manhatan Island. Pieter, along with many other men, wondered why the company had suddenly become so generous. No one could ever prove there had been an under-the-table deal, but not long afterward Governor Van Twiller suddenly had enough cash to buy the remainder of Nutten Island. The word about this spread, and Abraham de Witt, in his cups one night at Kock's Tavern, declared the island should henceforth be known as Governor's Island. It caught on immediately. From that day men spoke of Governor's Island as if that had always been its name. Eventually most people forgot that it was only a nickname.

During this time the boundaries of the colony kept expanding.

A few farmers went to the northeast corner of Manhatan and started bouweries on land purchased or, more commonly, leased from Michael de Pauw. They called it Harlem in honor of the Haarlem they knew back in Holland, but for a long time it continued to be known as Otterspoor, because of the great number of those sleek animals that lived on the sandy beaches and on the banks of the many streams that drained the land.

Jacques Bentyn and Adrianse Bennet started farms on the virgin lands of western Long Island, an area that was named Gowanus.

But even as the colony expanded outward, the complications of life in the small town of New Amsterdam increased.

Dominie Bogardus became more outspoken about the government with each passing month, and soon unfavorable reports about him were flowing back to Holland from the vituperative pen of Governor Van Twiller. Even though they were separated by an ocean, the burghers recognized Van Twiller for the incompetent he was and did their best to ignore his scathing letters. They tolerated Van Twiller only because they did not wish to antagonize the powerful Van Rensselaers.

A number of Huguenots settled in New Amsterdam in this year, among them a doctor, the first truly accredited physician in the colony. After their initial joy, the settlers looked upon his presence as a questionable blessing. His remedies for ailments often astounded the populace. A prescription for gout included "raspings from the bone of a human skull unburied." When Geertie Smit suffered pains in her back, he prescribed a "balsam of bats." Whether or not it would have cured the good mistress's pains was never known. The doctor stayed in the colony for a year, eventually giving up the practice of medicine to go sailing off to the Dutch East Indies, where, it was said, he made a fortune trading in exquisite porcelain vases made by the strange yellow men who lived to the north. Everyone breathed a sigh of relief when a ship carrying the well-meaning doctor sailed from New Amsterdam, and the people went back to the more reliable, plainer remedies taught them by the Indians.

A curious fate had also overtaken the schoolmaster, Carl Roelantsen. The colonists soon discovered he was a dreadful teacher and refused to allow him to instruct their children. When his income dwindled to nothing, Roelantsen looked for other ways to earn his living. As he was extremely limited in his skills and no one was disposed to give him other opportunities, the poor man was reduced to taking in washing. Even at this he proved a failure. There was a dispute with a client, David de Hatten, and Roelantsen sued the man for nonpayment of a bill. The case was brought before the governor, and de Hatten established that Roelantsen had ruined his clothing and said he therefore did not deserve to be paid. The governor concurred, and Roelantsen was down to his last penny without prospect of earning another.

Pieter de Kuyper heard of the man's plight. He took pity on the young fellow, because he had been one of the first to terminate Roelantsen's services as a schoolmaster. This happened after he had heard Young Pieter asking questions about the trees to be found in New Netherland. Roelantsen had stammered and sputtered and finally admitted he knew absolutely nothing about the local flora. He had then begun a long discourse about the bravery of the Greeks at a place called Marathon.

After the lesson was over, Pieter questioned the man about these Greeks. When he learned it had all happened thousands of years before, Pieter decided his son had no need for such useless information and cancelled his lessons. Before long, Roelantsen had received an avalanche of dismissal orders.

But now that the man was in serious trouble, Pieter came to his rescue with the offer of a job at the oil factory. This was a new business venture for Pieter. He had grown tired of sailing the *Bright Hope* home with a cargo of blubber only to see a good part of his profits go to the men who converted the blubber into oil for the lamps of the colony. So he started his own factory and was soon the leading processor of oil on Manhatan. When he offered employment at the factory to Carl Roelantsen, the man cried with joy.

The oil factory also provided Pieter with profits from an unexpected source. A Dutch trader filled his ship with barrels of oil, and paid for it with futures in tulip bulbs —an accepted and creditable method of payment in the Netherlands. Dealing in tulip futures was a highly volatile and risky business, but in this instance Pieter was lucky. Since the bulbs were of a varying quality, the price could rise or fall very quickly. This year the prices rose to new heights, and Pieter was prudent enough to sell and take his profits, even though other men urged him to wait and reap an even greater fortune.

The market peaked the next year, and since it was common practice to purchase bulb futures on credit, when it fell it caused a widespread panic in the counting houses of Amsterdam. Hundreds of speculators were wiped out, and countless bulb traders were ruined.

Pieter, however, had been content to take his relatively modest profit, and re-invest it in more tangible assets in the New World. While others floundered in debt, his own prosperity increased.

Christiana seemed in better spirits. The challenge of caring for the goat herd and making it profitable had kept her so busy for two years, she had little time to worry about much else.

The leaves dropped from the trees, and fall turned into winter. The first snow of the season was on the ground. It was an hour after dawn, and Pieter sat by the fire, warming his insides with a thick, hearty soup. Christiana came bustling into the room, her cheeks flushed in the chilly air. She smiled and kissed Pieter on the cheek. Both had fleeting thoughts of the previous night. They had made love, and for the first time in many months there had been no images to ruin her pleasure, or his.

"Have a good night?" he asked, a grin on his face.

"Mmm," she said as she ladled soup into a bowl.

"Off to the goats?"

"It's my morning to feed them," she said, reaching into her pocket and taking out a piece of paper. "If my figuring is correct, we'll make an even better profit this spring than last."

"That's good."

"And you said we'd never make a profit."

"I was angry when I said that," he admitted. "Besides, you proved me wrong last year."

"And the rest of the men—none of them thought we'd ever make money."

"Most of them were just jealous."

"Because they didn't want their wives to do something without them?"

"It's a natural feeling."

"There's nothing natural about it," she said. "Why shouldn't women be as good in business as men?"

"Why, uh, no reason at all," Pieter replied, not wishing to get into an argument, but secretly thinking it a foolish idea. "Business is the domain of men" was what he wanted to say, but didn't.

Christiana arrived at the pen and, as usual, couldn't hold back a smile. Everything was so neat and orderly, and the fresh snow on the ground enhanced the scene.

She opened the gate and started for the shed, but stopped when she saw Maria de Peyster coming through the door with a troubled expression on her face.

"What's the matter?"

"You'd better have a look," Maria said, and her voice quivered as she spoke.

Christiana entered the shed and went to the corner pointed out by Maria. A ewe lay on a pile of straw. Even in the dim light of the shed, Christiana could see something was wrong with the animal. She put her hands on the ewe's chest and then held the narrow head up to give herself a better look at the eyes. They had a glazed, unseeing look about them.

"Was she this way yesterday?" Christiana asked.

"No," Maria said. "I noticed her this morning when I came to clean the shed."

"Maybe a little food will help," Christiana said. She went to a bin and brought back some of the cornmeal the goats were fond of. But no matter how much she coaxed, the animal wouldn't eat.

The ewe was kept in a small area in the corner, isolated from the others. "Maybe she'll get better in a day or so," Christiana told the other women, who came as soon as they heard of the problem.

But the sickly ewe did not get better. She wouldn't eat and wouldn't drink any water. The poor thing seemed to shed her flesh before the women's eyes.

Christiana spent most of the next few days and nights in the shed. She tried everything. Heavy woolen cloaks were placed on the animal. An oil lamp was kept nearby for warmth. Warm broth was squeezed into the ewe's mouth.

Pieter came to the shed on the third day. Christiana showed him the animal. He felt the glands and the throat muscles. When he finished his inspection, there was a troubled look on his face.

"What's the matter?" Christiana asked almost in panic.

"I once saw a goat like this back in Holland."

"And?"

Pieter walked outside into the frigid air and rubbed his hands together. He stamped his feet on the frozen ground.

"Well, what about that goat?" Christiana said, pursuing him and waiting for an answer.

"The goat died," he said quietly.

"Oh." She was close to tears.

He looked into her eyes. He wanted to be honest and tell her the rest of what he knew—that the goat he had seen in Holland had been afflicted with some unknown disease that spread to the other goats and wiped out the herd—but he couldn't bring himself to do it.

"I'll go home now," he said. "Why don't you come with me?"

She shook her head and then, on an impulse, put her arms about him and hugged him for a long time.

The next morning the goat was dead. Christiana was the first to discover it. She had stayed in the shed for the greater part of the night, returning home for a few hours of fitful sleep.

"We must bury her," Maria de Peyster said when she arrived to find Christiana sitting near the dead animal.

"The ground is frozen," Christiana replied. "We'll have to put her in the bay."

The corpse was placed in a cart, and the women took it to the water's edge to consign it to the fishes. A group of workmen snickered when they saw the strange procession of women following a dead goat in a cart. Christiana stopped and stared at them until they felt ashamed of themselves.

And then the truth emerged, as the other goats began to sicken. One by one they stopped eating, grew thin, lost the strength to stand on their own feet, and died.

The dreadful procession with the cart became an everyday happening. Pieter, trying to keep his wife from torturing herself, offered to dispose of the bodies, but Christiana wouldn't hear of it. The goats had been her responsibility when they were alive, and would remain so in death.

Christiana fought for the life of the last goat. She couldn't believe this one too would die. A makeshift stove was placed in the shed, and she sat for two days and nights with the stricken animal's head on her lap. Those big eyes that had been so alert in the goat's search for food were now distant and empty. The strong legs and powerful haunches were now limp and flabby, disused strings of sinew and muscle. All through last night, while the stove glowed and the wind howled through the cracks in the roof, Christiana sat with the dying animal, petting his cheek and whispering vain hopes into his deaf ears.

In the morning she was still there. The fire had gone out and she was almost frozen, but still she sat with the head of the stiffening animal on her lap. The other women came and helped her to her feet. They gave her hot rum and rubbed her hands and arms to restore the circulation. And then they took the last animal to the beach and pushed it into the dark waters. Christiana stood immobile and watched, beyond tears, beyond despair, beyond caring.

"We'll try again in the spring," Geertie Smit said bravely, hoping to bring some cheer to her friend.

"No," Christiana said, "we won't. It's over. For good." And there was something in her voice that stopped Geertie from saying anything more.

Christiana never again went to the shed where the goats had been kept, and where her dream of doing something on her own had once flourished. When the last goat died, so did her dream. The winter passed and the ground thawed. Spring brought life back to the land, but Christiana did not feel its warmth.

It was 1637 and over the past two years Pieter's income from the *Bright Hope* and the oil factory had become substantial. He decided to invest its profits in the land he so dearly loved. He bought a large tract in the middle of the island, halfway between the fort and the village of Harlem. It was a beautiful but wild piece of land. The only road that came near it was an old Indian trail that followed the shore of a lake and disappeared into the swampy marshlands of the north.

Christiana was finally talked into making a visit.

On the day of the journey she was up at dawn, anxious to finish the doll she was making for Anne. She was sewing the dress together when her six-year-old daughter joined her.

"It's so beautiful," Anne said, timidly reaching a hand out to touch the doll's floppy arm.

"I wish you had the doll I had when I was a child," Christiana said with a sigh. "It had a delicate porcelain face. But we can't get anything like that here."

"I think I'll like this doll just as much," Anne said, with a serious look on her face.

"Of course you will," Christiana said, pulling the thread through the cloth for the last time before she bit off the end. "This is a very nice doll and she loves you very much."

"Do dolls know we love them?"

"Of course, and the more you love them, the more they love you."

Anne smiled and touched the doll's arm again. "I think I'll love her more than any doll in the whole world."

"Yes . . . well . . . but someday you may get a doll like the one I had as a child in Amsterdam," Christiana said, and her mind wandered as she thought of her own life when she was the same age as her daughter.

"You'd rather live there, wouldn't you?" Anne asked. A new perception about her mother was only beginning to dawn in her mind.

"It's so peaceful," Christiana said. "When I was your age we used to take long walks near the canals, admiring the flowers . . . there were so many of them, in freshly painted window boxes . . . and all the people would be in the streets. You never saw so many people . . ." And then she remembered that she didn't want to turn her daughter against this place where they lived. "Of course, our home has pretty flowers in window boxes, too," she said.

Anne wasn't fooled. She knew her mother disliked New Amsterdam. She didn't know exactly why; she couldn't understand what was wrong with the place.

"Here," Christiana said, holding out the newly made doll. "As pretty a doll as you'll find anywhere."

Anne took the little toy and held it in her arms. She knew her mother didn't think it was as nice as the dolls in Amsterdam, but she didn't care. It was the loveliest one *she* had ever seen. Then she put the doll down and hugged her mother. "Thank you, Mama, thank you."

Christiana held her daughter in her arms, and a gentle tear traced its way down her cheek.

Her reverie was interrupted as Pieter and their son entered the room, bustling with energy to begin the trip to the newly acquired land.

The journey took several hours, but it was a pleasant day and they arrived in good spirits.

Christiana stood at Pieter's side as he pointed out the heavily forested areas. She nodded her head as, exhilarated, he swept his arm to describe the gently rolling plains, whose contours were great statements of tall, lush grasses punctuated by sparkling lakes and streams.

"It is pretty," she admitted. But it was also wilderness, and she was convinced that wilderness, however pretty, meant hazards.

She watched as Anne walked happily through a field of wild flowers and worried for her daughter's safety even though Anne was accompanied by Young Pieter.

Anne had none of her mother's fears as she reached out and plucked a handsome yellow flower. "Look at the petals," she said to her brother. "I'd like to have a blouse with cuffs like this."

Young Pieter looked at the flower with interest and then pretended to be bored. "Just another flower," he said, "nothing special."

Anne was only a child, but she was quite aware of the undercurrents in the daily life of her family. She looked at her older brother. "You won't admit you like it because you're afraid of what Father will say."

Young Pieter was embarrassed. "Who cares what he says."

"You do."

"Why should I care what he thinks?"

"It's a beautiful flower," she said stubbornly. "Why can't you just say it?"

"Mother says the flowers here are nothing compared to the ones back home."

Anne looked curiously at her brother. "Why do you always call Europe 'home.' This is our home, you know."

"For the present," he said. "One of these days we're going to move back to Amsterdam." It was said with more hope than belief.

Anne continued to pick the yellow flowers until she had a bouquet that was almost too large for her to hold. "Let's give these to Mother," she said.

"I can't wait to see her face," Young Pieter said sourly, knowing full well what his mother thought of the land.

Anne gave Christiana the flowers with a little curtsy, and her mother bent down and kissed her on the cheek. "Thank you," she said.

"It's from the land," Anne said.

"To make you feel at home," Young Pieter said, carefully watching her to gauge her reaction.

Christiana forced herself to smile. "Of course I feel at

home. After all, your father owns this land." She looked nervously at Pieter. She was uncomfortable in this wild place, but was trying hard not to spoil the day for everyone else.

"Pieter," she said, "why don't you show us where you plan to build the house?"

Pieter was not fooled by his wife's feigned acceptance of this place. He would have been more pleased if she had said "our" house instead of "the" house; but he took Christiana by the hand, led her to a knoll, and singled out a pleasant grove that would make an ideal site for a house.

"How beautiful," Christiana said. "I can picture it all in my mind." She closed her eyes, but her vision did not include the farm that would be. She was once again back in the house on Pearl Street. And the house itself was not in the New World, but in Amsterdam.

In the house she could pretend the children were safe and living in a place of civilization. But here, they were in the wilderness, exposed to the ravages of nature and the unpredictable tempers of the local savages.

The Indians were in fact becoming a very real problem.

After years of contact with the men from Europe, their original good nature and innocence were wearing thin. No longer did they smile as the white men built houses and bouweries and then resold them, making huge profits over the original payments they had given the Indians. No longer did they gladly trade away furs and pelts for useless junk; they now demanded more substantial payment in the form of wampum, guns, and liquor. Moreover, the growing numbers of colonists were encroaching on their way of life, and since the white man showed no intention of changing his ways, the Indians became painfully aware it was they who would be forced to change. The list of grievances grew longer and longer, and the wisest and most far-seeing of the chiefs sat down in powwow and talked of their troubles.

It was becoming more and more difficult for their culture to exist side by side with the bustling haste of the Europeans. The values of each side were too far apart for true reconciliation. The patience of the Indians was frayed, and it was only the wisdom and moderation of the older chiefs and sachems that kept them from the warpath.

The Indians were angry and felt they had every right to be so. After all, was this land not their land? Had not their fathers and their fathers' fathers unto the beginning of memory fished and hunted these lands and waters as their own?

The white men had come, quietly, peacefully, and with great reassurances at first, but ever more boldly and with a growing arrogance as their numbers increased. These white men, with their foul smells and filthy habits, spoke of *their* colony and *their* rivers and *their* lands.

But the Indian knew the white man did not understand and spoke a mouthful of lies. At his most charitable, the Indian conceded the white man might act the way he did because he did not know the truth, did not know what the Indian knew.

The land was his. It had always been his.

4

Two-Dog and Others

40,000 B.C.

THE WARRIOR TWO-DOG STOOD ON THE KNOLL and stared in the direction of the Great Orb as it began to climb into the sky. In the far distance he could see the forms of a great herd of animals taking shape in the growing light. A few moments ago there had been nothing but a black mass of them, but now he was able to distinguish individual animals. Their great curved horns became defined: massive backs led up to the curving hump of muscle; broad bodies balanced delicately over legs as strong and elemental as young saplings whose roots were intertwined with the earth itself.

Two-Dog glanced at the warriors standing at his side. They did not speak, nor did they nod, but there was an instant accord between them that this would be a good day for hunting. Still without a word having been spoken or a signal given, the warriors started walking toward the great herd of animals grazing on the tall, dew-covered grasses.

The women and children watched the warriors leave, and then they too, silently and automatically, began the work of the day. They took down the tents, stitched together from heavy skins, and packed them on two slender poles that made an uneven X—the longer end past the axis dragging along the ground, the shorter end placed on a woman's shoulders, forming a primitive carrying sledge. Strips of hide held the top part of the X on the woman's shoulders, and the children piled their belongings onto the lower part.

The people set out toward the east in the direction

of the Great Orb. There were several families in the
group, attached to one another as a hunting unit and
led by the warrior Two-Dog.

He had been given that name because he was the
only warrior in memory who had two hunting dogs
that followed him. They helped him find and track
prey, and he shared his kills with them. Many warriors had one dog, but only their leader had been able
to bring two together so they were not always at each
other's throats. Perhaps it was because he had found
them as puppies and had raised them together. Most
warriors could not be bothered with puppies, and when
they came across the helpless creatures they either ignored them or, if the hunting had been bad, killed and
ate them. But Two-Dog had been persistent with the
puppies, and they had grown strong and tall together
and now worked as a team under his guidance.

The Great Orb climbed into the sky, passed its point
of greatest height, and was beginning its descent when
Two-Dog and the other warriors caught up with the
herd. The men crossed over a sloping hill, and there
before them, stretching almost as far as the eye could
see, were thousands and thousands of the beasts—
a living sea. These were big-horned bison, a relative
of smaller bison, those with short, curving horns, which
would survive into the distant future.

The big-horned bison stood seven feet at the top
of his mighty hump, and his head supported the weight
of a six-foot spread of horns. These were fierce creatures, powerful, seemingly indestructible. In their prime
they feared nothing that lived. Their only concession to
prudence was that they avoided the great shaggy mammoths; nor were they especially interested in disturbing
the huge bears that watched their passing with disinterest.
The scourge of the smaller bison—the dire wolf—meant
nothing to these mighty beasts, except when they grew
old and were left behind by the herd. Then the dire
wolves, sensing the failing strength of the bison, would
track him until that day when he could barely stand.
The wolves would close in and attack, but even though
he was almost dead, often the bison impaled a wolf or
two. The end of the drama, however, was always the
same, and the wolf pack would feast for days and nights

on thousands of pounds of the flesh of freshly killed big-horned bison.

Two-Dog sent several warriors downwind along the left side of the herd. When they had reached their positions far down the vast plain, Two-Dog and the remaining men charged from their cover and caused panic among the animals. The beasts at the rear bellowed and ran forward, exciting the animals in front of them, who in turn excited the ones further ahead, a process that kept repeating itself until hundreds, thousands, tens of thousands of terrified animals were charging forward in a mad stampede. The noise of their hooves built until it was a rumbling roar that could be heard twenty miles away, and the earth trembled beneath the impact of a hundred thousand hooves and millions of pounds of flesh.

Two-Dog had anticipated all that was happening. His warriors had charged in a way that allowed them to cut off a small group of animals from the main herd. These bison, perhaps thirty or forty of them, charged directly toward the warriors that Two-Dog had sent in advance.

The strength of any single big-horned bison was far greater than that of all the men put together, but Two-Dog's people had been hunting the bison for uncounted generations and had developed ways of overcoming the brute power of the animal. One way was to panic the beasts so they ran over the side of the cliff and were dashed to death on the rocks below. When there were no cliffs available, as today, the hunters used other time-tested methods.

When the bison came close to Two-Dog's crouching warriors, the men sprang from their hiding places and threw their spears at a single animal. These spears were stout poles with sharpened rocks held to their heads by animal sinew. The rocks could hardly be called spear-points, because they had not been chipped or flaked by man in any way; they were simply sharp rocks picked from the ground and used the way they had been left by nature. The age of the flint-worker was still in the future.

The animal singled out by the warriors was a middle-sized bull entering his third season. Five rock-tipped spears hit various parts of the bison's body. The shock and pain brought him to a sudden stop, and he looked around in bewilderment. Five more spears pierced his flesh, and the blood began to seep and drip from the openings. Two warriors immediately ran between the wounded animal and the others nearby, and with a snort the bison veered to the right to return to the herd. But warriors jumped in front of him, waving spears and shouting, so he turned to the left. The warriors allowed the animal to go in this direction, as it put more distance between him and the herd.

Now came the tedious part of the hunt. The warriors followed the wounded animal until his strength was sapped by the loss of blood and he began to move more slowly. Finally the bison could no longer walk; he sank to his front knees, his great tongue hanging from the corner of his mouth, his eyes empty of understanding, his life's blood draining to the ground. The hunters gathered around, still wary and respectful of the long horns, and delivered many stabs with their spears. The bison's eyes closed, blinked open, and then closed forever.

The warriors immediately began to butcher the carcass. When the remaining warriors and the women caught up with them, the freshly cut meat was put over a fire that had been started with embers from the last fire. This task, too vital to be left to a woman, was the responsibility of a warrior. The people of the clan of Two-Dog ate their fill.

This was but one of many kills made as the people of Two-Dog followed the herd across the plains in the direction of the rising of the Great Orb.

The sun was a thing of fascination to Two-Dog. Ever since he had been a small boy at the side of his father, his people had been following the herd, and always, but always, they moved in the direction of the rising of the Great Orb.

Warmed by the fire, satisfied by the day's hunt, and filled with bison meat, Two-Dog indulged himself in thought. He wondered why they never arrived at the land of the Great Orb. For twenty seasons he had been moving toward it, yet it never seemed to be any closer. How many seasons more would it take before he would be able to reach out and touch the orb, or at least see the lair from which it rose? He thought about it long after the others had pulled their warm furs over their bodies and crept beneath the stretched covering of hides.

Another problem bothered Two-Dog. After the Great Orb had followed its path across the sky and gone to its resting place, the sky often filled with bright dots of white light. It did not happen every night. There were nights when no lights could be seen, other nights when they were seen only here and there, and still other nights when the sky was so filled with them that, it seemed to Two-Dog, they looked as crowded together as a herd of big-horned bison. He spent many nights thinking about this and finally decided on the answer.

"Dead Ear, are you awake?" he said to another warrior who sat contentedly at the edge of the fire, his head nodding to welcome sleep.

Dead Ear had been given his name after a dire wolf had challenged him for the possession of a kill. The dire wolf had lost his life, but not before the man had lost one ear to the sharp wolf teeth.

Dead Ear came to full wakefulness when he heard the voice of his leader. His fur dropped from his shoulders, his hand grabbed his spear, and he looked around for wolves or other enemies.

"I have solved the problem of the bright lights up there," Two-Dog said, pointing at the sky.

Dead Ear looked at him with surprise. He too had seen the bright lights almost every night of his life, but they meant nothing to him. They could not be hunted and killed. They could not be eaten. They could not be worn. There was nothing to be done with them and so, naturally, he never thought about them.

"They are a herd followed by a Great Warrior who hunts them," Two-Dog said. "When the Great Warrior hunts, the herd hides and we see few of their number. But when the Great Warrior has made his kill and feasts, the herd knows it has nothing to fear and the animals graze in the open. That is when we see so many as on this night."

Dead Ear looked blankly at the other warrior. What was the matter with Two-Dog? he wondered. What was he talking about? Great Warriors? Herds? Lights in the sky? Dead Ear grunted, pulled his furs back around his shoulders, and went back to sleep.

Two-Dog continued to look at the stars. The more he thought about his idea, the more he knew he was correct. He was proud of himself, and in the years to follow he would tell others of his discovery.

Two-Dog's people continued to follow the herd, moving sometimes in a northerly direction, sometimes southerly, but always toward the east, always toward the land where the Great Orb was born each morning.

Two-Dog grew older. When he had now seen thirty seasons, he began to fear the day when he would be too old to hunt, or too old to defend a challenge from a younger warrior. But his fears were groundless, because he did not live to see his thirty-first season. His life was taken one day by a giant mammoth during a hunt. The warriors had trapped the animal in a ravine. They had already driven a dozen spears into his thick hide and bounced several dozen large stones off the top of his head, but he was far from finished. Two-Dog leaped into the ravine, threw his spear, and instantly retreated up the rocky wall toward safety. But on this day his feet betrayed him. He slipped from a ledge, plunging to the ground a few feet in front of the mammoth. The animal trumpeted in rage and lunged forward, one of his tusks smashing into Two-Dog's back, snapping his spine as easily as a man snapped a twig. The great mammal then pounded Two-Dog beneath his wide feet, crushing the body to jelly and screeching his triumph to the world.

Two-Dog was dead. But he had had sons, and these sons remembered Two-Dog's thoughts about the Great Warrior. They too wondered and talked about the Great Warrior. When they died, they left more sons who knew these thoughts. From the thoughts would come stories, and from the stories legends, and from the legends would spring the seeds of religion and theology. A vast gulf was being created between man and the beasts he hunted: the beasts accepted the world as they found it, but man felt compelled to explain it. And so the ideas and thoughts of Two-Dog did not die when the mammoth crushed him, but continued to live long after his name had been forgotten and the places where he hunted the big-horned bison had once again sunk beneath the seas.

* * *

Forty thousand years ago the continents of North America and Asia were joined by a vast land bridge. To find the beginnings of this bridge, we must go back to the beginning of the Pleistocene Epoch, one and a half million years ago.

From the beginning of the Pleistocene to the present day, the world has seen four great glacial advances, four vast rivers of ice with many fingers covering vast areas of the earth. The ice would advance and then recede. The advancing ice had been formed with water taken from the oceans, causing a sizable drop in the levels of the seas. At their peak the ice sheets buried almost a third of the land on the earth, gouging out solid rock to form rivers and canyons, sweeping away vast forests as if they were match sticks, digging huge holes in the ground and filling them with enormous quantities of ice that, after the sheet receded and the climate warmed, became enormous lakes.

The most recent ice-sheet advance began sixty-five thousand years ago, by which time the earth had witnessed the emergence of a new creature. He was modern man, a creature who was without sharp fangs, without claws, without protective coating of heavy fur, yet managed to hold his own with sabre-toothed tigers, ferocious bears, and the enormous mammoths and mastodons. In fact, he did more than hold his own, soon learning to master all the other creatures of his world.

Sixty-five thousand years ago, at the beginning of the last great ice age, man was well established in Asia, from the warm seas of the south to the cold tundra of the far north. The men of Asia had not yet learned to plant and grow their own food. They had not learned to raise animals other than the dog. They did none of these things because there was no need. Vast herds of animals roamed the plains, steppes, and tundra of Asia. All a man had to do was follow the herds and kill when he was hungry. He knew no other way to live, nor did he care to know. Two-Dog's people back to the tenth generation had lived this way, as they would live to the tenth generation after his death.

Today the continents of Asia and North America are separated by the fifty-six miles of freezing, fog-bound waters of the Chukchi Sea and the Bering Strait. But during the years of the great ice advances, this was not so. As the ice grew, the levels of the seas dropped between 150 and 300 feet. A 300-foot drop created a thousand-mile-wide land bridge between the two continents. A drop of only 150 feet created a land bridge 300 miles wide.

When the land bridges were created during the first three ice ages, man had not been there to cross them, but this did not mean they went uncrossed. The bridges lasted for thousands of years, and during that time they sprouted with vegetation, growing rich and green. This abundance of food attracted grazing animals, and over the years millions of beasts browsed their way across the land bridge from Asia to the Americas. Among them were herds of musk ox and bison, floods of moose and ground sloths. There were weasels, bears, opossum, and mountain sheep. Goats came, and two-humped camels with a resemblance so close to the camels of today that one would have a hard time distinguishing them. Birds came. Insects swarmed across the land bridges. And, as always in the wake of animal migrations, came the carnivores—the great fanged cats, the dire wolves, the foxes, and the carrion eaters.

The horse came and, for reasons we do not know, left. These primeval horses crossed one of the earlier land bridges, lived and thrived on the North American continent for hundreds of thousands of years, and then returned to the homeland of Asia across one of the later bridges. Their descendants did not reappear on the continent until they arrived with the conquistadores in the 16th century.

But man was on the scene when the last land bridge formed sixty-five thousand years ago. He did not cross the bridge in the spirit of exploration or because he was enticed by the adventure of visiting a new continent. In fact, he was not even aware he had crossed a bridge or set foot on a new continent. He came for the simplest of reasons. He followed the herds, because the herds were the nourishment of his life.

It is a mistake to picture the land bridges as landscapes of ice and snow, and it is false to create a portrait of these early men braving fierce polar winds as they made their way to a new continent, struggling through waist-high drifts of snow.

In reality, it was quite pleasant.

Glacial ice plays strange tricks on the world. It lowers the seas and creates vast new tracts of land. It brings more temperate climes to areas that are far colder at other times. During the last ice age most of Alaska was ice free, as was much of Siberia. The amount of snow and rain declined in the area of the Bering Strait, and the new land bridge blocked off the arctic winds and polar waters, allowing the bridge to be warmed by the mild currents of the Pacific Ocean. As the bridge widened, the birds came and dropped seeds; the winds swept over the new lands bringing more seed and pollen. Soon the landscape greened luxuriantly with various grasses. Tangles of dwarf birch flourished. Willows, heaths, mosses, lichens grew— all of the flora found today in the mild months of weather on the tundra stretching across Canada and Siberia. Lakes and ponds formed on the rolling land, complementing the abundant supply of food with an abundant supply of water. The great herds left Asia as they followed the mild weather and the lush vegetation across the land bridge. In their wake followed man.

The herds of big-horned bison were the key to the arrival of man in North America. The huge animals were perfect for his needs. They traveled in great numbers. They fed on grass, so they were visible on the open plains from great distances. A single animal provided a great deal of food. The bison led the way to water holes and salt licks. They left wide, easily crossed paths in their wake. For thousands of years these paths were the only roads known by man. And they were still useful when Daniel Boone followed an ancient bison path that became the Wilderness Trail over the Cumberland Gap.

The men followed the animals as they grazed, but preferred to live in the foothills of the mountains surrounding the plains. This was not for aesthetic reasons, but practical ones. The higher ground was drier and afforded more shelter. It gave the hunters a commanding view of the herds on the flatlands. And it was easier to defend oneself in the craggy foothills than out on the open plains.

At various times the ice corridors would shift, clearing places like the Mackenzie Valley, and the herds would follow these new openings, going south along the eastern flank of the Rocky Mountain chain, finding new openings with new promises of grass, spreading out onto the great plains of the south.

The descendants of Two-Dog, a people we know as the Paleo Indians, found prosperity and their numbers multiplied. The increase in population caused them to push ever outward into fringe areas. Prosperity; more food; more people; some are forced to move to fringe areas at greater and greater distances. In such fashion was man dispersed to the far corners of the New World.

Some went north, and from these men are descended the Eskimo. Others followed the herds as they doubled back along the land bridge and returned to the homeland of Asia. Still others dispersed to the south and the east, always following the herds.

These were great years for the race of man. Never had such herds of game animals existed in the world. They were numberless, an endless streams of animals, a primeval deluge of living flesh. The tens of thousands killed by the Paleo Indians had no more effect on the numbers of the herds than the bite of a mosquito had on the hide of a mammoth. By traveling with the herds and living in the foothills, the Paleo Indians enjoyed the best of two worlds without a worry about food or shelter. Following the herds, they populated the tundra of the north, the plains of the central continent, and the woodlands of the east.

Some continued south until three hundred generations later, a descendant of Two-Dog found himself staring at the sea from the rugged hills of Tierra del Fuego at the tip of South America. Of Two-Dog he knew nothing, but of the stories and legends that had been woven from his ancestor's thoughts he knew a great deal; they had grown into a body of beliefs and superstitions that ruled his life.

Man's easy living in the New World went on for thirty thousand years before a change occurred. Then again, it was because of the action of the glaciers.

The ice began to melt.

The glaciers shrank and retreated to their permanent northern homes, where they would slumber and lie in wait, gathering their strength, preparing for that day when they would again move forward upon the world to the south.

With their sources of unlimited water gone, the plants began to wither and diminish. Jungle turned into forest, forest into savannah, savannah into tundra and desert. And life turned into death.

The great land bridge narrowed and finally disappeared beneath the waters that closed above it. Once again there was nothing to stop the arctic waters, and they flowed south and touched the lands, chilling the air, frosting and killing the plants, creating swirling banks of icy fog, reaching out with frozen fingers of annihilation toward the bones of men and beasts.

And now the great herds began to die. It took long periods of time, but nature is the inventor of time and her decisions are thorough and final. The last of the great wooly mammoths died about ten thousand years ago; no longer would he be hunted by the descendants of Two-Dog; no longer would he keep them warm with his skins and thick, reddish-brown hair. The continent saw the last of the tapirs and ground sloths about ninety-five hundred years ago. The big-horned bison, so instrumental in bringing man to the new continent, no longer roamed in countless herds, and the last survivor fell to his knees and became a meal for wolves almost nine thousand years ago. Five hundred years later the camel and the giant armadillo were gone.

The loss of the herds profoundly affected the lives of the Paleo Indians. They were forced to turn to other animals and develop new hunting skills. They began to live off deer, elk, bear, and raccoon. But because these animals are not nomadic like the big-horned bison, the Indians began to settle down in one place. As they grew accustomed to this new life, they began to build permanent and more comfortable structures. They learned to make use of plants for medicine, food, and tobacco. They learned of dyes and herbs. They began to cultivate their own plants. More time passed, and peoples who previously had lived apart banded into tribes, and these tribes learned from one another, and from this pooling of knowledge came the various Indian cultures whose artifacts and customs have given us a fairly clear picture of their lives.

The Adena woodland culture spread from what is now southern Ohio to the tip of Louisiana, and east to the Atlantic Ocean. The Hopewell association of Indians

came into being out of economic considerations. These
peoples traded with their counterparts up and down the
length of the continent. The principal items of exchange
were pearls; mica; obsidian, which was used for the orna-
mentation of ceremonial knives; alligator teeth; large
conch shells; and a distinctive type of Minnesota stone
used to carve pipes in the shapes of animals.

As early cultures and associations dissolved, the Paleo
Indians became the men we know as the Archaic Indians. These were men who had learned to work flint and
create fine arrow points and blades from the hard stone.
We know them by the same names we have given their
beautiful carvings—Plano, Plainview, Folsom, Llano, and
Sandia. Their descendants created a great society of men,
and the groups they formed were the nations and peoples
alive when the white man first came to the continent from
Europe.

One of these groups was the great Algonkian people.
They inhabited the woodlands of the eastern seaboard
and paddled and fished the many waterways in their
canoes made from the trunks of trees. They took their
living from the land as well as the water, and developed
over thirty kinds of vegetables and spices. They hunted
bear, wildcat, rabbit, fox, beaver, muskrat, ground hog,
bison, and cougar. They knew the snake and used his
skin for decoration. They knew the skunk, and knew
enough to leave him alone. But of all the animals, the one
who gave the most to their lives was the deer.

Consider the harvest they took from this single animal:

skin—moccasins, thongs, and clothing
hair—ornaments and ritualistic instruments for their
    medicine men
antlers—tool handles and arrow points
dew claws—jinglers for belts and anklets
sinews—thread, bowstrings, and snares
bones—tools, handles, ornaments, carvings
paunch and bladder—ready-made containers for water

The meat, of course, was the very fibre of every Indian's flesh.

Many of the tribal names of the Algonkians are familiar to us. On Long Island lived the Canarsies, the

Rockaways, the Merricks, Matinacocks, Massapeaques, Nissequoquas, Sectogues, Setaukets, Unkechaugs, Corchaugs, Shinnecocks, Manhassets, and at the very end, the Montauks.

On the other islands and lands of the coastal plateau lived the Manahatas, the Wickquaskeeks, Tapaens, Esopus, and Raritan, among others. To the north lived their cousins—the Penobscots, Pennacooks, Narragansetts, and Pequots.

The race of men descended from Two-Dog had filled a continent, adapted to it, and lived off it while leaving it much the way they found it. They used, but did not use up; they built, but their building did not pollute; they lived and fought with one another, but their fighting was not enough to cause other races of men to die.

This was their land, not because they had bought it, not because they owned a piece of paper with their name on it, not because a king who lived far away granted them a charter.

There were stories and legends about ancient journeys from other places, but these were hoary with age and looked upon more as fable than fact.

The Indian looked at the matter with great simplicity of mind and heart.

This was his land and had been his as far back as the memory of man extended.

He could not understand why it would not be his land forever.

5

An Old Indian Dies

1643 - 1645

"THIS YEAR WE'LL HAVE A FINE CROP," CLAES
Vincent assured Pieter as the two men rode their horses
down the long lines of cornstalks. Although Pieter had
owned the land for a number of years, this was only the
third season the fields had been planted. The first two
had been disappointments.

Pieter was determined to make a success of his
bouwerie. It was not his home, because his whaling and
oil businesses still took up most of his time and it was
necessary for him to live in the settlement of New Amsterdam. But even if this were not the case, it would be
impossible to get Christiana to leave the house on Pearl
Street. She would never consent to live in what she called
a "wilderness."

So Claes Vincent had been made manager, and under
his guidance the bouwerie progressed swiftly. A farmhouse had been built, separate bunkhouse for the hands,
and a large barn for the animals.

"Are you sure you've planted nothing but Virginia
seed?" Pieter asked.

"Aye," Vincent said. "Every last seed."

"Let's hope we'll have a good crop of long-ears."

"My guess is ours will be twice the size of everyone
else's."

It had been something of a gamble, of course, to plant
nothing but the new, untried seeds, but Pieter had decided
it was worth the risk. The Indian corn that everyone
planted was short-eared and tough. Pieter had bought
the new seed from a trader who had gotten it from an

171

English planter in Virginia. The trader had shown them large ears of the "new" corn, which dwarfed the Indian "turkey wheat." The trader had not been willing to guarantee the new corn would thrive in the cooler climate of New Netherland, but Pieter could not expect any man to be so foolish as to guarantee anything in the New World. So he had bought the seed, planted it, and now could do nothing more than hope for the best.

"Are the fences strong?" he asked.

"We've been working on them day and night. S'help me, Pieter, nothing less than a herd of buffalo could bust through those fences!"

Pieter laughed. "I doubt we'll see any buffalo herds on the island this year. "They've never made it across the river. I guess I can rest easy at night."

"That you can," Vincent said. The dirt road to the house was neatly graded, and the horses made their way without any help from the riders. They knew, better than the men, where the barn awaited them.

They passed a group of hands who were chopping down a stand of trees to make way for next year's fields. With the addition of the new area, Pieter's farm was beginning to look as fine as any on Manhatan. Five full-time hands were employed, and Vincent was thinking of adding another.

Pieter was now forty-four years old, looking trim and fit, as if a lifetime of work had agreed with him, his sandy hair turning gradually to various shades of grey. His clothes were loose-fitting and his tanned face looked even darker because of the snowy-white collar that buttoned to the neck and flowed over the top of his jacket. He wore buckled leather boots on his feet and a wide-brimmed beaver skin hat on his head. He looked every inch the prosperous citizen of New Netherland—the sort of man the West India Company held up as an example to Dutchmen in Holland as they tried to convince more of them to cross the ocean and settle in the American colony.

The emigration rate was still a problem. The Netherlands was the richest country in Europe. The people ate well, lived in comfortable houses with rugs on the floors, and enjoyed more religious tolerance than prevailed anywhere else on the Continent. Their culture flourished, and they boasted of Rembrandt, Hals, and Steen, a new genius whose work was just beginning to be noticed. Dutch children were given educations—girls as well as boys, Holland being the only country in Europe where the education of females was even considered. Taxes were low, business thrived, and the government interfered little in the citizens' lives. No wonder the people did not want to leave all this and take their chances in a New World where much was still unknown.

Pieter and Claes Vincent arrived at the farmhouse.

"Master Pieter!" came a shout from the barn. Pieter turned and saw the giant figure of Manuel emerging through the open door.

Pieter turned his horse and met the man halfway between the house and the barn.

The huge man held the reins as Pieter dismounted. They threw their arms about each other in obvious affection. "It's good to see you, Master Pieter! Why, it must be more than a month!"

"Five weeks, Manuel. I've been at sea. The new ship, the *Christiana*, is bigger and takes twice as much blubber to fill her holds."

Manuel's arm dropped from Pieter's shoulder. "One of these days I'm going on that ship of yours. One of these days I'm going to get me a whale." His yearning was real and touching.

"Come to the house," Pieter said with a smile. "I have a present for you."

"A present? Master Pieter, you've already given me enough of a present to last a lifetime."

"Wait until you see what it is before you go giving it back."

The cozy farmhouse contained two rooms. One was a small bedroom used by Claes Vincent and his wife, Tryntje. The other large room had a kitchen area, a dining area, and a place near the fire with comfortable chairs for relaxing in the evenings and on the Sabbath. The dining area contained a long table with many chairs, which was not an indulgence, since the farm hands took all their meals with the manager.

Tryntje Vincent bustled around the kitchen. She gave the men cups of coffee and an enormous platter of soft, fluffy cakes still warm from the baking.

Pieter drank his coffee and then took a long, canvas-wrapped object from the crate he had brought up from town. He handed it to Manuel. The black man unwrapped the canvas, and his eyes lighted with excitement when he saw his present.

It was a harpoon. He touched the shaft as if it were made of fragile crystal. He touched the blades. He turned it over and over in his palms.

Suddenly he looked sharply at Pieter. "But what am I to do with it?"

"Practice. Learn to be accurate. Throw at haystacks. Learn to thread the eye of the needle. Learn to kill."

"But why?"

"You once told me your dream was to kill whales. After this season's crops are in, you become second harpooner on the *Christiana.*"

Manuel was stunned. "But my work . . . the farm . . ." he protested weakly, too bewildered to accept what was happening to him.

"There are others for the farm. Manuel," Pieter said quietly, "you once gave me my life. Now I'm giving you your dream."

Manuel started to speak. He stopped, swallowed hard, and said, "But once you gave me back *my* life. This," he said, holding up the shaft of the harpoon, "is more than I deserve."

Claes Vincent was afraid the black man would cry. "Let's have a drink," he said, going to the cupboard and bringing back a bottle of rum and three glasses. He filled them to the brim. "To whaling," he said, and the men downed their liquor.

It was true that Pieter had saved Manuel's life.

In 1639 the slave house had been moved to a new place far up the island. The fort was completed, and the slaves were sent to work on the company's tobacco bouwerie. The new "house" turned out to be a ramshackle hut close by the waters of the Hellegat. There was great dissatisfaction among the slaves. They complained and complained until one of the overseers, a black man who had once been a slave himself, became angry at the bickering and rushed into a group of slaves, lashing them with his whip. The slaves of New Amsterdam were not used to such handling. Their treatment had been fair, they thought, when they labored at the fort. The whip was rarely used, and then only as punishment for a breach of the rules. The slaves could hardly object to this; it was the same treatment given to free white lawbreakers. A man broke the law and he was tied to a stake and thrashed. That was proper.

No, it was not the whip itself that incensed the slaves, but the fact that the overseer had used it with no discrimination. He had simply dashed into their midst and flailed at everybody. This was the treatment accorded cattle; the treatment their fathers and grandfathers had endured aboard the slave ships and on the plantations of the Portuguese in Brazil. This was not to be tolerated.

The overseer was killed.

No one was sure who did it, because many took part in the savage beating. The manager of the company bouwerie had a problem on his hands. A man had been murdered, but it was impossible to identify the murderer. He made a unique decision.

"A man must be hung," he said to the assembled slaves. "I leave it to you to choose which of your number shall be that man. At dawn we'll hang the one you name."

At first there was great argument among the slaves. Each declared his innocence and argued fervently why he should not be the one to die. After listening for an hour, Manuel Gerait spoke up.

"You are not men. You are not even women. You are children, little children crying and begging for your lives. Stop worrying about who will die. They can hang me. It will be easier than listening to you. Now leave me alone," he finished angrily.

The others drifted from the hut, their heads hung in shame because they knew Manuel had spoken the truth. They had behaved badly, no better than cringing dogs. But their eyes also shone with the light of those who have been reprieved.

One of the slaves, a young boy named Thomé de Souza, was an admirer of the giant Manuel. When he heard his idol declare he would hang for the others, Thomé headed south as fast as his legs would carry him to bring word of the disaster to Manuel's sister, Zilla. The boy knew Zilla from the slave house at the settlement. When she brought food to her brother, she often gave some to him. Manuel and Zilla had been the only people who had ever been kind to him in the few years of his life. Thomé could not imagine either one of them dead.

When Zilla heard the news from Thomé, she collapsed in the de Kuyper kitchen. She began wailing and crying and the racket brought Pieter in from the garden, where he had been building a storage shed directly over the bones of Dirk Stratling and his companions.

Pieter finally calmed Zilla down. She told him the story, and Thomé begged Pieter to do something—anything at all, only Manuel must be saved.

Pieter did not disappoint them. He knew that what he was about to do was hardly legal, but the realization didn't stop him.

He went to his ship and rounded up a dozen armed sailors. Pieter, Thomé, and the sailors traveled north to the company bouwerie, arriving before dawn. Pieter roused the manager from his sleep. The man was angry and told him that what was happening was none of his business.

"You can't hang Manuel!" Pieter thundered. "He's one of the hardest workers on the island."

The manager was not a man of violence. He was an adminstrative sort, a lifelong employee of the Amsterdam burghers whose greatest ambition was to enjoy a quiet retirement in a cottage overlooking the Zuider Zee. He regarded his stay on Manhatan as a sentence in a penal colony and could not wait for his tour of duty to be over. He looked at Pieter and knew he wanted no trouble with him, and so he held up his hands and spoke mildly. "I have had nothing to do with choosing this man. The slaves themselves chose the one to die. There must be justice. I advise you, sir, not to interfere with the affairs of the company."

Pieter could be very practical. A man had been murdered and the manager sought justice, even if he did it in a very strange way. Pieter knew that if he interfered he would incur the wrath of the burghers. His concern was not for himself. If it had only been a matter of his own safety, he would have defied them all, taken Manuel away by force, and dared them to do their worst. But he was not alone. He had a wife, children, and employees who depended on him.

He solved the problem with guile.

The slaves and the free men of the bouwerie rose at dawn. Manuel was led to the gibbet. The manager took out a moth-eaten Bible and mumbled a few words. The rope was put around Manuel's neck. There was a long pause. The barrel was kicked from under Manuel's feet. The body dropped—

—and the rope snapped! Manuel fell unharmed to the dirt. With his hands still tied behind him, he gazed back at the other men who stood with their mouths open, not believing what their eyes were telling them.

Pieter stepped forward. "God Himself has proclaimed this man's innocence!" he cried. "Is there a man among you who would defy a sign from God?"

It was a well-rehearsed speach. He had gone over each word carefully since the moment he had used his sharp knife to cut the rope through to the last few strands. A few pounds of pressure would do the rest—and Manuel weighed in at two hundred and fifty.

The men looked at one another in confusion. It was no longer an issue of hanging Manuel, but of defying God Almighty.

"Free Manuel! Free Manuel!" the slaves chanted. It was picked up by the free workers and the sailors. The manager looked from the men to Manuel to Pieter. When the manager saw the smile of triumph on Pieter's face, he knew he was beaten.

"It's not for me to defy the will of God," he said. "Justice has been served. The man may go free."

"He'll come with me," Pieter said.

"I meant he shouldn't hang," the manager replied. "You can't take away company property."

"He was a condemned man whom you hung. Let the record show it that way," Pieter said evenly, his hand straying to rest on the hilt of his sword.

The manager was now thoroughly convinced he wanted nothing more to do with this matter. The man in front of him was very insistent, and he was backed by a dozen armed men.

"As you say, we hung and buried him," the manager said, wiping away the perspiration that had begun to bead on his lower lip. He hurried away toward his quarters for a much-needed drink.

The reciprocal bond between Pieter and Manuel had become the strongest sort of bond that can exist between

two men: each would not be alive if it were not for the
other.

Manuel was brought back to the house on Pearl Street,
where he stayed until Pieter began to work on his bouwerie.
Manuel and Claes Vincent were the first to work there,
and they built the farmhouse with their own hands.

After Pieter made his rounds of the farm, he returned
to town, remained a week, and boarded the *Christiana*
to begin another voyage after whales.

Manuel became a possessed man. In his spare time he
practiced with the harpoon—hour after hour—until Claes
Vincent warned him to slow down or he would die from
overwork. But to Manuel the work with the harpoon was
not work at all, but sheer joy.

At first he was content to hit the stack of hay. But as
his eye and arm learned to work together, the stack of
hay became too large and too easy a target. He painted
rings on it, and the more he practiced the closer the harpoon came to the center, until a time came when it was
unusual if he did not hit the center ring with every throw.

When the time came to hit the whale's eye, Manuel
would be ready.

The *Christiana* had been at sea for three weeks, and
the holds were filled with blubber. Pieter had sailed his
ship out to the waters at the end of Long Island to take
advantage of the great number of migrating whales there.

His crew stripped the blubber from whale after whale
within sight of Block Island, named for his first captain and
his friend, Adriaen Block of the *Tiger* and the *Restless*.
Block had discovered the island during the first voyage
of the *Restless*, and the crew had named it after him. Except for a few Indians who used it as a fishing camp during the summer months, Block Island remained unin-
habited.

There was another island that intrigued Pieter, a flat,
low-lying piece of land that appeared to rest between
the two jawlike spits that formed the northern and southern edges of Long Island. He had heard stories of a
strange Englishman living on this island, and since the
holds of the *Christiana* were filled almost two weeks before he had expected, Pieter decided to satisfy his curios-

ity. He dropped anchor in a cove of the island, and went ashore.

In such a chance manner did Pieter de Kuyper come to know Lion Gardiner.

The Englishman warmly greeted Pieter as one of the first visitors ever to come to his island. Pieter was delighted to find his host spoke Dutch. Lion Gardiner explained that he had spent many years in Holland as a mercenary fighting against the Spaniards and the Austrians. He had come to understand the country, its people, its language, and its customs.

In 1639 Lion Gardiner had been sent across the ocean by the English king to build a fort at Saybrooke, on the Connecticut River. When he completed his task he was rewarded with a grant to the island, which the Indians called *Manchonake* but which the king's charter termed "Gardiner's Island."

"I'm surprised you don't hunt the whales," Pieter said. "They come close enough to harpoon them from your shores."

"I'll leave the whales to you," Lion Gardiner said. "I prefer the peace and quiet of growing vegetables on my island."

"You have no problems with the Indians?"

"They're my friends. We treat each other as equals and have no problems."

Pieter was thoughtful. "I'm afraid most Dutchmen don't think of them as equals. Nor even as men. They call them savages and put them in the same category as the wolf and the wildcat."

"The English are no better," Lion Gardiner said. "They think they can take the land away as if the Indian has no rights. It's wrong, but it's happening."

"It's a shame we can't learn to live in peace with one another."

"The Indian would like that, but it is we, I'm afraid, who won't allow it. The Indian is an honorable man. I count several chiefs as my best friends. Most of the problems we have with each other could possibly be solved if we'd only sit down and talk about them."

Pieter and Lion Gardiner talked for several hours. The Dutchman was impressed by the other's wisdom about Indians. If only there were men like this in

New Amsterdam, he thought, men who understood it was possible to live in peace with the Indians if only both sides would take the trouble to learn more about the other. The New World, unlike Europe, wasn't filled with people; it was almost empty. Surely with so much space it was possible for men to live without killing each other or coveting their property.

When Pieter and Lion Gardiner parted, each man knew he had made a friend who loved the New World and shared a concern over what the white man was doing to it.

Anne de Kuyper nibbled on a cookie she picked up from one of the many trays spread on the table.

"You leave them alone," Zilla chided as she arranged a tray of sweetmeats. "They're for the guests."

"I took only one."

"See that's all you take," Zilla said, adding a few more tempting-looking pieces to her tray. There was no mistaking the tone of authority in her voice. Zilla, in fact, was the real ruler of the household. She had been given her freedom a number of years ago, but had elected to stay with the people she considered her family.

Anne waited until Zilla wasn't looking before she snatched another cookie. She was now a sparkling young girl of twelve, experiencing the onset of puberty. She had many friends among the children growing up in New Amsterdam. They collected flowers, tended the animals, counted the ships, learned to cook and sew, and, in general, spent as happy a time as any other children alive on the face of the earth.

"How many ladies are coming to the party?" she asked.

"About thirty," Zilla replied.

The party was in honor of Madam Wetherby. Her husband was an importer who lived in London and who had recently begun buying whale oil from Pieter. He was now in New Amsterdam, and Pieter had taken him out on his ship today. The party was designed to keep the merchant's wife busy.

"Seems like a lot of fuss just for one English-woman," Anne sniffed as she took another cookie.

"You keep quiet," Zilla said. "Her husband does business with your father."

"Oh," Anne said with great innocence. "I thought we were doing this because we admired the lady."

Zilla smiled and moved over to a work table where several pies were cooling. Little Anne was becoming quite saucy. Very often her humor was so dry it completely escaped the ponderous Dutch minds, but Zilla never failed to understand.

Christiana entered the room. "Do you think this Englishwoman will prefer white cakes or pink cakes?"

"She'll like them both," Zilla said.

"We don't have any of the kind with seeds on them," Christiana said petulantly.

"Englishwomen don't like seeds," Anne said blandly.

"They don't? Oh well, in that case we won't need any," Christiana said, taking her daughter's remark at face value.

Anne and Zilla exchanged looks and tried to busy themselves as Christiana flitted from table to table, looking over the platters and trays with their mounds of good-smelling food.

Christiana was now a handsome woman of thirty-six, living almost totally in a world of her own creation. She had finally gotten rid of most of her fears, but at a great cost. She no longer could tell fantasy from reality and had become scatterbrained. The doctor had examined her, but hadn't a clue about what to do for her. Pieter finally gave up and accepted that nothing could be done for his wife. Actually it wasn't all that bad, he thought. At least Christiana no longer suffered the way she once had.

She was, however, somewhat trying to be around, always forgetting what she was doing, or what she had said only a few moments ago. She was easily upset, but recovered as easily. Pieter and Zilla loved her and accepted her for what she was. Anne enjoyed making outrageous statements, which her mother usually believed. Anne's habit bothered no one except Young Pieter.

"Where's Pieter?" Christiana suddenly asked, looking around the room.

"On his boat," Zilla said.

"On his *boat*," Christiana repeated, with a note of horror in her voice. "Isn't he planning on coming to the party?"

"The party is only for ladies," Anne said.

Christiana stopped and made a great effort to think about the last remark. Suddenly her face brightened. "Of course. Pieter's taken Mister Wetherby with him."

"Maybe they'll bring back a whale," Anne said.

"Oh I hope not," Christiana answered. "What would we want . . ." and then she puckered her lips. "Now you stop trying to fool me."

Zilla shook her head and took the pies over to the already heavily laden table.

Young Pieter came in through the back door. "What's for lunch?"

Zilla pointed to a small trencher near the fire. "That's for you."

Young Pieter looked at it and made a face. It was a generous portion of warmed-up bear meat. "That's lunch? With all this other stuff around?"

"This other stuff is for the party," Zilla said. "So keep your hands off it."

"The party for mother's best friend, Madam Wetherby," Anne said.

"My best friend?" Christiana looked perplexed. "How can you say that? I've never even met the woman. Sometimes I wonder about you, Anne. You're always mixing things up."

Young Pieter glowered at his sister. He was sixteen years old, bright and introspective. He was embarrassed by his mother's condition, and he hated it when anyone—and it was usually Anne—had fun at her expense. He went over to his lunch, tasted the bear meat, and grimaced.

Christiana began taking silver goblets out of the sideboard, and then stopped. Her eyes rested on three small silver cups standing in one corner. The first was engraved "Pieter," the second "Anne," but the third was blank. She reached out and touched the nameless one, and a sense of loss was visible on her face.

Zilla noticed, and she immediately came over to the sideboard. "Now you said you were going to pick fresh strawberries. You go do that and I'll take care of this."

"Yes, that might be best," Christiana admitted. She forced herself to stop looking at the little cup.

"I'll help you," Young Pieter said. "I've some time before I go back to work."

The two of them walked to the door, and even Anne was careful not to make any remark.

The third cup was for Christiana's third child, Jan, who had been born dead. That was five years ago, but it was still a painful memory to the woman. Whenever she came across something that reminded her of Jan, she would come close to tears. Zilla often thought it would be better to throw out things like the silver cup, but Christiana was adamant about keeping them. She was at her most lucid on the topic of the stillborn infant; it was about the only sad thing she now allowed into her mind.

Anne and Zilla continued preparing the food while Christiana and her son picked strawberries. By the time they had filled a bucket, she had forgotten about Jan.

Young Pieter left the Pearl Street house and wandered down to the fort. He found a good rock to sit on and made himself comfortable.

Why was he the only one in the family embarrassed for his mother? Maybe it was because he loved her the most, he told himself. It pained him that his mother wasn't perfect. Zilla was kind enough, but sometimes she treated Christiana as if she were a child. That little snot-nose, Anne, was always making fun. And his father?

Young Pieter sighed. His father was usually too busy to bother with Christiana. Always out on his damned boat. Why did a man even want to be a whaler? the boy wondered. He had once accompanied his father on a voyage and had been sick most of the time. If it wasn't the motion of the ship, it was the smell of the blubber or the blood all over the decks. His father wanted him to go a second time, but he always invented an excuse to get out of it. He preferred books to whales, and solid land to the pitching deck of a ship.

It was time to get back to work at the oil factory. He wasn't in love with that either, but it was better than going to sea.

"Do you have more than one service on the Sabbath?" Madam Wetherby asked Anne.

"No, ma'am, only one," Anne replied. She was now dressed in a pale blue dress, and her innocent face gave no indication of the wicked wit that lay behind it.

The Englishwoman looked at this pretty little Dutch girl with some condescension. "Only one? Well, well, well. At our church, our pastor insists on an evening service as well as morning. He says it is the true Christian's duty to atone for his sins at least twice on the Sabbath."

Anne smiled. "Perhaps the people of England have more sins to atone for than we do," she said sweetly.

The Englishwoman was startled by this remark from the angelic-looking girl. She started to speak, stopped, and began rapidly waving her fan, although it wasn't very warm in the room.

Anne maintained her look of innocence but was secretly delighted with the woman's discomfort. Madam Wetherby had entered the house and looked around as if she were inspecting a zoo. The other women made it worse; they never stopped making a fuss over their guest, telling her how grandly she dressed and how important her husband was and how delighted she had made them by favoring them with a visit. It all made Anne sick, and she was enjoying this bit of revenge.

"I've been told that many churches in England hold two services in winter because it's the only place a person can get warm."

"Wherever did you hear that?" Madam Wetherby asked, her face contorted with shock. "Our houses back home are proper and grand, not at all like—" She let her eyes wander about the room. "Well, you know what I mean."

"Ah, the houses back home," Christiana said as she walked by on her way to the kitchen. "Everything is grander in Europe, I quite agree."

Madam Wetherby glanced smugly at Anne and then turned to Christiana, thinking she had found a kindred soul. "These youngsters who've grown up here simply can't appreciate our way of life back home."

"What do you mean?" Christiana asked vaguely.

"Why . . . what I meant . . ." Madam Wetherby stammered in some confusion, "was, well, life here can be so tedious after one has become accustomed to a place such as London. . . ."

"What's so different?" Anne asked, hoping for an opening.

Madam Wetherby did not disappoint her. "Well, for one thing, the Indians here—"

"As opposed to the Indians there?"

"There are Indians in London?" Christiana asked with surprise.

"Indians in London!" Madam Wetherby's face showed her confusion.

"Then there *are* Indians in London," Christiana said emphatically.

"Yes, tell us, ma'am, about the London Indians," Anne said with as much sweetness and innocence as she could muster.

"The London . . . no, no, you misunderstand," Madam Wetherby blurted. "There are no Indians in London . . . never."

"It must be a wonderful place," Christiana said blithely. "After we move back to Amsterdam we must pay a visit to London." She walked away. "I must see about the pastries."

Madam Wetherby was bewildered as she watched the other woman depart. "Your mother is a . . . most interesting woman," she said to the girl, who was fighting the smile that was trying to creep onto her face.

"Yes," Anne said, getting up from her chair and moving toward the door. "Many people mistake her for English." And then she was outside before the distraught woman could reply.

Anne walked to the window box. The flowers, in full bloom, were her responsibility and a task she cherished. Since she had been a little child, flowers had held a special place in her life. Their abundance was one of the things she loved most about New Amsterdam. Every spring the land seemed to sigh and a million buds burst forth from the branches and the vines. Within weeks the earth looked and smelled like a fairyland. She bent her head forward and sniffed a crimson bud.

"How's the party going?" a voice asked.

Anne turned to see David, Abraham de Witt's son, her senior by one year. "All right, I suppose," she said cautiously.

"You suppose?"

"Well, it's really kind of silly. All those women trying to impress that dotty Englishwoman."

"What's she like?"

An impish grin came on her. "Like a piece of English cheese—big, fat, and smelly."

David laughed. "Wonderful! My mother spent the entire morning dressing for the big event."

"All the women look as if they did."

David de Witt was a serious-looking lad. He had inherited his father's brains without the older man's acid tongue. "Care to take a walk with me?" he asked. "Or do they need you inside?"

"I have time for a short walk," she said.

They walked up Pearl Street as it followed the curve of the river. They crossed the wooden bridge that spanned the canal that had been made out of a stream down the middle of Broad Street and walked into more open country.

"My father tells me Young Pieter went to sea with your father aboard the *Christiana.*"

"Yes. He hated it."

David shook his head. "I don't understand your brother. I wish my father owned a ship. I'd love to go on a whaling trip."

He spoke so solemnly and in such awe of the idea that she reached out and squeezed his hand. "Maybe you and my brother should swap fathers," she said playfully.

David smiled at the thought. "Wouldn't that be a wonderful thing! To be able to change places with other people. Everyone would be happy."

"And after a time you'd probably want to switch back," she said, and turned to walk back toward the house.

"I suppose you're right," David said. "We all want to be something else, but it never lasts."

"Be someone else, or some*where* else."

David nodded. "Just a few weeks ago your brother was telling me how much he'd like to live in Amsterdam."

Anne pretended a sudden interest in a cat that was sunning itself by the side of the road. She bent down and scratched its ears, for which she was rewarded with a look of feline annoyance.

David realized the girl didn't wish to speak about her brother. He tactfully dropped the subject.

"You're not as bad as you used to be," she said when they resumed their walk.

"What do you mean?"

"I always thought you were horrid. You once threw mud at me and ruined a new dress. I cried for hours."

"I'm s-sorry," he said, blushing. "But . . . that was a long time ago."

"Do you want to visit Amsterdam someday like my brother?" she asked suddenly

"Sure," he said. "I wouldn't mind a visit. But I wouldn't go to live there. This is my home," he said with pride.

"Mine too," she said and leaned over and kissed him on the cheek. "I'm glad you're turning out to be so nice." And then she fled into the house.

David placed his hand on his cheek. His mouth was open and he stared in bewilderment as the girl disappeared into her home. He had been so thoroughly enjoying her company, he hadn't been aware they had come all the way back.

His cheek seemed to burn where Anne had kissed it. And then he looked at his hand and realized it was the one she had squeezed. It seemed to tingle.

David de Witt was light-headed as he walked back to his own house. New Amsterdam was becoming a more wonderful place every day, he thought. And one of its greatest delights was turning out to be Anne de Kuyper.

It was late at night. Christiana and the children were asleep when Pieter returned from a three-week whaling voyage. He sat near the fire sipping warm gin and gnawing on the turkey leg that Zilla had given him.

"Any problems come up?" he asked.

Zilla shook her head.

"My son's been going to work every day, hasn't he?"

"You ought to go easier on that boy. Let him find his own way."

"If he had his way he'd spend all day with his nose in a book," he grumbled.

"I don't see you picking on Anne."

Pieter smiled. "I don't because I have a feeling I'd lose."

"Just the other day she told her mother the French were breeding horses that could fly."

"And her mother believed her?"

"Oh yes, she thought it was a wonderful idea."

Pieter sighed. He didn't exactly approve of the way Anne played games with her mother, but he realized it didn't do any harm. No evil was intended, and Christiana was usually delighted with Anne's outrageous announcements. But tomorrow, he resolved, he would have a talk with his daughter. Something like this could get out of hand.

And Christiana? In the old days she would have been waiting up for him, no matter how late he came home. But those times were over, and now it scarcely made any difference whether he was around or not.

Zilla came over and poured more gin into his glass. She was very close, and he could feel the warmth of her body and smell her sweet flesh. He looked straight into her eyes.

Nothing was said, but they both knew. Zilla put the gin bottle back in the cupboard and went to her bedroom, which was in the new section of the house at the rear of the first floor.

Pieter remained in his chair, sipping gin. His thoughts were of his wife upstairs. He had long ago given up feeling guilty about his lovemaking bouts with the black woman. In all probability they would never have happened if Christiana had been able to give him what his body needed. Pieter had no desire to hurt her, but the fact remained he had normal appetites and desires.

He finished his gin and walked into Zilla's bedroom. He took off his clothes and got into the narrow bed. They were close together, their flesh touching and tingling. How many times has this happened? he thought. Twenty-five? Thirty? He had lost count, but what did it matter. This had become part of his life, and as long as he kept it to himself, no one would be hurt.

Zilla pressed her cheek against his chest and lay still. There were times when Pieter would come home from a trip and lie next to her and fall alseep before they made love. She understood. Returning home after his labors, he wanted tenderness and understanding from a woman—sometimes with sex, sometimes without.

From his peaceful breathing she decided this was one of the times without sex. It didn't matter to her. She was there to do his bidding.

Zilla was totally realistic. There could never be anything more for her than this. But she was content. It was a good life that Pieter de Kuyper had given her.

Young Pieter was aware of what was going on between his father and Zilla. He had always been a light sleeper, and once, a year ago, he had gone to investigate strange noises in the middle of the night. He traced them to Zilla's room and was about to enter when he heard his father's voice; and then Zilla's voice; and then more noises, and the boy blushed when he realized what they were doing behind the closed door.

He hated his father for this. He hated him once for himself and twice for his mother. In his anger he blamed his mother's "strangeness" on his father. He wanted to do something, anything, but he was only a boy.

He managed to keep his secret and never let on that he knew of the affair between his father and Zilla. Even so, his resentment could not be contained. He found himself staring at his father with unveiled anger. Pieter finally noticed it. "What's the matter with you?" he asked his son.

"Nothing."

"Something's bothering you. I want to know what it is," Pieter demanded.

Young Pieter hesitated. How could a son accuse his father of immorality? Even if it was true, which it was, a son could not speak of such a thing. "I don't like my job," he said finally in a halting voice. It was a weak statement, a bit foolish, but it was all he could think of at the moment.

Pieter made a sour face. He didn't understand his son.

First it was whaling he didn't like, now it was the oil factory. "Well, what would it suit you to do?" he asked.

Young Peter was now in too deep to back out. He thought desperately for an answer to give his impatient father. And then he remembered there was talk of adding a new building onto the factory, a new storage area to hold oil while they waited for the price to rise. "I want to build things, Father," he said, "that's what I like. You spoke of building at the factory . . ."

"I'm not sure we need it."

"If I could work with the builder and learn his craft, I'd learn a skill that would please us both."

Pieter regarded his son as he thought it over. It was true he had considered erecting a new building, and it was also true he had decided not to do so now. But the thought of seeing his son finally doing something he liked, something manly and useful, appealed to him. "Very well," he said, "we'll go ahead with the building."

Young Pieter was genuinely pleased at the prospect. It was the kind of work he would enjoy. It was only after he walked away that he remembered why he had been looking at his father with hatred. How could he forgive the man who had done such harm to Christiana? His own wife, my mother, Young Pieter thought bitterly. He has destroyed her, ruined her life. He would never forgive him for that.

Of course there was a part of Young Pieter's mind that told him this wasn't exactly the truth. He knew his father loved Christiana and never consciously did anything to hurt her. But one of the aspects of hatred is that it blinds us to those truths that disagree with it. So it was with Young Pieter. His mental images of his mother and father had little to do with reality.

It pleased him to dwell on them.

Willem Kieft, who had replaced Van Twiller as governor in 1638, was an entirely different sort of man from his predecessor. He was intelligent, feisty, waspish, energetic; a teetotaler possessed of a terrible temper that often got the better of his reason. The citizens sighed at his faults and made fun of his constant scurrying about and his rapid-fire speech, but most were convinced he was far better than Wouter Van Twiller, or "Wouter the Waverer," as they had taken to calling him.

One of the few exceptions was Pieter de Kuyper. "Van Twiller was an idiot," he said, "and a petty thief. But this new one, Kieft, is a madman. Wouter could give us only little problems. This one could get us in trouble."

Hardly anyone agreed, although they did not openly mock Pieter. He was one of the town's leading citizens, a man of some wealth and substance. They politely nodded their heads, but silently told themselves he was talking nonsense.

The governor invented an advisory council to help him with the business of running New Netherland. Pieter was on this council, as was Abraham de Witt, Michael de Pauw, David de Hatten, Samuel de Schuyler, Dominie Bogardus, Jan Van Tienhoven, Willem Verveelen, and Albert de Vries. The last two were substantial farmers who had taken advantage of the company's policy, effected in 1639, that made all the lands on Manhatan open for settlement—after purchase from the company, naturally. These men built their bouweries far to the north in the section known as Harlem. Because Pieter's farm was far enough north to qualify him as a neighbor, he often visited Verveelen and de Vries. Pieter knew the Harlem area. It was not far north of here he had wandered away from the yacht *Restless,* been captured by the Indians, and had his first real adventure in the New World.

Kieft's advisory council was not the "official" company council. The official council had only two members—Kieft and a doctor who called himself a lawyer, Jan de La Montagne. But this official council was a farce. De La Montagne had one vote, but Kieft had two. This, in the governor's own words, was "to prevent a tie."

Therefore no one was under any illusions. One-man rule existed in New Netherland, and the one man himself was the first to admit it. But even so, it had not proved to be as burdensome as it might seem. Governor Kieft held regular meetings with his advisory council, of which de La Montagne was an "honorary" member, and when the council members were united and they argued well and strongly, the governor went along with their wishes at least ninety percent of the time.

New Amsterdam had become a real town. The number of settlers in New Netherland was over two thousand, and almost seven hundred of these lived on Manhatan Island. The fort had been completed, and the citizens felt safer under the protection of its well-armed garrison and menacing twelve-pounders. The original countinghouse had burned down, but a new building within the walls of the fort served the citizens as well as the old one. The City Tavern, erected at 73 Pearl Street, served as a hotel, offering good accommodations for travelers and official visitors from Holland. The Church of St. Nicholas had been built within the fort, and it was made partly of stone, something Dominie Bogardus had insisted on when the governor's new house was finished in stone.

A wharf and a solid quay had been built, helping to speed the loading and unloading of cargo and to increase the colony's position as a port.

There were two fairs each year, held on the green outside the walls of the fort. The one in October featured cattle, and the one in November was for hogs. The fairs brought the people together—from all over the island and beyond, some traders coming from as far away as Fort Orange to do a brisk business with their Manhatan counterparts.

Several ferries made their way from Manhatan to the settlements on the other side of the Hellegat, but no one, including Kieft, had been able to convince any of the ferrymen to operate on a regular schedule. Nor was there any fixed rate. One ferryman would charge the same fee for a man as another would charge for a man and a horse. The subject came up often at the meetings of the advisory council.

Today, however, it was not on the agenda. Today there were only two problems to be discussed—the Swedish colony on the Delaware River, and the Indian problem.

The problem of the Swedes dated to 1638, when a group of settlers arrived under the leadership of none other than Peter Minuit. At first Kieft was beside himself with fury. This was his first year in the New World, and to have the man who had held his own job start a rival colony right at his doorstep almost caused the governor apoplexy. He ranted and raged, but it was to no avail: Minuit had secured the blessings of Amsterdam before he led the Swedes to their new home. The burghers had decided a nearby colony of Swedish allies would increase their strength against the constant poachings of the hated English.

In truth, the English were becoming a nuisance. They were spreading out from New England and Virginia, building settlements along the Connecticut River and on Long Island. They started a trading post on the Schuylkill River, but it hadn't lasted very long. The Swedes joined the Dutch in burning down this threat to their trading operations near South, or Delaware Bay. Because of the turbulent situation in Europe, the English monarch ignored this hostile gesture and did not attempt to rebuild the post.

Governor Kieft brought the advisory council to order. "The first matter before us is that of Fort Christina. The Swedes now have a whaling ship working along the coast in our own waters. What do we propose to do about it?"

Jan de La Montagne was the first to speak. "The Swedes have a legal grant to their lands and are sanctioned by the West India Company. There isn't much we *can* do about it."

"Nonsense," the governor said. "When it becomes a matter of our own survival, I say to hell with legalities! Does anyone have any ideas?"

Captain Van Tienhoven, a military man who had recently taken command of the garrison from Samuel de Schuyler, said, "We can harass them."

"How?"

The cadaverous Van Tienhoven stroked his beard. "Send a warship to Fort Nassau. Have them stop every Swedish ship that tries to leave the river."

"Excellent," the governor said. Fort Nassau was a Dutch settlement on the Delaware, just south of Fort Christina. It was in an ideal position to harass any Swedish ships.

"It is illegal," de La Montagne protested. "The Swedes will complain to Amsterdam."

"Let them," Michael de Pauw said. "It will take seven weeks for their protest to reach Europe. There will be weeks of argument and debate, and then another seven weeks for a ship to return and tell us to stop. That's a long time for their whaler to lie idle."

The governor smiled. This was the sort of talk he liked to hear, action talk without any nonsense about "restraints of law" and other rubbish. He turned to Captain Van Tienhoven. "Send a warship to Fort Nassau."

"Done," Van Tienhoven said, slapping the table with the flat of his hand.

Because the Swedish whaler was in direct competition with his own ship, Pieter had more to gain than any other man in the room. But he was not pleased. This sort of arrogance could only lead to trouble with the Swedes, and of all their European neighbors in the New World, the Swedes had proved to be the least hostile.

Anyway, there were plenty of whales. The real competition was in the trade with the Indians for furs and pelts. He brought this to the governor's attention.

"A good point," Kieft admitted. "Does anyone have any ideas about stopping the Swedes' trade with the Indians?"

The answers were interesting, reflecting the natures of the men who gave them.

Van Tienhoven was for taking an expedition and burning Fort Christina to the ground.

David de Hatten, who owned the forge, wanted to increase trade in ironwork with the Indians, giving them an edge over the Swedes.

Michael de Pauw was for bribing the Swedish government to bring an end to their own colony.

Samuel de Schuyler, whose trading interests were now among the colony's largest, recommended a blockade of all cargo ships returning to Europe.

Dominie Bogardus, pretending to be serious but with obvious cynicism, recommended abiding by the wishes of the governor, "since that is what we are going to do anyway."

This brought a black look from Kieft. Since the day of the governor's arrival, the dominie had been a thorn in his side, even as he had been a thorn in the side of Van Twiller.

The question of the Swedes was closed with nothing more than the ship's being dispatched to Fort Nassau, but every man on the council knew the governor would not rest until the Swedes were gone. The burghers in Holland also knew of his obsessive hatred of the Scandinavians, but even so, they had made him governor because of his undeniable vitality and energy. It was said he slept four hours a day and worked the other twenty, a welcome change from the lazy, inept Van Twiller.

Van Twiller was still in the colony. He owned a rich bouwerie on the banks of the North River, another house on Governor's Island, and a great deal of land obtained mostly through the offices of Michael de Pauw. He spent most of his time drinking himself into incoherence. Eventually his drinking would bore even him, and he would sell his property and return to Amsterdam, a wealthy but unhappy man.

"And now the problem of the Indians," Governor Kieft said to the council.

The men came to life. The Swedish problem was mostly Governor Kieft's making, but there was not a man in the room unaffected by the increasingly difficult relations with the natives.

Samuel de Schuyler came to his feet. "It's becoming impossible to trade with the devils," he said. "They've lost their reason to greed. They want a cod if they give a herring. When a deal is made for five fathoms of wampum, they bring forth their biggest man to use as the measure."

Pieter managed to conceal his smile at the last remark. The fathom, the traditional measure of wampum, was the distance from the tip of the fingers on one hand to the tip of the fingers on the other. A fathom of wampum, therefore, could vary a great deal. A small Indian with short arms could measure a fathom that was only a half of the fathom of a tall Indian with very long arms.

De Schuyler continued. "Moreover, they no longer accept beads or trinkets in trade, but insist on wampum, guns, and liquor."

"They'll get no guns!" the governor shouted.

"But the truth is they *are* getting guns," de Schuyler said calmly. From the English, the French, the Swedes, and—may God strike me dead if I do not speak the truth —from our own people."

"I'll teach them not to trade guns to the Indians!" the governor cried. "I'll whip them! I'll put them in the pillory! By God, I'll hang them if I catch them!"

The men of the council remained silent; they knew

such outbursts did nothing to deter the trade in guns. Few
men were above temptation when the savages were willing to pay for guns with a fortune in furs.

"These wild men complain that my sheep are destroying their cornfields," Albert de Vries said. "Can I help it
if my sheep must eat?"

"Your sheep must be penned," de La Montagne said
sharply. "You wouldn't permit them to wander about if
your bouwerie stood near the fort."

"But the cornfields the Indians speak of aren't culti-
vated fields, only patches of wild turkey wheat."

"That's not the point," de La Montagne said. "The law
is quite specific on this issue. Animals shall not be permitted free access to another man's fields."

The governor intervened. "But we've heard de Vries
say these aren't fields at all, only wild growths in the
woods."

"Last week the Indians killed three of my sheep who
went near their damned corn," de Vries complained. This
brought expressions of sympathy from everyone except
Pieter, Dominie Bogardus, and Abraham de Witt.

Pieter liked this last man a great deal. De Witt was a
tough-minded sort who had all the best traits of the Dutch
—industry, thrift, cleanliness, and a dislike of stupidity.
Pieter thought de Witt would have made a good governor,
but that could never be, since the burghers in Amsterdam
trusted only those who held the company's interests
above the interests of the colony. De Witt had proved
where his loyalties lay years ago when he had resigned
as provincial secretary and gone into business for himself.

"Perhaps you should revive the Indian tax," Dominie
Bogardus said with his tongue in his cheek. "After all, it
was quite a success the last time."

The governor smarted beneath the blow, and another
black mark against the dominie went down in his book.
"I don't think the savages understand the idea of taxes,"
he said, his red face going a shade or two brighter.

There were many smirks and concealed smiles among
the other men. Two years ago, Kieft had levied a tax—
to be paid with maize, furs, or wampum—on all goods
traded to the settlers by the Indians. The natives were
astonished at first, and asked why it was necessary for

them to pay this tax. Kieft told them it was to maintain the fort, under whose protection they lived. This caused great mirth among the Indians. The fort had never protected them; in fact, they hated it as the symbol of a way of life that was threatening them. After they had time to think about it, their mirth turned to anger, and for a while it seemed they would attack the fort and burn it down. The colonists flooded into the fort and waited behind the protection of palisade and cannon. They put up such a clamor the governor was forced to rescind the Indian tax. This mollified the chiefs, but the relations between the two peoples never went back to their previous pleasant state. Indeed, they grew uglier with each passing month.

The tax had been one of the governor's greatest mistakes, and he hated the dominie for reminding him of it. "Let's get on with our business," he growled. "Any more suggestions?"

Other men stood and explained their ideas. Willem Verveelen was a good farmer, but a bit slow in the head. He wanted to declare the entire island of Manhatan off limits to the Indians. Even the governor could scarcely remain polite in the face of such stupidity.

The meeting came to an end and few problems had been solved.

The more thoughtful members of the council were aware that many of the Indians' grievances had a solid basis. Their lands *were* being overrun, and their fields *were* being destroyed. And if they were now driving harder bargins for their beaver pelts, it was only because they had learned to do so from the Dutch. If they drank liquor it was because they got it from the Dutch, and if they used firearms it was because the Dutch had taught them how to shoot.

The earliest Dutch settlers had talked at great length of the wonderful opportunity to "civilize these savages." Now that the "savages" were becoming "civilized," the men of the colony were finding their "civilization" troublesome, though they had no one to blame but themselves.

Pieter left the council chamber and found himself walking alongside Abraham de Witt.

"Kieft is no fool," de Witt said. "He knows we can't treat the Indian as if he were some sort of two-legged animal."

"But he refuses to recognize them as equals."

"More's the pity, because the Indian is convinced he is our equal. Sometimes I wonder if he isn't *more* equal."

"Liquor is causing a lot of the trouble," Pieter said. "Most of the crazy things they do can be laid right to the last bottle of liquor somebody gave them."

"Yes, but how do we keep them from getting liquor?"

Pieter shrugged his shoulders. "A man who has a chance to get twenty beaver pelts for a single jug of whiskey isn't likely to pass up the chance."

"Have you ever given whiskey to an Indian?" de Witt asked.

"Yes," Pieter admitted. "I guess we are the cause of our own destruction."

Abraham de Witt looked at him with a twinkle in his eye. "What makes you think life has ever been any different?"

As Pieter and Abraham de Witt walked from their meeting with the governor, Anne, Young Pieter and David de Witt were tramping through the primeval woods that covered the hills in the middle of the island.

The two young men carried muskets, because this was a hunting excursion. David said he wanted to bag a fox to give his mother for her birthday. Actually it was only an excuse to spend the day with Anne.

Unfortunately from David's point of view, Anne had accepted the invitation not only for herself but for her brother as well.

"I don't want to hunt a fox," Young Pieter had protested when she told him. "And since when are you interested in hunting?"

"It's not proper for me to go alone with David," she said, a flush of crimson blossoming in her cheeks.

"Aha!" Young Pieter said, noticing his sister's embarrassment. "It's not a fox you're after, is it?"

Anne bowed her head as Young Pieter gloated. "It's young Master de Witt!"

"Don't say anything to Father," Anne said. "It would be . . ." she stammered, too embarrassed to finish the sentence.

Young Pieter put his arm around her shoulder. "All

right, all right, I'll go with you. I'm sure David will be delighted," he added with mild sarcasm.

They had started at dawn, for it was a good five- or six-mile trek to get to the place where David assured them they would find the elusive fox. After he had gotten over his initial dismay at learning the brother was included, David managed to enjoy himself. As they walked, his eyes followed Anne, but only when he was sure she and Young Pieter were not watching him. She moves gracefully, elegantly, he thought, as he watched the lithe figure dodge a tree branch or scramble over a rock outcropping.

"I see animal tracks over there," Young Pieter said, pointing to a patch of land still soggy from the last rain.

"Deer tracks," David said, looking closely. "Two deer."

Young Pieter shook his head. It was beyond him how anyone could distinguish one animal track from another. Except for size, they all looked alike to him. He watched as David patiently showed Anne how to read deer tracks. He was aware of the deference the boy paid his sister—and also of how fondly she looked at him. She never looks at me that way, Young Pieter thought, and then smiled when he realized his "baby" sister was falling in love. She seemed too young, too much a child, but then he remembered it wouldn't be long before other girls her age would be making marriage plans. If it happened to them it would probably happen to Anne as well. But as far as he was concerned, there was no sense in getting involved with any girl in the colony: one of these days he would be leaving for good.

This thought reminded him of his mother. How could he leave her? He sighed. His dream would have to wait. But even though it would be deferred, he didn't mean to forget it.

"Let's find a fox," he said irritably, annoyed with his own thoughts.

David surveyed the countryside and pointed toward a gully that narrowed as it wended its way upward between two hills. "That looks like fox country. Let's try up there."

Anne and David walked side-by-side, with Young Pieter a few paces behind. They entered the gully and began a slow ascent up the gentle slope. A trickle of water flowed from the heights down into the middle of the small lake behind them. Scrub brush and wild grass grew in profusion near the life-giving waters. A few feet back from the stream were the first trees, large pine and oak, their thick spines plunging down into the soil, rooting them fast to the earth, giving them strength to resist storms. This area was to remain wooded and unsettled for many years to come. Farms would slowly occupy the area, giving way to the design of streets as the city moved north, eventually returning to woods as the southern portion of Central Park.

An animal bounded from a thicket and David pointed his musket at it instantly. He lowered the muzzle when he saw it was a rabbit.

"I thought you were going to shoot him," Anne said.

"No. We're here for a fox. If we start shooting at the first thing we see we'll scare off every fox for miles around," David said.

This decisiveness was one of the things Anne liked about David. Even though he was young, there was nothing flighty about him. They had set out to hunt the fox; very well then, the fox it would be and nothing else.

They stopped when they were halfway to the top of the hill. David looked around through the trees. "It might be best if we separated. I'll go to the left," he said, and looked at the other boy. "You to the right."

Young Pieter looked at his sister and smiled. "You'd better come with me," he said and was rewarded by a black look.

David started to protest, but thought better of it. He realized there was nothing he could say without making a fool of himself.

Young Pieter decided the joke had gone far enough. "On second thought," he said, "Anne might learn more if she stayed with you, David."

Even though David tried not to show any emotion, his face refused to hide the happiness he felt. Anne, naturally, pretended not to notice it.

"Maybe it would be better if I just stayed here," she said to her brother, an eye peeled for David's reaction.

"It's all right with me," Young Pieter said, suddenly tiring of this game at which he wasn't much more than a spectator.

"Yes," she said, "you two go on. I'd like to rest here

for a few moments." She smoothed her skirt and sat down on the rounded top of a rock.

David looked crestfallen. "I don't know . . . you might not be safe . . ."

"Nonsense," Anne said, "you find your fox while I catch my breath. After all, I haven't the strength of you men." Her tone of voice clearly indicated she didn't mean a word of this, but still and all, this *female* had called them men. They both squared their shoulders and stood a bit taller.

"Very well," David said in a self-consciously deep voice. "We'll go on with the hunt."

Anne watched them make their way in different directions. Within moments the forest swallowed them, and she was left by herself. She waited almost ten minutes before she set off in the direction taken by David de Witt.

What fun it will be to sneak up on him, she thought. I'll bet I can get close enough to touch him before he knows I'm there.

She congratulated herself on this fine, playful idea. It served two purposes. For a time she would be alone with David. And she would take her revenge on Pieter for being such a smart aleck; he had known she wanted to be with David.

As she walked she looked for signs of a trail left by David, but could find none. It didn't particularly worry her, because she knew David would be wending his way up the hill. All she had to do was keep following the slope to the crest. Somewhere along the way she'd catch up with him.

The trees were very dense on this part of the hill, and the wild flowers sent their perfume adrift on the warm air. Everything was delightful. Then the trees thinned and she came to the edge of a small clearing. A jumble of rocks lay at one end of the open space, and wild grasses covered the area from one side to the other. It looked like a green carpet out of a fairy tale.

She was startled by a small movement on the far side of the clearing. Was it her imagination? No, there it was again. A low-lying branch rustled. A patch of brown appeared in the green. And then a small bear cub tumbled out from behind the protective brush and rolled over on the grass. He looked up once and then rolled over three more times, enjoying the feel of the blades of grass mixing with his fur.

Anne pulled herself back behind a tree and made herself as small as possible. Her lips curved in a smile as she watched the cub frolic in the warm rays of the sun. He was totally unaware of her presence, blissfully happy with the grass, the day, and the joy of being alive.

She didn't know much about bears. Her father had said they were dangerous and to be avoided, but it was obvious this particular bear was only a baby, born in the winter of this year. He could not possibly be a threat to anyone. She kept perfectly still, not wanting to scare away the little fellow.

The cub suddenly spied a patch of flowery vines that held ripe berries. He scampered across the clearing and began to pick the delicious fruit. He was very dainty, taking care not to squeeze the berries in his paws. Each one was plucked and brought unharmed to his mouth, where it promptly disappeared. After about five minutes there was the sudden, loud cracking of a twig on the far side of the thicket. Both the girl and bear cub looked toward the spot where the sound came from, the space between two large trees.

Anne's eyes widened as a dark form emerged from the trees. It was another bear—this time not a harmless cub, but a full-grown animal, the mother of the little cub. She was a hefty animal weighing close to three hundred pounds. Her brown-black coat was glossy. She looked about inquisitively, her pointed muzzle sniffing the air, her short ears and small eyes alert, inspecting the clearing. Nothing seemed amiss. She ambled over to the cub, who took a playful swat at her foreleg. The mother bear ignored her offspring and went to the berry vines. Her powerful paws found a clump of berries, and she brought it to her mouth, the sharp teeth puncturing the fruit. Some of the juices dripped down her muzzle and onto her chest, but she didn't seem to notice.

Suddenly she tensed. The cub was rolling on the ground, and she cuffed him lightly with her paw. The little fellow looked at her in surprise, and then noticed she was peering intently toward the far edge of the clearing, her nose wrinkling as it attempted to pierce the tangled wall of branch and scrub brush. The cub began to imitate his mother, the little nose wrinkling and his ears pointed forward.

Anne was also looking in the same direction. Her alert ears heard a noise. And another: footsteps on dried branches. Whoever was coming was trying to walk as lightly as possible, but not lightly enough to escape the notice of the girl and the bears.

The mother bear's lips curled back, exposing the teeth in a silent snarl. She moved forward a few paces and stopped, instinctively placing herself between the cub and any possible danger.

A twig cracked, and then the sound of a foot on dry leaves could be heard. A low rumble, barely perceptible, came from deep within the bear. The branches on the far side of the clearing moved, and David de Witt took a cautious step onto the grass. The bears were immobile, blending into the scene, and it was a few seconds before he saw them. He gripped his musket tightly and stood absolutely still, his heart pounding as he realized what he had stumbled upon.

He was almost thirty yards from the bears, and he hoped he could back off and retreat into the woods without a fight. With his eyes on the big bear, David stepped back one pace . . . then two . . . then three . . . a few more and he would disappear from view.

The large bear knew the smell of this intruder—an enemy. She snarled, and her body bunched for the charge.

David realized the bear was not going to let him get away without a fight. He also knew the woeful inadequacy of his weapon. One shot from a musket was rarely enough to stop a large bear. But one would be all he would get. The bear would be on him long before he had time to reload. He glanced at the trees. Several low branches that could be climbed. He quickly adopted a plan. Shoot. Then up a tree with his musket, up as high as possible. Reload before the bear could reach him; shoot again. He didn't like his chances of outclimbing a bear, but there was no other choice.

The bear looked at her cub, and the little fellow intuitively knew he was to stay where he was. She prepared a frightful charge that would carry her across the clearing in an incredibly short time.

But David knew about bears and how fast they could

move when they wanted to. He raised his musket to his shoulder and prepared to fire when she started her charge.

Anne had been a silent, unnoticed spectator to the drama. Suddenly she understood David was going to shoot the bear. Her reaction was totally unplanned and emotional. The bear was the mother of the sweet little cub. If David killed the mother, the cub would be marked for death. She didn't want that to happen.

"David, stop!" she cried, and took one step into the clearing. "Don't kill her!"

The mother bear and David both whirled at the sound of the girl's voice. A look of horror came over the boy's face. The bear became confused. One enemy was something she was able to cope with. Enemies popping up on all sides were a totally different matter. Confusion gave way to a controlled panic. In one motion she whirled, brushed against the cub as a signal, and charged off toward the side of the clearing, away from the two human creatures. The cub stayed at her heels, his short legs churning so fast they looked like a continuous whirr of fur. The bears crashed into the brush and vanished.

David's breath came in short gasps as he listened to the retreat of the bears, relaxing only when the sounds diminished and he was certain the mother bear really was retreating and not planning some treachery.

Anne came into the clearing and walked toward David. He took a step forward, but his gait was unsteady and his hands were trembling so badly he decided to let her come to him.

"You're crazy," he gasped. "Don't you know what you did?"

"I didn't want you to kill the mother bear," she said.

"Kill the— She might have killed both of *us!*"

"She never threatened me," Anne said calmly, and it was the truth, but a truth born of innocence.

David was not favored with such innocence, and he dropped to a kneeling position as his legs became too weak to support him. He was aware how close a call it had been, and how dangerous a bear could be—especially a mother bear with a small cub. He managed to undo the thong holding the goatskin of water to his belt, and he took a long, deep swallow. The water flowed down his parched throat.

"What are you doing here anyway?" he asked. "You're supposed to be resting there," he said with a vague gesture back in the direction from which they had come.

"I got bored."

"Bored?" David said in amazement.

"I don't know why you're so upset," she complained. "We weren't in any real danger." And then a moment of doubt. "Were we?"

David looked at her and could think of nothing to say. What was the use of trying to explain?

When the strength had returned to his limbs, they set out to rejoin Young Pieter. They found him at the foot of a tree, asleep, his musket laid carelessly at his side.

"It's time to go home," David said, roughly shaking his shoulder.

"Did we get a fox?" Young Pieter asked between yawns.

"No."

"It's been a lazy day," Young Pieter said.

"Yes, lazy," David said as they resumed their walk down the hill. "Very lazy."

He glanced at Anne, who had stopped to inspect a group of wild flowers. She was humming to herself.

David shook his head.

"Did you have a nice time?" Christiana asked her children when they arrived home.

"It was all right," Young Pieter said, helping himself to a handful of cookies from the jar in the cupboard. "We didn't even see a fox."

"Only two bears," Anne said.

"Bears?"

"One of them was only a baby."

"A baby, oh well, I suppose a baby bear is all right," Christiana said, forcing herself to remain calm. Although she was afraid of wild animals, she knew it was wrong to inflict this fear on other people, especially her children. She even managed to smile. "As long as no one was hurt."

Young Pieter looked angrily at his sister. "There were no bears," he said. "She's just teasing you."

"David was going to shoot the mother, but I stopped

him," Anne said, glaring back at her brother. "You weren't even there. You were asleep."

"Asleep? How could you sleep with two bears prowling about?" Christiana asked.

"There were no bears, Mother, she's making it all up."

"I am not!"

"Liar!"

"Don't talk to your sister like that," Christiana said sharply. "Now apologize."

Young Pieter mumbled a few words and walked angrily from the room, convinced his sister was playing her usual game.

"Were there really bears?" Christiana asked.

"Yes, but the little one was sweet," Anne said. "There was never any danger."

Christiana nodded her head. "Then everything is fine. I wonder why your brother acted the way he did."

"Because he didn't see the bears. He really was asleep."

Christiana smiled and headed for the kitchen. She felt quite proud of herself. Her children had been around bears and she had managed not to show any emotion when she heard the news.

It hadn't been that difficult, she thought. Yes, this was the way to handle such matters. Never become afraid. Never get worried. Let things happen as they will; that was the answer.

Her family had become so used to Christiana's distractedness that they thought she didn't know what was going on most of the time. This wasn't the case. She often knew exactly what was going on, but she had trained herself to force the knowledge out of her mind almost as soon as it had entered. It had been very hard at first, but over the years she had developed a singular ability to do so. It was never easy.

She began to peel vegetables as she forced the idea of bears from her thoughts. Work of any sort always helped calm her.

I'm not afraid, she thought to herself, I'm not afraid because there's nothing to be afraid of. And I won't be afraid of anything else that happens. It was a resolution she had made and was working hard to keep.

It would only be a week, however, before she heard something that would cause her to break her resolution.

Pieter returned to his home on Pearl Street late in the evening, having spent many hours haggling with a ship's captain over the price of a cargo of oil.

The Dutch captain who bought the oil had once been in the slave trade. He told Pieter he had gotten out of that business because of the increasing aggressiveness of the English, who were only now discovering the fortunes to be made with this new article of traffic. "Black gold," they called it, and ship after ship left England to scour the coasts of Africa until their holds bulged with the hapless wretches who would be sold in the colonies of the New World. The English had decided this was their trade and began to discourage ships of other countries from taking part in it. A Dutch ship left the African coast with a load of slaves and was never heard from again. Rumor said it had been sunk in mid-ocean by a British warship acting under orders from the Crown. No one knew this for certain, but the fact was the Dutch slaver disappeared—slaves, sailors, ship, everything down to the last link of anchor chain. The Dutch skippers, like the one in Pieter's office this day, began looking around for a less risky way of making their fortunes.

The Dutch captain pretended he was doing Pieter a favor by taking his surplus oil off his hands, but Pieter was too shrewd for this tactic. He knew there were captains of other ships who would be glad to buy his oil, and so he drove a hard bargain. The two began haggling in the late afternoon, and it was dark when they shook hands on the deal. Both sides were content. Pieter had sold the oil for almost twice the price he would have gotten from the settlers, and the captain was assured of tripling his investment when he delivered the oil in Europe.

Pieter came home to be greeted by a most unexpected visitor—Peter Minuit.

The ex-governor was seated in the kitchen talking with Young Pieter.

"Governor Minuit!" Pieter cried when he saw the beloved man who had done so much to bring the colony of New Amsterdam into being. The two men embraced, and their first words were a joyful babble. Finally Pieter regained control of himself. He poured drinks, and the two friends sat and talked.

"Does Kieft know you're here?"

"No doubt. His spies watch every ship. But I have a right to visit my friends."

"You should have heard what he said about you in our last council meeting."

Minuit shrugged. "He should read what I write about him in my letters to the company burghers."

"So what news do you bring me?"

"Your governor, Kieft, is causing great trouble with the Indians."

"You know this for a fact?"

"They don't trust him, and he gives them no reason to change their minds."

"He is a stubborn man," Pieter admitted. He trusted Minuit and loved him, but even so, Pieter had no wish to have his thoughts known by men in the Swedish colony.

"A foolish man," Minuit corrected him.

"How are things in New Sweden?" Pieter asked, attempting to steer the topic of conversation away from Kieft.

"There's a new governor."

"So we've heard. A man named John Printz."

"A gross fellow. Weighs over three hundred pounds. He was appointed against my wishes. But I couldn't do anything about it, since I'd already resigned. I guess I'm getting too old for all the headaches of running a colony."

"What is Printz like? Other than the fact he eats too much?"

"He suffers from the same bullheadedness as your own governor. He's convinced the Indians need to be 'tamed.' His ideas are a bit gamey for my taste. He hung one of them for being drunk, and then had his body torn apart by four horses."

"Yes, he sounds like Kieft," Pieter said.

"Printz is somewhat smarter. He's entered into an alliance with the chief of the Lenape Indians and that seems to have stopped most of the troubles. Actually, it's a good arrangement. Your governor ought to find his own Indian chief."

"I can see how it would be useful."

"You have no idea of the things we learn from our

friendly Indian," Minuit said slowly. "Whatever it costs, it's worth it."

Pieter began to realize Minuit had something on his mind, but seemed reluctant to come right out and say it.

"You know me well enough to speak your mind," he said. "What's bothering you?"

Minuit smiled. "You always were tough to keep a secret from, even when you were a callow youth. Very well, I'll tell you something you don't want to hear. There will soon be war among the Indians."

"Against us?"

"No, I said *among* the Indians. The Mohawks are readying themselves for an attack on the southern tribes —the Manahatas, the Wickquaskeeks, the Raritans, and the Canarsies. I don't have to tell you what could happen to New Amsterdam if it's caught in the middle of an Indian war."

The news hit Pieter like a blow to the stomach. For two reasons. First, he realized how much bloodshed there could be if the Mohawks attacked their neighbors—and because of where the fighting would take place, some of the blood that flowed would be Dutch blood. Second, the news came from the Swedish colony, while not a man in New Amsterdam had the slightest idea of what was about to happen.

"Who told you about this war?" he asked, barely able to keep the anger out of his voice. He was angry not at Minuit, but at himself and his own governor.

Peter Minuit smiled. "In many ways the Swedes have been more clever than the Dutch. Perhaps I helped them learn from the mistakes I made here."

"But how do you know of the war?" Pieter said again.

"We have Indian friends. They tell us the news of the forest. You don't have such friends, therefore you hear nothing."

The statement came as no shock. Governor Kieft and the Dutch administrators were thorough in their disdain for the Indians. Pieter could not think of a single important Indian who could be considered a friend, not one who—

And then he remembered Senadondo, the chief of the Wickquaskeeks on the northern end of Manhatan, the Indian who, thirty years ago, had called a young boy his "friend." Could Senadondo still be alive? And would he remember the boy named Pieter de Kuyper?

Governor Minuit remained for dinner. Pieter noticed that Christiana was unusually subdued. He suspected she had overheard their conversation about the Indian war. While they were at the table, the subject was never brought up.

"Aren't you excited about returning to Europe?" Young Pieter asked the guest.

"Yes and no," Minuit said. "I'm tired and need a rest; for that I'm grateful to be going. But there's so much work to be done here, it seems a shame to be leaving it all behind."

"He'd like to be going with you," Anne said, casting a spiteful look at her brother.

Young Pieter glanced at his father. "Well, yes, I'd like to go back . . . sometime," he said, not wanting to start any trouble.

"How about you, Christiana?" the governor asked. "Wouldn't you like to see your homeland again?"

"Oh, yes," she said, and a surge of joy came over her features. It faded as quickly. "Maybe we'll do that someday."

"When you get there," the governor confided, "you'll start wishing you were back here after a few days. People who live here for many years have a tendency to forget all the bad things about Europe."

"I'm sure that's true," Christiana said, but there was sadness in her voice. In a few minutes she made her excuses and went up to her room.

After talking late into the night with his host, Minuit took his leave and returned to his ship.

Pieter smoked another pipe and went to his bed.

He had decided to sail the *Christiana* northward in the morning to Spuyten Duyvil, where he intended to seek out the man whose name meant "Fox" in the Mahican dialect.

He only hoped that Senadondo was still alive.

Christiana shrank beneath the covers and stared up at the darkened ceiling, her thoughts racing in several directions at once. Curiously, the thoughts were cut from the same bolt of cloth. She had, indeed, overheard the conversation about the possibility of an Indian war. All her fears were beginning to be realized. This savage land and its fierce inhabitants were closing in on her, threatening her life and the lives of those she loved. The *wildmen* would come and kill them all. They were beasts, animals, *killers* who would spare no one. The white man would be destroyed, swept away in an orgy of murder.

She sat up in the narrow bed. For several years now she had slept in her own bed in her own room, without Pieter at her side. It was an arrangement she preferred. Although she managed to suppress her fears during the day, they often returned at night. The answer was to get to sleep early and stay asleep until daylight. But if she slept with Pieter and he moved or snored, she would wake instantly and there would be no more sleep for the remainder of the night.

But now she was awake. There could be no sleep after what she had heard this evening. There was a great danger, *but she was the only person who fully understood it.* It was up to her to warn the others. It was up to her to convince them to leave this place, now, before it was too late. It was a job that had to be done, and she was the only one who could do it.

She got out of bed and put on her heavy robe. She went to her son's room. Young Pieter was reading a book under the yellowish light of an oil lamp. He looked up in surprise when he saw his mother at the door.

"What's the matter?" he asked, coming to his feet.

She went to his side and spoke in low, hushed tones, looking over her shoulder as if she expected someone to enter the room in order to prevent her from spreading the warning.

"The *wildmen* are planning to kill us. All of us. We must leave while there is still time."

Young Pieter put his arm around his mother's shoulder. He loved her dearly, and it pained him to see her like this. "It's all right, Mother. No one is going to hurt us."

"The *wildmen* are coming," she said as if he had not spoken a word. "Governor Minuit said so."

He spoke soothingly for several minutes, and she finally calmed down. Her eyes lost their haunted look and she spoke of pleasant things. "In the Netherlands my father has a nice house. We can sit by the fire and be safe."

He let her talk until she ran out of words and sat contentedly in his room, her mind thousands of miles away. He took her arm gently and helped her back to her room. As he was placing the covers over her, she grasped his arm. "You must promise me something."

"Yes?"

Her voice was steady. "You must promise that you will return to Amsterdam. This is no place to be."

Young Pieter nodded solemnly. "I will return to the Netherlands," he said. As he spoke the words, he knew he was saying them more out of kindness than conviction. Christiana would forget everything by the next day. But it was better to lie. It would calm her fears and she could spend the night in peace.

A smile came over her face, and she settled down into the bed. Her eyes shut, and within moments she had drifted into the peaceful sleep of a child.

The young man returned to his own room and brooded over the thought of going to Amsterdam. The idea of living in a real city with great buildings and proper streets appealed to him. As much as the settlers of Manhatan boasted of their town, it remained a primitive toehold of civilization at the edge of a savage wilderness.

How nice it would be to sit in a coffeehouse and discuss books with people who had also read them. How nice to talk about ideas. Almost no one in New Amsterdam had the time or interest to read anything more than proclamations by the governor, or the postings of the arrivals and departures of ships. Men wanted to know about shipments and cargoes, not philosophy and painting. It was a poor place for a young man with the soul of a poet.

To go to Amsterdam . . . but he knew it was only a dream. His father would be against it. The colony was a fine place, according to the elder de Kuyper, who wouldn't even try to see the matter from his son's point of view.

But still, a visit to the Netherlands was an interesting thought. It wouldn't be too long before he would be old enough to stand up to his father and chart his own life. It would require great strength to oppose the older man,

but with each passing year Young Pieter was discovering
hidden well-springs of self-assertion.

While his mother slept fitfully, he remained awake,
brooding not over a sudden death caused by the tomahawk of a savage, but of the slow death he was enduring
by remaining in the colony.

The sun had barely cleared the horizon when the
Christiana got under way.

The wind was almost nonexistent. The ship moved
slowly as it cleared the end of the island and worked its
way across the river on a starboard tack. Pieter fretted and
paced the quarterdeck, but he was a sailor and knew that
nothing on the face of the earth could quicken the pace of
the ship until the wind grew stronger. He was certain it
would build during the day, turning brisk in the early
afternoon. With any luck they would reach the waters
near Spuyten Duyvil by nightfall. Even though the ship
was at the mercy of the wind, it was a faster journey than
going overland. Once a man passed the edge of the town
there were no roads at all, only Indian paths whose
meanderings confused the white men.

The new bosun, who had replaced Claes Vincent when
he became manager of the farm, was a Dane named Lars
Jorisen. He was efficient and thorough in his job, polite
and respectful. Yet Pieter distrusted him. He watched the
young Dane as he ordered the crew to make adjustments
in the set of the sails.

The ship neared the shore on the west side of the
North River, and Jorisen snapped out the proper commands. The wheel was turned at exactly the right
moment. The sails were shifted and the bow of the *Christiana* moved ahead on its new tack toward a point of
land on Manhatan. Pieter could find nothing to censure
in the young Dane's seamanship.

The *young* Dane . . . and then Pieter realized why he
disliked the bosun, and he felt ashamed. Jorisen couldn't
be more than twenty-one or twenty-two years old, and
Pieter realized he resented this very youthfulness.

He remembered himself at the same age. In those days
he had been struggling to convince the West India Company to found the settlement of New Amsterdam. It was
only twenty-odd years ago, but to Pieter it seemed a life-

time. In those days he did not have the burdens of a
sickly wife and a son he could not understand; nor the
burdens of business, which, no matter how many problems a man solved, always seemed to reappear in new
form; nor did he live with the threat of an impending war
among the Indians. Life had been simpler in those days.
Oh, he had his problems and his worries, and more than
once he had spent sleepless nights reviewing his troubles.

But they had been *youthful* problems and troubles,
uninfected by the cynicism that comes with years, softened
by youth's advantage of an unbounded supply of time.
If things went wrong, there would always be tomorrow,
and after that another tomorrow. But with the years comes
a growing comprehension that the tomorrows are not endless, as one had thought, and there are limits to a man's
days; and as the sum of one's remaining days diminishes,
each day becomes more precious as it is used up and left
behind, gone forever.

Jorisen moved to the other side of the quarterdeck and
checked the flow of wind into the sails. He had a serious
expression on his face, and Pieter envied him as he had
never envied another human being. The lad looked so involved in his work that one might think he was performing
the most important task in the world. Well, Pieter thought
with a mental sigh, perhaps to him it *is* the most important task in the world at the moment. No doubt he had
experienced the same intensity when he had been Jorisen's
age.

"Breeze is freshening, sir," the bosun said.

Pieter acknowledged by nodding his head.

"We'll make landfall before dark, sir. Never fear."

No, I shall not fear, Pieter thought, but he could not
bring himself to speak aloud to the lad. He went below
and napped in anticipation of the long search that might be
necessary if Senadondo had moved from the village
where Pieter had known him. Indians moved from time
to time, and a great deal of time had passed in thirty
years.

Many miles to the north, the chiefs of the Mohawk
sat in powwow. As each chief rose and spoke his thoughts
on the proposed war, he was heard with great respect. In
the end there were few voices raised for peace. The de-

cision was made: the Mohawk would attack the detested tribes to the south. A vicious campaign was planned against the Canarsies to avenge a Mohawk sachem who had been insultingly treated by these miserable fish-gatherers.

The warriors dabbed on their warpaint and readied their best feathers. Weapons were sharpened, oaths promising great deeds to come were sworn, and the medicine men prayed to the gods of forest and river.

Runners were sent to the other tribes of the Iroquois Nation—the Oneida, the Onondaga, the Cayuga, and the Seneca—to tell them of the Mohawk intentions. All were descended from an archaic Indian people who had worked their way across the continent from a place far to the south and far to the west. They had wedged themselves directly into the middle of the Algonkian populations who occupied the northeastern portions of the Atlantic seaboard. Warlike and violent, the Iroquois had no regard for the other Indians, who, by their standards, were weak and unmanly. Fierce as were all the tribes of the Iroquois, the fiercest were the Mohawk, whose name meant "maneater."

And now the "maneaters" were on the warpath.

There was an hour's light remaining when Lars Jorisen anchored the *Christiana* close to shore in a cove at the northern tip of Manhatan. After his short nap, Pieter had spent the remainder of the day pacing the ship. Now, as the davits swung out, his impatience took over, and he jumped into the longboat before it was lowered to the water.

Bosun Jorisen took the tiller as the six sailors rowed the boat to shore. They were heavily armed, for Pieter was taking no chances on being surprised by hostile Indians, be they Mohawk or the local inhabitants.

He led the party to where he thought the village might be, but there wasn't a trace of it. Thirty years can play many tricks on a man's memory, so, deciding this was probably the wrong place, he followed the bank as the river narrowed and became the Harlem River. They went half a mile, and there, in the middle of a clearing surrounded by a thick forest, was an Indian encampment.

The familiar longhouses were surrounded by a stout wooden palisade.

The movements of the white men had not gone unnoticed from the moment they had come ashore. Now dozens of pairs of eyes watched as the strangers came to the opening in the palisade. Several warriors stood there, blocking the way. Their behavior was neither friendly nor unfriendly, but they were armed and wary, which was not lost on Pieter. He approached the most important-looking warrior, the one who wore the finest skins and the longest feathers. Using a combination of hand signs, Dutch, and a few words of the Mahican dialect, he made his wishes known.

"Senadondo is here," the warrior said.

"Tell him it is Pieter from . . . many years . . . many, many years ago."

If this statement caused the warrior any surprise, he did not show it. He walked away, returned in a few minutes, and pointed at a longhouse. Pieter went to this building, opened the fur flap and passed inside. An old Indian was seated next to the fire. He looked up, and there was no doubt about his identity.

"Senadondo . . . it's me . . . Pieter."

The chief motioned for Pieter to sit near him by the fire. He did not speak. Two women materialized and placed bowls of food and skins of liquids in front of the men. When the women were gone, the chief looked Pieter over from head to toe.

"Pieter," he said.

"Do you remember?"

"I remember a boy. But now I see a warrior."

"Boys grow into warriors," Pieter said.

"And you have come back to see your friend."

"I hope I am still your friend."

This remark brought a glimmer of reaction from the stoical Indian. "When one man calls another friend, it is for life."

"I'm sorry. I should have known. We are friends."

"We are friends."

They ate and drank for a few minutes. The Indian did not speak, but waited, as was customary, for the guest to bring up the purpose of his visit.

"I have a question for my friend," Pieter said after

he thought enough time had passed to satisfy the Indian's sense of protocol.

"It is well for the white man to ask questions. He does not do it often enough."

Pieter accepted the rebuke, and the two men proceeded to talk. Pieter learned what he had come to learn, and he in turn answered the chief's questions as well as he could. Senadondo's stern manner relaxed. He even asked Pieter if he had sons, something a warrior of his dignity would never have done if he did not consider the other man a true friend.

It was after midnight when Pieter rejoined the sailors, who by then were half asleep by the wall of the palisade. They walked back to the longboat, and Pieter could sense the curiosity of Lars Jorisen, who walked at his side.

"There will be an Indian war," Pieter said. "The Mohawk has taken to the warpath."

"Against us?"

"Indian against Indian," Pieter said with a shake of his head. "But we'll be in the middle of it. Who knows what will happen?"

"The Indians wouldn't dare attack our fort!"

Pieter recognized the pride in the other's voice. He wasn't even Dutch, and yet the colony was becoming the only world he knew, just as it had become Pieter's only world. Which monarch sat on the throne of England or France mattered far less than the intentions of the Mohawk and the threat of a forest war. This place was their home.

The *Christiana* shipped anchor and rode southward with the current. The moon passed across the sky, its reflection dancing on the dark waters. The world was quiet, at peace. But the silence was ominous to Pieter. He knew it could be the calm before the deluge.

Later the next day, after Pieter had made his report to Governor Kieft, the tranquility of the town was broken by the arrival of a breathless, sweat-streaked, panting Manuel Gerait. Claes Vincent and his wife, Tryntje, had been murdered by an Indian.

The Indian had been drunk when he arrived at the farm with an armload of furs, wanting to trade them

for more liquor. Vincent refused. The incensed Indian
split his skull open with his tomahawk and then used it
to kill the screaming Tryntje. Manuel and another man
had chased him, but it was hopeless to try catching an
Indian in the woods.

The word of the double murder spread through the
community, and the naked face of terror hovered over
the settlement.

The governor was beside himself. He threatened to kill
every Indian on the island. Pieter argued against this.
He told of his visit with Senadondo and the words of
peace spoken by the chief. He argued that the other
Indians had nothing to do with the actions of one drunken
man. But his words fell on deaf ears.

"Kill them before they kill us," Captain Van
Tienhoven said, and the other settlers agreed.

The governor made his plans. He sent for an Englishman named John Underwood, who had recently
moved to New Amsterdam from New England, where
he had been a notorious killer of Indians in the Pequot
wars.

"I want to talk to you about Indians," the governor
said to Underwood.

"Dead Indians, I hope," the man replied. The two
talked for over an hour, and when the Englishman
emerged, there was a savage glint in his eye.

John Underwood was a complex and unusual man.
At the age of fourteen he had shipped out of England
as a hand aboard a packet. After two years he jumped
ship in Virginia. For the next six years he wandered
from place to place until, at the age of twenty-two, he
became a fur trapper in Massachusetts. The Indians
tried to kill him: they preferred the white man to buy
his beaver skins from them instead of trapping for himself. But Underwood was wily, catching his share of
beaver and thwarting the plans made for him by his
enemies. In fact, a few of them lost their lives before
they decided to leave this tough, resourceful man to
his own devices. In time he learned their language and
their customs, ate their food, wore their clothes, and
took an Indian woman as his wife. The Indians stopped
thinking of him as a white man, and accepted him as one
of their own. When he took his furs to white settlements,

at first glance he was often mistaken for an Indian. Several white men took exception to his behavior, but their dead bodies gave testimony that John Underwood was a man to be left alone.

Although he seemed more Indian than white, when the Pequot wars broke out in Massachusetts and Connecticut, he offered his services to the English governor. With his intimate knowledge of the Indians he was personally responsible for several massacres and did much to punish the Pequots for the temerity of wanting to remain on their own lands, rather than surrender them peacefully to the white man. Underwood was handsomely rewarded by the English, but soon decided to move to New Amsterdam. The bigoted Puritans would simply not accept a man who had an Indian wife. He arrived with the woman and their two small children and had become a successful trader in furs, this time leaving the rigors of trapping to the Indians.

But he was still the best Indian fighter in all the colonies, and after his talk with Governor Kieft, he took a detachment of soldiers aboard a ship. At midnight they crossed the bay to Staten Island, where many Raritans had taken refuge from the Mohawk. The soldiers surprised the Indians as they slept. It was not a battle but a massacre. Seventy-three Indians—warriors, women, and children—were slaughtered. A few warriors managed to fight back, and they killed two of the soldiers. Within ten minutes the "battle" was over and the ground strewn with bodies.

The soldiers acted more like beasts than men. They had been whipped to a frenzy by Underwood's stories of Indian atrocities during the Pequot wars, and they wanted revenge.

The killing had not been satisfaction enough. They hacked off hands and arms and raised these grisly trophies over their heads in triumph. They carried the bloody stumps when they returned to the town, as if they were laurel wreaths. The governor blanched when he saw them, but managed to suppress his feelings. He congratulated Underwood and his men on the "glorious victory."

At the same time as Underwood was attacking the Indians on Staten Island, another group of soldiers un-

der Captain Van Tienhoven exterminated forty more
at Laughing John's Hook on the shores of the Hellegat.
The "battle" went the same way as Underwood's. The
soldiers fell upon the Indians as they slept, and the
slaughter was almost complete. Only three or four of
the swiftest Indians managed to gain the safety of the
forest.

The teetotaling governor was so delighted with his
success that he ordered a fresh cask of rum tapped,
and the soldiers laughed and drank and retold their
adventures. Everyone was of good cheer. They had
taught a good lesson to the Indians. As Captain Van
Tienhoven said, from now on the Indian "would know
his proper place."

In fact, it was the beginning of two years of savage
warfare.

Appalled at what the governor had wrought, Pieter
de Kuyper predicted the Indians would exact a terrible
revenge.

His prediction was too mild.

The settlers in the bouweries of Pavonia and Hackensack were slaughtered, their homes and barns put to
the torch. The farmers on Long Island fled to the protection of the fort, leaving their homes and bouweries
to the Indians. The settlement of West Chester,
founded by the English but inhabited by the Dutch,
became a place of ghosts. The home of the redoubtable
Anne Hutchinson, a wealthy woman who had defied
the religious laws of New England and moved to Dutch
territory, was burned. The brave lady was killed and
scalped along with several of her children. Jonas
Bronck, the Danish farmer who had built the first
bouwerie on the other side of the Harlem River, escaped with his family, but his home and barn were
burned and his cattle slaughtered. The tough Dane
took refuge in the fort, but swore he would return to
his home and rebuild it. Only five bouweries on the
island of Manhatan escaped the Indian's torch as the
people flooded into the fort. But even the strong battlements and the booming cannons did not deter the Indians, and after several months of ferocious fighting,
the fort began to take on the aspect of a ruin.

But the walls were maintained, because inside them lived the entire European population of Manhatan. Every available foot of protected space was used. The barracks were filled to overflowing; people slept on the floor of the church. The governor's house was jammed, as was the church of Saint Nicholas. Each room of Dominie Bogardus's home was the dwelling place for a whole family. The de Kuypers were packed into what used to be the parlor.

Luckily, the winter had been mild. Many of the people were forced to live through it in tents pitched in the open spaces. But now it was the end of March, and the threat of freezing to death was passing.

But fear continued to grow. The cows were gaunt and scruffy, and only a few emaciated hogs remained. The twin spectres of hunger and disease hung over the head of every man, woman, and child. Bullets and arrows came over the walls in the middle of the night. Life was a matter of hanging on from day to day, not even daring to hope about tomorrow.

It was shortly after dawn. Anne de Kuyper was staggering under the weight of the two water-filled buckets she carried at each end of a pole slung across her shoulders. She stopped and set the buckets on the ground. She took a deep breath and wiped her grime-streaked forehead with the back of her hand.

David de Witt had just been relieved at his post on the wall and was on his way to get some sleep. When he saw Anne, he went to her side.

"Can I help?"

She shook her head in exasperation. "I don't know what's the matter with me. Two buckets of water can't weigh all that much."

David allowed his eyes to wander over her body. Anne had always been slender, but now she looked truly gaunt. "You're not getting enough food," he said in a quiet voice that almost implied he was to blame.

"Nobody is getting enough to eat," she answered.

"It must be harder on the women."

Her eyes flashed. "The women are holding up as well as the men. Maybe better."

David smiled at her defiance. "I surrender," he said.

He reached for the pole on top of the buckets. "Let me help you carry the water."

She snatched the pole out of his hand. "It's my job and I'll do it. I don't need any help from you."

He took hold of the pole. "To stay alive we have to help one another," he said softly.

She looked into his eyes, and her anger melted away. "I'm sorry," she said, letting go of the pole. "I guess I'm getting cranky as well as weak."

He carefully positioned the pole so that the buckets were balanced, and they walked across the courtyard. They passed several of the families who lived in the miserable tents. A few hungry dogs sniffed around for scraps, but there were fewer dogs to be seen these days. Everyone knew what was happening to them, but no one wanted to talk about it.

"When is this nightmare going to end?" Anne asked in a tone that said she knew there was no answer.

"It would be a lot easier if the Indians didn't have guns," he said.

"It's our own fault. We were the ones who traded them the guns."

"That was during peacetime."

"We should've known better."

"My own father spends half his time cursing the men who did the trading. He's conveniently forgotten he was one of them."

"Everyone has to share the blame," she said grimly.

It was the bane of their lives. Guns had been one of the items most desired by the red men, and the shrewd Dutch traders had happily exchanged weapons for furs. Now they were paying the price of this folly.

Anne and David arrived at the door of the house of Dominie Bogardus. David set the buckets down on the stoop.

"Have you eaten?" she asked.

He hesitated and then said, "Of course."

She looked closely at him. The still-handsome face was thin and haggard. The hollows of his cheeks made his eyes seem larger. His hair was matted and unkempt.

"Don't lie," she said sternly. "We have a little soup. It isn't much, but it's better than nothing."

"All right, I haven't eaten anything today."

A blood-curdling yell split the air. Arrows whistled and guns exploded on the other side of the wall.

"An attack!" David shouted.

Pieter and Young Pieter rushed from the dominie's house with muskets in their hands. No man was ever more than a few feet from his weapon during these times.

"Get on the wall!" Pieter shouted to the men who were coming from the buildings and tents. Some of them were partially dressed and only half-awake, but they moved quickly to defend their home. The men on the walls were already fighting back as the Indians poured from the fields and trees and abandoned houses outside the wall. They came like a maddened, howling river toward the besieged fort.

Anne ran to get her own weapon. She went into the former parlor of the Bogardus house and found Christiana and Zilla. The black woman had an axe in her hands, ready to defend herself.

Anne went to the corner where she slept and picked up a wicked-looking musket of the old wheel-lock variety. When the gun was fired, the heel of the stock would kick back like a horse and black powder would fill the air; the sound of the weapon was almost deafening. But a lead ball would flash out through the smooth bore, and it had enough power to blow off a man's head. She picked up the ten-pound weapon, checked to make sure it was loaded, grabbed extra powder and shot, and started back toward the door.

"Stay in the house, Anne," Christiana called sharply. "You might get killed out there."

"We'll all get killed unless we fight back."

Christiana nodded her head sadly. "I suppose you're right. I *knew* it would come to this," she said, suddenly indignant. "I always said this would happen but nobody ever listened to me."

She seemed almost proud that her worst fears about the Indians had all come true, almost as if she had been vindicated. And this conviction changed her and made her think and act much more lucidly. The burden of fear she had carried alone for all these years was now being carried by everyone. She took part in the work and was more affectionate toward her husband, even to the point where they occasionally made love in their tiny alcove, hidden behind a hanging blanket.

Anne ran out the door to take her place on the ramparts.

This Indian attack seemed more serious than recent ones. Almost two hundred red men were attempting to breach the walls. They fought with muskets, bows, tomahawks, and knives. They used poles and slender tree trunks in their attempt to top the walls. They constantly shrieked ferocious war cries, adding to the din of musket and cannon fire.

Young Pieter and David were crouched side by side at the wall. One would place his musket on the ledge, find a target, and fire. Then he would crouch down and reload while the other stood up and fired. A man who was good with a musket could load and fire about three times a minute.

Just as David stood up to fire, the face of an Indian appeared about a foot away. He was on the end of a long pole and about to come over the wall. He saw David and raised his tomahawk, but a booming sound erupted behind David and the savage was blown backward, his chest shattered by a musket ball. David turned and saw Anne standing in the middle of a cloud of swirling black smoke. She came to the wall and dropped down to reload.

David gave her a nod of thanks and went back to the battle. He saw one brave coming from the direction of his former home. He aimed and then slowly squeezed the trigger. Through the cloud of smoke he saw the brave fall to the ground and lie motionless.

The savages managed to breach the walls in several places, and now there were about twenty of them within the fort itself. They fell upon the settlers, and the sharp edges of their knives and tomahawks turned red and the blood of their victims drained into the earthen streets. A dozen men and boys left the walls to help their wives and daughters in the fight below. The men who remained on the walls worked at feverish pitch to take up the slack.

Anne, David, and Young Pieter worked as a team to defend their sector of the wall. One shot while the other two reloaded. Anne's face was black with gunpowder, and her shoulder ached from the fierce kick it received every time she fired the musket, but she was determined to do her share. They worked quickly and expertly—powder, primer, shot, flint; aim and shoot. They performed their task and ignored the guns exploding around them, the arrows, and the shouts and screams that had turned the fort into a hellish nightmare.

They spoke only once, when Young Pieter was reloading. "Maybe now we'll have enough sense to go back home," he shouted above the din as he placed some primer on the spoon.

"This is our home!" Anne shouted back.

Young Pieter looked at her in astonishment. "You want to stay here . . . after all this?"

"Do your job!" she said angrily.

"Some job," Young Pieter told himself as he placed a lead ball in his musket.

An Indian leaped over the wall about thirty feet away. Anne saw him, but she had just fired and her weapon was empty. She watched in horror as the Indian attacked her father. Pieter managed to swing his musket around and deflect the tomahawk. It bounced off the stock and cut his arm, but the wound was only superficial. Pieter smashed the butt of his musket into the Indian's groin. The man bellowed and doubled up in pain. Pieter raised the musket over his head and brought the stock down on the Indian's skull, crushing it like an eggshell and splintering the stock as well.

There was no time for rest. Pieter immediately went back to loading his weapon. Anne reloaded her musket and returned to helping David and Young Pieter.

One of the Indians who had made it over the wall found Christiana and Zilla in the parlor of the Bogardus house. He howled a war cry, raised his tomahawk, and leaped across the room. Zilla swung the sharp axe, and the surprised red man barely managed to leap to the side as the blade missed him by a fraction of an inch. But his maneuver knocked him off balance, and he crashed to the floor at Christiana's feet.

She dropped down on him like an aroused cat, screeching and clawing, her body pinning him down, getting revenge for the years of fear. Of course the Indian was far stronger, but Christiana delayed him for a fatal instant. He looked up to see the axe in the hand of the black

woman, and the whooshing noise it made was the last
sound he heard before Zilla split his skull in two.

Christiana came to her feet. She was panting and puffing, but there was a brightness in her eyes. "That's the
only way to deal with these Indians," she said proudly.

Zilla had to look away from her victim, because the
sight was making her sick to her stomach.

The battle had swung around in favor of the settlers.
What did it were the cannons loaded with grapeshot. One
blast of a cannon spewing out hundreds of lead balls
could wipe out half a dozen attackers at a time. The settlers would leave the part of the wall in front of a cannon undefended. The Indians would think they had found
a weak spot and attack. The cannon would boom and
the dead bodies would be strewn over the ground.

The last war whoop was heard, the last musket fired,
and silence came over the fort. Here and there the cries
and moans of the wounded could be heard. The settlers
paused, took deep breaths, and wiped the black powder
from their faces. And then they began the chores that always followed a battle: the burial of the dead, both white
and Indian; the caring for the white wounded, the finishing off of wounded savages; the shoring up of battlements
that had been damaged; the cleaning of weapons; the
taking stock of their dwindling supplies of powder and
shot. It was depressing work but necessary, and they had
done it so many times before that now they did it by
rote.

Christiana and Zilla fussed over Pieter's wound, even
though he made light of it. Then he lay down on his cot
in the alcove. Christiana came and sat beside him.

"I'm sorry this is happening," she said, "but I always
warned you it would.

"We'll survive and rebuild," he said.

"This place is killing us all. We must leave."

"We can't," he said quietly. "To leave would be to admit we've wasted our lives on foolishness."

"Like mine has already been wasted?"

Pieter was sad. Her fears and nightmares *had* ruined
her life. It was only now, in the middle of a bloody war,
that she appeared normal. This woman who had once
jumped at the sight of an Indian now seemed more at
ease than anyone else in the fort.

He felt a sudden spasm of guilt: he had been the one who insisted they remain in the New World. But there was nothing he could do about it now. He hugged her, and their tears mingled together as they both thought of what might have been, but now could never be.

The next morning Anne and David went to the top of the wall that faced out on the bay. They stood in silence as they gazed out at the majesty and serenity of the wide expanse of water.

"It's the most beautiful place in the world," Anne said in a soft voice.

"When it's peaceful."

"There will be peace again. This is where I want to live and get married and have children and . . . make my husband happy," she said without looking at him.

David put his arm around her and brought her closer. She felt so weak and thin. His thoughts became brave. He would die protecting her from any danger. She would not have to fear as long as he was at her side. His voice filled with emotion when he spoke. "When the time comes . . . I would like to be that husband."

She blushed and smiled shyly. "I always thought you would be."

He kissed her, and her face lost its gauntness and became radiant with the happiness of the moment.

They held each other, and both felt they were starting on a voyage that would last a lifetime. They were anxious for that voyage to actually begin.

"A ship!"

They both whirled about at the cry of the watch. They looked toward the Narrows. Yes, there it was—a ship!

The sight of the approaching vessel sent the beleaguered fort into a frenzy of activity. The governor placed Pieter in charge of a detachment of armed men and sent him to the wharf to greet the ship.

When the vessel had tied up, Pieter went aboard to welcome the captain and thank him for the sorely needed supplies.

"But these provisions are for the garrison at Curaçao," the captain protested. "We've stopped here only to take on water."

"You've stopped here to save a colony," Pieter corrected him.

The captain protested to the governor, but Kieft wouldn't listen. He ordered armed men to empty the ship. He then sent the Dutch captain packing with a written request for more men and supplies.

This gentleman had no choice but to return to Holland and complain to the authorities. It was his only hope of being paid for the provisions that Kieft had taken without so much as a guilder changing hands.

For the people of New Amsterdam, the provisions were a gift from God. Now they would be able to hold out for many more months. The provisions were stored in the cellar of the governor's house. David de Witt was appointed to the small detachment given the job of protecting the treasure. His chest puffed with pride as he took Anne on a tour of the community's new wealth, and he stole a kiss behind a stack of large barrels.

There were lulls in the fighting. At times most of the Indians would leave the vicinity of the fort for a week or two. A few scouts would remain behind to observe the settlers, but there was rarely any bloodshed.

During one of these quiet periods Christiana decided it was necessary for her to visit the house on Pearl Street. She wanted to assure herself that the only place on the island where she felt secure was still there, waiting for her. She realized, of course, that Pieter would forbid such a visit. How foolish of him! There was nothing to fear from the Indians; if one bothered you it was a simple matter to scare him away or kill him.

How easily they died, Christiana had often marveled since Zilla had killed the Indian in the fort. And she had worried about them for so long. She chided herself for her foolishness. They weren't monsters at all, only men, not even as dangerous as the rough sailors who came off the ships.

It was early afternoon. The fort was quiet as the inhabitants relaxed after eating the meagre fare that passed for lunch. On the worst days it was what they called "famine food." Indian corn was parched in hot ashes, the ashes were sifted out, and the corn was pounded into a fine powder. Three spoonfuls of this was a meal for one person, often the only meal of the day.

Many of the men dozed in the shade, taking advantage

of the lull in the fighting to build up their failing strength.

Christiana walked unchallenged through a gate while the guard was in a shed rousing his relief. She left the protective wall and walked toward the eastern shore of the island. She was amazed at the destruction all about her. Houses were gutted by fire, the roofs caved in, walls crumbled and blackened with soot. Fences were torn down, gardens abandoned. Wild grasses sprouted in the dirt paths. She passed the remains of Geertie Smit's house. The front wall was gone and she could see across the room. The hearth still stood. A cooking pot remained on its hook above the fire grill; it looked useless and forgotten.

The shed that had held the women's goats was a pile of charred ashes, the fencing twisted, trampled, broken. A pig poked his nose into a mound of earth, hunting for some unknown treasure. A skeletal dog passed.

She came to where the grain warehouses of the company had been, but there was nothing left except the stones of the foundations. Charcoaled wood covered the site. The remains of half a cart stood where the large doors of one warehouse had been. A yellowish, stained heap—bones?—poked out of the wreckage. Christiana shuddered and went on.

The houses on Pearl Street had fared better than those closer to the fort. None of the cannon shot had accidentally smashed into them, as had happened in the vicinity of the fort. The Indians had entered every house, looting and pillaging, but most of the structures remained undamaged even though they looked forlorn and abandoned.

The first thing Christiana noticed about the de Kuyper house was that the door was torn from its wood-pegged hinges and lay broken and cracked across the stoop. The brick gables of the corbel roof were intact, but a few holes had been punched through the planked walls. All the windows were smashed, and bits of glass remained wedged along the sides and in the corners of the frames.

She bit her lip as she entered the house, and gasped at the extent of the destruction. The large cupboard had been broken to kindling, and the other pieces of furniture lay about in confusion. She reached down and picked up a pewter cup. It was in perfect condition. She walked over to the wrecked cupboard and carefully placed the cup on a broken shelf. She clasped her hands together and surveyed the room.

She went to the hearth and looked briefly into the dead ashes. A doll, one of Anne's toys, lay on top of the fire's remains, half covered with dirt and soot. It was the doll she herself had made. She picked it up and brushed off the filth. She set the doll on the shelf running across the top of the hearth. That was better. Now the toy would be ready for Anne when she returned, Christiana thought, forgetting it had been many years since the doll was her daughter's plaything.

A noise startled her, and she turned back toward the open doorway. She wasn't even surprised to see the Indian. Nor was she frightened. She had seen Zilla kill the other Indian; why should she be frightened of this one? If he bothered her, Zilla would kill him, too. "Are you hungry?" she asked the wary savage, who stood with a tomahawk in his hand, his eyes darting about for signs of danger.

"Come, I'll fix some lunch," Christiana said, moving over to the smashed cabinets. She searched among the wreckage and found a jar of cured meat overlooked by the looters. She foraged among the splintered timbers and came across a small tin. Her face grew bright when she opened it and found a supply of coffee beans. She hunted through another pile and found the kettle. She took it to the pump Pieter had built in the house. Quite a convenience it was to have water indoors whenever you wanted it, she thought. Then she remembered there was no fire and looked crossly at the kettle. She walked over to the Indian and apologetically showed him the cured meat. "I know it's not much, but it's good if you're hungry."

The Indian had lowered his weapon and moved a few paces inside the house. On his face was an odd look of disbelief and caution. Christiana could hardly have known that if this had been an ordinary Indian, she would have been dead by now.

Stone Eagle, however, was not an ordinary Indian.

His mother was a Frenchwoman who had been abducted by a renegade Huron. His outlaw father had been killed before his child was a year old, and he had been raised in the small Huron village of Chief Running Deer in the lands between the two rivers—the Ottawa and the St. Lawrence. There had been no choice: the white girl and her half-breed child could not return to the French settlement. The girl was ashamed, and she knew the other women would turn her life into a living hell. God alone knew what they would do to the boy. The Hurons, at least, were willing to tolerate them, and so they lived quietly in the village for several years. And then the village was attacked by the fierce warriors of a Mohawk war party.

The feud between Mohawk and Huron went back to the days when the Huron had enlisted the aid of the French adventurer, Champlain, in a skirmish. For the first time, the Mohawk faced the deadly killing power of firearms. They were routed, but they soon learned more of guns and bullets. The Huron won the battle, but they lost the war, having earned the undying enmity of the fierce warriors to the south.

In the raid on the village of Chief Running Deer, as in most others, the Mohawk exterminated every adult—man and woman—and took as prisoners only healthy children between the ages of five and ten. The half-breed child was one of these prisoners, and as he was led from the burning village on a rope about his neck, he saw the body of his mother lying in the dirt. From her dress and general appearance there was nothing to indicate she had been a white woman, unless one noticed that her eyes were blue. At this moment, however, one would be less inclined to look at her eyes than at her throat, which was slit from ear to ear.

The little boy was brought back to the country of the Mohawk and made a slave.

It wasn't the worst of lives. The Mohawk treated their slaves far better than they treated their enemies, but this boy's situation was unusual. From the time he could remember, he had been set apart, different from the others, an outcast, a half-breed, and now a slave. He hated his life, and when he was old enough he escaped from the Mohawk and made his way south. He was young and strong, and when he came upon an Algonkian tribe of Mohicans, he was accepted by them. They did not mistreat him or make him a slave. As an outsider he was not important in the tribe, but it was enough for him that he was left alone.

He was quiet and kept to himself, spending hours in one position, almost motionless. A casual observer might think the brave was napping, but a closer look would reveal deep-set blue eyes that missed nothing. He was like an eagle. And silent. He spoke only in answer to a direct question. He volunteered nothing. No man could recall his speaking first, ever. These qualities led the Mohicans to give him his name. They called him Stone Eagle—and they left him alone, because they had seen him fight. The years with the Mohawk had not been wasted. When the war against the settlers began, it seemed only natural that Stone Eagle join the fighting as an equal of the other warriors.

This was the man to whom Christiana offered the bits of cured meat. He looked at her, and she reminded him of his childhood. His mother had been white like this one. He couldn't begin to remember what she had looked like, but he imagined she was not too different from this woman. Therefore he had no fear, nor the unreasoning hatred of his fellow braves.

If the Spirits of the Woods had decreed a different fate, he might have lived with the white people, been one of them, spoken their language, and had one of their women. It was an idea he had often entertained. Whenever he looked upon a white man, he took a silent satisfaction in knowing his mother had been like this person, wearing the same sort of clothes, worshipping the same gods, thinking the same thoughts. But the white man never knew this, and Stone Eagle's secret made him feel superior.

"This is for you," the white woman said, placing the meat on an edge of the broken table.

Stone Eagle didn't understand the words, but her meaning was clear. He stepped closer to the table and looked down at the food. It was the familiar dried meat his tribe kept for the snow and cold of wintertime. He took a piece and tasted it. Deer meat. He chewed it, never taking his eyes off the woman. Christiana picked up another piece and offered it to him.

And then the idea came to him. He resented this woman. He resented all white people. They acted as if they were better than anyone else. How could they do

that to him? He was half-white. He wanted to take this
white woman. It was as simple as that. Half of his own
flesh and blood was the same as this woman's. Was there
something different about this half? About this woman?
What was it like to have a white woman? The idea was
like a spark dropping into dry tinder. It passed instantly
from curiosity to conflagration. He dropped the piece of
meat and grabbed the woman by her upper arms. She
offered no resistance; in fact she smiled.

Stone Eagle was very strong. He pushed her down to
the floor and straddled her. She continued to smile.

Nothing was going to happen, Christiana told herself. It
would be like the last time. The Indian would look up
and Zilla would be there with an axe. She felt sorry for
the savage. Why did he have to do this? Why couldn't he
simply have eaten the food and gone on his way? That
was one of the problems with these wildmen, they hadn't
enough sense to realize what was in their own best interests. Of course they hadn't any of the advantages of being
born and raised in Europe, but that was no excuse. You'd
think they would learn by observing the ways of the white
man.

And while she dwelt in the cobwebs of her mind, patiently awaiting Zilla's axe, the Indian tore her dress and
ravished her.

When he was finished, Stone Eagle stood and peered
down in astonishment. The woman either didn't care what
had happened or, and this was beyond belief, hadn't noticed. She had the same smile on her face. Her vacant
expression indicated she was thinking of something else,
miles or years away.

Stone Eagle felt shame. It had been like taking a dead
person. There was no honor in such a deed. He glanced
around and assured himself that no one had seen his disgrace. He picked up his tomahawk and fled. As he passed
through the doorway he looked back once and saw that
the woman was in the same position, paying no attention
to him, the same faraway look in her eyes. He ran from
the house as if it contained the echoes of a thousand
devils, and prayed silently to the Wood God, who owned
his own spirit, beseeching him to keep the demon-in-the-
woman from pursuing him.

The house was silent, the savage gone. Zilla had not

appeared. And then Christiana became aware of what
had occurred. *It had finally happened!* For years she had
lived in dread of this moment, shuddered in terror that a
savage would violate her, and for years the horror had
been real, complete, only in her imagination and her
nightmares. But now it had happened, and she hadn't
realized it until it was over.

She straightened her torn clothes and stood up. It was
impossible that it could have happened, she told herself.
No, it had been another dream, a fancy. Yes, that was
the truth, the only truth.

She left the house and walked slowly back to the fort,
pausing now and then to look at the desolation of New
Amsterdam. It didn't seem important to hurry. After all,
what could happen? What could happen *now?* she
thought. It *had* happened. No! she told herself. Yes, she
said mildly; it happened and I scarcely noticed. A thing
I've been dreading for years happens, and I scarcely notice.

She returned to the gate at the fort and knocked on the
heavy planking. A surprised guard let her in. He tried to
question her, but she walked past him as if he didn't exist.

She returned to the house of Dominie Bogardus. No
one saw her enter. There was no fuss. She had not been
missed. She changed her torn dress, sat down on a chair,
and reviewed the entire matter, coldly and analytically.
There was no longer any doubt in her mind, no pretense
or illusion about what had happened. The Indian had . . .
yes, he had . . . why lie? It happened. And she was quite
sure of one other thing.

The Indian had planted his seed in her.

A year ago, even a month ago, this thought would have
sent her into paroxysms, driven her screaming and running from the house to throw herself into the dark waters
of the bay. But now she accepted it calmly. It was the
only way to deal with it.

Pieter came into the house and saw Christiana in the
chair. He walked over and kissed her on the forehead.
"A nice quiet day," he said. "Are you enjoying it?"

"I'm all right," she said, standing and forcing a smile.
"Can I get you something to eat?"

In the continuing struggle to find more supplies, a longboat was taken from the fort and Pieter was sent to the

Swedes at Fort Christina. While his one-masted little boat bobbed at anchor in the bay in front of the settlement, Pieter was brought to the Swedish governor.

The man heard Pieter's story and then refused to give him anything. If there had ever been a chance that the two colonies might work out their differences, it was gone forever.

"We ask for help against a common enemy," Pieter protested to Governor Printz.

"The Dutch are more our enemy than the Indian," Printz replied. He gave Pieter an hour to take his boat out of Swedish waters. The expedition was not a total loss: Pieter met a group of friendly Indians at the head of the bay, and they sold him a supply of turkey wheat.

The fighting continued, and the Dutch could claim their share of victories. John Underwood led many expeditions into the forest, where his knowledge of Indian ways allowed the soldiers to fall upon the unsuspecting natives with great success. Hundreds of Indians were killed. But hundreds of white men perished as well. With every day the death toll on both sides mounted.

Mohawk raiding parties scoured the lands on the west side of the North River as far south as Pavonia. Battles were fought with the Algonkian tribes on both sides of the Harlem near Spuyten Duyvil. The Mohawk and Algonkian fought each other, but when a white man came between them, both Indian groups would turn to the slaughter of the white before resuming their own battle. North of the fort, the island of Manhatan became an empty wilderness.

The Mohawk crossed to Long Island and attacked the Canarsies near the now abandoned Dutch settlement of Breuckelen. The Canarsies were readying themselves for an attack on Fort Amsterdam when the savage warriors of the northern forests swooped down on them. A great battle was fought, a blood feud to the death.

The Mohawk triumph was complete. The Canarsie tribe, for all practical purposes, ceased to exist. Only six of their number escaped—in a canoe to Governor's Island, where they managed to hide from their pursuers.

With this great victory the Mohawk lost his appetite for the war and returned to his villages along the upper reaches of the North River. In his wake he left a trail of death, burned villages, and extinction. Six Canarsie—one man, three women, and two children—were all that remained of a proud people who had once inhabited Long Island from the southern ocean beaches to the inlets and bays on the northern shores.

But still the war with the white man was not over. It continued, and the colonists huddled in their fort, hungry, desolate, close to despair.

Through the summer and fall, Christiana grew larger and larger with child. And now her time was at hand, in the middle of yet another winter with the family crowded into a single room of the dominie's house.

"Don't worry," Pieter said to his wife as she lay on the ragged bed in the tiny alcove. "Everything will be all right."

She said nothing but looked at him sadly. How could everything be all right? she thought. For one thing she was grateful. She had made love to Pieter at least twice not long before the incident with the Indian. He would be spared the burden of that sorrow.

"Maybe it will be the way it was with Jan," she finally said in a soft voice.

"Don't say a thing like that," he said quickly, not wanting the thought of the stillborn child to be in her mind for even a moment. "It will go well, as it did with Young Pieter and Anne."

"I'm sorry if I've been a burden."

"Please . . . "

"I only hope I'm not giving you an even larger burden."

"Christiana . . . save your strength."

"No, I must have your word that you'll love this child."

"Love him? Of course."

"The child is part of me. . . ."

Pieter gripped her hand.

"I pray he won't be a burden to you," she whispered, and it was as if she was pronouncing her own death sentence.

There were tears in his eyes as he looked at her. He did not see a frail woman in the last stages of pregnancy. He saw a young girl, slender and vibrant, standing on the wharf in Amsterdam, agreeing to go with him across the ocean as his wife. He saw a Christiana of great hope and happiness. She had not aged a moment, had never suffered, had never known the scourge of reality touching her soul. And Christiana knew what he was thinking.

Neither could say another word. Pieter stayed at her side until she fell asleep. He began to cry as he gazed on that gentle face, now marked by hunger and want. He cried until the wellsprings of his tears dried up, and then continued to cry in long, dry, wracking sobs that convulsed his body.

Anne was in the room. She watched and listened to all this until she finally couldn't stand it anymore. She fled the room and sat down on the stoop next to her brother. She too began to cry. Young Pieter tried to comfort her, but she pushed his arm aside.

"I'll never tease her again," she said.

"It's about time."

"And you must get along with Father."

This was another matter. Young Pieter barely spoke to his father and avoided him whenever possible. The bad blood between them had thickened, and had frozen his heart.

"You must, for her sake," Anne persisted.

He was silent.

"Promise me," she said, and there was an edge to her voice. It was as if she stood on a precipice and it wouldn't take much to shove her over the edge.

He nodded, and it was enough of an answer for the distraught girl. She took his hand and squeezed it until her knuckles turned white.

Christiana entered labor in the middle of the night, and it was after dawn when the child was born. It was a difficult birth, and the doctor did his best under the primitive conditions. He was assisted by Annetje Bogardus, the dominie's wife, and the Widow Smit, whose husband had been killed by the Indians during the winter.

A few moments before the birth, the people in the room witnessed a terrifying scene. Pieter, who was outside the closed door, heard every word and tried to break his way in, but was restrained by the doctor. Christiana became delirious and began raving. Suddenly, with a strength that was far beyond the capacity of her exhausted body, she sat up, throwing the Widow Smit and

Annetje Bogardus away with a powerful swing of her arms. "The Devil! The Devil!" she screamed in fright. And then the hysterical strength left her body, and she fell back on the bed. Within minutes her child was born.

The infant was a boy, and the doctor said he appeared to be perfectly normal, but that would be known for certain only with the passage of time.

The long and arduous labor had been beyond the strength of Christiana. She simply did not have the power or the desire to continue; and as the infant was born into this world, Christiana de Kuyper passed from it.

Pieter was desolate. When it came time to bury Christiana in the cemetery, on the east side of the Broad Way, he made excuses to Dominie Bogardus that it seemed a bad time because there were Indians about. Later that night, while most of the people slept, Pieter took Christiana's body and buried her inside the fort. This was clearly unhygienic, but he could not let her poor bones be placed in an unprotected place. She would feel safer, even in death, he reasoned, if she rested where Indians would not walk over her grave. After he had patted the last spadeful of earth on the unmarked grave, he wept unashamedly as he visualized the lovely face of this woman he had loved so dearly and to whom he must have been such a disappointment.

The infant was given over to the care of Zilla, and the black woman found a wet nurse to help the newborn in his fight for survival.

He was named Jacob Adam. "The names of my uncle and father," Pieter explained. "May he inherit only the best of each, and may he prosper in this New World."

The baby thrived on the wet nurse's milk and within a few weeks was a round, fat-faced cherub, content with life. When he was awake his deep blue eyes constantly watched anyone and anything that moved.

Several times Pieter wondered why Christiana had said this child would be a "burden." He failed to understand what she had been talking about. The baby seemed normal, healthy, filled with life.

If Zilla had affection for the other de Kuypers, she truly loved the baby. Since she had all the responsibility of the child, it was only natural that she came to think of him as her own.

Though his white skin contrasted with the black skin of his foster mother, Jacob Adam did not notice any difference, and he returned her love in full measure.

As the weeks passed, Pieter's concerns for the child's health lessened. The doctor made several examinations and finally pronounced the infant as healthy as any he had ever seen.

Jacob Adam was the only one who didn't act surprised. After all, he had known he was healthy from the beginning. He was the only person in the fort who was oblivious of the war.

As the fighting continued through a second year, it was marked by atrocities on both sides. Any ideas the Dutch had had about fighting a noble war disappeared as they lived with the realities of filth and lack of food, and the constant companion Death. The Indians too were despairing over this brutal and senseless conflict.

They captured two trappers who had dared to resume their normal activities, and burned them slowly to death. It would have ended with this except that the torture took place within hearing of a third trapper, who had managed to remain undetected by the Indians. The agonized moans of the doomed trappers lasted for hours before death brought silence to the night.

The story reached the people at the fort. John Underwood was dispatched to bring back Indian prisoners. He returned with five men, and these were dragged to the middle of the fort and forced to perform a bizarre dance of death while the soldiers jumped among them with whips and knives, beating and cutting until the unfortunate Indians dropped to the ground from exhaustion. The settlers beat them to death as they lay on the ground—with the exception of one wretch, who was dragged to the millstone and beheaded. The remainder of his body was hacked to pieces and fed to the starving dogs.

A great battle was fought on the Connecticut River near the abandoned trading post of Good Hope. Over a hundred Indians died along with fifteen Dutchmen. This event caused a victory celebration at the fort, but the very next day the colonists heard a tale of the slaughter of thirty whites who were trying to make their way down from Fort Orange.

The colony was in desperate straits. Food was meagre and of poor quality. Hundreds of people had died. The soldiers hadn't been paid in over a year. The town might have been lost had it not been for the arrival of a warship with one hundred and thirty soldiers aboard. These new troops encouraged Governor Kieft to send out more raiding parties. More Indians were slaughtered, but little was actually accomplished. The war dragged on and on, and it was becoming obvious that no one was winning anything except the increasing chance of an early death.

It was Pieter de Kuyper who finally thought of a way to end the slaughter. He went to the governor and made a proposal.

"Senadondo, Chief of the Wickquaskeeks, is my friend," he said. "I'll go to him and arrange for peace talks."

"Peace talks!" the governor said, leaping from his chair. "Now? Just when we have these damned savages on their knees?"

Pieter had just walked across the open area of the fort. He had looked at the people, their eyes hollow and empty of hope, their skin covered with the blotches and scabs of malnutrition and poor sanitation. The governor's statement was so ludicrous that, depite the desperate situation, he laughed. "On their knees? If anyone is on their knees it's ourselves!"

"I will not discuss peace talks," the governor said. "I will accept nothing less than total surrender!"

Pieter had expected the governor to act in a pigheaded manner. For this reason he had asked Dominie Bogardus to accompany him. If there was one man who could stand up to the governor, it was the dominie.

"Stop acting like a fool!" the dominie said in his sharpest voice. "You've made the wrong move at every turn. Another year of this war and there'll be no town, no New Amsterdam, no New Netherland, only a wilderness strewn with the bodies of dead men. And do you know who'll be blamed? Who'll have written this history? It will be you, Willem Kieft, it will be you!"

"Now listen—"

"We're through listening. Arrange a peace settlement!"

"I will not!"

"Then I swear before God I'm returning to Holland, where I'll preach up and down the country with only one message. I'll brand you a fool and a traitor! I'll make your name so loathsome that schoolboys of unborn generations will spit on the ground when they hear it!"

The governor was shaken.

Damn these pastors and their acid tongues, he thought. They can say what they want and people will listen and, what is even worse, believe!

Willem Kieft felt trapped. Despite his bravado, he was well aware the war was destroying the colony. On this point the dominie was correct. Another year like the last two and everything they had worked for would be gone. And if this happened while he was governor, he would be disgraced for the rest of his life. Yes, despite the fact he relished the idea of being The-Governor-Who-Crushed-the-Indians, he knew this was not to be. Since he couldn't win, the next best thing was to be sure he didn't lose. He nodded curtly at Pieter de Kuyper.

"Go to your Indian chief." He turned and stomped from the room, feeling robbed of a rightful triumph.

Pieter let his breath out in relief.

"The way to treat a bully is to bully him," the dominie said.

"Come with me to meet Senadondo," Pieter said. "I may need you."

The dominie nodded. "I think we both may need the help of God more than each other."

The next day the longboat was put into the water and headed up the river. As the little craft went through its countless tacks under the watchful eye of Lars Jorisen, Pieter and the dominie sat near the bow and talked.

"Kieft is a fool," the dominie said. "But he'll not be with us much longer. Nor, for that matter, will I."

Pieter's head snapped up. "What are you talking about?"

The dominie smiled. "The church has a way of hearing things. The company is very displeased with Kieft. Despite all the nonsense he sends back in the dispatches, the burghers know the truth. As soon as there's peace with the Indians, Kieft will be recalled and a replacement named."

"Who?"

"I'm not sure, but my sources tell me Peter Stuyvesant has been recalled from Curaçao and is the leading candidate."

"I've heard the name," Pieter said. "But I know nothing of the man."

"He lost a leg in battle, which was why he was brought home. Apparently the burghers had already chosen another man to replace Kieft, but with Stuyvesant available, they changed their minds. Who knows? Stuyvesant may be the sort of governor we need."

"Anyone would be better than this madman," Pieter said. And he smiled. "Sometimes I find myself wishing we had good old 'Wouter the Waverer' back again."

The dominie laughed. "If only the poor man could hear you say that, he'd die happy."

"I'm serious. Wouldn't you prefer Wouter to this maniac who's wrecking the colony?"

"I suppose you're right. Poor Wouter was weak and ineffectual, but at least he had the good sense to let the rest of us bully him into doing what was right."

"He was more interested in getting rich with Michael de Pauw's schemes."

"I try to find some good in every man. At least Wouter was kind to Indians," the dominie said with an ironic smile.

"That's probably because they didn't own any land he wanted."

The dominie looked closely at Pieter. "If life had taken a different turn, you'd have made a good governor."

"Maybe," Pieter said with a smile. "And then again I might have turned out to be worse than Wouter or Kieft."

"I doubt it."

"But now tell me, what is this about you going back?"

"Ever since Kieft arrived I've been his severest critic, and he's sent many reports back naming me as a troublemaker. Of course the burghers have long known of Kieft's shortcomings, but he is their official representative."

"Since they're recalling Kieft, I doubt if they'll recall you."

"Perhaps," the dominie said. "But I'm wiser than you about the burgher mentality. I say I'll be recalled."

It seemed impossible to Pieter that the burghers would believe Kieft's slander. Since his arrival, the dominie had been a tower of strength, his influence going far beyond his pulpit, elevating the moral tone of the entire community. To lose him would be a great blow. Not even the burghers in Amsterdam, with their heads hidden in their money chests, could act so stupidly. But then he had second thoughts when he remembered it was these same burghers who had appointed both Wouter Van Twiller and Willem Kieft; these were two blunders of monumental proportions.

The longboat was brought to shore in a protected cove. Pieter and Dominie Bogardus went ashore and met with Senadondo. At first the chief did not seem disposed to help bring about a peace. Pieter couldn't understand the man's reluctance and argued at great length to convince him. Finally the chief agreed to do what he could to end the slaughter.

Pieter and the dominie waited for a full week in the village of Senadondo. And then the chief told them an Indian delegation would be sent to New Amsterdam to discuss the terms of peace.

Pieter returned to the fort and helped draw up the treaty. Kieft wanted "unconditional surrender" on the part of the Indians, but the others voted him down; they knew this would be unacceptable to the natives. Pieter was surprised when the governor meekly bowed to their wishes. It was not in character, he thought, and then stopped worrying. It was enough that the governor went along with the majority.

On August 29, 1645, the bell sounded in the fort and the citizens gathered to hear the terms of the treaty. There were no objections. The men and women of New Amsterdam hungered for peace.

The next day the Indian chiefs, led by the stately Senadondo, came to the fort. They were resplendent in soft buckskins decorated with their finest feathers, pieces of whale's fin, and fathoms of both white and black wampum. They wore deerskin moccasins, and their flesh glowed with the sheen of fish oil and eagle fat.

The Dutch too were at their best, although in some

cases it was impossible not to show the ravages of war.
They wore their finest coats, three-quarter-length dou-
blets, the bottom four buttons of which were left undone
to show off the wide sashes tied about their waists. They
wore clean shirts with broad collars flowing over their
coats, and the sleeves of the shirts extended four or five
inches beyond the cuffs of the coat, revealing a gleaming
expanse of white. Their leather boots were shined and the
boot buckles newly polished. Their wide-brimmed hats
had been brushed and were worn with a rakish tilt to
the back of the head.

Both sides looked so manicured it was hard to imagine
they had been fighting a bitter war for the past two
years.

The terms were discussed. It was agreed that armed
Indians were to avoid the Dutch bouweries. No Dutchman was to go to an Indian village unless he was invited and came with an Indian escort. Cattle, sheep, and
hogs were to be kept behind fences. Specified fields of
wild corn were to be left for the Indians. Prices were set
for certain goods. Liquor was not to be traded for furs.
The Indians could buy a limited amount of firearms
every year.

Finally, a pipe was brought out and both sides smoked
it. The peace was made.

Both sides knew there would be future troubles. Sometimes the law would be broken by Indians, sometimes by
the Dutch, but these, it was hoped by both sides, would
be incidents that could be resolved without resorting to
warfare. The Dutch continued to think of the Indians as
wildmen, and among themselves the Indians referred
to the Dutch by the less-than-flattering term "turkey-
necks." But for the time being they were at peace with
one another.

One curious issue was the presence of several of the
Mohawk. It seems they had urged the Algonkian tribes
to make peace with the white man. The war had dragged
on for so long it was interrupting the trading patterns that
were the heart of the Indian's economic world. Even the
Mohawk, the most warlike of Indians, had had enough.

After the pipe of peace was smoked, there was a
great feast. Settler mingled with Indian, and they all
gorged themselves on food and stupefied their minds

with drink—the ban on giving liquor to the red men obviously not yet in effect.

Pieter and Senadondo talked late into the night.

"We must not have another war," Pieter said.

The chief nodded.

"We must live together in peace."

The chief nodded.

"We will both live and prosper."

The chief was now in his seventieth season, an old man who saw the end of his life approaching. He looked at this man he called friend, and there was a great sadness in his voice as he said:

"My people and your people are different. Very different. Too different. This year you are ten. Next year twenty. The year after, thirty. One day there will be too many of you to share this land with us."

Pieter disagreed, and the chief waited for him to finish. When he did, Senadondo continued as if the other man had not spoken a word.

"You do not understand my people. I do not understand yours. One day a final peace will come. On that day there will be only your people. Mine will have blown away even as the winds of the forest come, stay a moment, and then are gone forever."

Senadondo's view of the future disturbed Pieter. It spoiled his happiness over the peace treaty. He knew the chief spoke the truth as he saw it. He created a vision of hordes of settlers coming to fill the land with their houses and fields.

What *would* happen to the Indian? It saddened Pieter to think of this beautiful land without their handsome canoes, without their snug longhouses, without their exquisite wampum, without their silent passage in the forests. Without *them*. They were, as far as he was concerned, part of the beauty. Without them the woods would not seem as crisp, nor the rivers as sparkling, nor the air as sharp and clean. Without them something that had made the new world the New World would be gone.

And so on this first day of peace and joy, Pieter tasted the gall of despair.

Senadondo sat outside his lodge, watching a group of

children playing a game in the clearing. It was a hunting game.

One of the children wore a fur robe and played the part of a wolf. Another child, a little girl, pretended to be an unsuspecting squaw grinding maize near a campfire.

The "wolf" crept closer and closer, making menacing gestures that caused squeals among the children of the audience. The child grinding maize seemed oblivious of the danger.

At the last second, when it seemed impossible for the wolf to miss its prey, another child—a "warrior" in a huge war bonnet that kept falling over his eyes—leaped from the cover of trees and chased the wolf. The audience screamed its delight as the wolf tried desperately to escape, running first in one direction and then in another. But the ending was preordained. After a suitably long chase, the warrior bested the wolf and the predator lay dead at his feet.

And then a fourth child stepped from the woods. He carried a long stick in his hands, holding it as if it were a rifle. The audience became still. The newcomer was a "white man." He pointed the stick ominously at the dead wolf. Then he tapped his chest. There was no doubt of his meaning. The white man was claiming the kill as his own. He swaggered forward and placed one foot on the dead wolf.

The warrior looked, in turn, at the white man, the squaw, and the audience. The last screamed encouragement.

The warrior took a deep breath and then sprang at the white man. The fight was over in seconds. The triumphant warrior stood over the body of his two kills. He accepted the lavish praise of the squaw. The audience roared its approval.

There was no expression on Senadondo's face as he watched. The dreams of children, he thought, are the mirror of life. Or, at least, life as we would like it to be.

The chief noticed another warrior watching the children. It was the stranger, Stone Eagle, who had only recently joined Senadondo's people. Stone Eagle's tribe had been wiped out by the Mohawk, and the few survivors had joined tribes who would accept them. It had been easy for Senadondo to accept Stone Eagle, because he was a tall, broad-shouldered warrior, brave and able to take care of himself. He made a good addition to the tribe.

The chief assumed Stone Eagle had always been a member of the slaughtered Mohican tribe, and the latter said nothing to the contrary. He was quite willing to forget his history as half-breed and slave.

Senadondo made an almost imperceptible sign that he wished to talk, and Stone Eagle came to his side. It pleased Senadondo that Stone Eagle had seen the sign. Most men would have missed it. Stone Eagle had just passed another of the many little tests the older man had been giving him. The chief had been toying with an unusual idea for some time. And now he had made up his mind.

The chief picked up his pipe and took his time as he prepared it. He took a burning stick from the fire and pressed it into the bowl of the pipe. A thin swirl of smoke wafted up above his head. He passed the pipe to Stone Eagle, who took a puff and passed it back to the chief.

"I am an old man," Senadondo said. "My sons who would be chief after me are dead. The last was Konnoh, who was killed in this war." Stone Eagle said nothing. There was a long silence as the chief puffed on his pipe. He finally continued. "We have lost many warriors. There is none in this tribe who could be chief. They are all gone."

Stone Eagle looked at Senadondo with unblinking eyes. Not a muscle on his face moved. One listened. One learned. One accepted.

"I would have you as my son," Senadondo said simply, and hearing those irrevocable words, Stone Eagle knew he was the next chief of the Wickquaskeeks. There would be a ceremony. The blood of Senadondo would be mingled with his own. There would be a Feast of the Dead, during which the names of the departed would be called out to reassure and comfort their souls.

Stone Eagle was not surprised. He had often dreamed of being a chief, and, according to the Huron legend in which he was first steeped, dreams were the language of the soul. They were the soul conveying truths from previous experience and knowledge, speaking to the present world in the only way possible. These revelations that came during sleep were messages from a warrior's *mani-*

tou, his personal guardian spirit that shadowed him from birth to death. When a man had a dream, it was essential that it be fulfilled. If it was not, the *manitou* would turn on the body for denying the soul, and the man would experience agony, disaster, and failure.

Senadondo noted the other man's total lack of reaction and was pleased. A brave warrior accepted praise and torture in the same manner—as if they did not exist.

"I was alive to see the coming of the white man," Senadondo said. "You will not live to see his passing. Nor will your children, or their children. Teach our people to accept the white man. If we do not, our people will be no more."

No other word was spoken, but Stone Eagle knew he was dismissed. He stood up and walked over to a group of braves who were preparing to hunt. The Indians, like the settlers, were trying to pick up the threads of their lives, which had been torn apart by the disastrous wars.

Senadondo had no illusions about how thin and weak these threads had become. The colorful tapestry of the Indian way of life was turning rapidly into a time-frayed rag.

The colonists began rebuilding their town and their lives.

The hungry cattle, looking more like skeletons than living animals, were put out in the rich pastureland. They grew sleek, and then fat.

Ships of all sizes and all conditions were purchased as quickly as possible from the English in Virginia and Plymouth. The Dutch ships that once had anchored proudly off the island before the war either had been burned by the Indians, or had fled back to Europe. Pieter's *Christiana*, like her namesake, was gone. He was lucky enough to get a packet from the English; but it was such an ugly scow—with rotting decks and a leaky hull—that he refused to give it a name and vowed to replace it as soon as possible.

He also moved back to the house on Pearl Street. It had suffered a great deal of damage, and he spent the better part of a month making repairs. The baby, Jacob Adam, gurgled and warbled his happiness as he grew daily fatter and healthier under the loving care of Zilla.

There was much rebuilding to be done on Manhatan. Only three years ago the town had boasted over a thousand inhabitants. Now scarcely three hundred remained, the others having died or returned to Europe. Some of those who had left were beginning to drift back to Manhatan, together with first-time settlers, and the population began to grow once again. But it still had a long way to go to reach the prewar level.

Jonas Bronck moved back to his bouwerie on the other side of the Harlem River and, as he had promised, rebuilt his house and barn and put over a hundred acres under cultivation. The Indians called this land Wanachqua, or end place—the end of the mainland. A river ran through the land, and the Indians called it "Stream of the End Place," but the Dutch began referring to it as "Bronck's River." Eventually the sturdy Dane's name began to be used for all the land beyond the river, and people spoke of going to "Bronck's" or "the Bronck's." It was a name that would live on, in an altered spelling, long after the memory of Jonas Bronck himself had faded into obscurity.

The farmers returned to their bouweries on Long Island and the northern parts of Manhatan. They moved back across the North River, and the settlements at Pavonia and Hackensack were revived. Normal trading resumed, and once again the rich beaver pelts, shaggy bearskins, and other furs piled up in the warehouses of New Amsterdam before they were loaded onto ships and sent to Europe.

Governor Kieft retreated to his house and was not to be seen for days on end. The rumors of his recall became so insistent that not a man in the colony believed he would be around much longer.

Young Pieter became friends with Adriaen Van der Donck, a radical thinker who had originally come to the colony as administrator for Rensselaerswyck. Van der Donck was a man of many talents, and it did not suit him to spend his life tucked away on a bouwerie far up the river. He moved to Manhatan and proved himself adept at negotiating favorable trade agreements. As a reward for his services the company gave him a tract of land beyond

the Harlem. Van der Donck's country estate became the
site of a tiny settlement. The inhabitants honored their patron by calling the place Jonkheer's—the Young Lord's
Land. The English would change the spelling to Yonkers.

Young Pieter was fascinated by Van der Donck's so-
phistication, and he would listen for hours while the other
spoke of life in Europe and of the course of modern philosophy.

"There's no such thing as the divine right of kings,"
Van der Donck said. "It's an idea promoted by those who
have the most to gain—the kings themselves and their par-
asitic courts of nobles."

Young Pieter eagerly drank it all in. For the first time in
his life, he was hearing "ideas"—thoughtful words that
made one ask questions about the world one lived in.

"What other institution can you think of that defends
this right?" Van der Donck asked in a leading manner.

Young Pieter thought for a moment and then said, "The
churches?"

"Yes, the churches," Van der Donck said with a sneer.
"The churches are the lackeys of the kings. The ruler
threatens people with whip and branding iron, and then
to make sure they obey, he has the churches threaten
them with eternal damnation!"

"It is a powerful combination," Young Pieter said.

"Yes, but few in numbers. The kings, nobles, and priests
are outnumbered by thousands to one."

Young Pieter nodded in understanding. "If enough people band together they can remove the burden of king and
church."

"Exactly."

Young Pieter became very thoughtful. "The big problem will not be the kings, but the churches. A man might
be willing to lose his life, but I doubt if he'll risk an eternity
in the fires of hell."

"Do you believe in hell?" Van der Donck asked quietly.

"Sometimes I think hell is this place we live in," Young
Pieter answered with a rueful smile.

Adriaen Van der Donck's heart went out to the young
man. He had a bright, inquisitive mind, one that deserved
to be nurtured at a European university instead of lying
fallow in the wilderness of the colony.

He went to Pieter and suggested his son be allowed to go to Europe to receive an education. He argued eloquently. "It's the best for all—best for him, best for you, and best for the colony."

"It's best he remain here and learn the ways of his home."

"He's wasting his mind here. In Europe he'll learn."

"Learn?" Pieter said sourly. "What will he learn? To start wars? To steal lands and oppress people? To waste his time talking to fools like you?"

Van der Donck smarted under the insult, but he forced himself to remember he had come on a mission. "There are times when a man with an idea is worth a hundred men with muskets."

"Tell that to the Indians, or the English."

"You're an intelligent man, de Kuyper. I can't believe you dispute the value of ideas."

"You're absolutely correct. But *my* idea is to build New Amsterdam and make it great. I want my son to be a part of it. Tell me what's wrong with *that* idea."

It was no use, and Van der Donck finally gave up. He returned to Young Pieter and told him what had happened.

The young man received the news grimly. "The time will come when he will no longer be able to dictate my life."

"He thinks he's doing what's best for you," Van der Donck said placatingly. "That doesn't make him the worst of fathers."

A few days later Pieter said essentially the same thing to his son, and Young Pieter lashed back.

"Why must it be always you who decides what's best for me?"

"I'm older and have seen more," Pieter responded, with a shrug.

"My mother died because of this place," Young Pieter said savagely.

"She died in an attempt to build it. Her bones are now part of this soil."

"She was never a part of this place!"

Pieter controlled himself. "When you were born I promised your mother I would see you got only the best. It's a promise I intend to keep."

The statement was sobering. Young Pieter's head

drooped. He said no more and walked away. But he remained unconvinced.

Pieter sighed. He had no desire to argue with his son, but he thought he was doing what was right. Young Pieter should remain here. The New World needed bright, native-born sons. A day would come, of course, when no one would be able to tell him what to do. Pieter only hoped his son would have more sense by that time.

Later that day he returned to the side of Dominie Bogardus's house where Christiana was secretly buried. He said a few silent prayers and hoped that Christiana was listening and approved of the way he was dealing with their eldest son.

Anne de Kuyper regained the weight she had lost during the long struggle. She was now in her fourteenth year, looking radiant and beautiful. She returned to the house with a load of washing she had done in the stream at Maiden Lane. It was the custom of the local girls to take their washing to this small brook that bubbled from a spring and made its way to the East River. The water was crystal clear as it danced over the sandy, pebbly bottom. The local loafers came to watch the girls, and a wag named it Maiden Lane.

A few of the loafers were present on this day, and they made their predictable remarks. Anne ignored them, as usual. Along with most of the other girls, if asked she would complain about their impudence, but privately she was pleased by the effect her blossoming womanhood was having on men.

She left the laundry in the kitchen and went down to the pier to watch secretly as David de Witt supervised the unloading of a wagonful of grain. How strong he looked! He took command as if he already were a man. She kept imagining how nice it would be when they were old enough to marry and have a house of their own. David would come home every night and hold her in those strong arms of his. With these delicious thoughts she returned home and found Zilla feeding Jacob Adam in the kitchen.

"You look like the cat that swallowed the canary," Zilla said when she saw the girl.

Anne blushed. It was as if the black woman had the power to see into her thoughts. "I'm just so happy that everything is back to normal," she lied.

"Uh-huh," Zilla said as she spooned another mouthful of food into the infant. "That's why you look like a candle that's just been lit up."

Anne smiled. "I guess I'm just happy."

"I don't suppose David de Witt has anything to do with all this happiness, does he?"

The girl turned a darker shade of crimson. "David de Witt? What are you talking about?"

"I have eyes, child. I can't help it if they see what they see."

Anne affected lack of interest.

"He'll make somebody a wonderful husband," Zilla said playfully, watching the girl out of the corner of her eye. "But I don't suppose you ever thought of that?"

"Well, no . . ." Anne began. Then she gave up all pretense. "Isn't he wonderful! Whenever I look at him I get goose bumps all over my body!"

"Just take your time," Zilla chided her. "You'll have plenty of time for that when you're grown up."

"I grew up fast during the war."

Zilla put down her spoon. "The war is over and we have to take things a bit slower. Besides, your father must first talk to David's father."

Anne went to the table at the front of the room. As she brooded there, the cat came in and rubbed against her leg. Anne decided to write a poem, verse having become one of her hobbies. She got a quill and a sheet of paper.

> Kitten
> Small, delicate
> Warming, basking, purr
> Quiet, sly, sparkling
> Growing, prancing, play
> Soft, sleek
> Cat

She looked at it and wondered why she was bothering with cats. The only thing that mattered was David. And she couldn't have him. At least not for some time. She picked up the quill and decided to write about how she felt.

> Rain it comes down in buckets,
> rain it comes down in drops,
> tears they come down in buckets,
> tears they come down in drops.
>
> Why does it rain?
> Why do I cry?

And when she was finished she realized a tear was sliding down her cheek. Who was Zilla to say she couldn't have David? Who were any of these people—*her* father, *his* father—what did any of them matter? She and David were the only ones who mattered in this.

She left the table and threw herself on her bed in frustration.

The next day David took her out for a sail in a little borrowed flyboat. The boat belonged to a fisherman, and it smelled of its usual occupation, but neither of them paid any attention.

It was a blustery day, and the gusty winds indicated an approaching storm. Someone with more experience than David would have questioned the wisdom of going out on the water on such a day, but he was so interested in showing off for Anne that he failed to perceive the danger.

They went out on the bay, and the wind drove the little boat toward Staten Island. The rigging quivered and sang, and the mast groaned under the pressure. The whitecaps began to build, and the boat listed and heeled over, occasionally at alarming angles.

Anne sat close beside David, her legs pressing against his as they worked the lines and tiller. She felt as if she was in heaven. The thrill of being so close to David made her blind to the fact it was becoming dangerous to be on the water.

David had his hands full with the tiller, but even so he managed to keep glancing over at the girl. How beautiful she was! He felt proud to be with her, especially at this moment when he was in command of a boat. He noticed her admiring looks and sat up straighter. He pretended to be totally involved with the craft, but inwardly he glowed with pleasure.

And then a particularly strong gust hit them and drove the boat far enough on its side to make it ship water.

Anne jumped and let out a squeak. She looked nervously at David, who had turned a shade of green.

"There's nothing to worry about, is there?" she asked, hoping for reassurance.

"N-no, we're all right," he said, trying to look unruffled, but he knew he sounded unconvincing. And then another puff smacked into the sail and drove the boat over so she shipped more water. The dark clouds had scudded toward them, and now the first drops of rain began to fall from the angry sky.

David brought the boat around and headed it back toward Manhatan. But now its worrisome motion was even more pronounced: they were sailing into the tide and the wind was beating into them, a quartering wind from the starboard. The boat bucked and fought its way into the teeth of the wind.

"Take the tiller," he said. "I have to put a reef in that sail."

She took the stout piece of oak, and it immediately began to pull away from her.

"Keep the bow pointed toward the tip of the island!" David was shouting in order to be heard above the wind. The boat lurched back on course, off, and then back on again as Anne battled with the tiller. She looked ahead and was amazed that Manhatan was so far away. She hadn't realized how far they had come. It would take them more than an hour to get back, and now the rain was pelting down on them in force. The boat wallowed in a trough and she had another battle to control the tiller.

David hung onto the mast, manfully trying to lower the sail far enough to tie part of it down with the canvas reefing strips. But the force of the wind kept the sail as taut as the top of a drum, and it refused to be lowered. He pulled on the canvas with all his strength, but to no avail.

Finally, he gave up and came back to Anne's side.

"We'll have to turn her into the wind while I reef her," he said. He looked worried. "Do you think you can hold her steady?"

Anne nodded, but she had a sick feeling in the pit of her stomach. Holding a pitching boat steady into the wind with a sail up in the middle of a gale was a tricky bit of business. David would be standing up, working on the sail, and if she couldn't keep the boat headed up, the wind might whip the boom into David and knock him overboard. She doubted she had the skill to maneuver the boat back to pick him up. She was completely soaked, but her mouth felt dry and her knuckles grew white as she gripped the tiller.

"I'll help put her into the wind," David said. He pushed the tiller and the little boat responded instantly, slicing back through the water, cutting waves in two. Now they were pointing into the wind, the Narrows somewhere out there in front of them, and then they watched the sail go slack and begin to beat madly as the winds bore down on it from straight ahead.

David quickly went forward. He took the main halyard, but at that moment the wind caught the sail and started to drive the boat around. Fortunately David wound up on the windward side and the boom shot out in the direction away from him. Anne had tried to hold the sheets to keep the boom in, but the task was far beyond her strength. David jumped back and helped Anne in her battle with the tiller.

The wind was becoming more fierce as it slammed into the sail, driving the boat farther down into the water, farther and farther until the sail touched the water and the hull of the boat was parallel to the bay. David and Anne held onto the tiller for their lives. And now, because the wet sail was no longer held down by the air, the ballast at the bottom of the boat came into play. The ballast, acting as a counterweight, pulled the hull back through the water in the other direction, and the mast sped in a great arc from one side to the other. When it reached its farthest point of motion, the sail and mast hit the water and there was a loud *crack!* as the wooden mast broke apart. The boat righted itself and the mast came down, tearing off all the rigging, falling half in the boat and half in the water. Immediately the boat stopped heeling over and began to bounce like a cork. The mast was draped over one side, holding the boat atilt and allowing water to flow in. Soon they would be in danger of swamping. David tore frantically at the rigging, and Anne came to his aid. It was a struggle, but within two minutes they were able to shove the useless mast and boom over the side and immediate danger of swamping was over.

But they were still in a fearful predicament. They were a long way from shore, and the tide was pushing them toward the Narrows. Their boat had neither sail nor mast. And the rain was really coming down. In time it could fill the boat and sink them.

David grabbed a pair of wooden buckets. "We've got to bail," he said, and then he noticed how frightened Anne was. A pathetic-looking creature: soaked to the skin, with a mournful look on her face. On an impulse he put his arms around her and hugged her tightly to him. "I'll protect you, don't worry, I'll protect you."

She kissed him, and that act gave her courage and renewed her strength. They were on the brink of disaster, yet she no longer felt afraid.

They were still bailing an hour later when a homeward-bound whaler came by and rescued them. They were put ashore on Manhatan, wet and exhausted but—now that they were safe—thrilled by the adventure.

David brought Anne to the de Kuyper house, and Zilla made her go straight to bed with a mug of strong, hot rum. Later, when Pieter was alone with Zilla in the keeping room, she said, "Those two will get married. And the day isn't that far off if they have anything to say about it."

Pieter looked at her in surprise. "But she's only a child."

Zilla shook her head. "They grow up fast these days. She's older than her years."

Pieter thought about it for a moment and then said, "David is a fine young man. But he's too young."

"In a few years neither will be too young. Get used to the idea," she said.

She walked over to the cupboard and took out a bottle of brandy. Zilla still had a fine figure, and Pieter watched

her now. She noticed his interest and smiled. It didn't
happen as often as it used to, but she was still happy
that she was able to give him pleasure. She set the bottle
and glass on the table before him and went to her bedroom. It was curious the way this silent ritual had developed, but it had, and it never varied. She hummed softly
as she undressed and got into the bed. Pieter would finish
his brandy and, after a time, come to the room. Her flesh
began to tingle at the thought of what would follow.

During the week before Christmas an Indian warrior
arrived at the house on Pearl Street. He had been sent to
bring Pieter to Senadondo.

It was snowing heavily, so Pieter and the Indian
boarded the still-unnamed packet and sailed north rather
than attempt an overland journey through the huge drifts
and swirling powder.

The packet had no trouble, although an icy crust extended several feet from the shores of the river. The crew
was less happy than Pieter with the trip. An hour was the
limit a man could stay on deck, and then his fingers would
begin to freeze and his toes would numb, and his nose
and ears would redden and feel so brittle it seemed they
might break off.

The ship anchored at the mouth of the Harlem, and
the longboat took Pieter to shore, cracking its way
through an ice crust for the last few yards. Several Indians were waiting, and they took Pieter to Senadondo.

The old warrior looked as fit as ever. Pieter, as the
guest, waited for the other man to begin the conversation.
The chief decided they should first smoke a pipe. It was
almost ten minutes before a word was spoken.

"I have seen the future. I am going to die."

It did not occur to Pieter to question the old man.

"A man close to death sees the truth," the chief said.
He reached beneath his fur robe and brought out a deed.
Pieter looked at it and saw it was a legal document signed
by Governor Kieft. It made Senadondo the owner of
the place known as *n'ashave-kueppi-okk*—the "closed-
between place," the land between the waters of the
Spuyten Duyvil and the hills to the south and to the east.

A further notation recorded the transfer of this land from Senadondo to Pieter de Kuyper. Pieter looked up in astonishment.

"These are the lands of my people," the chief said. "But no papers will keep them from the white man. If my people cannot have them, they are best left in your hands."

Pieter tried to speak but could not. He attempted to hand back the deed, but Senadondo ignored it as if it did not exist. "The lands of my people must be in your hands and not those of another white man. If you do not take them my spirit will not rest."

Pieter was still astonished by the document he held in his hand. Kieft had had no right to do such a thing, and yet, obviously, he had done it. The land legally belonged to Senadondo, and now Senadondo was giving it to Pieter.

The old Indian was aware of Pieter's confusion. "You wonder how it is I have such a thing?"

Pieter nodded and held his hands up weakly.

"Your chief wanted peace very badly. He acted as if he did not, but he wanted it," Senadondo said, with what could almost be described as the flicker of a smile, although it was unthinkable that he would allow such a lessening of his dignity. "When you asked me to bring about the peace, I seemed unwilling. I was not. Your chief had already talked of peace in secret. I served his wishes —for a price. At the time you came, he had not yet agreed to that price."

Pieter understood at once. Despite all his bravado and bluster, Kieft had been desperate for peace. If he had lost the war, he would have been disgraced. The canny old Indian had squeezed the deed from Kieft as the cost of saving his hide.

"Come," Senadondo said, and the two men left the longhouse, passed the gates of the palisade, and walked through the snow-carpeted woods.

They climbed a hill and stood in the open, snow falling on their heads, the world as silent as a tomb. Senadondo looked out at the pristine glory of his world, muffled beneath its blanket of white: tall, majestic trees; a lone hawk in the sky; night's first star; the confluence of the

Harlem with the North River, the two bodies of water arguing and bickering with one another until they settled down to become one.

Senadondo and Pieter looked at this splendor in silence. And then, without once glancing at Pieter, the chief spoke. "The god Manitto remade the world after it had been destroyed. Manitto returns to us as a bird who causes the lightning. The world of my people is being destroyed. You must remake it. You are no longer Pieter; you are the lightning. You are Manitto."

They stood in silence again. Finally, Senadondo turned and walked down the hill. Pieter did not speak, nor did he try to follow. The chief reached the bottom of the hill. He crossed through the trees and came to the water. He turned east and was lost from view. Pieter stood silently for a long time and then returned to his ship.

Senadondo was never seen again.

6

Wars and Storms

1655 - 1659

PIETER STOOD ON THE GENTLY ROLLING DECK
of his new whaler, the three-masted schooner *Manhatan.*
The sleek craft, a low-lying ship with the look of a greyhound, was only a year old. The swept-back masts added
to its rakish appearance. The *Manhatan* was the finest
ship in New Amsterdam, and its master, Lars Jorisen,
now in his early thirties, anxiously paced the quarterdeck
and looked darkly at the owner. Pieter was well aware
that Jorisen was upset because the *Manhatan,* his pride
and joy, was being used for such work as it was doing at
the moment.

The two twelve-pounders and three eight-pounders
mounted on the starboard side roared to life and the can-
nonballs whistled through the air, pounding against the
palisade of Fort Christina.

The Swedes had started the trouble by attacking the
Dutch settlement at Fort Nassau, and the governor, Peter
Stuyvesant, had decided the New World would be better
off without the Swedes. The squabble had begun over
fishing rights, and the Swedes, spurred on by their in-
temperate leader, John Printz, had attacked the Dutch
fort and massacred over forty people. Printz was recalled
to Europe as punishment for his extraordinary bad judgment. His successor, Johan Rising, deplored Printz's folly,
but by then it was too late. He could do nothing to appease the irate Stuyvesant. A force of several hundred
men was raised by the Dutch, including over a hundred
warriors of the Mohawk, who had discovered a profitable
new business as mercenaries. To bring his force to the

Swedes the governor had commandeered several of the colony's biggest and fastest ships, including Pieter de Kuyper's *Manhattan*.

The ships continued their bombardment of the Swedish fort until the palisade was knocked down in a score of places. The Swedish artillery, never strong to begin with, was silenced. Now the ship's guns began to waste the town itself.

The Dutch prepared for a land attack. The troops, led by Stuyvesant himself, went ashore in longboats, and waited while the ship's guns continued to pound their targets. The Swedish defenders, their nerves frayed and their courage evaporating in the face of the cannon, seemed ready to surrender. It didn't seem as if there was any use in their continuing the fight.

"How much longer must this go on?" Jorisen asked Pieter.

Pieter looked toward the shore and his eyes stopped when they came to Governor Stuyvesant, standing at the head of his soldiers a few hundred yards from the shattered palisade. "We're to continue firing until the Governor tells us to stop. As of yet I see no signal."

"All this damn blasting away with the cannons will weaken our decking," the Dane complained.

"Then we'll put on new decking and send the bill to the governor," Pieter answered mildly. He was amused by Jorisen's concern for the ship. The Dane had become the finest sailor in New Amsterdam. When he was aboard a ship it was as if he became part of her, feeling every shift in the wind, knowing immediately the source of every creaking, every groaning. He didn't sail a ship, he *lived* it. Pieter tried to soften the younger man's discomfort. "The *Manhatan* is as strong as an oak. None of this will bother her."

"It isn't the physical part that bothers me," Jorisen said. "Nay, it's more what this could do to her soul. *Manhatan*'s made for blue water and whales, not for blasting away at a bunch of useless Swedes!"

Pieter managed to hide his smile as he turned away.

The cannons continued to fire, and the carnage behind the battered palisade increased. The Swedish governor wanted to surrender, but he was shouted down by the garrison commander, who said he preferred to die with honor than to live in disgrace. That was all very well and good for the soldiers, but the cannons had no way of distinguishing between a soldier and a civilian, and the dirt streets of the settlement were littered with the bodies of old men, women, and children.

Pieter walked the length of the *Manhatan* and, even under the circumstances, could not suppress his admiration for the beautiful vessel. That it existed at all was a joy, but that it actually belonged to him was the wonder of all wonders. When he thought back to his earlier ships —the *Tiger* of Adriaen Block, the *Sea Mew*, the *Bright Hope*, even the *Christiana*—all of them were scows compared to the *Manhatan*.

He walked to the end of the decking, where the bow narrowed to nothingness and the bowsprit began its haughty swing over the water. It was all so new and shiny and *intricate*. The bowsprit, bowsprit cap, jibboom, whisker pole, bobstays, forestays, preventers, lanyards, gaskets, foot ropes, the narrow and menacing dolphin-striker—each component with its own use, all brought together in a design that made them a single unit, a maze of beauty.

"Master Pieter," a deep voice said, and Pieter turned to face the grizzled countenance of Manuel Gerait. "How much longer are we going to do this?" he asked.

Ah, and you too. "You're beginning to sound like Lars Jorisen," Pieter said.

The black man nodded. "We love our ship, me and the Cap'n. We both hate to see her misused."

The remark came as a shock to Pieter. After all, this was *his* ship. He was the owner and master. Well, not exactly, he admitted to himself. He was the owner—but he no longer could claim to be master. That was Jorisen's title. And as he thought about it, he realized he hadn't spent that much time aboard the ship. No wonder Jorisen and Manuel were beginning to think of him more as a visitor than a real part of the crew. This was *their* ship, because it was their whole life.

"It'll soon be over," Pieter said. "Then you can go back to your whales."

Manuel smiled, his gold tooth much in evidence. The harpooner had it placed in his mouth after he lost his first tooth to a whale. He had been so close to the beast when he drove the harpoon deep into its flesh that the reaction of the whale had brought the lance back up into his mouth, splitting the lips and knocking out a tooth. He wore the gold tooth as a badge of his occupation.

"How's your son?" Pieter asked.

Manuel nodded. "He'll be two years old next month. Imagine," he said with pride, "a man my age becoming a father."

"You're not old."

Manuel shrugged. "When a man loses count of the seasons he has lived, he can be certain he has been here for a long time."

No one could be sure of Manuel's age. He had been born a slave, and no one bothered to keep records of such things for slaves. But Pieter guessed the black man's age was about the same as his own—fifty-six.

He didn't think of himself as being so old until he remembered that Young Pieter was twenty-nine. A man with a twenty-nine-year-old son was no longer a boy. Nor, for that matter, was the twenty-nine-year-old son.

"Zilla tells me you have a new house."

"Yes. We've been fortunate with the whales. Every time we go out, we return with a full catch."

"I know. I share in the profits."

The black man touched Pieter's arm. "Life has been good to me because of you. I never sleep before I ask God to watch over you and protect you."

Pieter was deeply touched. Of all the men in the world, the black man was closest to him. "Be happy with your house and family," he said as he walked back to the quarterdeck.

Manuel returned to his task of sharpening a harpoon. He was now first harpooner, a job he had taken over when the Basque, Santiago Equirra, had died five years before. They were out in the longboats, and Equirra had harpooned a whale. The line began to play out as the whale swam forward, but instead of whirling around the capstand, a coil flew back in a freak accident and wrapped itself around the harpooner's leg. Before Equirra could get the rope from his leg, the whale sounded and the man was dragged overboard. The tremendous strength of the whale, combined with the resistance of the water, created a force that tightened the heavy rope until it had sheared off Equirra's leg just above the knee. Flesh, veins, and bone disappeared, and where they had been was now only a small, rockhard knot in the rope.

Equirra's unconcious body floated to the surface, and by the time the longboat reached his side, it was too late. The breath of life was still in the man's body; but he had lost too much blood, and he died even as the men in the longboat were passing him over the gunwales of the mother ship. Manuel shuddered when he thought of poor Equirra's terror as he was dragged beneath the dark waters; he could almost feel his own leg being sliced off. They buried the Basque at sea, and Manuel succeeded to the post he had occupied. Accordingly, his pay was raised to a two-percent share of the profits. Manuel would have gladly forgone the added wealth if he could have spared the life of the taciturn man who had taught him so much of the ways of whales.

Pieter and Jorisen paced the quarterdeck for another hour before they received the signal to cease the bombardment. *Manhatan* continued to tack slowly back and forth across the river while the sailors watched the Dutch troops enter the ruins of Fort Christina.

On an impulse Pieter ordered a longboat lowered and went ashore with Manuel at his side. Lars Jorisen stayed aboard, preferring the roll of the deck beneath his feet to the unbending land. The Dane rarely went ashore, and then only when his duties forced him. He was becoming a legend in New Netherland, and men spoke of him as a "creature born of woman, but sired by a dolphin."

Pieter was appalled by what he saw inside the broken, smoldering palisade. The settlers surrendered, and the only remaining opposition came from the fortified tower, to which the last of the Swedish garrison had retreated. It was obvious these soldiers preferred death to surrender.

A Mohawk warrior approached Stuyvesant. "That is a strong tower, Wooden Leg," the Indian said, using the name given the governor by the natives.

"Do you have any ideas?"

"Fire arrows."

The governor allowed the Indians to try their burning arrows. The plan failed, because the Swedes had an am-

ple supply of water. As soon as a burning arrow struck
the wooden logs it was drenched.

The governor mounted a mass attack, but the troops
were driven back by a withering storm of musket fire.

"To hell with all this," Stuyvesant roared. He turned
to Pieter. "Do you think your gunners are accurate
enough to hit that tower, de Kuyper?"

"I think so."

"Then do it."

"Yes, sir!"

Pieter hurried back to his ship. As the longboat left
the dock, he noticed the Swedish settlers were already
being loaded aboard the ships that had been captured by
the Dutch. Stuyvesant planned to send them all back to
Europe with the threat that if they returned they would
be turned over to the Mohawk and left to their questionable mercies.

The *Manhatan* was brought into position as close to
the shore as Pieter dared. The cannons erupted, belching
fire and smoke. The first shots fell short. They fired a
few more times, and then the gunners found the proper
range. Volley after volley of shot smashed into the
wooden tower, splitting the thick logs, caving in the sides
and destroying the very floors beneath the Swedes. The
shot also hit the bodies of men, killing and maiming,
cutting off arms and legs and heads.

A white flag was raised. The cannons fell silent. The
remaining Swedes filed out, carrying their wounded and
their dying, their faces black with dirt, sweat, and gunpowder, their eyes filled with the haunted look of men
who have stood at the side of death.

A single pistol shot was heard, and when they went
inside they found the body of the garrison commander.
He had chosen death by his own hand over the ignominy
of surrender.

The troops—the living and the near-dead alike—were
packed aboard the Swedish ships, escorted to the head
of the Delaware, and told never to return.

Stuyvesant put the settlement of Fort Christina to the
torch, and by the next day all that remained of the Swedish Empire in the new world was a heap of ashes that
had grown cold through the night.

The Dutch ships returned to New Amsterdam in triumph, victory flags fluttering from their topmasts. There was a great deal of drinking, and even the governor joined the festivities.

Lars Jorisen would not dismiss his crew until they had removed the cannons and holystoned the decks, and all traces of the weapons were gone. But when the men went ashore, their master was not with them.

New Amsterdam's "trading post" look was being replaced by an urbanity familiar to visitors from Europe. It was becoming a miniature Amsterdam, a merchant town, determinedly Dutch. Most of the houses were one and a half stories tall, but two- and three-storied dwellings were not uncommon among the newer structures. Brick was the essential building material—the common red predominated, but there were many examples of the narrow, yellowish "Holland brick." Some builders preferred the local gray stone, because it looked dignified under a red tile roof. Interspersed among the newer buildings were wooden cottages with thatched roofs, but they were a dwindling breed, since Governor Stuyvesant had forbidden further construction of these fire hazards. Almost all the buildings had the customary "Dutch" doors. These were cut horizontally so the bottom half kept out animals while the open upper half let in fresh air. The Dutch loved sunlight, and their homes had many windows—large frames with many small panes leaded at the edges, all protected by stout wooden shutters. Many of the more expensive buildings had twin gables facing the street, double front stoops, and generous gardens at the back.

The marshes above Beaver's Falls had been drained into a canal, called the Great Ditch, that ran southeast toward the waters of the bay. The canal was sixteen feet across, and the unpaved walkways of Broad Street ran down both sides. A siding of wooden planks kept the earth from eroding and filling the canal. The Fish Bridge crossed the canal a block from where it emptied into the swirling waters of the Hellegat, or East River, as it was becoming more commonly known.

Many changes had occurred since the arrival of Governor Stuyvesant in 1647. The man was not a thief like Van Twiller and did not throw temper tantrums like Kieft. He was the well-educated son of a clergyman who had chosen a military career with the West India Company. He had served in the Indies as inspector-general of Curaçao and lost a leg to the Portuguese on the island of St. Martin. After a short rest in Holland, he was appointed governor of New Netherland and arrived with his wife, and his sister and her three small children.

Stuyvesant was a man of great energy and imperious ways. Upon arrival he passed a law that forbade taverns to open before two in the afternoon—except on Sunday, when they could not open until four. Innkeepers closed up when the town bell rang at nine in the evening; later the hour was changed to ten. Any man then still in a tavern could not go home, but was forced to spend the night, being let out only when the morning bell was rung at dawn. There were many objections to this law, but Stuyvesant was determined to stamp out the footpads and highwaymen, who were becoming a serious problem.

The finances of the colony were in a shambles, and the new governor levied taxes on liquor, furs, and gunpowder. In near desperation he sent two ships to the West Indies to prey on the Spanish galleons returning to their homeland laden with silver and gold. This, of course, was greatly resented by the English Sea Dogs who regarded the Spanish Main as their own private "hunting" preserve.

Stuyvesant had no use for his predecessor, and ordered him to leave the colony, but Kieft, in the middle of all his troubles, enjoyed a minor revenge. His constant attacks on Dominie Bogardus were finally rewarded when the pastor was recalled by his church at the insistence of the burghers. Ironically, Kieft and Bogardus departed for Europe on the same ship, the *Princess*. It was estimated that Kieft took with him a fortune of four hundred thousand guilders, almost certainly stolen from public funds. Both men claimed to be pleased to be allowed to plead their cases before the burghers. The dominie left with piles of documents that would be the basis of his defense; and it was said that Kieft intended to use a good part of the four hundred thousand guilders to insure himself of a favorable verdict.

What might have happened will never be known, because the *Princess* was caught in a storm and wrecked off the coast of Wales. Most of the passengers and crew drowned, the ex-governor and dominie among them.

Kieft's fortune was lost, and the documents of Dominie Bogardus disintegrated in the sea. All the documents brought by Kieft were also lost, and this loss would later prove troublesome to Pieter de Kuyper and others in the colony.

Relations with the Indians were no better than usual, and this uneasy state led, surprisingly, to a break in the warfare between Pieter and his elder son.

Stuyvesant worried about the lack of inland defenses, not only in the event of another Indian attack, but also against possible trouble with the English, who were spreading out from their Connecticut settlements. In 1653 the governor ordered a wooden palisade built across the island about a half-mile north of its southern tip. The palisade was to stretch from the banks of the East River to the banks of the North. The man assigned to supervise construction was Young Pieter. He didn't have the best qualifications for the job, and some men grumbled about unfair patronage.

Pieter was a constant visitor at the construction sites, pleased with his son, hoping he could handle the job. And in fact, Young Pieter was doing fine.

"This bank of earth is tall enough," he said to a group of sweat-stained workmen. "Start getting the logs in place."

He moved down the line, giving orders crisply and knowledgeably. He checked the earthwork and logs for signs of weakness. When he found a bad spot he ordered men to work on it at once. The palisade was ten feet high. The original intent had been to use whole tree trunks, but they had proved too cumbersome to handle and thick planks now formed the greater part of the structure. A walkway was being built so the defenders could look down on any attackers.

Young Pieter showed the plans to his father and explained them. "There will be two gates," he said. "The Land Gate will be at the intersection where the palisade crosses the upper reaches of the Broad Way. The Water Gate will be located where the palisade ends at the East River."

"The Land Gate will be of much use to farmers bringing their cattle and produce down to the settlement," Pieter said.

"And the Water Gate will give access to the bouweries north on Manhatan all the way to the village of Harlem," Young Pieter said. "We'll place several cannons at that point."

"You're building well," Pieter complimented his son as he looked at the thick earthwork and the stout logs. "You're making New Amsterdam a safe place."

Young Pieter knew what his father was getting at. "It's just a job I've been given," he said in an offhand manner. "I like to do everything as well as I can."

"Say what you will," Pieter said, "you're making the colony a better place." For the first time in years he was pleased with his son.

As the construction progressed, another blessing came to the de Kuyper family. Anne, now Mrs. David de Witt, gave birth to a child. The tiny bit of life was named Emilie. Tears came to Pieter's eyes as he beheld his first grandchild and held her miniature fingers in the palm of his hand. They were so small, and yet perfect. He only wished that Christiana had lived to see this sight. And Anne's wedding, he thought, not for the first time; Christiana would have enjoyed that too.

Anne de Kuyper's marriage to David de Witt had been one of the grandest social affairs ever seen in the colony. Both young people came from highly respected families, and everyone of importance, including Governor Stuyvesant, attended. People came from as far away as Rensselaerswyck.

Anne was a model of composure as she dressed for the great occasion. Zilla was more excited as she flitted about, helping the girl into her snowy-white gown. It was trimmed with the finest Dutch lace, which Pieter had ordered from Holland for this day.

"Now you stop looking out the window, girl," Zilla commanded. "You don't want to be late for your own wedding."

"We'll be on time," Anne said, continuing to gaze out at the sun-bathed garden behind the house. "It's the most beautiful day I've ever seen."

Zilla mumbled and grumbled as she struggled with the dress.

"Even the Almighty is doing His part," Anne said.

"I wish the Almighty would come help me get this dress on you."

The dress was finally on, and Anne stepped back. "Do you think I look pretty enough for David?" she asked.

"Oh for heaven's sake, child," Zilla said, picking up a pair of long white gloves. "You look like an angel just stepped down from heaven."

"I'm not a bit nervous, you know," Anne said as she worked the gloves over her slender, tapered fingers. "I've known this day was coming for a long, long time."

If the bride was calm and collected, the bridegroom was in a state bordering on helplessness. As he dressed for the last time in his room in his father's house—Pieter's gift to the couple was a brand-new house that was awaiting their arrival—he was all thumbs.

"Good God," Young Pieter said to his soon-to-be brother-in-law, "haven't you got that shirt on yet?"

"I . . . I can't seem to find the . . . find . . ."

"Here," Young Pieter said, taking charge and cramming the heavily starched shirtfront around David. "If I wasn't here you'd wind up going to the church naked."

"I'm sorry but . . . but this is all so sudden . . ."

"Sudden? You've been engaged for a year!"

David smiled, and his mouth felt as dry as if it had been stuffed with wool. He stood almost motionless while Young Pieter struggled to get him into his waistcoat and fancy throat scarf.

The wedding was held at the Church of Saint Nicholas, inside the walls of the fort. There wasn't an empty seat as Anne came down the aisle on Pieter's arm. The governor sat in the front row next to Young Pieter and Jacob Adam on the bride's side of the church.

Anne was radiantly beautiful, and the sight of her brought tears to the eyes of many a woman as she walked slowly and solemnly toward the waiting dominie and the nervous groom. At the party later that day, half in his cups, Young Pieter was to say cynically, "The reason women cry at weddings is they're no longer as slender and pretty as the bride."

Anne overheard. "The reason women cry," she said, "is their husbands are no longer as young and handsome as the groom." And as she said this she looked straight at her new husband, who was watching her lovingly.

David had been nervous throughout the ceremony, but had managed to get through it without disgracing himself. He didn't drop the ring. He didn't stumble. He kissed the bride at the proper moment. He didn't trip as he walked away from the dominie a married man.

As Anne swept out of the church on the arm of her new husband, no father could have felt prouder than Pieter. This exquisite creature was his own flesh and blood, the infant he had carried in the crook of his arm and tickled under the chin. David, of course, wasn't good enough for her, but he came as close as was humanly possible. Pieter was so pleased that he walked back to his house from the church arm in arm with his two sons. Jacob Adam thought nothing of it, but Young Pieter could hardly believe this unusual show of affection.

"Did you see that?" Young Pieter asked his brother after Pieter had gone off to see his guests. "He held me by the arm all the way home."

"So what?"

"He never does that."

"He just did," Jacob Adam said, with unflinching logic.

"Let's get a drink," Young Pieter said.

"No thank you."

Jacob Adam watched his older brother join the gathering mob of people hoisting mugs and cups filled with rum, gin, beer, and anything else they wanted. To him it all seemed silly, unnecessary.

Pieter and Abraham de Witt stood to the side and enjoyed the festivities. They had much in common. Both had been among the first settlers. Both loved their new home. And both were widowers who had never remarried.

"A wonderful day," Abraham said. "My son is the luckiest man in New Amsterdam."

Pieter agreed with his friend, but thought it too boastful to say so. "They're well suited to each other," he admitted.

"To think what we've accomplished since we've come to these shores," Abraham said, with a hint of nostalgia in his voice. "We've built a world from nothing. And now our children will carry on for us."

"Perhaps to do better than we did," Pieter said philosophically.

"I don't think we've done badly," de Witt said defensively.

"I didn't say we did, only that our children may do more," Pieter replied. "There are many who came here and haven't enjoyed as much good fortune as we have."

Abraham de Witt nodded. "True. Some have found as little here as they had in Europe."

De Witt was right. Two years earlier Governor Stuyvesant had started the town's first poorhouse as a place where the indigent might find a meal and a place to sleep.

Pieter had a sudden thought. "Let's share our good fortune," he said. "Let's take drink and food over to Beaver Street."

Abraham thought it a splendid idea. They gathered bottles of rum, brandy, wine, and beer, and filled a box with a delicious selection of food from the tables while Zilla badgered them to tell her what they were doing. They smiled at her, but wouldn't give her the satisfaction of an answer. They hurried over to Beaver Street.

The poorhouse had a half dozen inhabitants that day— a drunken sailor, a drunken town workman, two old men who had fallen on bad days, and a young Dutch couple who had just arrived from Europe without a penny in their purses.

It was these last two that brought moisture to Pieter's eyes. Young and innocent, they were frightened about having left Europe; and yet there was a spark of hope in their eyes, even a trace of defiance. They accepted the presents from the two older men, but they did so with dignity, and they bravely proclaimed they would soon be able to return the favor.

As the two men returned to the wedding party on the Broad Way, Pieter looked at his friend. "Were we like those two when we arrived?"

"Probably."

"They made me feel old," Pieter said. "I don't think I was ever that young and innocent, and yet I must have been." He stopped and grabbed his friend by the arm. "They made the right choice to come here. Twenty years from now they'll probably be celebrating the marriage of their own son or daughter and be sharing their happiness exactly the way we've just done. Life is wonderful," he said, and the two friends walked arm in arm down the street.

The party at the de Kuyper house lasted through the day and night and was still going strong when the next dawn came to New Amsterdam.

The newlyweds had departed long before, of course, retiring to their new house, where all of David's nervousness left him as he found himself gloriously involved in the nocturnal joys of married life. There was no hesitation on Anne's part. Despite her lack of experience, she was so much in love with David she instinctively knew what to do. They fell asleep in each other's arms, sublimely content, while the merrymakers still celebrated their nuptials.

The only other person who got any sleep was Jacob Adam. At ten o'clock he went down to the wharf and slept aboard the *Manhatan* in the cabin next to Captain Jorisen's.

It was sometime after midnight when Young Pieter got the idea that in honor of the occasion the cannon at the back of Kock's tavern should be fired. He led a group of men, most of whom carried at least one bottle, to where the cannon was mounted. It was only a four-pounder, mounted on a swivel base, but it was a cannon nevertheless.

"Powder!" Young Pieter shouted. After much fumbling and cursing the powder was set.

"Shot!" Young Pieter commanded, and two men stuffed the iron ball down the mouth of the cannon. There was a great deal of confusion about tamping the ball and setting the primer and wick, but eventually the cannon was ready.

"Fire!" Young Pieter shouted, and one of the de Schuyler brothers held a lighted taper to the firing wick. As the wick began to spark, he jumped away. The men cheered.

Young Pieter, who was standing next to the cannon, gave it a resounding *whack!* with his hand and casually sauntered back to join the other men. He suddenly noticed the look of horror on their faces. Perplexed, he turned to see what it was all about.

His hair stood on end and he was instantly sober. The cannon was pointed directly at him! No . . . it was moving away . . . And then he realized that they had forgotten to lock down the swivel and the blow he had given the cannon was making it turn in circles.

The cannon turned to face them . . . face away from them . . . back toward them . . . and Young Pieter threw himself on the ground together with the rest of the men. The wick sputtered.

Blam!

With a great roar and flash of flame the cannon erupted and the iron ball whooshed through the air, crashing at an angle through the wall of the top floor of the tavern, disappearing, then bursting forth a split second later into the open air, taking a sizable portion of the roof with it.

There was a deathly silence. A snicker. Another. And then Young Pieter began to laugh. "Did you see . . . ?" he started to say, and then the tears of his laughter choked off the words.

The other men began to laugh, raising bottles to their lips, pointing to the roof, kicking the ground happily, shouting and pounding each other on the back. As one gleeful mob, they returned to de Kuyper's house to share their mirth with everyone else. The members of the Dutch community—except those who had already passed out— thought it a very amusing thing. Even Frans Kock thought it hilarious when some of the men dragged him down to see his roofless tavern. The next day, of course, his opinion of this mishap was to change.

For weeks afterward the people talked about the wonderful affair—the wedding, the party, Kock's roof, everything—and agreed it was the best time they had had in many years. When the last guest had finally left, host Pieter de Kuyper was fast asleep in the chicken coop at the back of the house.

And now, a few years later, Pieter was looking at the first fruit of the union that party celebrated. The infant girl was the flesh and blood of his own body, his bid for eternity, passed along through an intervening generation.

His three children stood at his side as he peered into the crib. Everything in the family was peaceful.

Young Pieter left the room and went to the kitchen, where he got himself a cup of cider. Anne soon joined him.

"A beautiful baby," Young Pieter said.

"Yes, isn't she."

"I'm happy for you," Young Pieter said.

"How about yourself?"

"What do you mean?"

"I saw the way you looked at that baby," Anne said. "You'd make a wonderful father. When are you going to get married?"

He avoided her eyes. "One of these days."

"Almost everyone your age has taken a wife. I think it would please Father if you did the same."

"I'm not interested in pleasing him."

Anne recognized the tone. Whenever her brother spoke of their father there was a touch of anger in his voice. She tried to appease him. "I know he can be difficult, but deep down he only cares for your happiness."

"Good. I worry about him all the time, too."

"Getting back to marriage," she said, trying to shift the conversation away from their father, "there are many girls who'd make good wives."

"I'm sure there are," Young Pieter said. "And plenty of good husbands to go with them."

"We're talking about you."

"A subject I'd prefer to avoid if it's all the same with you, my darling sister."

"Well?" she said stubbornly.

"I haven't met anyone I want to marry."

She understood. "You're determined not to tie yourself to the colony in any way, isn't that it?"

Young Pieter shook his head. "No, I . . ." And then he smiled. "Since you know the truth, I might as well admit it."

She glanced over at Pieter, who was still admiring his grandchild. "It will break his heart if you leave."

"It broke our mother's life because he didn't," he answered sharply.

Anne walked away knowing there was little hope of reconciliation between the two men.

Young Pieter went back to work on the palisade and finished the job. Even before the palisade was completed, a street began to grow on the town side. It became known as the "Wall" Street. Over the years the palisade would fall into disrepair as the dreaded Indian attacks failed to materialize. The farmers would rip the planks down to use as building materials and firewood. The palisade would disappear, but the street, and its name, would not. The governor was credited with the idea, but for many years Young Pieter de Kuyper was remembered as "the Man Who Built Wall Street."

Pieter de Kuyper was a driving force behind the greatest of Stuyvesant's contributions to the colony. Their joint ambition was to change the status of New Amsterdam from a fief of the West India Company to a self-governing municipality reporting directly to the States-General.

"We must get out from under the crushing weight of the company burghers," Pieter thundered in the Council of Nine Men, the group of leading citizens appointed to advise the governor on colony policies. "All they care about is profit."

"What would you have, de Kuyper?"

"A recognition of the truth. We are not, as they seem to believe, a trading post, but a permanent settlement!"

Stuyvesant agreed, and for the better part of two years angry letters flew back and forth between the colony and the mother country. The Amsterdam burghers, naturally, wanted no part of this dramatic change, which would threaten their income.

Events in Europe, however, helped the Dutch government look with favor on the colonists' idea. The Thirty Years War, which seemed to have been going on forever, was finally ended in 1648 by the Peace of Westphalia. But now the Dutch were faced with a new menace— Oliver Cromwell. This latest defender of English Protestantism declared war on the Dutch and planned a conquest of their holdings in New Netherland.

The legal ruler of the United Netherlands was the *Stadholder*, William III; but he was only an infant, and the ruler was the appointed administrator, Jan de Witt. This de Witt was a first cousin of Abraham de Witt, who was on the Council of Nine Men in New Amsterdam.

Stuyvesant sent a delegation to Holland, and it seemed only prudent for Abraham de Witt to head it. It couldn't hurt their cause that his cousin would be the man to make the final decision. The delegation included Adriaen Van der Donck, acknowledged to be a man who knew his way around the councils of the States-General.

Abraham de Witt asked Pieter de Kuyper to join them,

but he refused. "I can be of more use here," he said, but the real reason for this reluctance was that he had no desire ever to see Europe again. However, an idea came to him. "But if you'd like to have a de Kuyper with you, why not take my son?"

"Young Pieter?"

Pieter nodded. "He can be your secretary, or something of small importance."

De Witt agreed, and Young Pieter could hardly believe his good fortune. At last! He was going to Europe! He was going to see Amsterdam! His *real* home!

It wasn't a completely altruistic gesture on his father's part. The older man truly believed that a firsthand look at Amsterdam would cure his son of all his romantic notions. He would learn the truth about the city and Europe, rather than the half-truths and fanciful images conveyed by books.

The only Amsterdam Pieter could remember was one of narrow streets, small attic rooms, freezing mornings, and a totally disagreeable life. It was to this Europe he was sending his son. He had no doubt he would return home cured and ready to make his life in the colony.

The young man's eyes shone as he embarked on his trip to the motherland. They burned even brighter when he saw the great city, with its church spires and immense guild halls. He delighted in the crowds of people and the tall buildings. There weren't enough hours in the day for him, and he rose before dawn each morning, anxious to taste new delights. But it wasn't all play. He worked harder than any other member of the delegation, until it seemed only proper to Abraham de Witt that the young man be given more responsibility than that of mere secretary. Soon he became one of the leading speakers of the delegation. Abraham de Witt found he had unearthed a gem.

Young Pieter's arguments rang through the chambers of the States-General. "If our colony is self-governing," he said to the assembled graybeards, "we will put up a stout defense against the mad English dogs! We will fight to the death because we will be fighting for what is ours!"

"It is yours now!" cried the leading company burgher, a desperate man fighting to preserve his wealth.

"No," Young Pieter said. "It is not ours—it is yours. We

will fight harder than you, because men fight harder for survival than for profit!"

"We are patriots, too!" the burgher screamed, knowing his back was to the wall.

"Patriots to your purses," Young Pieter replied. "If you were a true patriot you'd get your musket and sail back with us to the New World."

Which, of course, was the last thing the company burghers had in mind. Most of them did not even own muskets.

"I put it to you, sir," Van der Donck said, addressing his argument to Jan de Witt. "As a self-governing colony we will fight to remain under the Dutch flag. As an outpost of the West India Company we believe we would be as well off under English rule as any other."

Jan de Witt was no fool. He recognized the validity of the colonists' arguments. He forced a resolution through the States-General: New Amsterdam was now the first self-governing city in all the Americas.

In New Amsterdam the governor met with the Nine Men and elected the town's first officials—a prosecutor, two burgomasters, and five aldermen. Most of the Nine Men filled the new posts, and Pieter de Kuyper found himself an alderman. Together with the other officials, he reported to the governor, who in turn reported directly to the States-General. The influence of the West India Company was over, except through commerce.

Young Pieter returned home a hero, but hardly cared. He had discovered Amsterdam.

"How can you claim it was wonderful?" asked his dismayed father. "Did you have your eyes closed the entire time you were there?"

"It seemed that for the first time in my life they were really open."

"But the poverty . . . the dirt . . . the mean way people live—"

"And the towers . . . the vast harbor . . . the breath of men's thoughts in the air . . ." Young Pieter replied.

His father shook his head. It had not worked out as he had hoped. This young fool had only added to his delusions.

"This is your home," he said stubbornly before he walked away. "You must make the best of it."

Young Pieter hardly heard his father's words. He looked around at the settlement and knew this place was most certainly *not* his home. His only desire was to return to Europe.

This desire was fueled by the fact that Adriaen Van der Donck had remained in Amsterdam—and not of his own will. That wily administrator Jan de Witt had listened to Van der Donck as he eloquently pleaded the case for the colony. He decided the young man might not be satisfied until the colony became an independent body, free from all European encumbrances. Every time Van der Donck was about to return to the New World, he was given fresh excuses why his presence was required in Europe.

He became almost resigned to his fate as liaison between the States-General and the government of New Amsterdam. To fill up his hours he wrote a book—*Descriptions of New Netherland*—an account of the New World that was part expatriate's lament, part real estate salesman's brochure, and part fanciful depiction of the Indian as a noble savage living in an earthly paradise.

Oliver Cromwell, who because of his threats had been as responsible as anyone for the granting of a charter to New Amsterdam, never did come to the New World.

While the fighting raged in Europe, Governor Stuyvesant went to war against the many pigs that ran wild through the streets of New Amsterdam, rooting up gardens, undermining walls, and, in general, creating a great mess.

While the Europeans battled one another and died, their American cousins built houses, started farms, leveled great stands of timber, and drew riches from the forests and the seas.

Pieter de Kuyper spent the morning at work and then returned to his new ten-room house on the Broad Way. It was a more imposing structure than his former home on Pearl Street, and it reflected the prosperity of its owner. He kept the house on Pearl Street as a place of business from which he ran his enterprises—the whaler *Manhatan*, and the oil factory. In addition, there were the plans he was making for the tract of land along the Harlem River which he had been given by the Indian Senadondo, and his half-interest in a new windmill with Abraham de

Witt and a quarter-interest in the brewery started by Oloff
Van Cortlandt, who was one of the two burgomasters.
Pieter still owned the farm on the middle of the island, but
had never tried to work it since the tragedy of the Indian
war.

The decision to move from Pearl Street had been made
because of the growing commercialism of the area. Warehouses and a new "trade center" building had been
erected, and a new pier was also under construction nearby. Pieter did not want to live in the middle of all this.
The downstairs of the house became an office and the upstairs floor a storage area for the goods he often received in
payment for oil. Many of these trading goods were furs,
and Pieter would not resell them if the market for furs was
low; he could afford to wait until the prices climbed to
higher levels. He realized a great deal of extra profit in
this manner.

Pieter also bought the house next door when the owner, a
baker named Lacher, died and his childless widow decided
to return to Europe. He paid a fair price of three hundred
guilders, then rented the house for fifty guilders a year to a
man named Hedrick Jansen, who despite his name and appearance was a Mohammedan from Morocco. Jansen was
immediately nicknamed "The Turk." There was no malice
in this, since New Amsterdam was becoming a potpourri
of religions and nationalities and most people were tolerant. There were, of course, exceptions, and one worth
mentioning was the man who had replaced Dominie
Bogardus. Dominie Megapolensis was not a bad sort, but
he had an unnatural fear that the Dutch Reformed
Church would lose its position of preeminence amid the
many Huguenots, Lutherans and Catholics in the colony.
He preached many sermons warning his flock against the
"Papists, Jews, and other secret followers of Baal." Not
the most trusting of souls was the dominie.

As Pieter entered his house on the Broad Way, he heard
the happy laughter of a small child, and a smile came to
his lips. He hastened through the parlor and entered the
large kitchen. Zilla was holding a piece of candy, and the
child, his granddaughter Emilie, was attempting to take it
away, laughing and having a wonderful time.

"Father! Good afternoon!"

Pieter went to Anne and kissed her cheek. He turned

and picked up the child, who giggled and struggled to be free. He put her down, and Zilla held out the candy, which was instantly snatched from her hand.

"She reminds me of her mother when she was the same age," Zilla said.

"The prettiness or the greediness?" Pieter asked.

"Both," Zilla said solemnly, but there was a twinkle in her eye.

"Stop that," Anne said, but she smiled and cast an adoring glance at her daughter.

"How is your husband?" Pieter asked.

"Wonderful. Except he works too much," Anne said. "Right now he's away on a tour of the bouweries."

"Yes, I know," Pieter said. "He goes to the farmers and buys their grain in advance for the mill. Usually at a better price than if he waited for them to bring it to town. I never thought of it. Neither did Abraham. A bright young man, that husband of yours."

Zilla brought Pieter a glass of beer, and he sat on the cane seat of a straight-backed chair.

"Thank you, Zilla," he said.

Zilla was at least fifty years old, but she still did as much work as ever, even though there were three more servants to help her in the new house.

"You look like you've been working too hard," he said.

"I'm very content," Zilla said huffily, clearly indicating that she didn't want another of his you-ought-to-take-it-easier lectures.

"Look who's talking about working too hard," Anne said. "You act like you think you're still twenty."

"Work keeps a man young," he said.

"And dull," Anne said, not retreating an inch.

Pieter shook his head. Anne never changed. There wasn't another young woman in New Amsterdam who would speak this way to her father, and yet he adored her all the more because she did. "So now your father is a dull old man."

"I didn't say old. Really, Father, I think your hearing is starting to go, too."

Pieter smiled, and took his granddaughter aside and played with her for a few minutes before he excused himself and went to his study. He busied himself with a surveyor's report on lands along the Harlem. According

to the surveyor, the land was extremely fertile and would
be excellent for farming. Pieter sighed. He resisted the
idea of farming the land as long as the people of Senadondo still lived there. He could not bear to start the
process that would change the way of life of the people
of his old friend.

He next turned to a report written at his request by
Young Pieter.

There were a number of men in the colony who had
arrived as indentured servants. Each owed several years'
labor to pay off their debts or the cost of their transportation to the colony. Sometimes the "owners" of this labor
died, or moved away, or simply did not require the labor.
In such cases the contract of indenture was sold to the
highest bidder. Pieter had bought several of these contracts and had asked his son to determine the best places
among his various enterprises for the men to work.

Young Pieter had seized the occasion to condemn the
indenture system as another form of slavery. The contracts
of indenture should be torn up, he wrote. The men should
be offered a choice of jobs and then be paid as free men.

Pieter was furious. He had asked for a straightforward
report and had been given a philosophical treatise. It
wasn't that Pieter was an admirer of the indenture system;
as a matter of fact he wasn't. His anger stemmed from
the fact that his son could not be trusted to complete the
simplest of tasks without adding complications and irrele-
vancies.

He went back to the kitchen. "Where's my son?" he
asked Zilla, and his dark look told her which son he meant.

"He said he was coming back soon."

"Send him to my study."

Pieter left the room, and Zilla turned to Anne and
grimaced.

"The same old war?" Anne said, shaking her head at
the antagonism between her father and older brother.
They had been at odds ever since she could remember.

"It gets worse and worse," Zilla said. "Sometimes
I try to talk to your brother, but he's more stubborn than
ever. What he needs is a wife and a house of his own."

"That would help," Anne admitted. "But I think those
two will always find something to fight about."

While the women talked and little Emilie was teasing the cat with a long ribbon, Pieter fumed in his study.

He had few regrets in his life, but one of them was Young Pieter. If only the boy had turned out like David de Witt. David was a lad to be proud of—hard-working, practical, determined to be a success. But Young Pieter? A dreamer. Not that he lacked brains. Or ability. He had proved he had those when he built Stuyvesant's wall— and when he had gone with the delegation to Amsterdam. *My* mistake, that one, Pieter thought. The boy hadn't learned a thing. As soon as he had returned he had gone back to reading books. He must have worn blinders on his eyes the whole time he was in Europe.

It was in this black mood that Young Pieter found his father. "I understand you want to see me."

"Sit down."

There was a long silence, and Pieter finally threw his son's report across the desk. It landed a few inches from the edge. "What's this nonsense about?"

"You don't agree with it?"

Pieter's forehead turned into a network of lines and furrows.

"I suppose it must be nonsense," Young Pieter said easily, "if you don't agree with it."

Pieter managed to control his temper. "I asked you to do a simple task. It seems you're incapable even of that."

"I take it you approve of indentured men."

"That isn't the point," Pieter snapped.

Usually the son was anxious with the father, but today was different. Young Pieter stretched his legs straight out and looked completely relaxed

"What is the point?" he asked.

The young man's attitude infuriated Pieter. "The point is that you're a fool!" he said angrily, hastily, without really meaning it.

Young Pieter smiled. "I wasn't a fool when I built the wall, was I? Or when I argued your colony's case before the States-General?"

"Those were different."

"Were they?" Young Pieter asked softly, seeming to enjoy the situation. "Suppose you admit the real reason you think me a fool."

"And I suppose you know?"

"Yes. You think me a fool because I won't let you decide the direction of my own life."

"You must be practical—" Pieter began, but his son would not let him continue.

"And what, dear Father, is practical?"

"Doing what makes good sense."

"Exactly my own thought. And it makes no sense for me to remain in a place where I'm thought a fool."

"What are you talking about?"

"I leave on the morning tide. I have passage on a Danish packet, the *Valkyrie*. In seven weeks' time I'll be in Amsterdam."

The news came as such a surprise that Pieter forgot his anger. "You're leaving?"

"Yes."

"But we have so much work to do! Have you completely lost your mind?"

"According to you I haven't much of a mind to begin with. Why are you so worried about my losing it?"

"Don't play with words!"

"And as far as the work goes," Young Pieter said, tapping the crumpled report on the desk, "you're the one who doesn't think it's worth a damn."

"Have you lost your senses?" Pieter said, his voice rising as he pressed against the front of the desk, his hands gripping tightly to the edges.

"No. In fact, you might say I've finally found them. That's why I'm going to Amsterdam. Maybe there'll be some use for me there."

"But why Amsterdam?" Pieter asked, knowing full well the question was answered before it had been asked. But he could not help himself. "Who do you know there? Where will you stay? What will you do for money?"

"Still worried about your 'little boy,' are you?" Young Pieter said, his smile growing. With his finely chiseled features, slender frame, and elegance of movement, he bore a close resemblance to his mother. Except for his stubborn nature and tenacity, he had little in common with his father. "Shall I answer your questions one at a time?"

Pieter slumped behind his desk, glowering and unable to speak.

"Very well. Why Amsterdam? Because Amsterdam is

a city, a real city, not a little pisspot watering hole like this place. Who do I know there? Adriaen Van der Donck. Where will I stay? Adriaen writes that I may stay with him, as he has a large house. And as for money, Father, you've paid me a good salary for doing nothing and I've been thrifty with it. Any more questions?"

"New Amsterdam is not a pisspot!"

"As you wish. Call it the Garden of Eden for all I care."

"How long do you plan on staying there?"

"Until they bury me."

"And you'll spend all your time doing nothing, I suppose?"

"No. Adriaen assures me that a man with my brains will find something worthy of him in Europe."

"Van der Donck," Pieter said with distaste. "I might have known you'd take up with a man of his sort."

"What sort is that?"

"A fuzzy dreamer. A radical. Someone who ought to be taken out and hung," Pieter said, his anger getting the best of him. It had only been a few months ago that he told Abraham de Witt they had been lucky "to have a man like Van der Donck in Holland to make sure the States-General didn't ignore us."

Young Pieter stood up. "Adriaen Van der Donck is one of the finest men I know. I won't listen to you abuse him."

"Sit down!"

"No, Father, I won't sit down. I'll now take my leave."

Suddenly all of Pieter's anger and resentment vanished and he became a middle-aged father afraid he was looking upon his elder son for the last time. Forgotten were all the things he disliked about Young Pieter, forgotten were the disputes and the arguments, forgotten was the fact that the boy had never been what his father wanted, forgotten was the fact that the boy—

The boy? Yes, Pieter thought, maybe a great deal of the problem is my fault, for still thinking of him as a boy. He is twenty-nine years old and no longer a boy. He is a man and he is now rejecting the father who will not treat him as one, who has *refused* to treat him as one.

"Don't g-go—" Pieter stammered. "I will . . . try to . . . try to understand. . . ."

"The decision's been made."

"But there are . . . so many things. . . ."

The sight of Pieter speechless touched his son's heart. He was determined to go, but now he wished it might be more pleasant. "I would prefer to go with your blessing," he said.

Pieter wanted his son to stay more than anything in the world. He was willing to promise anything. But when Young Pieter asked for his blessing, all the years of angry bullying seemed to fuse.

"Blessing? I'll give you no blessing! Get out of this house! As far as I'm concerned I have no son! As far as I'm concerned you're dead!"

It was a statement he would regret for the remainder of his years. Young Pieter looked at his father with pity. It was truly finished. What had been undone could never be put together again.

He left the room and sent his trunk to the *Valkyrie*. He spent the night at the house of his sister, rose before dawn, and stood at the stern rail as the *Valkyrie* rode the tide carrying her toward the Narrows. Manhatan seemed to drift away, and soon it was lost in the morning fog. Long after nothing could be seen of the land, the young man stood at the rail.

The departure of his elder son left Pieter with only eleven-year-old Jacob Adam, and he determined not to make the same mistakes he had with Young Pieter. Jacob Adam would be allowed to be his own person. There would be no attempt to make him conform to his father's ideas of right and wrong. The tragedy of the first son would not be repeated with the second.

"Your brother has gone to live in Amsterdam," he said.

"Why?"

A chill passed through Pieter, as if someone had walked over his grave. He stared back into the unblinking blue eyes of the boy. Even if he had wanted to, he could never have acted with this son as he had with Young Pieter. This one was a boy, true, but he was also a wrinkled graybeard.

"Your brother . . ." Pieter started to say, and then changed his mind because it was too painful to speak the

truth. "He didn't really . . . like it here," he said lamely.
"He didn't like some . . . things."

"What things?"

The boy was making it difficult for him to spare himself. "Many things," he answered vaguely, knowing the words sounded false, but it was the best he could do. He managed a smile. "If there are some things you don't like, I hope you'll talk to me about them."

"Yes," Jacob Adam said thoughtfully. "Running away isn't a good answer to anything."

"What makes you think he ran away?" Pieter said, trying to salvage some pride.

"Didn't he?"

A long silence. "Yes."

"It was one of the things he always talked about."

"He talked to you, did he," Pieter said sadly, realizing he could hardly remember the last time he and his elder son had had a conversation that was not an argument.

"I am his brother."

Yes, Pieter thought, and I am his father and he could talk to you but he couldn't talk to me. "I hope you never think about running away," he said aloud.

"Why run away when we can change what we don't like."

Pieter felt awkward. He was the father and this boy the son, but there were times he felt their roles were reversed; the boy was more sure of himself than the father.

"Yes, that's a better idea," he said.

"After all," Jacob Adam said, "this place belongs to us."

Pieter felt a good deal better about his second son than his first. And a good deal worse. He understood that he could never guide this one. Or control him. Or never bring this one to hate his father as Young Pieter did because— he asked God's forgiveness for even thinking such a thing —this one couldn't be touched. He simply didn't worry about the opinions of other men. His resources all seemed to come from within himself. God help the man or woman who loved this one with all their heart.

Pieter decided to find solace from his daughter.

"I tried to stop him," Pieter explained to Anne and David as they ate dinner in the de Witts' house.

"I'm sorry I wasn't there," David said. "Maybe I could've talked him out of it."

"I doubt it," Pieter said, taking a sip of coffee. "Anyway it has nothing to do with either of you. It's an old feud and, I suppose, mostly my own fault."

"He'll be back," Anne said, with little conviction.

"A few months in stuffy old Amsterdam and he'll be wishing he was back here," David added.

"I'd like to believe that," Pieter said sadly, "but there was something about the way he left that was very final."

"You did give him your blessing, didn't you, Father?" Anne asked.

A long pause. Finally Pieter mumbled, "Yes."

But Anne knew he lied. And Pieter knew she knew.

Hours later, after Pieter had returned to his own house, Anne lay awake in bed next to David, thinking about the terrible anger that had forced a son to leave his father; and a father's anger so strong that he refused to give his blessing to his son.

David rolled over and realized his wife was still awake. "Can't you sleep?"

"I'm all right."

"Thinking about your brother?"

"Yes. And my father."

David propped himself up on one elbow and looked at Anne. She was bathed in the soft, silvery light cast through the shutters by the moon.

"Sometimes I feel guilty when I see how unhappy other people can be," he said.

"Because we're so happy in contrast?"

"Yes."

A smile came over her lips and he noticed it. "What are you thinking about now?"

"Can I make a confession to you?"

"A confession?"

"I used to dream about how life would be when we were married. They were wonderful dreams and I thought I'd die waiting for them to happen. But then we were married and I realized my dreams were only a small part of the true happiness you've given me."

David was silent, overwhelmed by her words.

"Even in my dreams, I had no idea it could be this wonderful," she said.

He looked at her smooth skin and her soft lips, and then he buried his head in her breast and slowly moved up until he found her lips.

They made love and fell asleep, Anne wrapped around David's body and all thoughts of her brother and father gone. Now there was only the two of them.

The floor of the forest was burning.

Stone Eagle, blood son of Senadondo, chief of the Wickquaskeeks, watched as the flames jumped from one pile of dry brush to another.

A dozen braves ran along the forest trail, stopping every fifty feet and putting their torches to fresh piles of dead undergrowth. The sounds of cracking leaves and snapping twigs filled the air.

And now an updraft caught the flames and they shot to the tops of the trees, burning the dead leaves, scorching the trunks, filling the forest with incendiary thunder. The flames sped across the tops of the trees, dancing, flickering, pausing as if to catch their breath, and then leaping onward. Soon the entire area from the inland lake to the grassy plain was ablaze as the fires swept across the trees down toward the river.

Stone Eagle shouted instructions to his warriors. The flames had to be complete and enveloping; the fires must totally engulf the area to have the proper effect.

This brush-burning ritual was performed every fall. Far from being destructive, it helped the forest rejuvenate itself every spring. The ash from the fire would work itself into the soil, enriching it, replenishing it, making it more nourishing for the new growths that would come after the passing of winter. The fires also pruned the forest, killing the weak and the dying, giving the healthy more space and room to grow. The bottoms of the trees would be scorched to a height of three or four feet, but the healthy ones would survive and sprout even more gloriously the following season.

The origins of this custom were lost in time, but the Wickquaskeeks never failed to observe it in the fall. They always chose different areas, and a plot of land that had been burned in one year would ordinarily not be touched again for many more.

The Indians did not do it for the good of the forest.

They did it for themselves. In a few days the fires would be out, the embers cold, and the floor of the forest covered with a fine layer of black soot. Then the animals would return, and they would leave clearly marked trails wherever they walked. The Indians would begin the Great Hunt of the year in preparation for the coming rigors of winter. Game would be hunted and killed as at no other time of the year. The lodges and huts of the red men would fill with preserved meat so the tribe would not go hungry during the long night of winter. To the Indians, brush burning was another way of aiding their hunting.

Stone Eagle saw that the fires had been properly set. Now the flames would dance their way to the river, and in a few days this area of approximately two square miles would become the scene of intense hunting.

He stood on a knoll and watched with satisfaction as the smoke wafted into the sky. The air was filled with the sight and sounds of confused birds that were being burned out of their homes. This did not bother the chief; he knew the birds would easily find new homes, or else go back in a few weeks and rebuild their old ones. The fires were only a minor inconvenience for the birds. As for the animals who lived beneath the earth or in burrows, or in the trunks of trees—well, there was no point in worrying about them. They would dig in and wait until the fires died down. They would then emerge, forage, and replenish themselves. They would survive.

Stone Eagle was startled by the sound of gunfire. He listened until he was certain of its source and then ran toward it, swiftly but with the easy economy of a deer. As he ran he looked in perfect harmony with the forest around him; as much at home here as the sharp-eyed otter who watched him pass. He came closer to the river and met a brave who was running from that direction.

The brave stopped and pointed back toward the waters. "White men," he said.

"They shot at you?"

"Yes."

Stone Eagle's expression remained impassive. "Go back to the lake," he said to the warrior. He resumed running toward the river and the white men. He skirted the edge of the burning forest and after a few hundred yards saw the white men, about a dozen of them, coming in his direction. He stopped, folded his arms, and waited for them to reach him. One of the whites raised his rifle to shoot, but another man stopped him. "I recognize that one. He's the chief."

Stone Eagle confronted the angry white men. They communicated in a mixture of signs and words from several languages.

Stone Eagle explained what his braves had been doing. It was not, he said, an act of hostility toward the white men. The settlers disagreed. Their village of Harlem was close by—and their fields and their homes. The fires were a threat to their lives.

"This part of the forest will not be burned for many years," Stone Eagle said.

"This part of the forest will never be burned again," the white men said.

"It is the way of our people," Stone Eagle explained.

"It has to stop," was the answer of the white men. And to give teeth to their threat they promised to raise a force of men and burn down the Indian's village if any more trees were burned.

The settlers turned and walked back to the village of Harlem. They were smug, sure of themselves, righteous. The only time we'll be safe, they said, is when these pesky redskins are gone. Burning the tops of trees, said another, what a crazy thing to do. Yes, agreed a third man, nothing they do makes any sense.

Stone Eagle's face did not reveal the turmoil in his heart and mind.

Another thing taken away from his people. And next year it would be something else. And so on and so on; for every year that they lived, there would be something taken away. Until, finally, there would be nothing left to take because his people would have nothing. And then his people would be no more.

All this did not surprise Stone Eagle. Had not Senadondo foretold it? No, it did not surprise him. But it did fill his heart with sadness, and his mouth with bitterness.

Stone Eagle returned to his village and told the warriors there would be no more brush burning. Some raised their voices in protest. They wanted to fight. Stone Eagle told them the days of fighting were over. The only way to survive was to learn to live with the white men.

"And if the white man does not let us learn?" one warrior asked.

"Then we will fight," Stone Eagle said. But he knew his words were empty.

A few weeks later Stone Eagle was hunting with two warriors. They came across a hastily made campsite where a French trapper was preparing to spend the night. The Frenchman was alarmed at first, but he relaxed a bit when he saw the Indians were not Mohawk.

"You are far from home," Stone Eagle said.

The Frenchman nodded and told of his travels. He had wandered far afield in his search for rich pelts. And now he was bringing his wealth to New Amsterdam to sell instead of trying to take it back to Montreal. It would be easier to make the long return journey without so many furs. Anyway, he said, the Dutch would pay as much as he could get in New France.

The two braves were eyeing the furs, and Stone Eagle knew their thoughts. With a gesture he made it known that the white man was not to be harmed. The braves showed no disappointment, although Stone Eagle knew they thought it foolish to pass up such a chance. Here was a lone white man from far away, a *Franchy* from the north. The farmers of this region did not know him, nor would they care what happened to him. It was a golden opportunity. But Stone Eagle was the chief and there could be no questioning his commands.

Stone Eagle sat beside the Frenchman's small fire. He wanted to hear about the people of his long-dead father. He asked a few innocent questions about conditions in the north.

The trapper spoke freely of the Huron, the Mohawk, and the French. Stone Eagle pressed the man about the Huron, the people of his blood.

"Mohawk savages trying to kill them all," the man said. "They hate them worse'n they hate the French."

Stone Eagle sat in silence and waited while the man took a long drink of whiskey from a skin. "My guess is," the trapper continued, "the Mohawk is going to succeed."

"The Huron are your allies?" Stone Eagle asked.

"In a way, that's true."

"You will help them?"

"What's it to me? I'm a trapper. What those Indians do to one another is none of my business."

"They are your friends," Stone Eagle said.

The Frenchman laughed and took another drink. "There are times when I've been accused of being too good a friend to some of them Indians."

Stone Eagle did not understand, and the Frenchman explained. "I took a woman from the Huron. Some might say she's a wife. I even have a kid. Nice little one, even if he is half-breed."

"You would allow the Mohawk to harm these people?"

The trapper shrugged. "I didn't start the trouble between Huron and Mohawk."

"But the boy is your son."

"I didn't make him Huron. That's the part the Mohawk hate the most."

Stone Eagle's face did not show the contempt he felt for this man. He sat with him a while longer only because he wished to hear as much as possible about the Huron. Finally he rose and walked away from the fire. He stopped when he reached his braves, who were squatting on the ground a short distance away.

"This one is a coward," he said. "Do not eat his heart."

Stone Eagle vanished into the forest, leaving the Frenchman to his fate. He would not have permitted it to happen except that the man had abandoned a Huron wife and son. The Huron were the people of his father's blood, the people who had been kind to his mother.

He also realized his mother had been French, the same as this trapper. Stone Eagle felt ashamed as he walked the floor of the forest with this French blood running through his veins.

From a distance he heard the first agonized scream from the trapper. His braves would be in no hurry. The white man would be many hours in dying. Maybe a full day if he was strong. And unlucky.

From the time his brother left New Amsterdam, Jacob Adam was allowed a great deal more freedom than before. His father involved him in the plans for the Harlem lands and in the expansion of the oil factory. He was encouraged to go with Lars Jorisen on a whaling expedition aboard the *Manhatan*.

The night before the ship sailed, Pieter handed the boy a handsome sheathed dirk.

"This was given to me by Captain Adriaen Block. It once belonged to Henry Hudson," Pieter said. "And before that it had been a gift from Queen Isabella to Christopher Columbus."

The boy took the knife. He extracted the blade from the sheath and ran his finger across the sharp edge. "It must be worth a lot of money," he said.

Pieter shook his head. "It is worth nothing, because we can never sell it. That knife was one of the first to come to the New World, even as we are among the first families. Keep it. It is now yours until the day you give it to your own son."

The boy replaced the blade in the sheath. "I will remember," he said.

Jacob Adam did not go aboard the *Manhatan* as the idle son of the owner, the way his older brother had. Jacob Adam was a working member of the crew. The eleven-year-old bunked in the fo'c'sle, ate the same food as the others, and was taught how to throw a harpoon by Manuel Gerait.

Jacob Adam was equal to every task. He did not complain. He did not shirk responsibility. Captain Jorisen took him into his cabin every evening, and the boy learned of ship handling and navigation. Jorisen, who had begun to regret that he had no sons, was almost fatherly with the young crewman. If the teacher was superb at his task, the pupil was worthy of him. Jacob Adam took to ship's life as naturally as if he had been born on the ocean. Within a week he was standing his watch at the wheel, and there wasn't a man on board who doubted his ability to steer a true course.

He was even allowed the great adventure of going aboard a longboat when it went after a whale. He stood beside Manuel, looking frail and small next to the huge black man, whose muscles rippled in his naked arms and back. But when it came time for the kill, both Manuel and the boy held the harpoon. They threw it, black muscles and white muscles working together, and the razor point struck true and sliced deep into the flesh of the whale.

The mighty beast sounded, and the rope hummed as it

whirled around the capstan. The whale surfaced, and Jacob Adam was treated to a twenty-minute ride at fifteen knots. His eyes shone as never before. He helped row the longboat back to the *Manhatan* and spent the afternoon happily cutting up chunks of blubber and fitting them into the barrels.

The *Manhatan* was out for six weeks, and Pieter was on the quay when she returned to port. A young man with the look of eagles in his eyes came ashore. He barely resembled the young boy who had sailed from this very spot only a short time ago. How different a response to the sea from that of his brother, Pieter thought.

Michael de Pauw was over sixty years of age and in poor health. But if his body had slowed and kept him in constant pain, his mind was as quick and aggressive as ever. He decided to challenge the validity of Pieter de Kuyper's claim to the lands along the Harlem. He secretly moved a dozen settlers onto the land. They erected a crude barn and a few huts, and began to clear a section of the forest. The Indians, aware that their chief, Senadondo, had long ago given these forests to Pieter de Kuyper, sent word of what was happening to New Amsterdam.

The *Manhatan*, fortunately, was in port. Pieter boarded the ship and sent it scudding up the river on a day when the wind howled and the waters were mostly froth. Lars Jorisen drove the *Manhatan* as if he was possessed: he knew how much the lands meant to his employer. They anchored in the cove that had become as familiar to Pieter as his own house in the settlement.

Backed by a force of twenty armed sailors, Pieter came upon the barn and the huts of the farmers. It wasn't long before he realized the farmers were only dupes of de Pauw. His anger lessened, but he was firm. He burned the barn to the ground, took the tools, and brought the farmers back to the ship under guard. He confined them below decks until the *Manhatan* had returned to New Amsterdam.

He left the ship and went to the City Hall, which had been the town tavern until the States-General gave the town its charter. He registered a complaint against the farmers and the man who had sent them. To his surprise

he was informed another complaint had already been issued—this one by Michael de Pauw against him.

De Pauw's complaint stated that Pieter had no legal
right to the land; that the deed given him by the Indian
chief was worthless.

Moreover, the complaint stated that Pieter was guilty
of malicious destruction, interfering with peaceful settlers,
and maintaining an armed force of his own within the
boundaries of the colony.

Pieter, incensed, swore to himself he would have
shot de Pauw if the man were present. But he was nowhere
to be seen; there was only his complaint. That it had been
registered so quickly told Pieter the entire affair had been
carefully planned. De Pauw had known what Pieter's reaction would be when he heard about the settlers.

There was nothing Pieter could do but to go home and
wait until the morning. He planned on returning to the
City Hall to ask for a court trial as soon as possible—
that very day, he hoped.

He did not speak during dinner. Zilla sensed that something was very wrong. She ate quickly and busied herself in another part of the house. Pieter sat at the table
and brooded under the watchful eye of his son.

Talking more to himself than to the boy, he told what
had happened. Jacob Adam listened quietly. He had already learned that one would know more by listening than
by talking.

"And it all comes down to this," Pieter cried at last.
"Will a deed from an Indian hold up in court?"

"What's the basis for Michael de Pauw's claim that
you don't hold a legal title?" the boy replied.

"I hadn't thought of it. Damn! I've been so mad it
never entered my mind."

"He must have some reason to believe he'll be successful."

Pieter agreed, but it seemed a hopeless task to find
this reason. Michael de Pauw would be guarding such
information as if it were a treasure. Pieter said as much
to his son.

"When men are angry they say foolish things," Jacob
Adam said. "If de Pauw became angry enough, maybe
he'd tell you what you wanted to know."

The nimbleness of the boy's mind startled Pieter. "I

don't think it possible to get de Pauw angry," he said. But this thought gave him another, and he worked it out as he talked. "That doesn't mean there isn't another way to find out, though. Ever since Stuyvesant retired Commandant Van Tienhoven, the man spends most of his time at Kock's tavern. Van Tienhoven and de Pauw are as close as two hogs in a wallow. The commandant isn't half as intelligent as de Pauw. If he were angered enough, and drunk enough, he'd talk until his tongue fell out."

Pieter stood up and patted his son on the shoulder. "At any rate, it's worth a try." He put on his hat and went out the door.

Pieter arrived at Kock's Tavern. He took a table near the door, ordered a beer, and looked around the room. As usual, Jan Van Tienhoven was at his table with several friends, halfway to a drunken stupor. Pieter ordered a round of beers sent to the table.

Van Tienhoven looked across the room as the serving girl pointed out his benefactor. He waved to Pieter and indicated he was welcome to join them.

Pieter took his mug and pulled a chair up to the table, sitting opposite the commandant.

"You're becoming a big man in the town," Van Tienhoven said pleasantly, but there was an edge to his voice. The three other men, middle-aged cronies of the former commandant, and all half drunk, smiled at Pieter and then looked back at their friend. Van Tienhoven was known as a wit among them, the more so as they became drunker. None of them had been men of much accomplishment, and in their company the man who had once been the proud commander of the garrison emerged quickly as the leader. They now welcomed the chance to see him play his cat-and-mouse game with Pieter de Kuyper, whom none of them particularly liked because he seemed too successful.

"Things go well," Pieter said mildly.

"I was down at the quay and I saw them unloading a shipload of blubber," Van Tienhoven said. "The sea's making you rich."

"I do well by sea . . . and by land."

Van Tienhoven gazed sharply at Pieter. "Yes? Pray tell us about it."

Pieter pretended to be nothing more than an affable

man having a few drinks with companions in a cozy tavern. "Why talk about business now?"

"No, really, I'd like to hear about your successes on land."

Pieter smiled. "If you insist. I have the oil factory, which has just been expanded because business is going so well. I have an interest in Van Cortlandt's brewery. There are the houses on Pearl Street. And then there's the partnership with de Witt in the grain mill. Yes, things go very, very well."

The words, spoken conversationally, seemed harmless, but they were aimed directly at Van Tienhoven's weakest point. Pieter was well aware that since his retirement the ex-commandant had tried several commercial ventures. Most of them had failed, and none had turned a profit. This talk of another's success was guaranteed to annoy him. Now that Pieter had stuck the knife in, he proceeded to twist it.

"But these are only a beginning," he confided to the men at the table. "I have plans for something that will make any other ventures seem insignificant."

The three affable drunks became interested, but Pieter was gratified more by the jealousy that came into Van Tienhoven's face.

"Yes," he persisted, "a great venture. And would you believe that my good fortune rests on the gift of another?"

"And what is this gift?" Van Tienhoven asked.

Pieter sat back and smiled again. "One doesn't speak of great crops before they are in the barn."

"Please tell us, Pieter," one of the drinkers asked. He was William Lambert, a former sailor and jack-of-all-trades who now lived with his married daughter at the expense of his son-in-law. "Perhaps you need investors and we might be allowed to share a crumb or two from your table."

Van Tienhoven's face became flushed. Lambert was his greatest admirer, and now here he was, his stupid moon-face aglow, begging de Kuyper for information that might bring him a guilder or two. This defection choked Van Tienhoven with anger.

"Perhaps I'll give you a hint," Pieter teased. "My new venture has to do with land."

"The land along the Harlem?" Van Tienhoven said in an ugly voice.

Pieter pretended to be flustered. "The land along the . . . what are you talking about? I never mentioned the Harlem."

Van Tienhoven would not relent. "It *is* the land on the Harlem, isn't it?"

As if he were a schoolboy caught in a forbidden act, Pieter dropped his eyes and made a confession. "I can see there's no use denying it. Yes, the land along the Harlem."

A look of triumph came across the commandant's face. In that instant Pieter knew the man was aware of Michael de Pauw's plans. Now the problem was to get him to talk. He must be goaded to a point where he would forget caution and say anything to prove himself right.

"Ah well, since you've guessed my secret . . ." Pieter paused dramatically and cocked his head. "I take it that it was a lucky guess, eh, Commandant?"

"Take it however you want."

"Well then, this guess of the commandant's, this *lucky* guess—"

"It was not a guess!"

"Come, Van Tienhoven, there is no possible way for you to have known of plans. When you spoke of the Harlem lands, it *had* to be a guess. Why, I've never even spoken to you about them."

"You're not the only one to talk to."

"No?" Pieter said, forcing himself to remain unruffled. "Then who else should one talk to?"

The commandant almost spoke, but his anger was still controllable and he managed to choke back the words. He reached for his mug, drained it of beer, and spun around in his chair.

"More beer!" he called out to Frans Kock, who was standing behind the bar. "More beer for everyone at this table!" He turned to Pieter. "You're not the only one who can treat his friends."

Pieter did not allow himself to be thrown off the path. "Ah, but now you won't answer my question. You claim other sources of information, Commandant, but you decline to say what they are."

"Don't worry about my sources, they serve me quite well, sir!" the commandant said, his anger rising again.

"I don't blame you for pretending to know what I'm up to," Pieter said. "It will be the greatest coup yet seen in the colony. If the mood suits me, sir, I might even find a minority interest for you."

Van Tienhoven exploded. The gall of the man on the other side of the table took him past common sense. "Damn you! I don't want your leavings, especially when there'll be nothing left by the time we get through with you!"

"We?"

"Yes, we! Michael de Pauw and myself! What good will all your plans be when we take the Harlem lands away from you?"

"You can't do that."

"Can't we?"

"I own legal title to those lands," Pieter said in an even voice. Please, please, he thought, go on just a bit further and tell me of de Pauw's plans.

Van Tienhoven did not disappoint him. "Damn me, sir, you hold no legal title! Kieft took the recordings of sales with him back to Holland and they were lost at sea!"

"What?" Pieter said, and this time his astonishment was more real than feigned.

"You may have a piece of paper, sir," Van Tienhoven said, now beyond all common sense, knowing only that he would destroy the detested man who had no right to be so damned successful, "but it's worthless!"

So that was it.

Michael de Pauw planned to use the loss of Kieft's records to declare Pieter's deed a fraud. Now that he knew, he was no longer compelled to play the part of a grinning simpleton. His smile disappeared as he stood up.

"Thank you for telling me of Michael de Pauw's plans," he said and started to leave the table. He stopped and smiled once again. "You really shouldn't drink, Van Tienhoven. You're a big enough fool when you're sober."

He was gone; and Van Tienhoven's ruddy face began to turn white. That damned de Kuyper had tricked him! And now his anger melted into fear. Good God, what if de Pauw heard what had happened! He'd be furious!

Van Tienhoven looked quickly at the other men to see

their reactions to the last exchange. They were staring at him with interest. He decided to bluff it out. "Well, that de Kuyper's a horse's ass if I ever saw one!" he said with a great laugh. "Caught him out I did, so he leaves in a huff. Drink up, boys, the next round's on me!"

His gruff self-assurance convinced the drink-fogged men to view the situation his way. They raised their glasses and toasted each other.

But as Van Tienhoven drank, his thoughts were of the wrath of Michael de Pauw, and of what could happen because he hadn't been able to keep his big mouth shut.

He had been promised the job of agent for the Harlem lands after they had been taken away from de Kuyper. But that was before this latest incident. If de Pauw heard what had happened, he would probably cut Van Tienhoven out of everything.

Van Tienhoven was upset. It was important for him to be involved with de Pauw, because his present enforced idleness was driving him crazy. He was a man of action who withered when there was nothing to fill his days.

The commandant drank a great deal that night, but try as he did, he could not get drunk. The blissful stupor he sought evaded him, and long after he went to bed, he remained awake with his fears.

The next day the case was heard by the governor.

The city prosecutor, Jan de La Montagne, presented Michael de Pauw's complaint against Pieter. He listed the several charges, the most important being that Pieter was not the legal owner of the lands in question.

When he talked on this point of the complaint, de La Montagne acted as if he were sorry he had to be the bearer of bad news. "There is no question of the integrity of Pieter de Kuyper," he said. "We all know him to be a good and honest man. Therefore, we do not imply in any way that he should be accused or found guilty of fraud."

De La Montagne was very skillful in presenting his arguments. "But can we say the same of Willem Kieft?" he continued. "There was a man capable of fraud! Nay, not capable, but *involved* with fraud! And that man's fraud is the reason we find ourselves in the unhappy state of arguing this complaint against a good man named Pieter de Kuyper."

Pieter awarded a point or two to the prosecutor, even though he realized it meant a point or two against himself.

"Kieft—who thanks be to God is no longer our governor—gave a worthless piece of paper to an Indian. That piece of paper ended up in Pieter de Kuyper's possession. But it is not Pieter de Kuyper's fault. And it is not the fault of the poor, deluded savage. No, it is the fault of Willem Kieft. Would that he could be here to stand before the bar of justice!"

Pieter was again forced to admire the other's skill. It involved no risk at all to wish a man on the stand when the man was dead.

De La Montagne moved closer to the governor, and his voice, while not losing any volume, took on a more confidential tone. "Is it not clear what happened? The Indian gave the deed in good faith to Pieter de Kuyper. De Kuyper, also in good faith, truly believed the land to be his. But good faith is not enough for the law. The law concerns itself only with facts. The facts are: the land in question was bought from the Indians by Peter Minuit; there is no record in the registry files of this land ever being sold again; the Indian certainly gave a deed to Pieter de Kuyper; it was a false deed created by Kieft to gain favor from the Indian; the land, in fact, was never sold to anyone."

Governor Stuyvesant appeared uncomfortable. He gazed around at the men in the crowded room. Most were solid merchants and farmers, and all were landowners. They were intensely interested, because many of them held title to lands bought during the time of Willem Kieft. If Pieter de Kuyper's case was not upheld, there was a chance the legality of their own holdings might be called into question. Nobody was quite sure just how many of the registry records had been lost at sea with Kieft, but they all feared the worst. A great deal was at stake and the courtroom was filled with tension.

The governor was uncomfortable also because he liked Pieter de Kuyper and did not want to render a decision that would harm him. In addition he was not very fond of Michael de Pauw, whom he thought interested in nothing but his own riches.

But Stuyvesant sat as governor and magistrate, well

aware he was required to pass judgment within the cold
and narrow confines of the law. He could not let his
personal likes and dislikes interfere with his decision.

He nodded at Pieter. "Do you wish to present your side
of the argument?"

Pieter rose from his seat and looked over at Michael
de Pauw, who had a smug expression on his face. The old
brigand was dressed in an expensive coat, but, despite his
finery, looked as if he were halfway into his grave. Beside him sat his twenty-year-old son, Robert, the issue of
a late marriage with an ugly woman whose dowry had
brought him an excellent farm and other valuable property.
The wags said de Pauw totally ignored the woman after
the marriage ceremony, but the son and heir who sat
beside him was testimony that on at least one occasion the
couple had exchanged more than words. Robert was a
pallid fellow, good-natured but thoroughly overshadowed
by his domineering father. It was also said he was slow
in the head, but then no one had ever given him the
chance to prove himself.

Pieter couldn't help but think of Young Pieter and how
his relationship with him had been much the same. The
realization that he shared this paternal narrowness with
Michael de Pauw made Pieter shudder. He looked away
from the de Pauws and gave his attention to the governor.

"I wish to file a complaint against Michael de Pauw
for settling people on my lands, thereby causing an invasion of my privacy. Here are the particulars," he said,
placing a sheet of paper on the governor's desk.

De La Montagne was on his feet. "Were these people settled on the lands in question at this court?"

"They were."

"Then I don't understand," de La Montagne said in
mild confusion. "How is it possible for you to file a petition for invasion of privacy on lands you don't own?"

"Has it been proved that I don't own them?"

"That is the function of this court."

"Exactly. But this court has yet to make its decision.
In the meantime I hold a patent on these lands. Michael
de Pauw saw fit to ignore it without benefit of the judgment of this court. I claim he acted outside the law. The

question is—who decides ownership? This court or Michael de Pauw?"

"I believe this court takes precedence over Michael de Pauw," Governor Stuyvesant said dryly.

"Very well," Pieter said. "Since this court has not yet rendered a judgment, I submit Michael de Pauw invaded my privacy."

"That is not the issue," de La Montagne said quickly. He faced Stuyvesant. "This court must rule on Pieter de Kuyper's legal ownership of the land."

"Are you telling me how to run this court?" Stuyvesant asked. There was an ugly glint in his eye.

"Not at all," de La Montagne said smoothly. "I am merely pointing out the facts."

Stuyvesant scowled. "We'll deal with any question of invasion of privacy at some later time. But I agree with the prosecutor that we must return to the question of who owns these lands. Without proof of ownership there can be no trespass."

He turned to Pieter. "Please confine yourself to the issue under discussion."

Pieter bowed. He hadn't won the battle, but he had been able to score a few hits. He couldn't have hoped for any more than that, and knew it.

"Here is a deed," he said, holding up the folded document. He placed it on the desk in front of the governor. "It is a legal deed, valid and signed by Willem Kieft, then governor of this colony. It indicates the land was sold to an Indian named Senadondo, who sold it to me. That the registry contains no record of this deed is an invalid argument, since we all know that a good many records were taken by Governor Kieft and lost at sea. The records are gone, but this deed exists. I petition this court to confirm its legality and also to confirm my rights to the lands described in the deed."

Pieter sat down. The governor nodded at him, but addressed his next remarks to Michael de Pauw. "As petitioner in this case I presume you are prepared to present evidence of your ownership of this land?"

Michael de Pauw rose. He was thin and his fine coat hung loosely from his shoulders. The broad white collar made his neck look chickenlike.

"No, my Lord Governor, I am not."

"No evidence?" Stuyvesant said, and his jaw dropped. "None."

De La Montagne stood. "Our petition is not filed in Michael de Pauw's name, but in the name of the City of New Amsterdam. It is our contention that the city is the proper owner of the lands in question."

"And if this petition is upheld, what are your intentions for the land?"

It was Michael de Pauw who answered. "I'll try to buy some of the land and settle it with people."

"You do not plan to buy it all?"

"No, sir," de Pauw said, with a slight glance in Pieter's direction. "It's far too much land to be owned by one man."

De Pauw had scored heavily, and Pieter knew it. His heart began to grow heavy. The land had been given to him as a sacred trust by Senadondo. And now it seemed he had a good chance of losing it. He knew his emotional promise to a dead Indian would be a useless argument in this court of law and logic.

"Are there any further arguments to be given, or evidence to be submitted?" the governor asked.

No one offered to speak, and the governor ordered a short recess.

The prosecutor started to object to the recess, but the governor cut him off savagely. "Are you attempting—*again*—to tell me how to run my court?"

The prosecutor said nothing. He bowed and was happy to see the angry Stuyvesant leave the court without another word. He wondered what had gotten so deeply under the man's skin to cause such an overreaction.

Jacob Adam de Kuyper had been seated in the rear of the room during the entire proceedings. At his side sat Abraham de Witt and his son, David. As the governor clumped from the room on his wooden leg, they walked outside and were joined by Pieter.

"What do you think?" he asked his friends.

"You did well," Abraham de Witt said.

"You have the only deed. What more can they ask for?" David said.

"Yes, I have the deed," Pieter said to his son-in-law. "Too bad there is no record in the registry."

Abraham became angry. "If they reject your deed

simply because that scoundrel Kieft ran off with a pile of records—why, dammit, what of the other records? I have deeds signed by Kieft. Will I lose my lands as well?"

Samuel de Schuyler was standing near by. "Do you really think that could happen?"

"If it can happen to Pieter why can't it happen to the rest of us?" Abraham said.

De Schuyler shook his head. He too had bought several pieces of property during Kieft's tenure as governor. If none of the records pertaining to the purchases could be found in the registry, might he lose them?

He turned and began arguing vehemently with other men who were standing in a group. Their reactions indicated they were owners of lands acquired during the governorship of Kieft. A decision against Pieter could set a precedent that might bring many of them to the brink of ruin.

"They can't take away your lands," David de Witt said. "Why, it could be the beginning of a rash of foreclosures that could reach out to half the men on the island!"

"The governor will not decide against you," Abraham said, more in hope than belief.

"What do you think?" Pieter asked Jacob Adam.

He answered carefully. "I think the governor is your friend, Father. When he looks at you his face is kindly, but when he looks at de Pauw he scowls."

Abraham de Witt clapped the boy on the back. "Yes, you're right!" He looked at Pieter. "I think Jacob Adam has given us the answer. The governor will decide in your favor."

Pieter was watching his son closely. There was more on the boy's mind. "Is that what you meant?" he asked.

"I said the governor is your friend. If he intended to decide in your favor, I think he would have done it right away. I think he called the recess because he is unhappy he will decide against you."

The older men were startled. Jacob Adam's argument caught them by surprise, and yet, as they thought about it, they began to appreciate its logic.

Pieter put his hand on his son's shoulder. "We'll have to wait and see, won't we?"

The bailiff announced that court had reconvened, and

the men filed inside and took their places. There was a
great deal of rustling and nervous coughing.

Governor Stuyvesant returned to his chair. The bailiff
called for silence, and the governor began to speak as if
he was unhappy with his own words.

"Unless civilized men are governed by a body of laws,
they are no better than savages. And if these civilized
men, even with the most noble of intentions, attempt to
bend some of the laws, it will only be a matter of time before all the laws are bent and the civilized community
returns to a state of savagery."

He paused and let out a great sigh. "The case we have
before us is, perhaps, an unjust one in many ways. Pieter
de Kuyper has a deed that he claims had been registered
according to the law. Unfortunately, the record of this
has been lost beyond recall. This gives us a thorny problem. If we rule that de Kuyper's claim is invalid because
there is no record in the registry, we open the floodgates
to invalidate hundreds of other claims issued during the
Kieft years and of which there are no records.

"However, if we decide in de Kuyper's favor, how
many more men will come forth with deeds they claim to
have received from the Indians? And how many of these
deeds will be false? How will we tell the good from the
bad?

"It is wrong to disallow all claims simply because the
records were lost by Kieft. And it is equally wrong to set
a precedent that will allow dozens of false deeds to pro-
liferate. Therefore . . ."

Every man in the room leaned forward and scarcely
dared to breathe.

"All land patents issued direct by the government to a
settler will be held valid—whether or not there is a record
of the transaction in the registry.

"All land patents obtained from secondary, Indian,
sources will be held *invalid*—unless there is a record in
the registry.

"Therefore, in this matter of Pieter de Kuyper's Indian
deed, of which there is no record in the registry, we declare it to be invalid. The lands belong to the city of New
Amsterdam.

"This hearing is now closed."

The governor stood, looked at Pieter as if to say he

was sorry, and walked from the room, his peg leg pounding the wooden floor with every step.

The decision was hardly a surprise to Pieter: he had been told what would happen by his son. He looked uneasily at Jacob Adam, but tried to show no emotion.

Several men, including Pieter and Michael de Pauw, immediately filed petitions to buy parcels of the land along the Harlem. Pieter was especially anxious to regain ownership of the northwest corner of the island, which held the palisade of the people of Senadondo.

All the petitions were made in vain. Governor Stuyvesant declared a moratorium on the sale of these lands for at least a year. When pressed on the precise meaning of "at least," he was vague and querulous. "At least" was a very flexible term, and Stuyvesant explained the moratorium could last as long as he was governor, which could be ten years or more.

Nobody was pleased by this moratorium, but nothing could be done to make the governor change his mind. Even though he had lost the land, Pieter had the solace of believing that at least part of it would be sold back to him. His promise to Senadondo was not completely broken.

The *Manhatan* once again rested at anchor near the cove at the northern tip of the island. Pieter went ashore with Captain Jorisen and Jacob Adam. He pointed out the place where, as a boy, he had first met Senadondo.

Pieter had come here to tell the present chief, Stone Eagle, about the problem with the deed to these lands. There was nothing he could do about it, but he wanted the news to come from him personally.

At the village they were told that Stone Eagle was out with a party of bird hunters.

"It is not far," a brave said, and Pieter decided they should go out to meet the chief.

They set out in a southeasterly direction and after a mile saw the hunters. Bird hunting was not the most vital of activities to the Indians: there were still more than enough four-legged game animals on the island and in the surrounding areas. But the Indians enjoyed the sport. They took pigeon, partridge, woodcock, pheasant, and quail; and in the marshlands there was an abundance of curlew, plover, and snipe. The birds were not the easiest game in the world to catch, but they were among the most delicious.

Without great concern Stone Eagle watched the white men approach. He only wondered what new indignity they planned to thrust upon his people. Therefore he was pleased when he spotted Pieter among them and learned the neighborly reason for his visit. They returned to the village, where they sat around the chief's fire enjoying food and drink. A pipe of peace was brought out and smoked. There was a genuine friendship between Pieter and the chief.

When the hour of departure came, Stone Eagle walked with his guests to where the longboat rested on the narrow strip of rust-colored sand.

"You are a friend," Stone Eagle said. Pieter mumbled his thanks and hoped his visit would salve the hurt he felt for betraying these people of the forest, however unwillingly.

The Indian turned to Jacob Adam and looked him over from head to toe. The boy was no less frank in his study of the tall chief.

"You must be a good son," Stone Eagle counseled him, "so you will make a good man like your father."

Looking at both the chief and Jacob Adam in profile, Pieter was startled. There was a resemblance between them despite the great difference of size: in the strong chin, the straight forehead, the proud nose—but most of all in the way they held themselves, the way they stared with unblinking eyes and closed, inscrutable expressions. You could stare at this pair for an hour, he thought, and never have the slightest idea what they were thinking.

Even their coloring was similar. Stone Eagle was light-skinned for an Indian, and Jacob Adam had always been a shade darker than the other Dutch children.

It was uncanny, Pieter thought, and his skin crawled at the idea of his son being so much like the tall savage.

"Will you be such a man?" Stone Eagle asked.

"I will do what has to be done," Jacob Adam replied quietly.

"Sometimes men are called upon to do things that are beyond them," Stone Eagle said.

Jacob Adam said nothing. There was a wordless communication between the two that told the chief all he needed to know.

"And there are some men whom nothing is beyond," the chief concluded.

Jacob Adam knew he would be one of these men, and Stone Eagle shared the thought. Of what use were words?

The longboat set out into the water, and the sailors bent their backs as they rowed out to the anchored *Manhatan*. Before they were aboard, Captain Jorisen was barking commands and the process of getting underway was begun.

Pieter stood at the railing, his son at his side, looking back at the motionless figure on the shore. The Indian stood like a tree, his face as steady and quiet as his body.

Pieter was deeply troubled. He could not explain his feeling, but he would be happier if his son and Stone Eagle never met again. He patted Jacob Adam on the shoulder and retired to the master's cabin.

The son watched Stone Eagle become smaller as the *Manhatan* caught the tide and moved downriver. They rounded a bend and the lone figure was lost from sight.

Stone Eagle had reached out and touched his soul. It was the first time this had ever happened—a deeply moving, mystical experience. It did not trouble Jacob Adam, or lead him to questioning. It had happened and he accepted it. The mysteries of the world are not always to be solved.

Anne de Kuyper de Witt decided it was time her father remarried. Christiana had been dead for many years, and enough reverence had been paid her memory.

"It will be good for him to have a wife," she said to her husband.

"Maybe he's happy the way he is," David suggested.

"Nonsense," Anne said, dismissing the idea that a single man could be content. Especially an older single man who had once been married.

Early deaths were not uncommon in New Netherland, and most widows and widowers remarried. It was a sensible solution, accepted by society and church. Life was difficult enough for a married couple, doubly so for one alone. Her father, of course, was hardly alone in the world. He was a man of substance, with Zilla, three servants and a son living in his house. He also had a married daughter and a grandchild. Still it would be best if he had a wife, Anne thought with the certainty of one who decides what is best for another. She proceeded to make a thorough survey of all the available females who by age, temperament, and situation might make a good wife for her father.

Anne settled on the Widow Lysbeth Godyn, because the woman was known to be a generous supporter of any charity and one who would weep when a drayman whipped his horse to increase his pace. These were admirable qualities, to be sure, but Anne didn't look beyond them to decide if the woman was exactly what Pieter would choose for a wife.

Anne paid a social call on the Widow Godyn.

The good widow was in her early forties, her chubby face and extremely full figure attesting to her robust health. Her husband had been a successful trader who had died the year before, and it was well known that he had left his wife in handsome circumstances. The woman would bring a cheerful disposition, two grown sons, no obvious problems, and a handsome dowry to a new husband. Anne was delighted with her choice.

Interesting the widow in the match was no problem. She was most anxious to remarry, and the thought of being the new wife of handsome and distinguished Pieter de Kuyper fairly took her breath away. The moment she divined why Anne had called on her, she said quickly, "Oh, my dear, you and your father must come to dinner this Sunday. Oh, and I suppose it would be nice if you brought your husband."

"I'm not going," Pieter said when his daughter informed him of the invitation.

"Why not?"

"Because I know what you're up to."

"I'm not up to anything."

"Ha!" Pieter said, extremely pleased that his son-in-law had tipped him off about what was on his daughter's mind. "Forget it. I'm not going."

"Yes you are," Anne said. "I've already accepted the invitation."

"You have no right to speak for me."

"It's only a Sunday dinner."

"I told you I wasn't going."

Anne recognized his determined tone and the stubborn jut of his jaw. She quickly changed her method of persuasion.

"I hardly ever ask you for anything," she said with a slight but audible sniffle. She sat down in a chair with her back toward him. "And now I ask something *for your own good,* and you want to make me look like a fool."

"You're trying to marry me off."

"It's only a dinner invitation," she insisted, forcing him to continue the argument on her grounds.

"Now, Anne, you know I wouldn't—"

"The Widow Godyn didn't even want to do this. I practically had to force her."

"But—"

"Don't worry about my feelings; after all, I'm only your daughter. Your *only* daughter."

Pieter sighed and bowed to the inevitable. "Very well. But only for dinner, and only this one time."

Anne's face was wreathed in a smile as she came over and kissed him on the top of his head. "Of course, Father, you know how careful I am never to interfere with your privacy."

Pieter looked over at his son-in-law, and they exchanged knowing smiles.

Sunday came, and after church services Anne led her father and husband to the Widow Godyn's house on Marcktveldt Street. As they approached the door, Pieter looked beseechingly at his daughter. "Can't we do this another time?"

Anne didn't bother to answer. She held him firmly by the arm while David used the heavy door knocker to announce their arrival.

Lysbeth Godyn bubbled over with goodwill, joy, and ample flesh as she showed them into the house. Within seconds the men had large tumblers of good West Indian rum in their hands, and Pieter took full advantage of his portion. Before the widow had a chance to sit down, he was holding out his tumbler for a second draft of the fiery liquid.

"It's so good of you to spend a few hours with a lonely widow," Lysbeth tittered and looked coquettishly at

Pieter. "I have so much time on my hands," she added with a sigh.

"I hardly have a free moment myself," he said, hoping to forestall any further implicit invitations she might extend.

"I just adore seeing a man keeping as busy as a bee," the widow said, choosing to misinterpret his remark. "This place hasn't seemed like a home since—*sniff*—Henryk—*sniff*—passed away—*sniff*—"

"He must have been a wonderful man," Anne said, playing the good guest.

The widow's face burst into a big smile. "But we mustn't talk about the past, must we?" she said, with a cheeriness so sudden and emphatic that it startled her guests. "The present and the future are the only things that count."

Pieter managed a feeble smile toward the widow, who had directed this last remark at him.

The conversation continued along similar lines for half an hour, and then the widow announced it was time to sit down at the table for dinner.

"You must try this . . . and make sure you get enough of this . . . and, oh, I can't wait to see your face when you taste this . . ." These and similar remarks flowed from the widow as she and the servant girl brought platter after steaming platter to the low table. The amount of food was staggering, and Pieter wondered if they would live through the end of the meal. He placed portions of each dish on his trencher, but it wasn't enough to satisfy the widow, who insisted he take more of everything. He was about to resist, but a look from his daughter convinced him it wasn't worth an argument. The one container he didn't mind refilling was the tumbler of rum, which was now augmented by a large goblet filled with a good Madeira. The servant girl refilled both drinking cups every time they were empty, and in this manner Pieter managed to make it through dinner, despite the fact that the widow had twice replenished his trencher, each serving being as much as he would have taken for his usual meal.

God Almighty! he thought, no wonder she's so fat! She stuffs the food away as if she were starving. Indeed, the widow's chubbiness was not surprising to anyone who had been privileged to dine with her. Spoonful after spoonful of vegetables disappeared into her mouth, interrupted only when she cut off another chunk of meat or some of the good dark bread of which there were four loaves on the table. One for each of us, Pieter thought sourly.

The abundant meal was finally over, and Pieter wanted nothing more than to take a walk to relax his stomach muscles. First, however, the widow insisted they all have chunks of a thick fruit pie and cups of scalding-hot coffee. Into each huge mug the widow placed thick slices of sugar, which she shaved off a nine-pound sugar loaf.

Pieter gave the sugared coffee a good lacing from the rum bottle that the servant girl had thoughtfully left on the table.

The rum and Madeira he had consumed since entering the house were beginning to take effect. He felt mellow, even happy. The constant babbling of the widow bothered him hardly at all.

David de Witt was having a wonderful time. How his wife had ever imagined her father would find Lysbeth Godyn attractive confounded him. Christiana de Kuyper had been slender and elegant, a quiet beauty. The good Widow Godyn was a hausfrau, a fat, happy, brainless hausfrau. There were men who liked the type, but David could see his father-in-law was not one of them. The situation was so ludicrous he had to keep reminding himself not to laugh out loud. Anne noticed the constant smile on his face, realized the reason for it, and was annoyed.

"Having a good time?" she asked, with a forced smile.

"Very good," David said innocently.

"I'm happy for you."

"Maybe your father would like some more pie," he said, taking another mouthful. "It's not every day he gets to eat like this."

Lysbeth Godyn was totally unaware of these asides as all her considerable attentions were devoted to Pieter.

"A wonderful meal," Anne said, directing a meaningful look toward her father.

Heeding the signal, Pieter said, "Oh yes, yes, best meal I've eaten in a long time."

"We eat like this every day," the widow said in triumph, and looking at her, Pieter could well believe it.

"The smoked meats are delicious," Anne said.

"We do it ourselves, in the attic by the chimney," the widow said, nodding her head in joy. "Bacon, sausage, ham, turkey, pheasant—everything."

"Isn't that interesting," Anne said to her father. She turned back to the widow. "These bachelors . . . they hardly keep a bite of food in their houses."

The look she received from her father made her smile. How miserable he was! It served him right for drinking so much. And for not appreciating all she was doing for him. An evil thought came to her mind. "Why, do you know," she said in great seriousness to the widow, "sometimes my father gets so hungry, he has to come to my house for a good meal."

At that moment, Pieter would have liked to break a heavy wooden trencher over his daughter's head. The widow looked at him in feigned horror. It was the opening she had been waiting for. "My poor man, you must never let yourself go hungry again! Anytime you need a good meal you must come to me!"

"But . . ."

She was determined. "Now promise Lysbeth you'll remember." She looked over at Anne and winked. "I'll fatten him up," she said gaily. And then back to Pieter. "You don't have to let me know. Just come to the house."

"Oh, no," Pieter protested, sensing an escape, "that would be too much bother."

"But it's no bother," the widow said, appalled that he might even consider such a thing, "no bother at all."

"You mightn't have enough extra food," he said, grasping at any straw.

She waddled quickly around the table, and before Pieter knew what was happening she was dragging him by the arm toward the cellar door. "Come, you must see how well stocked we are. How could you even *think* you could be a bother?"

She whisked him through the door and down the stairs. That he was able to keep his footing despite the quantities of rum and Madeira he had drunk was testimony to the fact that his body was in good shape.

In the cellar the widow pulled him about, pointing out the treasures to be found. It was, he had to admit, a vast hoard of edibles. There were large wooden bins of potatoes, pecks of turnips, mounds of apples, a mountain of parsnips, a lifetime supply of beets. There it was, filling the cellar, threatening to burst through the wooden planks of the floor above: row upon row, stack upon stack, pile upon pile of food. Pieter's proud hostess showed him barrels of salted pork, tubs of ham salted in brine, caskets of salted deer meat, cords of cured bacon ends, hogsheads of corned beef; it went on and on—kegs of pickled pig's feet, tubs of souse, tonnekins of salt shad and mackerel, firkins of butter, kilderkins of lard. If one got thirsty there were pipes of Madeira, kegs of rum and gin, vats of crab-apple cider, barrels of maple-sugar beer.

Pieter emerged from the cellar dazed. Never in his life had he seen so much food in one place. He reached for his tumbler and downed another four ounces of rum to quiet his nerves.

"Henryk—*sniff*—my late husband—*sniff*—was a trader in foodstuffs," she explained. "We always made sure we had a good supply on hand."

Somehow Pieter made it through the next hour. He was helped considerably by more glasses of rum and hard cider. He hardly remembered leaving the widow's house. The only thought that stuck in his mind was that she had deliberately brushed against him as they were leaving. No, not brushed, *crushed* against him. That large chest had pushed against him as if she meant to squeeze the breath of life from his body, her great white teeth smiling so close to his ear he was afraid she might get hungry suddenly and bite it off.

At last they were in the street. He gulped the fresh air as his daughter and son-in-law walked him back to his house. His head reeled, and he knew that if he didn't make it to his bed within the next few moments he would not make it there on his own two feet. Without a word he plunged through the open door, ignored the inquisitive Zilla, staggered up the stairs, and stumbled into his room. As he fell onto the soft down quilt he was already blissfully asleep.

Zilla looked at the young couple as if to ask, "What's the matter with him?" Anne giggled and led her husband back into the street.

"Do you think Father enjoyed himself?" Anne asked, tongue in cheek.

"Definitely," David said, with an innocent look on his face. "I think he'd like to do it again next Sunday."

"It wasn't such a good idea, was it?"

"You could say that."

"Maybe Lysbeth is the wrong person," Anne said. "Maybe there's someone else . . ."

"Would you really like to please your father?"

"Why do you think I went to all this trouble?"

"If you really want to please him, I think you'd better drop the whole idea."

Anne made a sour face; then it was banished by a smile. "It really was a funny day."

"The look on Pieter's face when . . ." But David burst into laughter before he could finish the sentence. Anne looked at him, and then she too began laughing. By the time they reached home, they were holding onto each other to keep from falling.

A year passed, and something happened that caused Pieter, and everyone else, to forget about such things as bountiful meals and marriage.

There had been a series of storms in the previous months, but they were not unusual. The low thunderheads rolled in from the sea. Claps of thunder roared through the heavens and flashes of lightning streaked down to char tree trunks, at times causing fires that were soon quenched by the rains. The people of New Amsterdam went about their business. They had seen storms before; no doubt they would see many more in their lifetimes. Besides, rain was good for the fields, and it brought a clean, fresh smell to the town. When the rains came, many of the women rushed to hang out their dirty laundry so it would get a good soaking.

And then a new storm came.

At first it seemed no different from the others. The wind built up, and men clung to their hats lest they be carried away. Women called their children indoors. They came with reluctance, because they knew one of life's great joys was to run through the wet fields, the rain pelting down on their heads, soaking their clothes, making them feel free and part of nature.

The clouds came, great angry swirls, growing darker and darker, crowding one another as if they were jealous of their space, growing thicker and thicker until the sun was a memory. And now the rains fell. They did not seem any heavier or any wetter than the rains of the previous storms.

The difference was the winds.

As with the other storms, the winds started as gentle puffs and then grew in steadiness and intensity. But the winds of the new storm did not decline as usual. They grew stronger and bolder until it was not enough for a man to hold onto his hat to keep it from blowing away; it was necessary for him to cling to some well-anchored object before the winds blew *him* away.

They swooped from the sky, these winds, immensely powerful, howling across the waters of the Upper Bay, churning them, picking up the tops of waves and mixing them with the falling rain until it was impossible to tell seawater from rainwater. The space beneath the low clouds became an impenetrable gray, filled with water that blew in every direction including up. It was a mad dance of wind and water.

The whitecaps, which had risen with the wind, began to disappear. So strong were the winds that they sliced the frothing white water from the darker water beneath, and the whitecaps became part of the maelstrom, leaving the waters beneath to brood sullenly.

The winds uprooted trees on both sides of the Narrows, sending them crashing into the water like thrown spears.

The winds crashed down with stupefying force on the communities of Breuckelen and Flatbush, tearing up fences, lifting roofs off farmhouses, snatching bushes from the earth as if they were rootless tumbleweed. The tall, slender silos fell as if they were pins in a giant's game of Bowls. A barn creaked and groaned; its roof disappeared in a gasp of wind; the hens and roosters squawked and flew for the first time in their lives as they were sucked into the air and carried off into the darkness. The heavier animals—sheep and cows and horses and pigs—dug their feet into the ground and tried to hold their own, not always with success. A sheep would be on the ground one second and the next he would be gone, and even a man who had been looking at the very spot could not say he had seen the sheep disappear.

These were the winds that came from the sea, howled

across Long Island, and then leaped across the bay and descended with paralyzing force on New Amsterdam.

The fort, with its thick stone walls, shuddered and trembled in the face of this satanic power that struck head-on at first, and then wormed and wiggled its way into every crevice and crack, like a thief in the night. Where the crevice or crack showed weakness, the winds attacked with greater force until walls that could withstand cannon shot began to splinter and split in shrieks of agony.

The roofs of houses began to disappear, and the people huddled in the cellars, their heads buried beneath blankets, even the irreligious among them closing their eyes in prayer.

Emmanuel de Landis's bouwerie at the north edge of the town was hit particularly hard. His farm lay at the end of a series of small hills that created a funnel in which the winds were squeezed together, their velocity increasing as they raced down the tube until they burst out at the other end at a speed that defied imagination. The de Landis farm was leveled—every fence, every building including the house, the barn, the chicken coop, the hog pen, and even the creamery, which was made of heavy stones piled one on top of the other. The animals were driven to the ground and killed, or else they disappeared into the sky, their bodies tossed about as if they were feathers, their lungs crushed to the bursting point by the smothering air. Emmanuel de Landis, a God-fearing, churchgoing man, and his wife and five children simply disappeared as if they had never existed; no trace of them was ever found.

Anne de Witt had taken her child, Emilie, to Pieter's house on the Broad Way. Zilla hid her in a snug corner of the cellar where she and the other servants tried to escape from the wrath of the storm.

Worried about David, Anne tried to get back to her own house. As she rounded the corner onto Broad Street, a heavy gust grabbed her and knocked her to the ground. It rolled her over several times, shifting just before it would have swept her into the canal. She could see her house down the street and tried to crawl toward it, but the lashings of the wind were sapping her strength. She crawled forward until she reached a small tree. Anne held onto the trunk for her life. The wind stung and bit and she started to cry, not out of fear, but out of frustration at being able to see her goal and not being able to make it.

The door of the house opened, and David peered out and saw his wife. "Anne!" he cried and stepped immediately into the street, bending low to avoid being dashed against the walls of his own home.

Dirt was flying through the air, making it difficult to see, but Anne caught a glimpse of her husband coming toward her. "Go back! Go back!" she tried to shout, but the wind forced itself into her mouth and the words came out in a weak garble.

David didn't hear her, but it wouldn't have made any difference. His wife was in trouble and he was going to her rescue. He kept his head lowered and his body crouched as he came down the street. He managed to keep his footing to the last moment—and then a vicious gust knocked him to the ground at his wife's feet. She screamed as she realized he was unconscious.

It was a fearful predicament. She could not leave her husband, but neither could she remain in the street with him. A flying bit of debris could crack her skull or David's at any moment. There was only one thing to do—get to the house and take David with her.

She inched away from the tree, crawling on hands and knees, dragging the deadweight of David . . . inch by inch . . . finally a foot . . . and then another . . . it was painful, so painful . . . And then she stopped and realized she had moved only about six feet and her strength was gone . . . she couldn't go any farther . . . there was no use in trying . . . the terrible winds would pounce on them and consume them . . . it was over, all over. . . .

"Go!" a voice shouted in her ear. "Go on!"

She looked up blankly at the face of Jacob Adam. "Go!" he shouted again. "I'll take care of David!"

She understood as she watched her younger brother grab David's body and start pulling it toward the house. She sobbed in thanks and began to crawl after them. The wind howled and plucked at them, but then there was a momentary lull in the gale and Jacob Adam managed to get David to the house. He opened the door, pushed David inside, and went back to his sister. He put his arm around her shoulder and got her to the house. Just in time: an explosive blast of wind hit the street, whipping the waters of the canal to froth, tearing down the wooden railing that had been built to keep people from falling into the old creek.

Anne's last look at the street included a view of the tree she had been holding. As she watched, the proud little elm was torn out of the ground by its roots and flung across the street, where it bounced against a house. And then an updraft caught it and the tree disappeared over the roofs of the buildings.

Jacob Adam slammed the door. "The cellar," he shouted above the din. The house seemed alive with groans and screeches as the walls and timbers uttered protests against the battering they were receiving. "We must get down to the cellar!"

Jacob Adam managed to carry David down the stairs. Anne followed, stumbling over the third step from the bottom and falling, an accident that went almost unnoticed after the ordeal she had been through in the street. David was propped up against the wall.

Jacob Adam looked at his sister. She tried to open her lips to thank him, but hadn't the strength. She could do nothing but sit and listen to the noises of the storm as bit by bit it tore the house apart over their heads.

The windmill owned jointly by Pieter and Abraham de Witt came apart in stages. The first parts to go were the sails—heavy canvas stretched over thick lengths of wood, each almost forty feet and weighing several hundred pounds. The fingers of the wind effortlessly tore them away and sent them flying toward the river. The roof went next. Then a crack in the sturdy wall widened and a section of bricks collapsed. The winds raced through the opening and the windmill was ravaged from inside and out. With an almost audible sigh amid the din of the storm, it crashed into rubble. Many of the bricks didn't reach the ground but were hurled by the winds toward other structures that dared to test their strength.

When the storm arrived Pieter was at the governor's house in the fort, attending a meeting of the trade commission, on which he served as a member without pay. The walls of the fort were the best defense the town had against the ungodly wind. They broke much of the force

before it hit the governor's house. The house itself was
built of brick and stone, and it had the strength to defy
the invisible forces that tore and pounded at its door.
Indeed, a man could sit comfortably inside and not notice
the storm—provided he was deaf and could not hear
the shrieking that was so loud it made conversation
inpossible between two men a few feet apart; and provided he did not look out the window to see the flying
debris; and provided his fireplace was not burning, for
the winds would blow the smoke back down the chimney,
filling the room with soot and fumes.

Pieter found a place near the window that faced away
from the wind. He watched with fascination and horror
as a cart sailed past and smashed to kindling against a
wall. His horror increased when the donkey that had been
pulling the cart appeared, still wearing torn traces of har-
ness. The donkey was knocked to the ground and rolled
over until the stubborn animal dug his hooves into the
dirt. With more courage than sense the donkey struggled
to his feet, only to be knocked down and rolled over
again. Finally the winds knocked him against a wall.
The tenacious beast got to his feet again, but this time
his right flank was braced against the wall. It was all the
support he needed to fight the winds. Pieter cheered the
brave animal.

Something hit the roof of the governor's house with a
great clatter, and then fell down into the street in front
of Pieter's window. He recoiled when he realized it was
a tangle of spars and rigging from a ship. A bit of canvas
sail was caught in the middle of the tangle, and it flapped
frantically as if it were trying to escape.

The ships!

Now the winds were destroying the ships! What of his
own ship? The *Manhatan?* He did not stop to think of
what he was doing; he knew only that he had to see his
ship. Nothing mattered as much as seeing if the proud
lady was still afloat at her anchorage.

He reached the door and tore it open. Even though
the door stood in the lee of the building and received
only a fraction of the force of the winds, he was shoved
backward and the strength of the gust took away his
breath.

"De Kuyper!" a voice shouted.

Pieter looked over his shoulder as the governor came up to his side. "What the hell are you doing?"

"I must see my ship."

"Are you mad? Close that door!" the governor shouted. "A man could get killed out there!"

The governor's words came as if they were a cue in a stage play.

No sooner had he spoken than they saw Jan Van Tienhoven. The ex-commandant was dressed in his uniform and wearing his sword. He came toward them from the direction of Kock's Tavern. The winds pressed against him and he struggled and swayed, not only from the buffeting he was taking, but also from drunkenness.

The governor and Pieter watched as Van Tienhoven miraculously remained on his feet while he fought his way toward the house. He came within thirty feet, and then an object flashed down from the sky and knocked him as flat as if he had been a blade of grass.

Pieter stared at the thing that had hit the man. "My God!" he cried. "That's a cannon cradle!"

The governor looked at the solid chunk of wood whose rounded curves had once held the barrel of a cannon. "A wind mighty enough to wreck a cannon," he whispered in awe, and although he whispered, Pieter heard every word.

A miracle! Van Tienhoven was not dead. The cannon cradle was heavy enough to have felled an ox, but the man was struggling to his feet! The horrified watchers could not see his features, because blood flowed across his face from a gash that started on the top of his head and came halfway down his forehead. He managed to take several steps, and then a mighty gust blew down over the walls and Van Tienhoven was swept upward into the air. As his body cleared the far wall it began to twist and tumble, and then it was lost in the gray swirl. The governor and Pieter knew they had seen the last of Jan Van Tienhoven, ex-commandant of the fort, a man for whom they had had little use in life, but for whose soul they now uttered silent prayers.

Pieter stepped out through the door again and for an instant thought he would be swept away. But he kept his back against the wall and began to inch his way along.

"Come back, you damn fool!" Stuyvesant shouted,

taking a step outside. Immediately his head and shoulders became as soaked as Pieter's.

"I must see my ship!" Pieter shouted back.

"You'll be killed!"

Pieter ignored the warning and continued on his way, hugging the wall to avoid the brunt of the wind. He came to the end of the building and stopped. He decided a quick run would be the best way to bridge the gap between the corner of the building and the wall of the fort, which was some fifty feet from the back of the house.

He figured the house to be about forty feet deep. Adding that to the fifty feet of garden between the house and the wall, he knew he would have to cross about ninety feet of open ground. It was that or returning to the house. He took several big gulps of air, filled his lungs a final time, and plunged around the side of the building.

It was like nothing he had ever experienced.

The winds tore at him, snatched at him, pulled and clubbed him with an angry fury. He was fortunate to have filled his lungs with air, because the wind on his face was so strong that it would have been impossible to breathe. He ran in a crouched position with his arms over his head. Several times he was struck by flying objects, but they were small and neither hurt him nor slowed him down. He had covered half the distance when a gust knocked him to his knees. He struggled to his feet and began to run again. Something smacked into his hand, and the pain made him give thanks that it had not struck his head.

He had thirty feet more to go . . . twenty . . . ten . . . and his feet were whipped out from under him and he was thrown sideways. He struck the ground, and his remorseless pursuer rolled him over and over until he finally managed to brace his arms and legs and bring himself to a stop. He kept his face near the ground and let the air out of his tortured lungs. He took another breath and his nostrils burned with a mixture of air, salt, and fine dust. He came to his feet and the winds again singled him out, but this time they were not strong enough to knock him down. The winds beat on his body, tore at his face and throat, and punished him for daring to defy them. He ran forward, his only thought the left leg, the right leg,

the left leg, the right leg again . . . pumping, driving,
straining while his muscles screamed in agony.

He realized he should have come to the wall. But he
had not.

He kept his hands before his face and made a small
opening between two fingers. He squinted ahead. There
was no wall. He looked to the left and saw the side of the
governor's house. He looked to the right and saw the wall.
It was almost sixty feet away. When he had been knocked
off his feet and tossed, it had confused his sense of direction. Good God! He had been running the wrong way.

There was nothing else to do but start for the wall
again. Objects continued to fly through the air, and they
struck him as he ran. But this time he was not knocked
down. He felt the wind go slack as he suddenly ran into
the wall and almost fell over backward.

In the lee of the wall he was protected. The wind struck
the top and plunged down over it at an even greater
speed, but it did not drop straight down; rather, it came
at a slight angle, just enough to create a small area of
relative calm at the foot of the wall.

The wall, however, had been only his first objective.
Now he had to climb the stone steps to the top, get himself to a gunport, and brace himself before he would be
able to look upon his ship in the bay.

The steps caused little trouble, since they enjoyed the
protection of the wall except at the very top. The winds
at the top almost managed to pitch him off the wall, but
he dropped to the ground and squirmed his way to the
stone barricade at the front of the wall. He came to a
gunport, but there was no gun. Torn away from its restraining chains, it sat on the ground a few feet away,
looking like a beached whale.

Now Pieter was beneath the opening of the gunport.
All he had to do to look upon the bay was to poke his
head up. But he had been taught a reverence for these
winds, and it took several moments for him to ready himself to take the brunt of their full force. He faced the
gunport and took hold of the remaining links of chain
embedded in stone on either side of the opening. Holding
onto the chains as tightly as possible, he raised himself
up and peered through the open port.

If he had thought the winds strong before, he now knew
he had felt only their shadows.

A house no longer protected him, nor did a wall offer shelter. Now there were only the winds, and they struck him in the face and would have hurled him backward had not his grip on the chains been so strong. They pulled out bits of his hair and ripped the collar from his shirt. His nose seemed to flatten against his face, and the howling in his ears almost deafened him. His eyelids drooped under the force and he had to fight to keep them open.

And then he looked at the scene on the waters of the bay and forgot about himself.

The sea was chaos. Water swirled and blew in all directions—up, down, to the left, to the right—and it was difficult to define the limits of the sea. Before the storm there had been twenty ships moored in the harbor, a half-dozen more berthed at the quay. Now there were no ships at the quay and only three afloat. The others had either disappeared completely or survived as skeletons, unholy messes of masts, spars, booms, planks, and bottoms that were being churned together and disintegrated.

The *Manhatan* was one of the ships still afloat. No longer the sleek, proud mistress of the Upper Bay, she now looked more like a tortured animal screaming in her death throes. Her decks were littered with a tangle of broken masts, barrels, and deck planking; her bowsprit was gone, and the rigging from the foremast was draped over the bow, worn like a veil to cover her ashamed face. Whipped by the winds, the heavy shackles and cleats beat a tattoo on her sides, gouging her handsome finish. The railing along her port side was gone and only half remained on the starboard. The heavy storm anchor somehow hand managed to hold, and even in the midst of her destruction the *Manhatan* pointed her bow straight into the face of the winds.

As Pieter watched, another mighty gust, a wind from the black tunnels of Hades, pounced on the *Manhatan* and snapped her fore anchor cable. Immediately the harried ship began veering to starboard, swinging until her bow was parallel to the shore and one flank exposed to the nonexistent mercies of the winds. As if sensing they were close to another kill, the winds and the seas wasted no time. They combined to push the ship with great force until she crashed lengthwise against the quay. It seemed impossible she could survive the impact, but she was

stoutly built and reeled back from the quay as if in a
drunken haze, though still in one piece. Now the sea
dragged her back and pulled her on top of the next wave.
Once again the *Manhatan* was hurled against the quay.
This happened five times before she gave up the ghost.
The keel, the very backbone of the ship, snapped, and
the decks buckled and began twisting at crazy angles.

Pieter could hardly believe his eyes as he watched two
figures emerge from a pile of tangled rigging. The men
fought and clawed their way through the mess as if it
were a hostile jungle. One of them tried to crawl under a
broken boom, but the ship lurched and the boom split
again, the lower part crashing down on top of the man.
He was knocked unconscious to the deck.

"Get up! Get up!" Pieter shouted into the wind, although he knew it was impossible for the man to hear
him. As if in answer to his shout, the other man happened
to look back and saw his unconscious shipmate.

The man was naked to the waist. His skin was black.
There could be no mistaking that giant form—Manuel.

The black started back for the other man, and Pieter,
at this point hardly aware of what he was doing, began
screaming for Manuel to save himself.

Manuel picked up the other man and started back to
the side of the ship.

Despite the pressure that kept trying to close his eyelids, Pieter could see the unconscious man's face. It was
Lars Jorisen, his blond hair in stark contrast against Manuel's black skin.

Manuel bulled his way across the ship, away from the
side that was being pounded to pieces against the quay.
To jump from the ship on the shore side was impossible
—a man would be crushed between the hull and the
quay. To jump from the other side was to plunge into the
sea and take one's chances. As small as these chances
were, there was no alternative.

Pieter decided to go down to the beach to help Manuel.
He didn't know what he could do, but he knew he had to
do something. He couldn't stand by and watch two of his
oldest companions lose their lives.

He was lucky. The mighty gust that had hurled the
Manhatan against the quay and broken her back seemed
to have been the storm's final fury. The winds, while still

harrowing, began to diminish. They were a threat, but a lesser one.

Pieter ran along the top of the wall toward the steps that descended to a portal that went through the walls and would give him access to the beach. He ran at top speed as the wind bit into him. Flying debris gouged his skin, but all this was nothing to a man who had faced into the mightiest gusts and lived. As he came to the head of the steps he looked at the *Manhatan* in time to see Manuel, the unconscious Lars Jorisen in his arms, timing his leap to coincide with the arrival of a wave that carried the ship back toward the quay. It was the correct thing to do. As the *Manhatan* went in one direction, Manuel and his burden went the other way, minimizing the chances of being crushed beneath the ship.

Pieter saw no more as he dashed down the steps and came to the portal. The door was off its hinges, as was the one on the outer side. Pieter made his way through the passage and had to step over the body of one of the garrison soldiers. The man must have been standing in the passage when the door blew off and hit him. The heavy oak door weighed three hundred pounds, and the part of the body that lay beneath it had been crushed to an unrecognizable mixture of bone and flesh.

Pieter reached the beach and the winds howled about him, but they were even more diminished than when he had made his run along the top of the wall. As quickly as the mighty storm had risen it seemed to be passing, moving on to seek new victims.

Pieter stood at the edge of the water and the frantic waves snapped and snarled at his feet. He looked for the two men, to the left, to the right; but there was no sign of them. And then a wave brought them to its crest and he saw them—far out from the beach. The wind was blowing toward the shore, but the tide was pulling them out into the bay. Manuel was handicapped because the burden of Jorisen forced him to swim with only one arm. To add to his troubles, the wind flicked the water into angry splashes that came from all directions, so that no matter which way he faced, water flew into his eyes and nose, blinding and choking him as he tried to swim toward the shore.

It was an unequal struggle. Pieter knew the strength of

his black harpooner was twice that of a normal man, but even so it was finite strength. The strength possessed by the winds and the waters approached the infinite. No matter what Manuel did, it was only a matter of time before he lost the battle and slipped beneath the dark waters, fodder for the animals who lived on the floor of the bay. Of course, it might have been possible to save himself if he shed the unconscious Jorisen. Pieter knew that it would never occur to Manuel to abandon his friend.

It was up to him to save them both.

But how? He looked frantically along the beach. But what was he looking for? he asked himself. A rope? No, it would be impossible for him to throw a rope. Seventy or eighty yards separated him from the men in the water, and the gap was widening with every second. And then he saw it.

A small dinghy had broken loose from its place on one of the sunken ships. It had been tossed ashore and now lay on the pebbly beach with its bottom turned to the sky. Pieter quickly overturned it. Oars were wedged beneath the slats that served as seats.

He wasted no time in getting the dinghy into the water. As he began rowing, the bow lifted and then dipped down as it passed an incoming wave. Pieter rowed with every ounce of strength in his body. Another wave crested and the dinghy rose, not as sharply as before, then leveled out and slid down the back of the wave. Now there was nothing between Pieter and the two men except open water.

But this was open water only in a technical sense. It splashed and hammered at the dinghy's sides, spinning it, turning it, twisting it, and half of Pieter's effort was spent in keeping the boat on course toward the two men. If only Manuel did not weaken. If only he could hold on until the dinghy arrived.

As Pieter rowed he was witness to a terrible sight. The *Manhatan,* her spine broken in several places, her starboard side crushed to firewood, her masts down and the spars being tossed about with such force they were punching holes through the decks, her rigging wound about the bodies of sailors—whether dead or alive it was hard to tell, but certainly soon-to-be-dead because they could never free themselves—the poor *Manhatan* was smashed once more into the quay. The force of this blow ripped her from bow to stern and she broke up, no longer a ship, no longer even a hulk, but a collection of driftwood debris. As the undertow dragged her back to the sea, the front third broke away. The rest filled with water and quickly sank, leaving a boiling, bubbling froth as the air escaped through the water with a loud *whoosh*. The suction created a vacuum, and a whirlpool began to form in the water. Pieter rowed even harder as its swirling tentacles greedily reached out toward him.

He came closer and closer to his goal. Manuel stopped his futile attempts at swimming and conserved his strength by treading water. Pieter put his back into the task, almost afraid he was going to pull his arms from their sockets. But there was an end to his pain as the boat came close enough for Manuel to reach out and close his fingers around the narrow gunwale.

"Lord! I was never so happy to see a man!" Manuel said.

Without a word, Pieter reached out and grabbed Jorisen's coat. Manuel lifted the Dane with one arm and shoved him into the boat. Even though he was exhausted almost beyond thought, Pieter couldn't help but be amazed by this display of strength.

Pieter grappled with Jorisen's deadweight. He placed him on the deck of the dinghy, but saw this would never do. The little boat was half filled with water, and if the unconscious man was left on the bottom, the water would cover his head and drown him.

He finally solved the problem by wedging Jorisen into a sitting position between the side of the boat and one of the narrow slats that served as a seat.

Manuel had held on to the side of the boat while Pieter took care of the Dane. Now he carefully eased his bulk into the boat, taking care not to capsize it.

"Better get some of this water out, Mister Pieter," Manuel said, wasting no time as he sat down and picked up the oars. He brought the bow around until it pointed at the shore and began rowing. "Don't see nothing for bailing. Best use your hands."

The dinghy was riding low in the water, with a scant two inches of clearance at the low point of the sides. At least six inches of water filled the bottom of the boat.

Pieter cupped his hands and began bailing as fast as he was able.

During the time it had taken to get the men aboard, the strong tide had carried the dinghy out another thirty feet. They were over a hundred yards from safety.

Until now Pieter's strength had been that of a possessed man. But with the rescue of his two friends, this strength fled. He was, once again, a man in his fifties. Manuel was the same age, but there was no weakness in his back or arms, and the oars whipped through the water. Pieter watched them bend and was afraid they would break.

The shoreline came closer and closer, and Pieter stopped bailing. There was still a good deal of water in the boat, but he was totally exhausted. He slumped in the bottom of the boat, his breath coming in panting gasps, assured he was safe in Manuel's hands.

The mighty winds had now passed, and the ominous sky began to lighten as the clouds moved away. The roaring wind became a brisk breeze, and then turned to a gentle passage of air.

The storm had gone. And half of New Amsterdam had gone with it.

It was only later, hours afterward when he was back in his house on the Broad Way, that Pieter realized how much physical abuse he had taken. His muscles ached and began to stiffen, making movement painful. There were many cuts and scrapes on his hands and arms and face, mementos of the flying debris that he had scarcely been aware of as it struck him and broke the skin. He had a deep wound in his left thigh and there was a sliver of wood embedded in the skin. He could not remember how or when it happened.

A few hours after Lars Jorisen was put to bed, he woke up and started to rave. Zilla gave him a potion and it was another twelve hours before he awoke, perfectly lucid. The last thing he could remember was arguing with Manuel because he had wanted to stay aboard the *Manhatan* and go down with his ship. The black man had convinced him that in this case there was no honor to be derived from the tradition, and the two of them had been trying to get off the ship when Jorisen was struck on the head. He knew nothing of Manuel's heroic rescue.

Even though he was in pain, Pieter dragged himself about the house to make sure everyone was all right. The only person who seemed normal was little Emilie. She came out of the cellar with a piece of string in her hand, and a cat chasing the string.

Assured there was nothing to be done in his own home, Pieter made his way toward his daughter's house. He was horrified by all the wreckage he saw, and even more horrified when he came to Anne's house. The entire structure above the ground had been carried away or pounded into debris on the spot.

"Anne!" he called loudly. "Anne, are you there?!"

"Is that you, Father?" It was the voice of Jacob Adam.

"Yes, yes. Is Anne with you? And David?"

In the murky light beneath the shattered bits of wooden floors and walls, Jacob Adam looked over at his sister and brother-in-law. They were fast asleep in each other's arms. "Yes, they're both here."

"Thank God," Pieter said as he began to dig his way into the ruptured house.

Jacob Adam came to the foot of the stairs and began to move some of the debris out of the way. The noise woke his sister. It took her a few seconds to realize where she was. She saw David and it all came back to her. She reached out and touched him on the cheek. He woke and looked around in bewilderment.

"The storm is over," Anne said. "I'm going to help my brother."

David's eyes seemed glazed, but he nodded his head. He watched Anne crawl over to the stairs.

Each movement was an agony for her as she kept discovering new cuts and bruises, but she began to work alongside the boy. She suddenly remembered her daughter. "Emilie!" she cried out. "Is Emilie safe?"

"She was playing with the cat the last time I saw her," Pieter answered.

The idea of her daughter playing with a cat while New Amsterdam lay in ruins broke Anne's mood of despair. She laughed. Jacob Adam looked sharply at her as he continued to work.

"It's over," she said, "thank God it's over," and her laughter was drowned in her own tears.

Men came to help Pieter, and soon the three young

people were brought to the surface. They returned to
Pieter's house on the Broad Way, and Zilla bolstered them
with a thick, hot soup and great mugs of coffee liberally
laced with rum.

The next afternoon Pieter and Jorisen went to the little
house where Manuel lived with his wife and son. Manuel
looked fit, and it was hard to believe he had just been
through a terrible ordeal. His wife served cider and
seemed embarrassed by the presence of two such important men in her humble house.

"The *Manhatan* is gone," Manuel said.

Pieter nodded.

Lars Jorisen clapped his hands together. "The finest
ship in these waters. The best." He looked worriedly at
Pieter. "You *do* plan on buying another ship?"

Pieter had been wrestling with the same question. The
storm would have a catastrophic effect on his finances.
He had spent the morning visiting his properties and was
appalled by the damage.

The windmill was completely gone. Abraham de Witt
had advised him that he didn't want to spend the money
to rebuild it, because he wished to devote all his resources
to the grain brokerage business started by his son. Pieter
was not sure he could afford to do it alone.

The oil factory had sustained great damage and would
require substantial sums to fix it.

The two houses on Pearl Street seemed to have come
through the storm with only minor damage. Many windows had been blown out, and the roofs needed work,
but he didn't think the repairs would cost a great deal.

The house on the Broad Way needed work. The roof
would have to be replaced, and the south wall had
buckled. The chimney was gone, as were all the fences
and bushes.

He would have to pay a quarter of the costs of fixing
the brewery he owned with Oloff Van Cortlandt.

The *Manhatan* was gone.

The final calculation of all these expenses brought a
sick feeling to the pit of his stomach. Two days ago he
had been one of the town's most prosperous citizens. Now
he faced bills that would leave him almost a pauper. But
the work would have to be done. If he didn't fix the oil

factory, he would have no income. The same was true of the Pearl Street houses.

He looked sadly at Lars Jorisen and Manuel Gerait. "I don't think I can afford to buy a ship at this time."

Manuel looked away, and Pieter could feel his sadness. Aside from his little family, Manuel had no other interest but chasing whales.

The look in Jorisen's eyes was even worse. It was unthinkable for him to be without a ship. Pieter was certain the man could find other employment; his reputation had spread along the entire seaboard. But at this moment Jorisen knew only one thing—he was a ship's captain without a ship.

Dammit, Pieter thought, here I am with two men who have helped me over the years, who have contributed to my success and profit, and who now look to me for help and I tell them they can't have it. He made his decision. "I'll get another ship," he said fiercely. "By God! We'll have a ship on the water. Soon!"

Jorison smiled. "It may not be the *Manhatan*, but it will be a ship."

"I will kill whales from dawn till dark," Manuel said. "We will make money again."

Pieter found their joy infectious. "We'll buy the finest ship in these waters."

In the weeks that followed he became painfully aware of certain realities. Most of the ships in the area had been totally wrecked, or else they needed costly, extensive repairs. And he was quickly using up most of his capital with the repairs on the houses and the oil factory.

He raised money by selling his quarter-interest in the brewery back to Van Cortlandt. But this was still not enough to order a first-rate ship to be sent from Europe. Pieter considered selling the houses on Pearl Street, but he couldn't bring himself to do so because of the sentimental value of the first one, and the second was attached to it.

He finally sold the oil factory to Cornelis Brenwyck, a ship owner whose two vessels had been lost in the storm, and who vowed never to own another ship.

In the midst of his hunt for a ship, Pieter found more and more of his time taken up by his duties as alderman. The aldermen and burgomasters met regularly with the

governor to work on all the new problems of the settlement. The storm had badly hurt the town, and much
work had to be done. All the slaves were put to work on
the roads and public buildings. Emergency loans were
made to citizens who needed the money to reestablish
their businesses. Payments on debts between private individuals were suspended for ninety days.

New Amsterdam began an orgy of rebuilding, and
every man, woman, and child worked to restore property.
Houses had to be built before fences. This led to trouble,
because the cattle and sheep, no longer confined, wandered into Indian fields and ate the wild corn. Tempers
flared and it was with a growing uneasiness that the
settlers and Indians continued to live side by side.

The situation needed a single spark before it exploded. The spark was not long in coming.

A farmer on Staten Island saw an Indian taking a
peach from one of his trees. The farmer, known as a hot-
head, went to his house, got his musket, and came back
and shot the thief.

The "thief" turned out to be a twelve-year-old girl of
the Raritan tribe. The Indians were incensed and went on
the warpath again. The fighting spread and soon extended
to Long Island and the settlements along the banks of the
Connecticut. The Indians attacked the English settlers as
well as the Dutch. This, in turn, caused further complications, because the English felt sure the Indians had
been sent by the Dutch.

The fighting was savage; several battles were fought.
Over one hundred whites were killed, and property damage was over two hundred thousand guilders.

This infamous "Peach War" came at a time when New
Amsterdam had more than its share of other problems.
But there was a major difference between this war and the
earlier one: the settlers didn't retreat to the fort, and
never considered that they might lose. Their numbers
were now greater, and the Indian population had remained constant. Nobody liked the war, but the whites
didn't live in the sheer terror that had been their lot in the
war of '44.

Finally the governor arranged a powwow with the
chiefs, and another treaty was signed. Peace returned, but
it was a peace of cynicism. Most men knew it was only a

matter of time before they would be forced to put the Indian in his place once and for all time. The virtual extermination of the red man became a foregone conclusion.

Pieter was becoming desperate to find a new ship he could afford. Together with Lars Jorisen he haunted the docks, inspecting the vessels for sale, tramping their decks, getting the feel of the rigging, descending into the bilges. They found nothing that would make a first-rate whaler.

It was Governor Stuyvesant who solved the problem. "What sort of a ship are you looking for?" he asked.

"A whaler," Pieter answered. "Fair speed and good storage space. And in good condition. I don't want a ship that will take six months to fix."

"Would you like to buy the *William?*"

Pieter lost his voice. The *William* was a three-masted, two-decked frigate—not only one of the first frigates in the New World, but one of the first ever built. It was owned by the Dutch government and named after their infant prince.

He finally managed to say, "Did . . . you *did* say the *William?*"

"Yes. She was in the South Bay during the storm and escaped without a scratch."

"But the *William* is a warship."

"You couldn't use it as a whaler?"

"Of course. But it belongs to the Netherlands. How can you sell it?"

"They claim its upkeep is too expensive. I don't agree, but that's beside the point. I have instructions to sell it."

"How . . . how much will you sell it for?"

The governor quoted a low figure.

"But it's worth at least twice that," Pieter protested.

"Do you want to buy it or not?"

"Yes!"

Within three days the money was paid and the sale recorded. Pieter now was the legal owner of the frigate.

The governor smiled. "There's a reason why the price was so low. I want you to keep the *William* armed."

"All the cannons?"

"Yes. I disagree with the States-General that we do not need a warship."

Pieter assented, scarcely aware of how soon the governor would call for the services of the *William,* a ship that he was no longer required to maintain, but that would be around when he needed it. It was a good deal for the shrewd governor, but it was also a good deal for Pieter. He now had a fine ship, and it had cost him far less than he normally would have had to pay.

Pieter and Lars Jorisen took the ship on an extended shakedown cruise.

"A beauty," Jorisen said. "She doesn't have the sleekness of the *Manhatan,* but by God! is she stoutly built! The storm doesn't exist that could sink her!"

They took the *William* all the way to Boston to buy the superior naval stores of the English.

On the way back they stopped at Gardiner's Island. While the *William* sat with bare poles, riding gently at her anchor, Pieter rested in Lion Gardiner's house, drinking sherry with his host and talking of whaling, Indians, family, and other matters. Finally Gardiner came to an uncomfortable subject.

"Pieter, you know these lands and waters as well as any man alive. You're aware of the vastness of this land."

"Yes. Enough for ourselves, our sons, and for countless generations to come."

Lion Gardiner nodded in agreement. "That's what I say, but there are men in England who disagree. There are Englishmen *here* who disagree."

"What do they say?"

"That the Dutch have no legal claim to the lands."

"Nonsense. Manhatan was discovered by Henry Hudson, who was in the employ of the Dutch East India Company. We also paid the Indians for our lands."

"Hudson was an Englishman."

"But he *was* in the employ of the Dutch."

"As far as your payments to the Indians are concerned, many of my countrymen don't even consider that."

"That's their problem, not ours."

Lion Gardiner was not to be put off. "The problems have deep roots. Many of them are a reflection of conditions in Europe. England and the Netherlands are at each other's throats. There are some who would extend this situation to the New World."

"My God!" Pieter said in dismay. "I thought most of us came here to get away from those conditions!"

"Some of us. But there are other men whose greed is greater than their reason."

"What will happen?"

Lion Gardiner smiled. "I'll be the last man to know the answer to that question. I only repeat what I hear from my visitors. There will be trouble. Perhaps not this year or the next, but it will come. The earls and dukes of England are looking across the ocean and they see great estates for themselves. At the moment most of them do nothing but dream about it, but the day is coming when they'll not be content with dreams."

On the voyage back to Manhatan Pieter thought a great deal about Lion Gardiner's words, his happiness with his new ship marred by the sobering prospect of trouble with the English.

Walking the quarterdeck of his frigate, Pieter became aware of a sailor at the railing of the main deck. As the man stood, his lips moved as if he were talking to himself.

Curious, Pieter climbed down the ladder to the main deck and came up without being observed. The man was saying some sort of prayer in a strange language. Pieter was about to walk away and leave the sailor to his private communion with God, but the man sensed his presence and turned around. He smiled nervously.

"Don't let me bother you," Pieter said. "Continue with your prayers."

Pieter thought the sailor was embarrassed because he had been caught in an act that other sailors would look upon as a sign of weakness. To put the man at his ease he said, "What language do you pray in?"

The man hesitated and then said very softly, "Hebrew."

Pieter was as tolerant as any man of his day, but there were Jews in New Amsterdam, but he had not known there was one aboard his own ship.

The man noticed the look and decided to forgo any deception. "I am a Jew."

Pieter was as tolerant as any man of his day, but there was nothing in his experience that had allowed him to become friendly with or even understanding of the Jews. As far as he knew they were a race that had been persecuted because of some heathenish beliefs, exactly what he wasn't sure. He thought he had nothing to do with them, but now he found one who was a member of his crew, part of his own "family."

He peered more closely into the man's face and recalled seeing him aboard the ship; he was a good sailor who worked hard and knew what he was doing. It all flashed through Pieter's mind in a moment, and he realized that if the man was enough of a sailor for Lars Jorisen, then he was also enough of a man for him.

What difference did it make anyway? New Netherland was not Europe, with all its ancient hatreds and prejudices, with all its persecutions and atrocities. The New World gave a man a fresh start, and it was time to forget the old hatreds. New Amsterdam had Methodists and Calvinists and Lutherans and even a few Papists. What harm would be done by adding a few Jews to the stew?

The sailor had become very nervous under Pieter's scrutiny, and his hands began to tremble. Pieter quickly tried to put him at ease. "I'm glad you're aboard," he said. "What's your name?"

"Isaack Seixas, sir."

"How long have you been aboard my ship?"

"I served over a year on the *Manhatan* and I've been aboard the *William* since the day you bought her."

"And how long have you lived in New Amsterdam?"

"Three years, sir. I came from Brazil."

When the man said he was from Brazil, Pieter vaguely knew his history.

Many of the Jewish refugees who had fled or been expelled from Spain and Portugal in the sixteenth century had gone to Holland. When the Dutch began to colonize Brazil, the Jews emigrated there, but they were unlucky and their persecutors were not far behind. Recife, the last Dutch stronghold in Brazil, fell to the Portuguese in 1654, and the Inquisition once again caught up with the Jews. Twenty-seven managed to escape with their lives. A French ship brought them to New Amsterdam, and the hard-hearted captain auctioned off their few possessions as payment for their passage. Never before or since had a group of immigrants arrived in the New World with less of the world's wealth.

The Jews had been a topic of discussion in the New Amsterdam City Hall. More of them had arrived from

Curaçao, and Governor Stuyvesant did not want to permit them to remain. "I do not want them to *infest* my colony," he wrote to the States-General in Amsterdam. The Jews, the States-General replied, are shareholders in the West India Company, and their money is as good as anyone else's. As long as they could take care of their own poor and did not become a burden to the community, they were to be allowed the remain, the burghers said.

Stuyvesant could do nothing about the situation. Even though their occupational opportunities were limited—initially the only jobs available were as slaughterers of livestock—the Jews managed to survive and prosper. As time passed they were allowed to work at other trades, to start their own businesses, and to open trading companies dealing with Europe. They enjoyed most of the rights of the other citizens, with the exception of holding public office. This exception was Stuyvesant's doing. He refused to listen to arguments in favor of the Jews as officeholders, and not one of them held any post during his long tenure as governor.

Pieter de Kuyper knew these things, and yet he was still surprised to find that a Jew had become a sailor. "Where did you learn the ways of the sea?" he asked.

"In Brazil," Seixas said. "My father was a trader who supplied ships. I discovered I loved ships more than trading and became a sailor when I had the chance."

"How old are you?"

"Twenty-three, sir."

"And it makes you happy to pray to your God?"

"God is important to me, sir," Isaack Seixas said.

God was, indeed, important to the Jews. Two months after they landed in New Amsterdam, they held the first Rosh Hashanah service on the North American continent. They were not sure of their new home, and after so many centuries of persecution they weren't taking any chances. The service was held in secret in the attic of a warehouse on lower Pearl Street. The group took the name of Congregation Shearith Israel, and they held regular services, but it would be years before they dared to do so openly in the midst of all the Calvinists and Methodists. It would be even longer before they dared to build their own synagogue.

The one public facility they required was a place to

bury their dead. The Christians would not hear of a
Jew being buried in the grounds that had been blessed
and were reserved for their coreligionists. So the leaders
of the congregation went to Stuyvesant and asked permission to start a cemetery.

The governor, despite his bluster and anti-Semitism,
was not a dedicated persecutor of Jews. He would have
preferred not to have them around, but since they were
in New Amsterdam he tried to make the best of the situation, which to him meant ignoring them as much as
possible. After the horrors of the Inquisition and the
years of hideous treatment by the Spaniards and the
Portuguese, this behavior came as a relief to the Jews.
They would have been content if everyone treated them
the way Stuyvesant did. In turn, they did their best to
stay out of his way. If he tried to pretend they didn't
exist, they were most happy to oblige him.

But men die, and there was no getting around the
need for a cemetery. Stuyvesant granted them a small
plot of ground just north of the palisade on Wall Street.
The first man was buried, and so the Jews joined the
other immigrants who gave their labors and their toil to
the New World; who gave their hopes and dreams, and
ended by giving their very flesh to be mixed with the
soil of their adopted home.

Isaack Seixas breathed a sigh of relief at Pieter's
reaction on learning he was a Jew. Pieter had seemed
surprised at first, but he also seemed accepting.

He remembered the day he had applied for the job.
Lars Jorisen had asked him many questions about ships
and seamanship. Satisfied with the answers, the captain
had pushed the log book toward Isaack and told him
to sign it. After he had written his name—a distinction
in itself, since most men could only make their mark—
he hesitated before leaving. The captain looked questioningly at him, and Isaack blurted, "I think you should
know, sir, that I am a Jew."

Lars Jorisen's face remained calm. "I don't ship with
Jews," he said, and Isaack's hopes were dashed.

"I don't ship with Calvinists or Methodists either." The
captain continued. "I ship with sailors. Be aboard at first
watch," he said, turning to interview the next sailor.

There had never been any trouble aboard ship, and

now the owner himself put his hand on the young Jew's shoulder and said, "I'm pleased you're on my ship."

As Pieter walked away, Isaack Seixas thanked his God there were men like this Dutchman and places like New Amsterdam.

The *William* went on many sailing voyages during the next year, and then Governor Stuyvesant summoned Pieter.

"We're having a devil of a time with English pirates," the governor said. "I need you and the *William* to stop them."

Pieter felt trapped. It was part of the deal for buying the ship so cheaply, but he decided he owed himself at least a token resistance. If the *William* was used to hunt pirates, she would be prevented from earning the money Pieter needed to replace his lost fortune. "The *William* is supposed to leave for the end of Long Island the day after tomorrow. The whales are running."

The governor said nothing. He looked sternly at Pieter for a moment, and then a smile crossed his face.

Pieter knew he had been caught, and a matching smile came to his own lips. "We are at your service," he said.

They spent the next few hours discussing the situation. When he left the governor's house, Pieter had learned that the pirates were led by an Englishman named Thomas Baxter. He had lived in New Amsterdam in the late '40s and had killed a man in a tavern brawl. There was a warrant out for his arrest, and if they caught him he would, no doubt, leave this world at the end of a rope.

The pirates were operating out of the many uncharted coves on Long Island. They apparently had two ships— a caravel and a schooner—and their method of attack was clever. The swifter schooner would engage a ship and drive it toward the shore. While the ship was busy defending herself from the schooner, the slow but heavily armed caravel would come out from its hiding place along the shore. The attacked ship would now be caught between both pirate vessels.

Pieter and Lars Jorisen ate dinner in the house on the Broad Way as they made their plans against the pirates. The Dane was far from happy. He was hardly a coward, but his love of ships was so great he hated to see them battered by cannon fire.

While the men sat at the table and discussed the coming venture, fourteen-year old Jacob Adam entered the room and took a chair. The men paid no attention to him and continued their conversation. Finally Lars Jorisen stood up to leave. "Well, young laddie, what do you think of these pirates?"

"They must be stopped."

"Would you like to be with us when we stop them?"

"Yes."

"Impossible!" Pieter said. "It'll be far too dangerous."

Jacob Adam ignored his father and spoke to Jorisen. "Will you take me?"

"It'll be no place for a boy," Pieter said.

Jacob Adam looked Lars Jorisen straight in the eye. "Do you think I'm only a boy?"

Pieter looked at the Dane, hoping to engage him as an ally, but the man could only speak the truth as he saw it. "I see a boy in the size of your body," he said to Jacob Adam. "But in your mind and heart you're a man."

The boy said nothing, because the Dane had said it all. He turned and looked at his father.

Pieter was about to reject the request, but he stopped himself. He remembered the resolution he had made to treat Jacob Adam differently from the way he had treated his other son. He did not want to lose him the way he had lost Young Pieter.

"You may come with us," he said in a quiet voice.

"Thank you, Father, I'll not disgrace you."

Lars Jorisen rested his hand on the boy's shoulder. "It's good to do as much as possible when you are young. It helps you avoid foolishness when you're older."

Zilla was less than pleased when she heard the news. She said nothing to Jacob Adam, but turned her wrath on Pieter when they were alone. "It's wrong to expose that boy to such dangers."

"He wants to go," Pieter said. "I have to give him his head. I can't repeat the business of my other son."

There was no sense in arguing, Zilla realized. She knew how strong Pieter's feelings were on the subject. "Don't let anything happen to him," she said in a quavering voice. "I couldn't stand it if anything happened to him."

Pieter looked at her and saw she was crying. His voice was very gentle. "I understand how much you love him."

"Do you? Do you know I love him as much as if he was my own flesh and blood? I raised him. I helped him through his sicknesses. I want him to grow up fine and strong. I want him to marry and have children. I want him to have everything life has to offer. Do you understand?"

Pieter placed her head on his shoulder and gently stroked the graying hair. He understood. Yes, Zilla wanted Jacob Adam to have children. Because then they would belong to her as well. She would think of them as her grandchildren, and she would lavish all her considerable love on them. It was a natural ambition. Did it matter that she was black and the children would be white? Did it matter that they would not carry a single drop of her blood? No, it didn't matter, didn't matter in the slightest. She would have grandchildren and she would be happy.

Pieter understood, and his affection for this woman had never been greater.

It was the hour before dawn. Jacob Adam was dressed, and preparing to leave the house. He passed through the kitchen, where a fire was already burning; he knew Zilla was up. He paid no attention to the crackling sounds and the sweet smell of the wood. He slipped out the door and walked out onto the Broad Way.

A hint of silver covered the eastern horizon, but even now, before the day had begun, the town was awake.

The sounds of oars rattling loosely in wooden tholepins echoed across the calm, flat water as fishermen took to their boats.

A gang of slaves moved along, picks and shovels on their shoulders, looking dejected and tired before starting their day's work on a new road they cared nothing about.

The men of the watch were beginning to drift back toward the fort from their posts.

The foodstuff dealers by the wharfs yawned as they opened their stalls. It was an ungodly hour to be selling salted meat and vegetables, but necessary if they were to provision the ships that would be catching the early tide on their way to Virginia, the Indies, or Europe.

Jacob Adam missed none of it as he padded silently and swiftly toward the anchorage area. When he reached the fort he followed the walls until he came to a point of land that gave him a clear view of the hulls of ships squatting like large dark beetles on the still waters.

A strong smell of damp seaweed assailed his nostrils. The *caw* of seabirds resounded in his ears. He could imagine the crackling noises made by the barnacles, the soft chafing of lines and hawsers, the slap of water against planked hulls.

"Thinkin' of runnin' away from 'ome, laddie?" a voice said.

He turned and saw a dirty one-eyed man who wore a filthy handkerchief on his head.

"For a small coin I can get ye aboard a ship wot leaves on the tide," the man said, his mouth twisting as he talked.

"Go away," Jacob Adam said in a low voice.

The man looked at the boy and decided he was fair game. He came closer and his face glowered in anger. "Lissen 'ere, you little muck, give us some money or I'll bust your face."

He took another step toward the boy and then stopped dead in his tracks. From somewhere—he hadn't seen it happen—a vicious-looking knife had appeared in the boy's hand. It was pointed at his heart. He looked more closely into the boy's eyes. What he saw convinced him not to push his luck. The boy had seemed a harmless lad, but the eyes and the knife told him otherwise. He backed off and disappeared around the wall of the fort.

Jacob Adam resumed walking toward the anchorage area as if nothing had happened. He went aboard as the *William* was being readied to get under way.

She boasted twenty-two guns—nine along each gunwale, one on either side of the bowsprit, and two in the stern. Herself more than a match for any pirate ship she might encounter, she was also accompanied by two swift armed schooners. Soldiers of the garrison were aboard all the ships. Pieter was given the title of commander-in-chief of the naval forces of New Amsterdam.

He stood with his son at his side as the *William* began to ship anchor. The men worked the heavy winches, and the cable pulled the anchor clear of the bottom. The *William* took the leading position, and the schooners fell into line in her wake. They crossed the Upper Bay and passed through the Narrows. When they reached the middle of the Lower Bay, they changed course and headed for the south shore of Long Island.

For almost two weeks the ships sailed along the coast of the south shore, inspecting hundreds of coves and inlets. They came across many Indians who were fishing the rich waters, and once they encountered a Dutch sloop, but they saw nothing of pirates. The men grew bored. The garrison officer held drills to give his troops something to do, but these were listlessly performed on the crowded decks.

Pieter became annoyed. It was one thing to go out against a pirate, but it was quite another to waste his time inspecting Long Island's shoreline when he could be replenishing his lost fortune with whales.

Only Lars Jorisen, who was never unhappy at sea, and Jacob Adam did not seem to be bothered. The young man spent a great deal of time in the captain's cabin poring over the maps and charts. At first Pieter thought it only a boy's whim, but then he realized his son was quite deliberately becoming an authority on the waterfront land of the colony.

At the end of two weeks Pieter was ready to return to Manhatan. He decided to give it two more days. And then a swift sloop came over the horizon and headed straight for the *William*.

A courier from Stuyvesant came aboard from the sloop. "It was the pirate," the man said, "attacked a ship he did, on the other side of the Narrows."

"Inside the Narrows?"

"Yes, sir."

"But we've been patrolling these shores for two weeks. If he had passed through the Narrows after the attack, we would have seen him."

"Then he didn't come through the Narrows," Captain Jorisen said. "His hiding place must be somewhere in the Upper Bay."

"The nerve of the man!" Pieter said.

"The question to be answered is where does he hide?"

"Perhaps my son can help," Pieter said.

Jacob Adam was brought to the cabin. With his father and Captain Jorisen he studied the maps of the Upper Bay. He said there were many places for a pirate to hide, but the two best were the watery marshlands along the kills behind Staten Island, and a many-pronged inlet near the Breuckelen settlement. Of the two, he preferred the latter.

"Why?" Jorisen asked.

"A ship could hide in the inlet while a lookout stood on the hills and watched the approaches to Manhatan. He could see all the ships and pick his targets."

The captain nodded his head in appreciation of the boy's solid thinking. "Yes, yes, that would be a good spot for a pirate." He turned to Pieter. "Well, what do we do?"

"I think we're wasting our time out here in the ocean. Let's get back inside the Upper Bay."

The three ships, joined now by the sloop, set course for the Narrows. A thick fog rolled in from the sea and cut visibility to almost nothing. With the fog came a loss of wind. The ships drifted slowly and silently through the afternoon. The fog thinned for about an hour, and visibility increased to almost one hundred feet. The *William* was alone. They hailed the other ships but received no reply.

And then the fog returned with the night and it was impossible for a man to see two feet in front of himself. The wind was negligible, but Jorisen kept the sails set, and he stood at the helmsman's shoulder and gave slight changes of direction. The crew thought the captain was daft. How could a man know which way he was heading?

The morning came, but the fog did not lift. The light of the sun illuminated the dense blanket, but it was still impossible to see more than five feet away. The danger of running aground was minimized by their sluggish pace. If they did sail into one of the rocky outcroppings that abounded along these shores, they wouldn't crash into it, only nudge it. This was the only comforting thought left to the sailors and soldiers, who were becoming spooked by the unearthly conditions.

By midmorning the fog was still quite thick, but now

a man had visibility of thirty or forty feet. And then
something happened that snapped everyone into a state
of alertness.

Lars Jorisen was the first to hear it—a faint scraping
sound, the sort made by the rings of a gaff as it was being raised along a mast.

Pieter stood beside the captain as the *William* was
headed a few points more to starboard. "There's a ship
out there."

"And getting under sail," Jorisen said.

"The pirate?"

Jorisen shrugged.

The men watched in silence. The soldiers gave their
weapons a final check. The gunners took up their sta-
tions. The sailors awaited their captain's orders.

The noises grew louder as the *William* drifted toward
the other ship. And then the sound of voices could be
heard.

"They're speaking English," Pieter said.

"I think we have our pirate."

The *William* inched ahead, and then, out of the fog,
the form of the other ship became visible. It was a caravel! As the vessels closed, the men on the other ship saw
the looming hulk of the *William*. If there had been any
doubt that the caravel was the pirate, it was dispelled as
a man aboard her raised a musket and fired at the approaching craft.

All hell broke loose on both ships.

The *William* had the advantage. She had known she
was going into battle, and her crew was ready. The starboard guns began to hurl shot at the caravel. The distance closed, and the guns found their target. Round
after round crashed into the caravel, stoving in timbers,
tearing through the rigging, bringing sails and gaffs tumbling down to the decks. One round cracked the oak
foremast, and it floundered in its own guys and forestays,
making it impossible to raise her sails.

The *William*'s gunners punched holes in the side of
the caravel, and screams of agony could be heard as the
iron balls chopped men to pieces. The men aboard the
caravel finally began to return the cannon fire, but most
of their panic-stricken shots whizzed harmlessly over the
decks of the *William*. One struck a cannon and killed

three of its crewmen. Another put a hole through a fore-sail, but it passed miraculously through the rigging without touching it.

The guns of the *William* were proving far superior to those of the caravel. But then the Dutch ship was hit by a round of shot from the opposite side.

It was the pirate schooner: now the *William* was trapped between the ships of the enemy. The schooner fired again and killed several soldiers.

At first Pieter thought the arrival of the schooner meant disaster, but his fears were groundless. The *William*'s firepower was superior to that of the other ships combined. The schooner had only four guns, and two of these were on the side facing away from the frigate and thus useless.

The port guns of the *William* opened fire and soon had scored ten hits. Bits of rigging came crashing down on the pirate's deck. One of her guns took a direct hit and was put out of the fight. Another shot carried away her bowsprit, and the foresails came crashing down. The schooner was finished in five minutes, and she began to drift away from the battle. The *William*'s port gunners scored two more hits before the schooner was swallowed by the fog.

But now the fight with the caravel was intensifying. The pirate captain decided he could not trade cannon fire with the frigate, and the two ships came closer and closer as the pirates prepared to board the enemy. The *William*'s cannons continued to blast away, the shot smashing into the hull of the caravel, tearing up the timbers, knocking men into pieces, creating havoc.

The pirates threw their grappling hooks, and they caught the sides of the frigate, locking the two ships together in a fight to the death. Some of the pirates boarded the frigate in the face of cannon fire that flung their mutilated remains back at their shipmates. It was not a pretty sight, but the buccaneers were not finished. Barely a third were still alive, but these came aboard with a blood lust in their eyes.

The soldiers and sailors met them with musket fire and killed many, but soon the decks were filled with a fighting, cursing mob. Several pirates leaped from the rigging onto the decks. Pieter calmly shot a pirate who jumped on the quarterdeck. Jorisen fired his pistol at another and missed. The captain and the pirate were soon rolling on the deck, locked together in combat.

Jacob Adam had moved to the far side of the quarterdeck. His father had ordered him below when the ships closed, but Pieter was so preoccupied he did not notice that his son disobeyed.

A huge pirate with a long black beard landed on the quarterdeck. He drove his sword into the side of the helmsman's neck, almost down to the heart. He turned and was about to attack Pieter when a falling spar hit the Dutchman on the head and knocked him to the deck, dead or unconscious.

The pirate looked for another opponent and saw Jacob Adam. As he charged forward, the boy picked up a belaying pin. The pirate, suddenly realizing the youth of his adversary, swept the belaying pin aside. He laughed and would have grabbed the boy, when a knee crashed into his back and a hand grabbed his throat.

The blow from Manuel's knee might have killed an ordinary man, but this pirate was almost as large as his attacker. He twisted around and tried to slash the black man with his word, but Manuel seized his wrist, and the two of them stood locked in a titanic struggle. Their muscles bulged, sweat popped out on their foreheads, and they groaned in their exertion. Finally the superhuman strength of the black man began to tell, and the large pirate was forced backward. He fell to the deck, and Manuel was on him with the quickness of a cat. One huge forearm went under the bearded jaw, and he began to pull the chin back. Jacob Adam watched as the head was brought back farther and farther until there was a loud snap. Manuel tossed the body to the deck, the bearded head lolling at an awkward angle.

Lars Jorisen finally managed to overcome the man he had been grappling with. He succeeded in finding a belaying pin on the deck, grabbed it, and belted the pirate on the head. He stood up, shook himself and then a bullet caught him in the left arm above the elbow. A sailor quickly applied a tourniquet to halt the flow of blood, and the captain carried on as if nothing had happened.

Pieter came back to his senses and shook the cobwebs from his brain. His son helped him to his feet.

But the battle was over. Six pirates remained alive, and these surrendered. The soldiers treated them none too gently, sending them into the hold with kicks and curses and the butts of their muskets. One of them died before he could be chained, and his corpse was dragged back to the deck and thrown over the side.

Pieter went aboard the caravel and was amazed at the pile of booty he found. There were chests and barrels filled with the loot taken from other ships. He came across the body of a man wearing a captain's cap and assumed it was the corpse of Thomas Baxter.

Several garrison soldiers were left on board the pirate craft to guard her until she could be towed to New Amsterdam. Pieter wanted to get back as quickly as possible to care for the wounded men.

"But the schooner," Jorisen protested. "We must go after her."

"In this fog?" Pieter was incredulous.

"The fog will lift in an hour. Besides, the ship is hurt badly and we'll have no trouble catching her."

Pieter remained skeptical. He pointed to the tourniquet on the other's arm. "Shouldn't something be done about that?"

"It'll wait."

Pieter finally agreed, and the captain set his course as the commander-in-chief inspected the wounded men. He came to Isaack Seixas.

"How did it happen?" Pieter asked, pointing to the wounded leg.

"A sword," Seixas said. "I killed the man who put it there."

"You'll be all right."

"Yes, and live to tell my grandchildren of this," Seixas said with pride.

Pieter smiled and moved on.

The fog lifted and the wind increased. The sails of the frigate filled, her bow bit deeper into the water, and the spray splashed alongside the hull. After the almost motionless passage in the fog, it seemed as if the ship were flying. The fresh air revived everyone.

They saw the sails of the pirate schooner in the distance. The ship was limping along with about half of its normal complement of sails, and the *William* closed rapidly. The men on the schooner were trying to make their way to an inlet.

"We'll beat them to it," Jorisen assured Pieter.

The *William* responded as if anxious to prove that her captain was a man of his word. She sliced through the water, and the schooner was soon within cannon range.

From the looks of the activity on the decks of the schooner, Pieter decided, the pirates were going to make a fight of it. He looked around the decks of his own ship and saw the wounded men. Many of the "nonwounded" wore bloody bandages and limped as they prepared for the next ordeal.

Pieter made his decision. "There will be no closing with that ship and no attempt at boarding."

Jorisen nodded.

"Blow her out of the water."

Jorisen tacked the *William* so that it would cross the path of the schooner at an angle that would allow his gunners to rake the other craft with a full broadside.

The *William* came closer and closer, and then her guns opened up. As she passed the schooner all nine guns of the starboard side fired twice, and of these eighteen rounds, twelve found the mark. It wasn't so much an example of good shooting as it was of superb ship handling on the part of the captain.

The pirate schooner attempted to fight back, but she managed to fire only one round from her remaining cannon before it was blown apart by a shot from the frigate.

Jorisen jibed the frigate about and brought her past the schooner so the port guns could rake her.

With this double broadside the battle was over. The schooner was sinking. There seemed to be total confusion among the pirates. The single longboat was launched, but its bottom had been hit by a round of shot, and it sank as soon as it went into the water. In minutes the schooner slipped beneath the surface of the water, leaving the sea covered with debris and the floundering forms of thirty men.

The *William*, by this time, was a good distance away. She turned and started back to rescue the men in the water. The soldiers readied their muskets in expectation of the new batch of prisoners.

Before the frigate could reach the pirates, they became

the victims of a fate far worse than the one awaiting them on the gallows of New Amsterdam.

Many of them had been wounded, and their blood mixed with the sea water. The blood attracted one shark. And then another. And then a great many sharks. The first bite. The first scream. Then more bites, more screams; more blood in the sea. And now the sharks began to feed. They dashed forward, sank their teeth into a man, and tore away great hunks of flesh. Arms and legs were ripped away as the men screamed and bled to death in the water. The sharks went berserk. They began to bite each other, and their blood mingled with the blood of the men. They dashed through the water, their mouths open, their teeth flashing, and they slashed and ripped at anything that moved. The sea bubbled and frothed as fifty of the sleek monsters thrashed about.

By the time the *William* reached the spot, none of the pirates was alive. None of them was even whole. The men on the frigate gaped in horror at the savage scene, and Pieter was aware that his son had not missed one fragment of the evil drama. He shook his head. It was not a sight meant to be seen by a man, let alone a boy of Jacob Adam's years.

The *William* headed back for New Amsterdam and was hit with a stroke of bad luck. The wind died again, and the ship drifted through the rest of the day and through the night before it landed the next morning at the quay. By this time several of the more severely wounded men had died.

Captain Jorisen collapsed. The doctor removed the tourniquet, and when he saw the arm he knew it would have to be amputated. The tight bandage had been left on too long.

The battle was over and pirates were gone, but a number of good men had died; others would carry their scars to their graves; and Captain Jorisen would have to learn to get along without a left arm.

Pieter went home. He noticed that Jacob Adam remained at the quay for the arrival of the caravel. The men who had served in the expedition were to share the booty of the pirates as their prize money, and Jacob Adam wanted to know what his share would be.

*   *   *

After the damage to the *William* had been repaired, and half the cannons removed with the reluctant permission of the governor, it returned to the business of whaling. In command was Lars Jorisen, lacking one arm but retaining all his courage and zeal for the sea. The seemingly indestructible Manuel was aboard as first harpooner, and his new assistant, at the request of Pieter de Kuyper, was Isaack Seixas.

Since the storm had almost ruined him, Pieter's caution had become marked, and he was no longer a bold entrepreneurial adventurer. Whaling being a somewhat risky proposition, his one sure source of income was the rental of the two houses on Pearl Street. Hedrick Jansen, "the Turk," still rented one, and the other, which used to be the de Kuyper residence, was leased to an Englishman named John Riverton.

Riverton had recently come to New Amsterdam with his family and a sizable fortune, which he said he had made "in the Caribbean trade." When questioned about the nature of his cargo, he would speak vaguely of its "value and worth," but no man could get him to tell more.

He built a new house near the home of Oloff Van Cortlandt, which was on Stone Street, the first paved thoroughfare in the city and hence its name. The street had been paved because Mevrouw Van Cortlandt disliked getting her shoes muddy when it rained. It achieved a goodly amount of fame, and farmers and settlers from the hinterlands would come to the city to look upon this phenomenal sign of civilization.

Riverton built the city's largest sugar refinery. Ships coming from the Indies brought their cargoes to him, and his business prospered. Settlers as far away as Plymouth and Boston became his customers. He was a man with many business interests, and when he signed a five-year lease on the Pearl Street house, he said his intention was to "start an importing company." Pieter thought little of the matter, being pleased with the assurance of a steady income.

When Riverton finally finished the house on Stone Street in the fall of 1658, one of the first men he invited to dinner was Pieter de Kuyper, who came with his son. Dinner was plentiful, with a good deal of wine and beer. The Englishman was more open and talkative than usual.

His wife was a quiet woman who spoke only when a question was directed toward her, but even then in the stingiest amount of words. Otherwise she said nothing. This was hardly the case with Riverton's daughter, Elizabeth, a beautiful girl of eighteen who had a sparkling smile, a quick wit, a swan's neck, and other features that caused Jacob Adam to fall in love with her immediately, even though he was several years younger. Throughout dinner and afterward he found himself sneaking glances at her and, to his embarrassment, getting caught at it. Elizabeth would look up suddenly and put on her most dazzling smile. Then she would flutter her eyelids and look away.

None of this was lost on Pieter. He realized the girl was too old for his son and probably would be married and caring for several children by the time Jacob Adam was ready to take a wife. But he approved of his son's mooning; it was a very human thing. Jacob Adam had surrounded himself with a hard shell, and Pieter hoped this display of softness would be duplicated in other situations.

Pieter and his host walked into the garden after dinner, and Riverton pointed out his new plantings and expressed his hopes of turning this spot into another Garden of Eden.

"Don't bother with strawberries," Pieter advised. "They grow wild all over the place outside the wall. By the end of the season you'll be sick of them."

"Ah, that's the truth, I suppose," Riverton said with a sigh. "But the wife wants them, and there's no talking her out of them. I guess I'll have to humor her. After all, 'tis not been an easy life for her. Many a year she scarce saw me 'cept between voyages. Now that we have a good home, let her enjoy it a bit, I say."

Pieter was curious about the man's past. "You've spent a good deal of time at sea?"

"That's the truth."

The man seemed in an affable mood, and Pieter decided to press the issue. "And what cargo made your fortune?"

Riverton hesitated. He looked at Pieter. The Dutchman was an alderman, a member of the council, and a known friend of the governor—in short, a good man to have as his own friend. Riverton was cautious, but he had consumed more than his share of spirits. He also knew that his past, and present, activities were soon to come out, so he decided to answer the question directly with the hope of having his honesty repaid with Pieter's friendship.

"It was several cargoes. A three-legged trade—the Caribbean to Europe; Europe to Africa; Africa to the Caribbean. Cargo on every leg, and profit as well."

Pieter stiffened. The African trade could mean only one thing.

Riverton was aware of Pieter's reaction. "That's right," he said. "I was in the slave trade."

The slave trade, Pieter thought, and his heart turned against the other man.

It was a curious thing about slaves. They had been in New Amsterdam almost from the first days of the colony —not in any great numbers, since the economy did not require them—but they had been there, and almost every man had owned a slave at one time or another. Pieter himself had owned slaves, although he had since given all of them their freedom. But no matter that slaves were accepted as a part of daily life, there was still a stigma attached to the men who traded in black flesh. Men like Dominie Bogardus had preached against the slave trade, calling it "an abomination and an evil to be burned out of our lives." Even Governor Stuyvesant condemned it, though for very different reasons. The governor said, "It caused white men to grow lazy and lead idle lives while the blacks do all the work."

Why, Pieter asked himself, was the presence of slaves accepted, but the slave trader regarded as unclean? Perhaps the main reason for this distinction was that the farmer or merchant who owned slaves treated them fairly, provided for them, and sometimes came to respect them as fellow human beings. None of this was true of the traders. The horror stories of their brutality and sadism became the grist of tales to frighten small children. The trader was not a man who bought a slave to help with honest labor. No, a trader was a demon who packed the blacks into the stinking holds of his ship. A third of them died as they crossed the Atlantic in their stifling coffins, and the remainder were sold at a great profit. Somehow *owning* a slave was acceptable, while *trading* human flesh was not.

Pieter realized that this was not sound logic; that the man who bought a slave from a trader was as guilty of perpetuating the system as the trader himself. As long as there were men willing to buy human flesh, there would be men willing to sell it.

"You don't approve?" John Riverton said.

"It's not up to me to approve or disapprove," Pieter said after a moment of soul-searching.

"But you don't like it?"

"No, I don't like the traffic in human flesh. But I've owned slaves myself, so who am I to judge?"

"You must understand how I came to be a slaver."

"It's not important."

"I was dirt poor," Riverton said as if the other had not spoken. "I had nothing, nothing at all. And then one day I signed aboard a ship that dealt in slaves. It was a *Dutch* ship." He paused to let this sink in. "After several voyages I had made more money than I thought I'd ever make in my entire life. I took the profits and bought my own ship."

Pieter was thoughtful. "It's a cruel world and we must make our way as best possible."

"Exactly."

"A man should not always be judged on his actions of the past. Anyway, I'm glad it's all over."

The Englishman hesitated, but he knew that since he had come this far, there was nothing to do but continue. "Only it's not all over. I still own the ship. My cousin's son is now her captain."

A horrible thought occurred to Pieter. "You told me you plan to use the house on Pearl Street for your trading ventures. What ventures?"

"I plan to keep slaves there before they are sold."

Pieter staggered back as if he had been struck a blow in the stomach. "Use my house . . . for slaves?"

Riverton nodded. "It's a stout building suited for the task."

"My God!" Pieter cried. He moved forward until his jaw almost touched the Englishman's. "My children were born in that house! It will not be a charnel house for your chained slaves!"

Riverton was a big man, toughened by his years in a brutal occupation and accustomed to brawls, but he backed away from the primal anger of the other man.

"You say you don't feel fit to judge your fellow man in this matter. Why do you change your mind?"

Pieter stepped back again and took a moment to calm himself. "You are correct. I don't wish to be a judge. But that house has been my home. You are planning an abomination for it."

The Englishman attempted to appease him. "It will not be an abomination. I don't intend to mistreat Negroes. They're valuable property, and only a fool mistreats his own property."

"And I suppose you capture them in Africa with kindness?"

"I have never captured a single one of them. I buy them from the Portuguese or from other black men."

"And what of the voyage? I've seen the condition of slaves as they come from those foul ships."

The Englishman shrugged. "It's a business. The greatest profits are made by fitting as many Negroes aboard as possible. Some die. It's a fact of life."

"It's a vile, unspeakable sin!"

"Do you take pity on the whales?"

"Whales are not men."

"If it were not me, then it would be someone else."

"How do you sleep at night?"

The Englishman was stunned. Pieter had asked about the problem that was the bane of his life. He sat down on the wooden bench next to the freshly planted flowers. "Why do you ask?"

"Some men are brutes and no task is too low for them," Pieter said. "I don't think you're one of those men. You're intelligent and you care for your family. Therefore, it's a very logical question. How do you sleep at night?"

"Badly," the Englishman admitted. "But is it wrong for a man to want to give his family a good life? Is it wrong for a man to want his share of the world's wealth?"

"There are other ways to obtain wealth."

"I was a creature of the slums. As a child I cried myself to sleep because of the hunger in my stomach. I begged for scraps of bread. I stole crusts. I ate food that had rotted and been thrown away. Am I wrong because I managed to escape from those horrors?"

"I will not judge you," Pieter said. "You've become your own judge and I think you've found yourself guilty."

"It's too late to change the world. I'll continue with the trade that has taken me from the streets."

"You'll not do it in a house of mine. I'll have no slaves chained to the walls that have heard the laughter of my children."

"I have a lease! You've already taken my money."

"The money will be returned. As for the lease, it can be broken. I think you'll find I have more influence here than you."

The Englishman wrung his hands together. "I need that house. It stands near the new wharf. Forget the terms of the lease. I'll pay a double amount."

The idea of the extra money appealed to Pieter. Times had not been the best, and— No, no, no, dammit! I will not do it, he thought.

As if he were reading the other man's mind, Riverton said, "I'll pay triple the amount."

Pieter did not hesitate. "No. Be damned with your money!"

A crafty look came over the Englishman's face. "I'll make a deal with you, de Kuyper."

"I want no 'deals.' "

"This one might interest you."

"I doubt it."

"I'll take this extra rent," Riverton continued, ignoring Pieter's objections, "and place it in trust with the governor's office. A special fund to buy freedom for deserving slaves."

"They shouldn't be slaves in the first place."

"Ah, but they are, aren't they? And will continue to be unless . . . unless you help use this money to free them."

Pieter mulled over the proposition. He shrank from the idea . . . but still . . .

"If I don't lease your house I'll find another," Riverton said. "At least if you accept my offer you'll be able to do some good."

The man was correct, Pieter thought. He would find another house . . . the slaves would come . . . they would be sold . . . the crime would continue. But if he accepted Riverton's offer at lease some of the poor devils could be helped . . . it was the lesser of two evils.

"Very well," he said. "Triple rent."

"Done."

"Have the papers sent to my office and I'll sign them."

"Two-thirds of the triple rent will go to the governor's office. The other third to you."

"All the money with the governor to go toward the freedom of a slave," Pieter said, but his words carried an edge of sadness. He knew, despite any rationalization he made, he was compromising his principles.

"Of course."

The Englishman did not smile in triumph. He had the building, but he had also hoped to have Pieter de Kuyper's friendship. Now it could never be.

Pieter left the house and took Jacob Adam with him. As he walked with his son, who was still mooning over the girl, he knew he would never again set foot in the Englishman's house. Nor the Englishman in his.

The house on Pearl Street became a barracks for the newly arrived slaves. The wretched black men and women, covered with sores and wasted from their long voyage, lay on the floor and moaned as their overseers fattened them up before placing them on the block to be sold like cattle to the highest bidder.

Pieter refused to go near the house. It was enough that he knew what was happening there. He did not want to see it. For a long time after the arrival of the slaves, he had trouble getting to sleep and he felt as if he had made a pact with the devil.

Jacob Adam continued to be madly in love with Elizabeth Riverton. He would go out of his way to pass the house on Stone Street in hopes of catching a glimpse of her, even though he knew his father's feelings about the house on Pearl Street and realized the two families had no future together.

He was walking down Stone Street when he saw Elizabeth coming from the opposite direction. He gathered his courage and spoke to her. She gave him her most radiant smile and seemed to encourage his advances. She acted as if she had done nothing but pine for him since that day they had dined together.

This happened several times, and he began to be certain that somehow, some way, when the time came for him to take a wife, Elizabeth would still be smiling, waiting for him.

And then one day she was walking down the street, both hands holding on to the arm of a tall, handsome man who was wearing the cap of a sea captain. She laughed, grasped his arm more tightly, and gave him a little peck on the cheek.

Jacob Adam saw all this and turned his head, hoping that she would not see him. "Look who's here," she said with a pleasant laugh.

Jacob Adam managed to look at her and smile.

"This is Jacob Adam de Kuyper," she said to the man on her arm. "Jacob Adam is an admirer of mine. He takes care of me when you aren't here." She giggled.

"I'm Robert Barrow," the man said, extending his hand.

Jacob Adam mumbled his greetings as they shook hands, his own buried in the huge paw of the other. "Elizabeth has told me all about you," Robert Barrow said. "I understand your father is our landlord."

Jacob Adam stared at the man in puzzlement.

"Robert is the captain of my father's ship," Elizabeth explained. "He's also my second cousin, but we're not going to let that stop us."

"Stop you?"

"From getting married," Elizabeth said. There was a devilish gleam in her eye, and in that instant Jacob Adam knew the girl had only been leading him on.

Jacob Adam had remarkable control. He was filled with anger, but kept it completely within himself. "I wish you both great happiness," he said coldly.

The captain was genuine in his appreciation, but Elizabeth had a cruel look in her eyes. To think that this *boy* had presumed to believe she could become interested in him. But now her eyes told him that she had put him in his place and her triumph was complete.

Jacob Adam went home and threw himself on his bed. He wanted to cry, but no tears would come. He couldn't even remember the last time he had cried.

A week later Elizabeth married her sea captain, and they had two full weeks together before his ship took on a cargo of dried fish, hides, and naval stores. These would be taken to Europe and unloaded, and then the captain would take his ship down to the coast of Africa for another cargo of "black gold."

John Riverton gave a lavish wedding for his daughter,

but very few of the leading citizens of New Amsterdam attended. They were content that Riverton live among them and add to the general wealth of the colony, but the man was a dealer in slaves and they did not want him as a friend.

Anne de Kuyper de Witt gave birth to another child. She was one of the first to have her baby at the colony's first new hospital. She was attended by Doctor Varrenvangen, the talented surgeon who had given up his practice in Amsterdam to found the hospital.

The child was named Paul.

Pieter came to visit his new grandson. Of his three children, Anne was the only one who gave him pleasure. She had married well and had now made him a grandfather for the second time. It was a shame the child would bear the name de Witt. Pieter would have liked to know that future generations would also recognize the name de Kuyper, but for this assurance he would have to depend on his sons.

Young Pieter, of course, could not be counted on. He had remained in Holland even after his friend, Adriaen Van der Donck, had returned to the colony and opened up a law office. Van der Donck had given Pieter news of his son. Young Pieter had flourished in Europe, was thinking of marriage, and would never return. If he had sons, they would almost certainly remain in Europe.

This left only Jacob Adam.

There seemed little doubt this son would remain in the colony. He would marry and have children, and they would be the future de Kuypers of New Amsterdam.

The thought was comforting and at the same time quite unsettling to Pieter. There was much about his youngest son that he did not understand. Even more than that, there was something about his youngest son that troubled him.

Because the winter had been long and hard, David de Witt was pleased when he looked through the window and saw that the first spring thaw was due any day. He was in the back room of the warehouse that served the grain brokerage company of Abraham de Witt & Son.

The door opened, and he looked up at his unexpected visitor.

It was his brother-in-law.

"Come in. Stand by the fire and get the chill out of your bones."

Jacob Adam took off his cap and gloves and rubbed his hands together as he stood by the fire. David handed him a cup of coffee, which he drank in silence.

"Will you be shipping aboard the *William* this year?" he said to open the conversation.

Jacob Adam put down his cup. "Why should I bother with whales? And why do you bother with grain?"

David de Witt had learned to respect his fifteen-year-old brother-in-law. Jacob Adam had a brilliant mind, cold and calculating to be sure, but as tough and stubborn as a bear trap. David waited for him to come to his point.

"Oh, there's a living in whaling. And a man can be happy with the profits from grain brokerage, I suppose. But both are very limited and not very satisfying," Jacob Adam said, bringing a chair close to the fire and sitting down on it.

"And what is more satisfying?"

"Making a fortune in land. It's there, you know. You just have to know how to go about it."

"Any particular land?"

"No. The land on Manhatan. The land on the other side of the North River. The land on Long Island. It's everywhere. Think of how the colony continues to grow. The man who owns land will own what people need. When you own what people need, you own *them*."

"Agreed," David said.

Jacob Adam drew a bulky document from inside his coat. He turned a few pages and proceeded to read: ". . . those who remove to New Netherland with five souls above fifteen years, to all such our governor there shall grant in property two hundred acres. . . ."

He stopped reading and looked at the other man. "Anyone who brings in five settlers gets land."

"Two hundred acres," David said impatiently. "I know that. Everyone knows that. It's been a law for years."

"A very ambiguously worded law. One could easily interpret it as giving two hundred acres for *each* of the five souls settled."

David reread the paragraph. "Yes . . . I suppose it could be interpreted to mean that."

"Not only could, but will be interpreted to mean that."

"What are you talking about?"

"I retained the services of Adriaen Van der Donck. He petitioned the governor, and Stuyvesant has agreed to give the sponsor of five settlers not two hundred acres, but a thousand."

The smile that started to form on David's lips disappeared as a cloud entered his mind. "So what? Five settlers split a thousand acres instead of two hundred. Where's the fortune in that?"

"The sponsor doesn't tell the settlers about the thousand acres. He tells them about two hundred. They come to settle and they split two hundred acres. The sponsor keeps the other eight hundred for himself."

David laughed. "That sounds like a fair split."

"Especially for the sponsor."

"But how do you expect to find settlers? Few farmers in the Netherlands show any interest in leaving. What makes you think you can get them to come here?"

"By not bothering with the farmers in the Netherlands. They're too fat and content with their lives. We must get settlers from a place that's in turmoil. From a place where the farmers are starving. From a place where people fear to go to sleep at night."

"And where is this place?"

"England."

David de Witt was astounded. "You'd bring English settlers to fill a Dutch colony?"

"English, French, Swedes—what difference does it make?" Jacob Adam said, dismissing the problem with a wave of his hand. "When settlers come here they forget where they came from. They become like us. This is our home and this is what we care about. Tell me, David, do you really care what happens in Holland? Or London? Do you really give a damn about the entire continent of Europe?"

"I suppose you're right," David said. "People change when they come here. God alone knows how many kinds of people we have in New Amsterdam, and they all seem to get along fairly well."

"Exactly. When people come here they're no longer interested in fighting the battles of Europe."

"But these English settlers will want their full share of the lands granted them by the government."

"They'll get it. Two hundred acres—split among them."

"But the contract—"

"—is in Dutch. How many hayseed English farmers can read anything in their own language, much less in Dutch?"

"They'll find out someday."

"Yes, and by then it will be too late. Trust me."

David de Witt sat down behind the long table that served as his desk and pondered the proposition.

Jacob Adam did not interrupt, but allowed his brother-in-law time to sort the details for himself. He had baited his hook and dropped it, and now there was nothing to do but bring it in. But a man was like a fish. You had to give him enough line. If you became impatient, the line would snap and you'd lose your fish.

The idea had its attractions for David. For some time now he had been impatient working for his father. The older man was too cautious, he thought, always resisting change. It would be wonderful to get into a business of his own, and out from under his father's thumb.

After a few minutes of silence, he raised another question: "What inducement will you offer the settlers to get them to come?"

"We'll pay their passage and guarantee the land. In addition we'll give each of them a bonus of ten English pounds. We'll get this money back by charging them a quitrent fee of two pounds a year for five years."

"That could amount to a lot of money. Do you have it?"

"No."

"Your father?"

Jacob Adam shrugged. "He wouldn't give it to me once he learned what I planned on doing with it."

David threw up his hands. "But I don't have such an amount of money. And my father wouldn't give me a penny if he knew we were talking about English settlers."

"We also need money to charter a ship."

"Then what's the use of talking about this?" David asked in annoyance. "It's a good plan, but it takes money and we haven't got any. So that's an end to it."

"Not quite."

"You know how to get the money?"

"Of course. You don't think I'd come to you with half a plan, do you?"

"How do we get the money?"

"We bring in a third partner. Someone who wouldn't be interested in taking an active part. Someone who couldn't care less if the settlers were Dutch or English or yellow heathens from the land of the Great Khan. And our partner must be a very wealthy man, one who has enough vision to understand the sort of profits to be made."

"Do you know of such a man?"

"Yes."

A long pause. "Who?"

"It must remain our secret."

"From the way you talk, I might not want my name publicly connected with his. Who is this person?"

"Michael de Pauw."

It was after midnight when the two young men left the town house of Michael de Pauw. One of them, de Kuyper, wasn't much more than a boy, de Pauw reflected. But the lad was shrewd, and this outrageous plan was obviously his.

At first de Pauw had been wary when the two young men called upon him. Pieter de Kuyper was an old enemy, and Abraham de Witt was no friend. The appearance of their sons brought out the old brigand's suspicions that they had been sent by their fathers. But as the young men unfolded their plan, de Pauw became certain their fathers knew nothing of it.

In the end he conceded they had an excellent idea. They had already obtained the governor's agreement on the thousand-acre grant. They had selected a place to recruit settlers. They had worked out a bonus system. They had even talked to an English captain about chartering his ship.

All they needed was the money to get the scheme moving.

De Pauw chuckled to himself. The young rascals! They knew that the plan would be irresistible to him. In the first place, the profits would be huge. In the second place, if it ever caused a scandal the city government would be loath to punish two enterprising young Dutch-

men for taking advantage of English settlers. Dutch
pride would come to their rescue. Furthermore, the plan
was to settle only the lands on the western side of the
North River, at least in the beginning. Since the governor was having enough problems with Manhatan, he
didn't give a damn what happened across the river.

There was another reason de Pauw liked the plan. His
two partners were the sons of men who had opposed and
fought him over the years. What better way to avenge
himself than to make their sons his partners?

And so he had agreed to put up all the money and let
them do all the work.

Michael de Pauw looked up at the sound of coughing.
It came from his son, Robert, good-natured, pleasant,
and empty-headed.

"Yes, Robert," he said in a voice that ended with a sigh.

"Perhaps it would be a good idea for me to go to England and personally select the settlers. We do want only
the best sort, don't we?"

"That's good of you to offer, son, but you must remember that you can't be actively connected with this scheme.
If you became involved, everyone would know that I
was, too."

Robert's head bobbed up and down. "Oh yes, of
course. We're to be silent partners. It does seem strange,
though. I mean, here we own a third of the venture but
must pretend to know nothing about it."

"It will work out for the best."

A cheery smile came over Robert's face. "Well, I'm
glad it's settled. I must be off to bed. Good night, Father," he said and left the room.

Michael de Pauw watched him go and shook his
head. It was unfortunate that his son had inherited his
mother's brains, or lack of them.

He sighed again. A man could chart his own course
through life, he thought, and he could outwit the world
and make a fortune, but he had absolutely nothing to
say about the sort of children sent by the Lord. If
Michael de Pauw had been given a choice, he would
have picked a son like Jacob Adam.

It wasn't fair. Pieter de Kuyper could never understand
such a son if he lived to be two hundred years old. He
deserved a harmless ninny, a son who was pleasant and

honest, who would be well liked and who would never amount to anything. He deserved a son like—de Pauw winced at the thought—a son like his own Robert.

A stab of pain hit his chest and he gasped and rested against the back of the chair. The pain lasted only a short time, but it left him weak and trembling. The pains seemed to come more frequently, and each time the agony was a bit worse. He wondered if the time would come when he would willingly surrender his life rather than endure the pain.

When he had regained sufficient strength, he went to the sideboard and poured himself a glass of brandy. It had become his only solace. He swallowed the brandy and refilled the glass. He walked slowly back to his chair and sat down.

Jacob Adam de Kuyper, he thought. And after I am dead how long will it take this Jacob Adam de Kuyper to slice up my own son?

Anne de Witt inspected the row of candlewicks covered with tallow. There were a half-dozen of them hanging from a long pole. "These are ready," she said, moving to the second row for a closer look.

"A few more dippings and this row will be done," Sarah Seixas said as she hefted the pole and carried it from the shed into the house. She lowered the pole carefully over the two-foot-wide kettle, and the embryo candles were submerged in the boiling tallow. She paused a second and then lifted the pole. The candles were bright and shiny with a new layer of tallow. She took them back to the shed and placed the pole so the ends rested on the backs of two chairs. The tallow was already dull as it cooled.

Anne picked up a second pole, carried it to the kettle, and repeated the process. Six candles-in-the-making hung from each pole. After twenty dippings the original double-twist of wick would have accumulated enough tallow to be a proper candle. When the tallow set to a hard finish, the candles would be removed from the pole and replaced by new wicks so the process could be repeated.

"We'll make almost fifty candles today," Sarah said with pride. "Our best day."

Anne picked off a bit of dripping tallow that was

hardening into an irregular-shaped ball in the middle
of a candle. Such imperfections would spoil the finished
work.

She looked across the shed for a moment to watch the
two women who were preparing new wicks. The women
twisted the strands of milkweed until they were tight
and strong enough to hold their shape. These were then
tied in double thickness to a pole, soon to begin the
process of dipping in the tallow. When the women had
fashioned enough wicks to last awhile, they would turn
to cutting up the various bits of fat being used to make
the tallow. No odd piece of fat was overlooked in any of
their kitchens—deer suet, moose fat, bear grease.

"Let's take a rest," Anne said to Sarah, and they returned to the fire and sat near the two kettles that held
the tallow. One or the other was constantly over the fire.

The ground floor of the Seixas house was one large
room. It was kitchen, living room, and dining room all
in one. Upstairs were several tiny rooms, which held the
sleeping alcoves. Heavy drapery hid all the beds; not one
could be seen during daylight hours. This was not a
custom of the Seixas family or the Jewish community, but
one they had adopted from the Dutch. The house was
tidy and spotless and did not reveal that because of economic conditions it was the living and sleeping quarters
for seventeen people.

"I can't thank you enough for helping us," Sarah said,
filling two cups with cider as she talked. She handed one
to Anne, who wiped the perspiration from her brow before quenching her thirst. The making of candles was
hard, hot work. The heavy kettles had to be shifted
constantly back and forth. The poles gathered weight as
the tallow accumulated. But the most tiring part of all
was the tedious business of watching that each wick and
dipping was precise. One could never hurry the work. An
improperly fashioned wick would make a useless candle,
as would a sloppy or careless dipping. If the tallow
was not exactly smooth and even it would crack when
hardened, and the candle would have to be thrown away.

"You're doing fine work," Anne said.

"It was all your idea to make candles," Sarah protested. "Such a wonderful idea . . . you have no idea how
much this money means to us."

Anne knew. The idea of helping the small community of Jews had occurred to her when one of their women had come to her door begging to be allowed to do some washing. She looked hungry and offered to do the work for a pittance so small Anne's heart ached. Something had to be done for these people, she decided.

The problem stemmed from Governor Stuyvesant's stubborn refusal to allow Jews to engage in commerce. They could slaughter cattle and dress meat, and they could work on ships—and at first that was all they could do. Things had begun to ease up, but most Jews found in other trades were usually in the lowest-paying jobs. Being realists, none of them dared even to dream of holding public office. They were allowed to take their places among the night watch, but most men, Jews and Christians alike, considered this chore a dubious honor.

Anne's idea was to start a local candle industry among the Jews. Candles were needed by everyone, and yet, because almost all were imported from Europe, many people simply couldn't afford them. At a price of four pence each they were beyond the means of a great many families. Even the wealthier people who could manage the expense were very judicious in their use of candles. A tin or pewter candle box near the fireplace was a recognized sign of affluence.

Anne didn't know any Jews, so she asked her father for his advice. Pieter replied that he had a Jew—Isaack Seixas—aboard his own ship and he would mention Anne's idea to him. The next morning Isaack's wife, Sarah, had shown up at Anne's door, eager to learn about the new business.

It had been only two months since Sarah and two other Jewish women had joined Anne in the enterprise, but already they were on their way to success. The first few days were the worst. None of them knew very much about the manufacture of candles, and for every good one made they ruined three or four others. But their determination paid off: they learned how to make perfect wicks and how to dip them properly in the tallow, and now they ruined no more than three or four candles a day.

"We received an order from people on Staten Island," Sarah said. "How on earth did they hear about us over there?"

"At two pence each our candles are a bargain," Anne replied. "In time I wouldn't be surprised if we weren't filling orders from the English settlements."

"This is the first business my people have started in New Amsterdam," Sarah said. "Until now we've only been allowed to work for other people."

Anne knew next to nothing about Jews and their customs. She was indifferent to the fact they professed a different religion and had "strange" customs. "Has it always been this way with your people?"

"Oh no," Sarah said. "My family, and many others, were merchants when we lived in Brazil. And my grandfather before that in Spain."

"Then you haven't always been poor?"

"No," Sarah said with a sigh. "I guess you might even say we were wealthy. But then we were forced to flee Brazil and the pirates robbed us of everything. The little we brought with us to New Amsterdam was auctioned off to pay the French captain who brought us here on his ship."

It surprised Anne to hear these Jews had once been people of substance. Because they had arrived in an impoverished state, the New Amsterdam burghers treated them as paupers who desired nothing more than to get on public relief. There was little fear of that. Governor Stuyvesant promised to hang any Jew who asked as much as a copper from the public coffers. Needless to say, no Jew could be found who was willing to test the governor on this particular promise.

"Do you hate Governor Stuyvesant?" she asked quietly.

Sarah Seixas looked thoughtful as she answered. "No, he's not all that bad. It's true he's imposed restrictions on us, but I think he's much harder on the Catholics."

That was probably true, Anne thought. Only a week ago the Governor had flogged several Catholics, simply because they were Catholics, and shipped them off to indentured slavery in the Indies. He was equally harsh with Lutherans and Baptists.

"Stuyvesant is an old crank," Anne said. "He worries about all the wrong things."

"At least he allows us to lead our lives," Sarah said with a smile. "I've heard he's been told about our candle business and has granted us permission to continue."

It was Anne's turn to smile. "Yes, he has granted that

permission." It was Anne's own father who had informed
the governor about the venture—on Anne's orders.
Pieter told the governor in no uncertain terms that for the
good of the community at large Jews must be allowed to
become useful, productive people. How could they sus-
tain themselves if they were not allowed to engage in
commerce, Pieter's argument went. If you do not let
them earn money you will be forcing them to steal or ask
for public relief. The governor could not help but see the
wisdom in allowing the candle business to continue un-
molested.

Sarah Seixas was not exaggerating when she said many
in the Jewish community had been people of substance.
They were Marrano and Sephardi Jews. The Marranos
and Sephardim were educated men and women who had
been merchants in Spain, North Africa, and South America. The forefathers of the Marranos had been Jews who
lived as Christians in Spain—some for hundreds of years.
The Sephardic ancestors had been men of the world, men
of commerce and literature, men accepted as men, and
quite incidentally as Jews, by the Moorish-influenced
culture that had flourished as a bright jewel in the
darkened crown of Europe. Most of them spoke Spanish,
dressed as Spaniards, and lived as Spaniards. The
bearded old men hunched all day over a venerable
Talmud belonged to another world. But the lives of the
Sephardim changed with the ascent to the throne of
Ferdinand and Isabella. In the year 1492, the same in
which Columbus first gazed upon the lands of the New
World, the dual monarchs instituted the beginnings of the
movement that was to see the meteoric rise of the
Dominican Friars as fanatical purgers of all heresies. It
was the beginning of one of the blackest pages in
Europe's history.

"Do you miss Brazil?" Anne asked.

"I miss the lovely home we had," Sarah admitted,
looking around at her present room and laughing. "This
whole house would have fit in our front parlor."

"Why did you leave?" Anne asked, innocently unaware of the Inquisition, which had never come to New
Amsterdam.

"Well," Sarah said with hesitation, and then decided
if there was one person in the world she could trust, it

was Anne de Witt. "The Catholic priests arrived and . . . it was impossible for my people to stay."

"Why do the priests persecute your people?"

It was a touchy subject, and Sarah had been conditioned to avoid the topic at all costs, but somehow it didn't seem right to be evasive with Anne. "We have a different belief about God."

"Yes?"

"We believe God is One," Sarah said, and when she saw that Anne did not understand, she decided to test the extent of the other woman's friendship. "We don't believe that Jesus Christ is God."

Anne's eyebrows raised. She had never heard anything quite like this. But she quickly decided it was not her role to act as a spokesman for God. "Neither does my older brother," she said, and Sarah's last fear was put to rest. "So all of you left Brazil to come here," Anne continued.

"Not all of us," Sarah said in a quiet voice. "Some were sent back to Lisbon before they could escape."

"What happened to them in Lisbon?"

"They were burned at the stake."

Anne shuddered at the horrible idea. At least such things couldn't happen to people living under a Dutch flag, she thought. The Dutch might not exactly clasp Jews to their breasts, but they treated them in a reasonably civilized manner. And it benefited both sides—witness the contribution they were beginning to make with the candle industry. And others would be sure to follow.

"It's time to apply more tallow," Anne said, rising from her chair. She wished to hear no more about such things as people being burned at the stake.

They went back to the tedious process of dipping the wicks, allowing them to dry, dipping again, drying, dipping, until finally they had a row of finished candles. Then new wicks would be tied to the poles and the process begun once again.

Anne returned home as the sun was setting. Pieter was in the kitchen enjoying a hot flip of rum, beer, and sugared nutmeg. He often stopped by at the end of the day to see his grandchildren. "How is my little candle maker?" he asked in a teasing voice.

"Tired," she said, ignoring the gibe. She came to his

side and kissed his cheek. "But happy. I feel good about helping those people."

Pieter nodded. "Isaack Seixas is one of the ablest, hardest-working men on my ship," he said. "If he's an example of what those people are like, we're lucky to have them here."

Anne bustled around as she began to prepare the evening meal before David arrived home. "Will you eat with us tonight, Father?"

"Thank you, no. Zilla will be waiting for me. And Jacob Adam. I'll just relax awhile with my drink."

"You're welcome to stay."

"I know."

He sipped his warm drink and watched his daughter as she worked. He felt a moisture in his eyes as he tracked her every movement. She reminded him so much of Christiana. Certain mannerisms, certain words she used, certain ways she thought were an inheritance from her mother. Starting up this candle business with the women, for example. How Christiana would have approved of that.

He recalled Christiana's goat cooperative. He remembered the long days she had spent at the pens, caring for the goats, milking them, currying them with a stiff brush, worrying about them. The long hours she had spent on the ledgers, keeping track of what was coming in and what was being spent, even on winter nights when she would finally be forced to stop working because the room grew so frigid the ink froze in its well. And, finally, how she had mourned when the goats sickened and died; how she had wept and turned her face to the wall, crying herself to sleep.

The moisture in Pieter's eyes became tears, and he looked away so his daughter could not see them. The years were passing like milestones on a long road, and at each cold stone a man left a bit of his life, never to be seen again. Someday the road would end and there would be nothing left of a man but what he had lost along the way.

In November of 1659, Michael de Pauw died. Pieter refused to go to the funeral.

"But you knew him for so many years," Anne protested.

"And hated him for just as many."

"Don't speak that way of the dead!"

"I'm sure de Pauw would have nothing good to say of me if the situation was the other way around."

"I still think you should go," Anne said, turning to her brother for help. "What do you think?"

Jacob Adam shrugged. "It's up to Father."

"See," Pieter said in triumph. "That makes sense. No de Kuyper should be caught within a hundred yards of that funeral."

"I plan on going," Jacob Adam said.

"What?"

"Robert de Pauw is my friend."

"That ninny!"

Pieter wanted to order his son not to attend, but knew it would be wrong. Besides, Jacob Adam would go anyway if that was what he wished.

"I'll go with you," Anne said defiantly to her brother.

Pieter shook his head and grumbled, but in the end he too went to the funeral.

Michael de Pauw's white face looked peaceful. More peaceful than he's looked in years, Pieter thought as he looked into the casket.

He was surprised that he no longer hated the man.

"Rest in peace, Michael de Pauw," he said softly. "Rest in peace."

7

His Excellency, James, Duke of York

1664 - 1667

THE ENGLISH FLEET CAME AROUND CONEY IS-
land, passed through the Narrows and anchored in the
Upper Bay. There were four men-of-war, carrying 450
regular troops. The force was under the command of
Colonel Richard Nicolls. The date was August 28, 1664.

The news caused consternation in New Amsterdam.
Dutch relations with the English had been deteriorating,
but the mother countries in Europe were presently at
peace with one another. What was the explanation for
the strong English force?

The people of New Amsterdam were kept waiting
twenty-four hours for an answer. Then a small boat put
out from the fleet. Two officers sat near the stern as the
broad-backed sailors rowed the boat toward the quay.
A white flag of truce fluttered at the bow.

Governor Stuyvesant led the burgomasters and aldermen to the end of the quay. Several other important
men followed a few paces behind, and two hundred
others—men, women, and children—watched from a
respectful distance on the shore. The soldiers of the garrison were at their positions along the walls of the fort.
The cannons were loaded and primed, and the gunners waited patiently for the governor's command.

The sailors raised their oars as the longboat pulled
alongside the quay. Hands grasped the landing's planking, made of solid tree trunks, and the boat came to a

stop without rippling the water. The two officers stepped
ashore, their uniforms bright and clean, their swords and
decorations polished and gleaming in the early-morning
sun.

They were young men.

Too young, Pieter de Kuyper thought, as he stood
with his fellow aldermen by the side of the governor. The
assembled burghers were, almost to a man, grizzled
graybeards, weathered and seasoned by the years, tempered and tried by sorrows and triumphs. But the English
officers looked rosy-cheeked, new, and untried. Pieter
couldn't help comparing them to his twenty-year-old son,
Jacob Adam. If these young Englishmen were anything
like his son, they were not to be dismissed lightly.

Governor Stuyvesant stepped forward, his face a
hostile mask. He placed his hands on his hips; his legs
were spread, the wooden leg placed defiantly in front
of the one made of flesh and blood. "Old Silver Nails"
was not in a pleasant mood.

The senior English officer saluted and asked if he was
addressing His Excellency, Governor Peter Stuyvesant.
The governor ignored the question and reminded the
officer that England and the Netherlands were not at
war.

The officer remained unruffled. "Quite so, sir, quite
so."

"Then what do you want?"

"Colonel Nicolls, the commander of His Majesty's
fleet in these waters, begs to inform you that these lands,
and all the lands from the west bank of the Connecticut
River to the east bank of Delaware Bay, have been
given by Royal charter to His Excellency, James, Duke
of York. Colonel Nicolls begs to inform Your Honor
that he must now take possession of said lands in the
name of Charles, by grace of God, King of England,
Scotland, Ireland, and Wales."

Pieter, along with every man within earshot, was
stunned. They looked toward the governor, whose face
was turning red with anger.

"I tell you our countries are not at war! This is an act
of piracy! You have no right to be here!"

The Englishman ignored the outburst and handed the
governor a sealed envelope. "These are Colonel Nicolls's

terms for your surrender, sir," he said politely. "I trust you will find them most generous."

Stuyvesant looked at the envelope in his hand and then, in a rage, tore it up and threw the pieces on the ground. "Be damned with your terms of surrender! Get off this island before I order the cannons to blast you back into the arms of your maker!"

The young officer saluted and turned smartly. He walked calmly back to the longboat, followed by his aide. They stepped into the craft, the sailors pushed off, and the boat drifted away from the quay. The oars were lowered and the longboat headed back for the fleet anchored at the head of the Narrows.

Governor Stuyvesant went up to the ramparts along the top of the fort's wall and began inspecting the cannons and their crews. It was obvious he intended to fight.

The colonists were in a state of confusion. They did not wish to knuckle under to the English, but four men-of-war carrying hundreds of troops was a very strong force, and they were painfully aware of their own lack of defenses. The entire colony of New Netherland now had over ten thousand people, but only fifteen hundred lived in New Amsterdam. Of these people, one hundred and sixty were garrison soldiers. Another two hundred composed a sort of militia, but it was poorly organized and badly trained. Even this paltry number might have been enough if they had stout fortifications and defenses. But the palisade along Wall Street was in sad repair. Great stretches were missing from one end to the other, torn down for firewood or to make passages for cattle and sheep. Both banks of the river were completely undefended. The only stout defense was the fort, but even this was not all it seemed. It would be possible for the English troops to land and place themselves on the hills near the Broad Way. From there they would look down into the fort. The gunners along the walls would be vulnerable to their fire. As to sustaining a long siege, the fort contained no well, and they couldn't last long without water. But even before they ran out of water they would run out of gunpowder, which was in short supply.

Jacob Adam de Kuyper stepped forward and began gathering the torn pieces of Colonel Nicolls's terms of surrender. The other men crowded around while he patched the pieces together. He proceeded to read the document.

The English, according to the terms of the letter, would not interfere with private property, inheritance rights, or local customs. They would respect freedom of conscience and religion. Public records and buildings would not be disturbed. The colony could maintain direct trade with Holland and other countries. City officials would retain their jobs until such time as a new set of free elections could be held. Finally, in assuming his rights granted by the Royal charter, the Duke of York would do all in his power to help the colony prosper even as it had in the past.

Almost to a man the townspeople thought the terms generous. They wished to surrender. After all, why should they risk their lives for the Netherlands? What had the fat burghers of the States-General ever really done for them? And who was Governor Stuyvesant to decide they should die to satisfy his misguided sense of honor?

"But this is our home," Pieter de Kuyper cried. "We are Dutchmen flying the flag of the United Netherlands. We are free men."

"Yes, free to die!"

"We cannot hand over our homes to the English," Pieter insisted.

Many voices were raised, but only a few agreed with him.

One strong voice raised against him was, surprisingly enough, that of Abraham de Witt. "Why should we resist the English? What do we owe the people in Holland? For over forty years the wealth of this land has been sent to them by the sweat of our brows and by the blood of the people who have died here! I say to hell with them!"

"No—" Pieter started to protest, but Abraham de Witt would not allow him to continue.

"Look around you! Are we an army? Are we soldiers trained to battle an English fleet? No, we are not. We are merchants and farmers who have just gone through several terrible years! Would any man here like to relive the past year? Is there a man among you who has not suffered? I say to hell with fighting the English! Perhaps they come as the will of God to change our fortunes!"

It was an impassioned speech, and Pieter was deeply shaken to find that he and his old friend were at such odds.

Jacob Adam brought them all off their soapboxes and back to cold reality. "Look toward the Narrows," he said.

The four men-of-war were getting under way. They moved majestically, their sails unfurled. The high gunwales were pocked with open gunports, behind each of which there was a dark, sinister cannon. At this distance the guns could not be seen, but the Dutchmen knew they were there.

"Of all that has happened this year, this could be the worst," Oloff Van Cortlandt said, and the men stood on the shore and pondered his words.

It had been, in fact, a year of unrelenting disaster. An earthquake had shaken the colony. Walls tumbled, houses cracked apart. Barns were destroyed and fences uprooted. Two old warehouses were turned into ruins. A group of people were praying in the church courtyard and an old windmill toppled into their midst, killing several and wounding others.

Pieter's houses on Pearl Street were disrupted by the quake and slightly damaged. Men were put to work restoring the property. In the course of their labors they came across the bones of three men buried in what had once been the back of the garden and was now a canvas-covered storage area.

Pieter ordered the bones covered up again and the workmen did so without argument. What were a few old bones in a place like New Amsterdam?

"Must be left over from the Indian War," one of the workmen said.

"That must be it," Pieter agreed, but he knew these bones had nothing to do with Indians. They belonged to Dirk Stratling and his two henchmen who had come, many years ago, to kill him. Instead they had found their own deaths.

Jacob Adam had been standing nearby. He looked closely at the bones. Although it was impossible to tell from the lack of expression on his face, Pieter knew he was interested.

"Indian bones," Pieter said.

Jacob Adam said nothing, but something in his manner disturbed Pieter.

"You have doubts?"

"They are not the bones of Indians."

"Why do you say that?"

"Because I know. They are the bones of three white men who came to kill you."

"How do you know that?"

"My brother told me."

And then Pieter put aside any pretense, because he remembered his oldest son had been a witness to the killing, the burial, all of it. Obviously he had related the story to his little brother. "He told the truth."

"They deserved killing," Jacob Adam said. "I would have done the same."

Yes, Pieter thought, so you would have. And done so without a backward glance at the bodies. His son was perfectly correct, of course, but why did he have to be so icy about everything?

"I wouldn't give it a second thought," Jacob Adam said, reinforcing his father's ideas about him.

The bones were buried once again beneath the damp soil, and Pieter couldn't put them out of his mind. He speculated whether they would ever be dug up again in the future. It gave him a certain amusement to think of some man of a later generation being confronted with this mystery. Who knew but it might even be one of his own descendants.

After the earthquake the spring rains had fallen in amounts not seen before. It was not a great storm, but a steady deluge that went on and on. The ditches filled. Ponds and lakes spilled over their sides, and the waters spread over the land. The soil absorbed as much as it could, and then was able to hold no more. The waters formed new streams and brooks that snaked across the farms and turned the streets of the town into waterways. The water began to stream down from the hills, increasing until it became a flood, racing over the fields, ripping out plants and seedlings, carrying soil to the rivers, drowning small animals and fowl. The waters also brought total ruin to the spring crop. The people prayed they would not return to ruin the fall crop and thereby cause a famine.

"I want to die, I want to die!" eleven-year-old Emilie de Witt had shouted as she ran through the house and threw herself on her bed.

"What's the matter?" Anne asked, but the only reply she got was a mumbled "the cellar, the cellar." She went to the cellar door and opened it, then stood back in dismay. The cellar was flooded, and she could see the bodies of three dead cats that had been trapped there.

It was weeks before Emilie began to act normally. Anne understood. Her daughter loved cats the way she herself loved flowers. Both flowers and cats had suffered much because of the waters.

This past year had also seen more trouble with the Indians. A farmer at Esopus had gotten into an argument with one of them. The verbal abuse turned into a fistfight, and the Indian got the worst of it. No one knew what the argument was about, or who had been in the right, nor did it really make any difference. The Indians massacred twenty farmers and their families, and it looked like the beginning of another war. Farmers carried guns as they worked in their fields. Traders kept one eye on their goods and one hand on their weapons. Finally the tension slackened and the Indians returned to more peaceful ways, but most people did not sleep very well and it was a time of great uneasiness.

As if all this were not enough, an epidemic of smallpox broke out. The masters of ships refused to unload their cargoes. Many people died. And the children were shut up like wild animals to keep them from contracting the dread disease.

It was then Anne de Witt earned the title "Saint." When the pox broke out she moved her own children— Emilie and Paul—to a farm in the north of the island. Then she took on the self-appointed task of caring for the sick. Every morning she would venture forth from her home with baskets of food and medicine to dispense at the houses of the victims.

"But you'll get the pox," David objected.

"Not if I'm careful," she replied.

"You must go up to the farms in the north with the other people," he insisted.

But nothing he could do or say would dissuade her from making her rounds of mercy. Though she was cautious never to enter the houses of the sick, instead stopping at the door and passing the food inside, she always had a few words of hope for the suffering victims.

"Sarah will get better," she said to Isaack Seixas, keeping his distance inside the open door of his house.

He took the basket and shook his head. "It's good of you to say that, but I'm afraid you're wrong. Sarah is wasting away."

"Nonsense. She'll get well. She *must* get well. What will the candle makers do without her?"

Isaack managed a weak smile. "She says the same thing. She's dying and she still thinks of the candles." His eyes brimmed. "We have never forgotten your kindness."

Praise made Anne uncomfortable. She quickly changed the subject. "Have you heard from your children?"

"Yes. A note was brought to us."

"That's good," Anne said, and thanked God for this much at last. The Seixas children, along with many others from the town, had been taken away to the clean ground and air of lands north on the Hudson. A small village already existed at this place, but as yet had no name. It would remain for the English to coin a name that would stick. They would give it a designation that had a familiar ring to them—Greenwich Village.

"And how are you feeling, Isaack?" Anne asked.

"So far I feel nothing," he said, but then added philosophically, "but this is a poxed house."

"That doesn't necessarily mean the disease will get you."

"I leave my fate to the Creator," he said with a shrug.

A few days later it became obvious that Isaack Seixas was not to be spared. His body broke out with pox sores, a fever consumed his body and mind, and his incoherent rantings would end only with his death. Sarah passed on, and her husband joined her but a few hours later. Their bodies, along with those of the other victims, were carried off in the death carts ordered by Stuyvesant, and the corpses were burned in the common pit near the

Collect Pond. Isaack Seixas didn't know it, and there would have been no satisfaction if he had, but he and his wife were the first Jews to be "buried" alongside Christians in New Amsterdam.

And then Anne herself was stricken. The symptoms were all too familiar. She developed severe headaches and backaches, and alternated between high fevers and chills. She became weaker and weaker as the virus worked its way through her system. And then she could no longer rise from her bed and lay there in a state of delirium.

David was beside himself. He walked around the house like a man possessed, refusing to let anyone come inside for fear they would contract the disease. Pieter came every day and talked to David through an open window, and then he would turn and go home looking like a man who was carrying the world on his shoulders. David watched him go one day and felt so helpless and frustrated that he began beating on a door with his fist. He pounded it so hard he splintered the wood and took the skin off his knuckles.

On the fourth day of the illness Anne began to feel better. She could sit up in bed and eat a bit of food. But she knew enough about pox not to be fooled. This was the lull before the storm. "You shouldn't stay in the house," she told her husband. "You might get the pox."

"I have to take care of you."

"But you can see how much better I am."

"You know what's going to happen. I'm staying with you," he said stubbornly.

The next day the characteristic itchy rash began. It came first on her arms, then her legs, and finally her face. The skin lesions were vicious-looking red vesicles, puffing up the skin, filling with pus. The desire to scratch them became more than she could bear, but to do so was an error, often a fatal one, because then the disease would spread even more. David tied her to the bed. He stood off helplessly to the side as he watched her moan and cry. He finally was able to get her to sleep with some herb medicine Zilla brought over.

It went on for a week, and David looked as if he could take no more. He had lost weight, hadn't shaved, and there was a hopelessness in his gaunt eyes. But then the rash suddenly abated, the vesicles dried up and formed scabs, and the urge to scratch was gone. The scabs would fall off and leave Anne's skin pitted. But the pit marks wouldn't be very deep. For all her misery she had been stricken with a fairly mild form of the disease. She was young and had been in good health.

"It's over," David said in a tired voice. "I have you back."

"You're lucky you didn't get it from me," Anne scolded. "I told you to move out."

"The way you moved out on those poor people you helped? That's why you became sick, you know, helping other people."

"Someone had to show they cared."

"You're a saint," David said.

He repeated the remark to others. They nodded and agreed, and the legend of Saint Anne of New Amsterdam was born. It was a legend that would be revived a hundred years later during another plague, and people would pray to this Saint Anne without ever knowing who she really was.

When the smallpox epidemic was over it had carried away about thirty percent of the population. So when Oloff Van Cortlandt said, "Of all that has happened this year, this could be the worst," it made a deep impression on the people.

The English fleet was now closing quickly on the tip of the island, and many soldiers could be seen lining the rails of the transports. The cannon mouths loomed larger and more ominous. There was much activity on the decks as the gunners prepared their weapons.

Jacob Adam and David de Witt stood on a small knoll and observed with growing concern. "There's going to be a fight," David said.

"It's crazy. Those warships will pound us to pulp," Jacob Adam said.

"What can we do?"

"Appeal to the governor. Maybe there's a chance yet."

"If they start shooting I'm taking my family out of town," David said.

Jacob Adam nodded. "Do it now. Just in case. I'm going over by the governor."

David turned and walked toward Anne and his children. If there was to be a war, he didn't want them to be part of it.

Others shared his sentiments.

Abraham de Witt, David's irate father, pointed to the figure of Governor Stuyvesant, who was standing next to a cannon. "We must stop him," Abraham de Witt said, "before he gets us all killed!"

A loud cry of agreement came from a dozen throats, and the townsmen, as if they were a single large animal, swept up the stairs, went along the rampart on top of the wall, and descended upon the governor.

The first English ship was starting to come onto a course that would allow its gunners to blast the fort with a broadside. The other three ships had dropped off, and now they were falling into line behind the leader. If Stuyvesant resisted, the ships would fire broadside after broadside at the fort, the town, and the people.

"Stop this madness!" Van Cortlandt shouted.

"Surrender!" The voice was Abraham de Witt.

The commands were echoed by a dozen men.

"I had rather be carried a corpse to my grave than to surrender the city," the governor said.

The men held their breath as a gunner approached his cannon and put his hand on the firing lanyard. He looked toward the governor.

Samuel de Schuyler, who had been getting signatures on a petition asking for surrender, hurried up to the governor and thrust the paper in his face. "There are ninety-one signatures on this paper. All God-fearing men who demand that you surrender!"

The governor took the piece of paper and looked shaken. Samuel de Schuyler was a brave man, and a loyal one. If he did not wish to fight, no doubt many other brave and loyal men did not wish to do so either. The governor was no longer so sure of himself.

"You say you would rather be in your grave than surrender?" a clear voice asked, and Stuyvesant saw it was Jacob Adam de Kuyper who spoke.

The governor nodded.

"That is, of course, your right. But as for myself and many others, sir, we are too young to be in our graves."

The governor averted his eyes from the steady gaze of the young de Kuyper. If his people would not stand behind him, if they would not fight, then he was beaten. He called off the gunner who stood by the cannon. In a few moments a large white flag was raised above the walls.

The leading English ship immediately broke from its course as sailors climbed up the ratlines and through the shrouds like monkeys and began to furl the sails. The other ships followed, and soon the fleet rode at anchor. Several longboats were lowered; the English commander came ashore.

Stuyvesant was not there to greet him. His face contorted with anger and defeat, the governor had retreated to the Whitehall, his handsome three-story town house near the Battery. Within the hour he left for his bouwerie farther uptown.

Pieter was among the aldermen and burgomasters who officially greeted Colonel Nicolls. He appeared to be a pleasant man, well educated and hardly the ogre or barbarian some of the people had feared. The colonel was taken to City Hall, shown around, and even offered the use of Stuyvesant's private office. He declined.

"We are merely taking legal possession of our rightful lands," he said in precise and fluent Dutch. "We have not come as conquerors."

"Your soldiers are aware of this?" Pieter asked dryly.

"They have their orders," the colonel assured him. "They'll behave."

But an ugly incident occurred within an hour after the troops had been landed ashore.

They were lusty, healthy men who had been confined aboard the ships for more than two months, and discipline aboard a British warship was harsh. Once ashore, half the men were given their liberty. There was a brisk trade in gin, and the bottles were passed about. It had been a long time since any of them had drunk anything except the short rum ration issued on the ships. A good number of the men became soused.

One of these was a farm boy of no more than sixteen years. He was standing with a group of his fellows, wobbly-kneed and glassy-eyed from gin, when Anne de Witt came by with Emilie.

The soldiers hungrily eyed the woman and the girl, but they had been given their orders and knew what would happen if they disobeyed. Colonel Nicolls was a stickler for discipline. Nothing would have happened if the men had not taunted the boy.

"The older one is nice but the little one's too young," a soldier said.

"Not for 'im," another soldier said, jerking his thumb toward the farm boy. "Just about right I'd say."

"'E wouldn't know what to do with 'er," scoffed a third.

"Is that right, boy?" the first soldier said. "Are you just a baby:"

The boy was very drunk. And annoyed. The men were always taunting him about his tender years and the fact that he didn't shave. Now his gin-soaked brain decided enough was enough. He would show his mates what he was made of. He stepped onto the dirt roadway and confronted the women. Before anyone knew what was happening, he grabbed Emilie and kissed her. The girl shouted and pushed him away.

Anne stepped between her daughter and the boy, and the latter grabbed her arm because he was losing his balance.

"Get your hand off me," Anne said, and slapped him in the face.

The farm boy had a bewildered look on his face as the other soldiers rushed up and grabbed him.

"Beggin' the missus' pardon," one of them said to Anne, "but this one 'ere didn't know what 'e was doin'."

Anne looked at the boy. She could see how frightened he was, and also drunk. "I'm s-s-sorry," the boy stammered, "I didn't mean—"

Anne suddenly saw the silliness of the situation. She turned to the older soldier. "Better keep your eye on him until he sobers up."

The soldier nodded. "Yes, missus, we'll be doin' that. 'E be only a boy."

Anne took Emilie's hand, nodded at the soldier, and continued down the street. "He didn't hurt you, did he?"

"No," Emilie said. "I wasn't even scared. Boy, did he smell of gin."

"It's the fault of the older men who gave it to him."

"He *looks* like a nice boy."

"He probably is," Anne said. "Well, nobody got hurt and it's all over."

But it wasn't over. The incident had been witnessed by a Dutch soldier on the walls of the fort. He reported it to the commandant, who immediately went to Colonel Nicolls and complained. "Your men have only just stepped ashore and already they're making free with our women."

"It was only one man?" the colonel asked in a steely voice.

"One," the commandant said. "But if he goes unpunished there will be more incidents."

"By your leave, sir," Colonel Nicolls said, "there will be no more incidents." And then he snapped out several orders and a lieutenant went scurrying to carry them out.

Anne and Emilie met David near the City Hall. They were standing near the Whitehall when Anne saw the young farm boy being dragged down the street. She saw his frightened expression and realized they were leading him to the whipping post.

"They can't do this to him. He's only a boy," she said, and related the incident to her husband.

David was unsympathetic. "If he can't behave himself when he drinks, he shouldn't drink."

"But he really didn't do anything, Papa," Emilie said.

"He must be taught a lesson," David said sternly.

The three of them watched as the boy's shirt was ripped from his back. He was very white below the neck. A master-at-arms opened a canvas bag and drew out a vicious-looking cat-o'-nine-tails. The strapping master-at-arms took up a position behind the whipping post as two other soldiers tied the boy's arms with strips of rawhide.

Emilie was wide-eyed and close to tears.

"This is terrible," Anne complained again to her husband. He looked at her and shook his head.

"They've got to be kept in line."

The boy was tied down, and the master-at-arms looked toward the lieutenant for his orders.

"Three dozen. Well laid on," the lieutenant said in a crisp, businesslike voice. "Commence punishment."

Anne's mouth was dry as she watched the burly man

raise the lash and bring it around in a swift, whistling arc. There was a sickening thud as the nine knotted thongs cracked against the boy's back. He grunted and his body strained forward toward the front of the whipping post, but he did not cry out. Nine crimson lines appeared on his naked flesh as if by magic. He began to whimper.

"One!" a sergeant cried out.

"Two!"

"Three!"

And now the boy began to scream with each lash, a high-pitched scream that broke off into chokes and sobs. The red lines were all over his back now, and the blood was beginning to drip, spreading from lash mark to lash mark, turning his back into a field of red.

"Where is this Colonel Nicolls?" Anne said angrily to David. "He's got to stop this!"

David pointed to Nicolls, who was standing with a group of men farther down the street. "But it won't do any good," he said.

"Don't let Emilie watch," she said, and walked very rapidly toward the English colonel. Six! Seven! Eight! The sounds of the lash as it connected with bare flesh continued. The screams were becoming hoarse and more desperate.

"Colonel Nicolls," Anne said to the Englishman. "You must put a stop to this!"

"I beg your pardon, madam?" the startled man said.

Pieter was standing with the group around the colonel. He stepped forward. "Colonel Nicolls, may I present my daughter, Mrs. Anne de Witt."

"A pleasure, madam," the Colonel said, and bowed.

"Sixteen! Seventeen! Eighteen!

"Stop beating that boy," Anne said.

"He disobeyed orders, madam. He knew what to expect."

Anne looked to her father for help. "What the boy did was nothing. I know, I was there. Can't you make the colonel understand?"

"I believe the colonel must maintain discipline," Pieter said, attempting to quiet her down.

Anne looked at the two men and shook her head.

"Men!" she said, as if it were the vilest epithet she knew, and turned on her heel and walked away.

The colonel looked at Pieter. "I too have a strong-willed daughter, sir. I understand."

The crowd watched the whipping in fascination. The screams stopped at the twenty-sixth stroke, when the boy lapsed into unconsciousnes, but the blows continued until the assigned punishment of three dozen had been delivered.

"Thirty-six!"

Anne forced herself to look at the limp figure in the whipping post. The boy's back looked like raw, bloody mincemeat. The flesh was mush, and in places it was possible to see exposed bone. She went back to Colonel Nicolls and asked if the whipped boy could be brought to her house to be cared for. The colonel gave his consent, and the farm boy lived in the de Witt house for two weeks as his back healed. Some of his comrades called on him; the English had begun to mingle with the Dutch.

It wasn't much of a chore to bring the two peoples together. Many of the townspeople had English blood in their veins, and they viewed the newcomers as "cousins." A good many of the others had grown tired of the imperious ways of the States-General in The Hague. They were happy enough to cut these ties.

One who was unhappy was Pieter de Kuyper. He had been among the first to come to this colony, one of the first to settle permanently, one of the first to bring a wife and start a family, one of the first to learn to love this island and this land. But he was a Dutchman and he had loved it as a Dutch possession. It did not seem right to have expended so much Dutch sweat and so much Dutch blood simply to hand it all over to the English.

He could not sleep, and was still awake when the insistent voice of a rooster greeted the first day of English rule.

The first week passed, and the second. And the first month, and the second. As an alderman Pieter attended all the meetings that Governor Nicolls scrupulously held to prove he was keeping his word about "self-government." The aldermen would discuss the issues, vote, and affix their signatures to the various documents. There were arguments and debates about some points, but the Dutchmen were clever enough to know which laws the English governor wanted passed, and which he didn't care about. They were careful not to disappoint him.

Pieter's voice was often the only one of dissent, and he was always voted down. He tried to pretend he didn't care, but inwardly he seethed, his stomach churning until it caused him great pain. Even his own family offered little solace, because more often than not they seemed to agree with the governor and not with him.

"Why do we have to change our name?" Pieter complained at Anne's house as they sat around the dinner table on a rainy Sunday afternoon.

"So now we're New York and not New Amsterdam," Anne said. "I don't see that it makes any difference."

David de Witt was something of a scholar, and he explained it was only natural for the Duke of York, as proprietor, to name the community after York, his own venerable cathedral town in England.

"Actually, New York is quite an apt name," he said. "York is a corruption of the old Roman name 'Eboracum,' which itself is a version of two ancient celtic names that mean 'place at the water.' I would say 'New York' describes us rather nicely."

Pieter ignored his son-in-law's logic. "And the other changes?" he complained. "Why must Fort Amsterdam become Fort James? And Fort Orange isn't good enough; no, it must be Albany from now on."

"Albany is one of the duke's titles," David explained, but there was no stopping Pieter.

"Massachusetts is Duke's County, Long Island is Yorkshire Island, and the North River becomes Hudson's River. For the love of God! Hudson was sailing under the Dutch flag when he found the river. The good duke conveniently overlooks that fact," he said triumphantly.

He came home one day roaring with laughter. "Nova Caesarea," he said between guffaws. "Nova Caesarea!" When he stopped laughing he told them the story. The Duke had arbitrarily given a patent for the lands on the western bank of the Hudson to two friends—George Carteret and Lord Berkeley of Stratton. These estimable gentlemen promptly named their lands Nova Caesarea after the Latin name of the home of the Carterets, the island of Jersey.

"The hell with that," Pieter said, and in all further council meetings he referred to the place as New Jersey. Since no one could pronounce the Latin name anyway, Pieter's name stuck. After a time Carteret surrendered and Nova Caesarea officially became New Jersey.

There was one name change that Pieter would not speak of. The Hellegat became the East River. The first name was retained as "Hell Gate"—specifically describing the place where the waters of the Upper Bay met those from Long Island Sound. Pieter could only remember himself as the young boy who, on his first visit to the New World, had dubbed the river "Hellegat." The arbitrariness of the English, in this case at least, seemed to be personally directed against Pieter de Kuyper.

It was all in his mind, of course, because Colonel Nicolls found him more honest than most men and trusted him accordingly. For this reason Pieter was chosen to head the delegation sent to the Dutch settlement of Fort Amstel on the Delaware River. His task was to persuade the settlers to come to terms with the English.

"It's the only way," Pieter said to the Amstel burghers, and went on to describe the might of the English forces. His heart must not have been in it, because the commander of the Dutch garrison decided not to emulate Governor Stuyvesant's surrender. Sir Robert Carr was dispatched to Fort Amstel with two frigates and several hundred troops. The frigates pounded the fort with a series of broadsides, the troops stormed ashore, and the fighting was over. Either because the resistance had angered him or because he was not as much a humanitarian as Colonel Nicolls, Sir Robert allowed his troops to loot the fort and the homes of the settlers. They carried away everything that wasn't nailed down, including the underwear of the former Dutch commander, Alexander Himmoyossa. The Dutch soldiers were packed aboard the frigates, shipped to Virginia, and sold into bondage. When Pieter returned and informed the New Amsterdam Council, these men were doubly assured they had done the correct thing in surrendering.

This harsh action also sobered up the men in the other Dutch settlements. The people on the Passaic said nothing when the British took over and renamed their settlement 'Milford' in honor of the home town of the British representative, Sir Robert Treat. They got their revenge by simply referring to the place as Newark, supposedly the hometown of the English pastor, Abraham Pierson. But the *real* reason was that the Newark in England was where Treat was rumored to have fathered a bastard, and this name passed into common parlance. Sir Robert was either too much of a gentleman, or too embarrassed, to complain.

Pieter dutifully attended the sessions of the council held under the direction of Colonel Nicolls. It was, of course, with a certain amount of cynicism that he signed all the documents of the new Duke's Laws. The only man who steadfastly refused to sign anything was Governor Stuyvesant.

Colonel Nicolls made one last attempt to get the former governor's signature on a document of formal surrender. To help plead his case he persuaded Pieter to accompany him to Stuyvesant's bouwerie.

"You have no right to be here," Stuyvesant insisted.

"We have a legal claim, sir," Colonel Nicolls said politely. "In 1606 the Crown issued a charter claiming the Atlantic coast lands from the 34th to the 45th parallel. Subsequently, we founded settlements at Jamestown in 1607 and Plymouth in 1620. Our rights extend to all the lands between them, including New York."

"But Dammit, we've been here for fifty years."

"But not before the charter was issued," Nicolls said easily, yet fully aware on what flimsy ground the English claim stood. There was a great deal of truth in the observation that the English take things coolly, but they take them.

"I won't sign," Stuyvesant said stubbornly.

"Whether you sign or don't sign will make no difference to the outcome," Pieter argued. "But perhaps it will bring a firmer unity to the Dutch community."

Stuyvesant refused. "I will not surrender that which has been illegally seized," he said angrily.

"I do not agree with your terminology," Nicolls said

in his driest voice. "I prefer to think that a trespassing government has been expelled."

This comment brought a smile to Pieter's face. But on the way back to his house he felt ashamed that he hadn't remained as adamant and stubborn as old Stuyvesant.

He sighed. Perhaps such thick-headedness would have been better for him personally, but taking the long view it was best for the Dutch if they did not resist the English. Theirs was a lost cause and he knew it.

The English are our cousins, he told himself, and it helped to soften the hurt somewhat. The problem was that as often as he told this to himself, he really didn't believe a word of it.

The day began as most other days. Pieter rose, dressed, and went to the kitchen to eat the breakfast prepared by Zilla.

"Another meeting today?" she asked.

"Of course," Pieter said between mouthfuls of food. "Our leader, Colonel Nicolls, likes nothing better than meetings. Yesterday it was a meeting about cattle. Today we are to discuss the land patents. Tomorrow, no doubt, we will meet to debate the amount of dirt we have under our fingernails."

Zilla sat down at the table and regarded him with a concerned eye. "I don't mean to pester you, but you should try to relax. All this worrying and fretting is aging you."

He looked at her and smiled. "What would I do without you? No one else worries or cares about me. But as long as I have you, I don't need anyone else." He reached across the table and patted her hand.

"Don't you try to soft-soap me, old man, I know you too well. No one cares for you indeed! Your daughter loves you as much as any girl ever loved her father. Your grandchildren *adore* you. And Jacob Adam—oh, I know he has his cold ways, but he loves you, too."

"I suppose you're right," Pieter admitted. "But when I come home you're the only one I can count on to be here."

"The others'd be here if you needed them."

"Will you forgive an old man for being selfish? I'm glad I never lost you, because I'd be that much poorer."

The black woman smiled. "I know it. Why do you think I never left?"

"Well, I have a few things to do before I must go to City Hall," Pieter said, rising from his chair. "Damn! I hate these meetings. So much pointless talk. I almost wish the English acted like conquerors instead of being so polite and proper. It might be easier to take."

He left the house and walked through the streets with the intention of paying a visit to his daughter. He went down Stone Street, still the only paved street in the city. He was passing John Riverton's house, which, true to his word, he had never again set foot inside, when the door opened. Elizabeth Riverton Barrow came out with her five-year-old daughter, Jennifer.

Pieter had not seen Elizabeth for many months, and this was one of the few times he had ever seen the child, her mother rarely allowing the little girl to play anywhere but in the garden at the back of the house.

Elizabeth looked at Pieter. "Good morning, Mister de Kuyper."

Feeling the way he did about her father, Pieter would have preferred not to speak with the girl. But he was a fair man and did not blame the children for the sins of their elders.

"Good morning, Elizabeth," he said. "And this young lady gets bigger every time I see her."

"Make your greetings to Mister de Kuyper," Elizabeth said.

The little girl smiled shyly and bent one knee in her five-year-old's version of a curtsy.

Pieter solemnly bowed in return. He looked at the mother and smiled. Elizabeth's beauty was still with her, but it had hardened and there was a bitterness to the line of her mouth. The eyes were as wide as ever, but the sparkle was gone. When she smiled it was perfunctory, and one had the feeling she had forgotten how to laugh.

Pieter suddenly remembered something. He reached into his pocket and held out a bit of candy he had been taking to his own grandchildren. The child's eyes widened.

"It's all right, Jenny. Take the candy and thank Mister de Kuyper."

A tiny hand darted out and the candy disappeared behind her back. The child mumbled something and then hid behind her mother's skirts.

Pieter tipped his hat and continued on his way to his daughter's house.

As usual the children greeted him with exuberance in anticipation of the treasures he always had for them in his pockets. Today it was candy—minus the piece he had given to the Barrow child, but they didn't know about that. Emilie was now eleven, and Paul had turned six. Paul took his candy and darted from the house, and his sister followed at a more leisurely pace as befit someone of her years. Pieter sat in the kitchen and watched them in the garden. It occurred to him that he hadn't been much older than Emilie when he had first come to these shores. At the time he had thought of himself as a man, but Emilie appeared to be still a child. She will be tested as I was, he thought, and then she will blossom into a woman even as I turned into a man.

Anne gave him coffee and cake and joined him at the table. She was still very pretty, despite the tiny pits in her skin that bore testimony to her survival of a bout with the pox. There was so much of Christiana in his daughter; he again felt the pain of his loss. And the daughter was no longer his to claim, but her husband's . . . David de Witt . . . *lucky* David who now had more than he himself . . . who— he silently chided himself for being jealous of his own son-in-law.

Age makes us more foolish than we realize, he thought to himself.

"You look tired, Father," Anne said. "You should relax and try to get more rest."

It was like hearing an echo of Zilla's words. "Nonsense," he said. "When a man gets to be my age, he always looks tired to someone your age."

"And David agrees that you're not looking well."

Pieter smiled. "If I listened to you I'd think that half New Amsterdam spends its days worrying about my health."

"Only the family worries," she said. "And you really should start calling the town by its proper name. New York."

He sighed, and she realized how troubled he was by the English seizure of the colony. She reached over and hugged him. He put his arms around her, and they were the father and daughter of many years before, close and content with the love they felt for one another.

"When you were younger you used to write poetry, do you remember?"

"Of course, but I haven't written anything in years."

"Do you remember the one about the candle?" he asked.

Her brow furrowed as she dipped back into her memory. "Yes, I think so. That was a very important poem to me. I wrote it when I was in love with David but we were too young to get married."

"How does it go?"

She reviewed it in her mind and then recited it aloud slowly, struggling in a few places for the exact words.

> "Candle
> Burning, dripping, melting
> Living forever and ever
> I stare at it in a dazed way
> Then comes a refreshing breeze
> and
> blows
> the
> candle
> out."

There was a silence and the words hung in the air. "I was so upset when I wrote that," Anne said in a faraway voice. "It seemed I would never get David."

"And has he turned out to be the husband you wanted?"

She smiled. "What do you think?"

Pieter was pleased that his daughter had found such happiness. It made his own life seem more worthwhile.

But that still didn't solve his own problem. "I remembered your poem because I feel as if the English breeze has come and blown my candle out."

"I think you're being foolish," she said. "So the English have taken the colony, renamed it New York, and stuck up their flag. What difference has it made? We live as we did before, we eat the same food, sleep in the same beds. Business goes on as usual. I don't know why you let it upset you."

There was no use trying to offer an explanation, he thought. Anne was a child of the New World. This was her home. The flag that flew over the fort was simply a decoration without any meaning. She had no memories of another life in another world. How could Holland possibly mean anything to her? He understood her point of view. But it was not his own: he was sixty-five years old, had been born a Dutchman, had lived as a Dutchman, and would die as a Dutchman. No matter what anyone said to him; no matter that his own youth in Amsterdam had hardly been idyllic; no matter that throughout his adult life he had grumbled as much as the next man in the colony about the high-handedness of the burghers—it hurt to be living under the English flag.

"Your husband seems to prosper," he said, changing the subject to one less painful. "He looks more like a rich Amsterdam burgher every day."

"I suppose the grain business is doing very well."

"And the land business?"

She looked at him blankly.

"Surely you know he's involved in several land schemes with your brother?"

"Oh yes," she said in a manner that showed she had little interest in her husband's business affairs. "They seem to spend a lot of time together."

As if to prove she was telling the truth, the door opened and David entered with Jacob Adam. They exchanged greetings with Pieter, and Anne bustled to get more coffee and a platter with a pile of little coffee cakes.

"I hear the two of you are doing very well in the land business," Pieter said. Actually he knew very little of his son's affairs. Jacob Adam never invited questions, and Pieter's pride prevented him from asking.

"Quite well," David said. Pieter looked at his son, but Jacob Adam allowed David's answer to stand for both of them.

"If you have some exceptional values, I might be interested in buying," Pieter said, not meaning it, but hoping to draw them out.

The younger men exchanged glances. This time it was Jacob Adam who gave the common answer. "At this time, Father, we only buy land; we don't sell it."

The finality in his son's voice told him that he could pry as much as he wanted, but he wasn't going to learn anything. But he knew that Jacob Adam was up to something. He was always up to something.

During the first week of the English occupation there had been a general halting of business. All trading stopped while people waited to see what would happen. Jacob Adam had gone around buying as much wampum as possible—all at greatly reduced prices because of the general climate of fear in the town. Many men thought the English would ship them all back to Holland, where their wampum would be worthless.

When life returned to normal the traders found there was a scarcity of wampum, seriously affecting their business with the Indians. The natives would accept goods —clothes and, though it was illegal, liquor and guns— for their furs, but only up to a point. The hard currency of the realm was wampum.

The traders became desperate, and it was then that Jacob Adam announced he had plenty of the shell money and would be most happy to sell it. On learning he was selling at twice the normal rate of exchange, the traders at first resisted; but when it became obvious that Jacob Adam had the only available supply, they began to buy from him. Within a day they had driven the price up, and Jacob Adam sold his wampum for four times the normal rate.

All in all, Jacob Adam had made a good deal of money. Pieter was happy that his son prospered, but unhappy that he had taken advantage of his fellow Dutchmen when they were in trouble.

"I spoke to Elizabeth Barrow this morning," Pieter said.

A frown came over the younger de Kuyper's face. The injury to his pride had happened a long time ago, but it had left a deep wound and his anger had not lessened.

"She looks as if life is not treating her well."

Jacob Adam's frown eased as if he had just heard a bit of good news.

"I saw the child as well," Pieter said. "She'll look like

the mother. It's good she doesn't take after her father. A man who traded in slaves must be suffering the fires of hell."

"She knew what he was when she married him," Jacob Adam said. "He deserved to die before he saw his own child."

Pieter shrugged. "He deserved to die, but I shudder at the manner of his death. That wasn't a good death for any Christian, no matter what he'd done."

Jacob Adam said, "Of course." But it was clear he thought no death too mean for a man who had taken something he had wanted.

The slave ship of Captain Robert Barrow, so the story went, was in midocean when the slaves rebelled. They had been brought on deck for exercise when they turned on the whites. The crew was ill prepared. The rebellion was one of the few successful ones on record.

Most of the crew were killed, but the captain and a few others survived the fighting. They were chained in the hold that had previously housed the slaves.

The Negroes took over the ship. None of them, of course, had the slightest understanding of how to run a sailing vessel, and the ship drifted aimlessly over the ocean. The ex-slaves ate the food and drank the rum and water, but then the supplies ran out.

The black men became crazed with hunger and thirst and turned to cannibalism.

It was two months before another ship came across them. The sailors became sick when they saw the hellish tableaux on the decks and in the holds. There was no one alive, only emaciated bodies, many with pieces of flesh missing. The white men in the holds had been cannibalized while they hung from their chains. Barrow, as the chief symbol of their hated enslavers, had been singled out by the black men: his body, or what was left of it, wore his captain's cap and coat.

The entire ship reeked with a stench that made the captain of the other ship fear disease and pestilence. He ordered the slaver set afire and watched as it burned and finally sank to the bottom with its loathesome record of horror.

"The man walked with the devil," David said. "It is fitting that he join him in the next world."

Pieter had had enough of this sort of talk. He kissed his grandchildren, patted his daughter on the cheek, and took his leave of her house.

It was a beautiful day, and he decided to take a walk along the shores of the Hudson. He left the streets with their early-morning traffic of farm carts and flocks of animals being driven to pasture. Walking along the clean sands of the riverbank, breathing deeply of the crisp morning air, and gazing across the sparkling waters that danced in uniform rows toward the open sea, he was filled with a sense of well-being.

He turned back into town and passed the house with the bell outside that one rang to summon the ferryman whose boat crossed the Hudson to Bergen. This ferry had begun operating in 1661 and was as thoroughly unreliable as the one on the other side of the island that went to Breuckelen. The ferryman was also a farmer, and if he chose to tend to his fields instead of his ferry, one had no choice but to wait until he was ready.

Pieter went down Broad Street and smelled the odors coming from the shops of the tanners. He crossed the bridge over the canal and walked toward Bowling Green, where he could see the belfry of Dominie Bogardus's Church of St. Nicholas peering over the walls of the fort. In its shadow, on the other side of the Broad Way, the cemetery shimmered under the morning sun.

He turned back to Whitehall and went past the jail and the stocks, which held no prisoners on this day. Here the air held a strange commingling of the sourness coming from several nearby breweries and the sweetness emanating from a bakery. He continued his walk until he came to Pearl Street, and as he rounded the curving road on his way northward, he could see his destination, the City Hall at 73 Pearl. But before going on he stopped at the East River slip, where the construction of several new wharfs was under way. A dozen ships were tied to the pilings, their anchors trailing into the water. Pieter spotted the ship he wanted, made his way carefully over planking that had been thrown down for temporary walkways and looked up at the bow of the *William*.

Like himself, he thought, the ship was beginning to show her age. She was still beautiful and stout, her planking as strong as ever, but time had weathered her skin, and brought the slightest sag to her masts and spars. She seemed to ride lower in the water, weighed down with the years she had lived and the sorrows she had seen.

He went aboard and found Lars Jorisen in the aft cabin. The Dane's bulk had increased over the years, and the empty left sleeve of his coat was pinned up. His eyes, however, still had that clarity common to blue-water sailors.

"I plan to take the ship here," Jorisen said, stabbing the map at a place about forty miles south of the mouth of the Delaware. "The whales should be running on those coasts."

This discussion of plans for a voyage was only a formality. Pieter might be the owner, but the running of the ship was left entirely to the Dane.

They returned to the main deck. The cannons installed at the insistence of Governor Stuyvesant had long since been removed, their places now occupied by empty barrels waiting to be filled with blubber.

"I hear a man in Virginia has a special stove that will allow the oil to be taken from the blubber while a ship is at sea," Pieter said.

"Aye, so I've heard," Jorisen said. "But 'twould be a shame to bring such a stench aboard a ship. 'Twould turn her into a floating sausage factory."

"It would mean a ship could be able to take twice as many whales."

The captain conceded the point, but wasn't about to give up his position on the subject. "Maybe so, but before I'll have such nonsense aboard my ship, I'll join the fishes at the bottom. The *William* does not deserve such shabby treatment."

Pieter managed to conceal his smile. He knew nothing could ever convince Jorisen that extra profits would be worth turning a ship into a "sausage factory."

He was about to leave when he saw Manuel, who was talking to another black man. He walked over, and Manuel introduced the other man. The name—Thomé de Souza—was familiar, but Pieter couldn't place it.

"Thomé was only a boy when he ran from the company farm to tell you they were going to hang me," Manuel explained, and Pieter's memory raced back over the years and conjured up a picture of a young black boy, skinny as a spider and on the verge of collapse from his long run. He had changed a great deal and now looked like a man who had seen much of the world.

Pieter greeted him warmly and learned that for the past twenty years he had been a sailor and there was not a sea or ocean he had not known.

"Have you returned to stay?" Pieter asked. "Perhaps we can find a berth for you on board the *William*."

"Thank you, Mister de Kuyper," Thomé answered, and pointed to a ship at another piling. "But three years ago I bought my own ship. It is that one with the yellow gunwales."

Pieter admired the ship. It was a handsome vessel. Thomé had done well for himself, he thought.

"Do you bring cargo to New Amsterdam?" Pieter asked, purposely not using the hated new name for the town.

"Yes, and in good health. They go on the block the day after tomorrow," Thomé de Souza said.

Pieter was startled. This black man was in the slave trade. A black man selling other black men? He looked at Manuel. The giant was embarrassed and looked away.

Thomé de Souza had become used to this reaction from white men. "I saw no reason why only white men should make a profit from men whose skins are black," he said.

Pieter nodded. In a few moments he invented an excuse to take his leave. He did not wish to remain with a slaver. He felt the same revulsion for de Souza that he felt for all men who traded in human flesh. There were many people who claimed the Negro was an inferior being, and they even questioned that he possessed a soul. To Pieter all of this was nonsense. The Negro was a man. A man had a soul and was a creature of God. No creature of God should be treated as less than he was. So went Pieter's argument; but he never did anything about it. He was only one man, he told himself, and slavery was a fact of life. There were other men who believed as Pieter did. And, like Pieter, they did nothing to change the situation.

* * *

Richard Nicolls rose to greet Jacob Adam de Kuyper. They exchanged pleasantries, and both sat down in the comfortable chairs near the window. The governor waited for his visitor to explain the purpose of his call.

Richard Nicolls was slightly more than forty years old, gray-eyed and curly-haired. He was an urbane and patient man, the son of a wealthy lawyer, a university-trained scholar who read the classics in the original tongues. He spoke fluent Dutch and French, and quickly put visitors at ease with his friendly and charming manner.

He also understood the ways of changing governments with the least trouble. One of his first acts as governor was to issue an edict allowing any Dutch citizen the right to return to Holland with all his possessions. The townspeople were reassured, although not one of them accepted the offer.

Jacob Adam wasted no time in getting down to business with the governor.

"You intend to honor all former contracts?" he asked.

"Yes."

"This includes land patents?"

"Of course."

"What about lands whose purchase was begun, but at this time has yet to be completed?"

"Perhaps you could explain in more detail?" the governor asked.

"My partner and I have bought a tract of land from the Indians. The land is on Long Island. We would, in due course, have applied for the patent to these lands from the Dutch government. But under the Dutch terms of patent, we would have been required to bring settlers to this land. The settlers receive a certain amount of land, and my partner and myself receive the remainder."

"Who is your partner?"

"My brother-in-law, David de Witt. At times we have a third partner, Robert de Pauw, but he's not involved in this particular venture."

"What exactly do you wish of me?"

"Several things. The first is, will you honor the beginning that has been made toward a patent?"

"I see no reason why not."

"Good," Jacob Adam said. "The second point, will you require the settlers as a condition of patent? You see, sir, it made sense for the Dutch because it was difficult to convince Netherlanders to come here. This is not the case with the English. In your Province of New England you already have over thirty thousand people, whereas the Province of New York has slightly less than ten thousand, many of whom aren't even Dutch. I suspect the numbers of settlers in New York will increase now that we live under the English flag."

The governor looked more closely at this young man. He knew what he was talking about. He knew what he wanted. And he seemed politely determined to get it. The governor became more wary.

"If we don't require any settlers, what do you intend to do with the land?"

"I'll develop some of it into farmland—to be sold or leased to tenant farmers. Some I'll retain for sale in the future. And finally, I'll give a third portion to the provincial government if it is agreeable to my terms."

"And what are those?"

"The land must be used as a racecourse."

"What?"

"There are sound reasons for this. The bloodlines of our horses are very weak. If we build a racecourse, our people will begin to value superior horseflesh the way it has been valued in England. If the land is granted to me, I'll give it to the province. The province will pay for the construction of the course. I'll pay for the construction of a grandstand, provided the government allows me to be repaid by keeping the monies obtained as admission charges."

The governor was most impressed. It was a superbly clever scheme. It was well known that Nicolls owned a racing stable in England and was a supporter of improving breeds. Any plan that included a racecourse would appeal to him. The governor was well aware of what the young Dutchman was doing.

"Will people be interested in racing?"

"People are people," Jacob Adam said with a shrug. "It's an exciting sport and it gives them a chance to wager. That's as much a Dutch failing as it is English."

The governor smiled. "I think it unfair that we should

pay for the course and not receive any of the admission charge."

"What would you consider fair?"

"An equal split. Half to you and half to the province."

"Done."

The governor was surprised. "I was told the Dutch are great hagglers and traders. Aren't you going to haggle even a little bit?"

This time it was Jacob Adam who smiled. "The burghers in Amsterdam have a saying: Fifty percent of a good profit is better than one hundred percent of no profit."

"You say this land is on Long Island?"

"Yes. Good flat land covered with grass. It will be perfect for a racecourse."

"And the land for farming?"

"Rich, loamy soil."

"How much land are we talking about?"

"Two hundred acres for the racecourse. Eight hundred acres to be divided into farms immediately. Four thousand more to be held by my partner and myself for further development. Five thousand acres in all."

"Five thousand acres!" the governor said, unable to contain his surprise. "How in the name of God do you arrive at such numbers?"

"Under the Dutch system my partner and I received eight hundred acres for every two hundred we used for farming. I ask the same of you. The eight hundred for farming plus the two hundred to be used for the racecourse adds up to a thousand acres. Therefore, my partner and I receive four thousand. It's the same ratio as before."

"What if I were to say no?"

"Then you say no."

The governor began to like this self-assured young man. There was no doubt in his mind that he would do something constructive with his land, for he was hardly the type to allow it to lie fallow. And finally, he admitted to himself, he could not resist the idea of starting a racecourse. The young Dutchman had certainly known what he was doing when he had thrown that into the potpourri.

"Very well," he said. "I'll approve the patents when they're submitted."

"Thank you. You'll not regret it."

"I have a feeling that I won't."

The Dutchman rose to leave, his business concluded. When they came to the door the governor stopped him. "There is, however, one other point."

"And what is that?"

"What do you intend to name the racecourse?"

"I hadn't thought about it."

"Good. It will be called the Newmarket Course in honor of the track outside London."

"Where, no doubt, you have had many winners."

The governor looked at the young man and then broke into a hearty laugh. "Damn you! Do you have the ability to see into a man's mind?"

"It was a lucky guess."

"I don't believe that for a minute. De Kuyper, it was worth the ocean voyage just to meet a man like you."

They parted, and both men were more than pleased with the arrangement.

The governor would have his racecourse, half the profits from the admissions, and the certainty of new farmland to be settled by hard-working, God-fearing Englishmen.

Jacob Adam was also pleased, but not because of the racecourse and his share of the profits. They were unimportant. If the governor had pressed the issue, he would have given away all the profits from the admissions.

The important thing was the four thousand acres. He had entered the governor's office to get them; the other matters had been only camouflage.

"You're out, Paul!"

"Paul's the goat! Paul's the goat!" the children shouted with glee.

"Everyone out of the chairs," Anne de Witt said, and the children stood up, all eyeing the dejected Paul de Witt, who was now out of the game. Emilie, as second-in-command to her mother, removed another chair, and the hired fiddler began to play as the children circled around the remaining seats.

There were over fifty children at the party in the new de Witt house on Tuyn Street—to be known in a later, more mercenary age as Exchange Place. Tuyn was only a block south of Wall Street, and David had thought it a bit too far uptown. "It's for the good of the children," Anne had said to convince him of the benefits of this more countrylike residence.

The party was in full swing, and most of the guests' hands were sticky from candy and honey confections. The music stopped, and this time it was little Jacobus Van Rosenvelt who was left without a chair. The other children hooted and stamped their feet. It seemed as if the lad would cry, but Anne quickly handed him a gooey piece of candy and his look of failure vanished. He gazed with triumph at the other children as he bit into his "reward."

After the game of musical chairs was over, the children were fed large hunks of a delicious nut-and-strawberry cake that had been baked by Zilla.

"How is it, Joshua?" Anne asked an eight-year-old boy who was attacking a piece of cake that was almost as big as his own head.

Joshua Seixas could hardly speak because his mouth was so full, but he managed to say, "Ver—very good, Mrs. de Witt."

"Think you'll have room for more?"

The boy was very serious. He thought for a second and then nodded, "Oh, yes."

She patted Joshua on the head and walked away shaking her own. How many bellyaches there would be tonight, she thought.

David came into the house as a rousing game of billygoat was being played. The object of this game was to avoid being butted by the blindfolded "goat." The present goat was his own son, Paul, who was doing his best to terrorize the others with his rubber horns.

"A success?" David asked his wife as he kissed her on the cheek.

"Best party of the year."

David noticed the dark eyes and hair of the Seixas boy, and although his face displayed no emotion, Anne knew what her husband was thinking.

"You're not sure the Seixas boy belongs, are you?"

"Not everyone shares your feelings about Jews. Some of the other parents might object to him being here."

"I dare them to tell me that."

"They won't," David said. "As families go in this place, we're old stock."

"Good. And in another generation the Seixas family should be 'old stock' as well."

"It's not quite the same."

"It should be."

He smiled. "You really are a saint. Most of the time."

"What do you mean by that?"

He leaned over and whispered in her ear so none of the nearby children could hear. "When you're in bed, you're a devil," he said, giving her a pinch on her bottom.

"Stop that," she hissed, looking around to make sure none of the children were watching. But then she smiled, and her look promised she would live up to his compliment.

She walked back to supervise the game of billygoat, and David's eyes followed her. She was no longer the slender nymph he had first known, and they had now been married more than a dozen years. Yet she still excited him as much as she had on their wedding night. David de Witt was a man with few regrets.

Pieter decided to visit Holland.

His family and friends wondered about this, because he had always claimed he had no interest in seeing his birthplace again. Perhaps, they speculated, it was because English flags now flew over Manhatan. Or perhaps he was just bored with his life. None of them voiced the thought that all of them had, that Pieter was an old man whose life had almost run its course and he wished to see his native home for a final time. He let them speculate.

He found himself standing at the bow railing as the 450-ton *Hope of Orange* passed through the Narrows and churned up white water as it headed for open ocean.

The voyage was uneventful. There was a brief, nasty storm, but the *Hope of Orange* was a stout vessel and had no trouble. The skilled Dutch sailors went about their business as if they were sailing on a smooth millpond.

When the sun was shining, as it did a good deal of the

time, Pieter spent long hours at the rail watching
the waves coming from as far away as the eye could see,
marching toward the ship in endless rows, then slipping
under the keel and continuing their journey to the far
ends of the earth.

He also enjoyed watching the myriad life of the ocean.
Birds drifted across the sky, their wings still, their bodies
carried on the unseen currents of air. Flying fish soared
out of the water, chasing a bit of food, or perhaps being
chased themselves. They would skim alongside the ship,
and it seemed that a man with a net could reach out and
take them in midflight. There were the dolphins that swam
alongside the ship, playfully leaping out of the water in a
tower of spray, returning in a graceful arc, acting as if
they enjoyed the company of the strange creatures who
walked the decks of the ship. But most of all he loved the
whales. He once had hunted these leviathans and had
no fear of them. Nor they of him, he realized. The whales
were the lords of their world, and the passage of a floating
pile of wood meant nothing to them.

The *Hope of Orange* rounded the point at Land's End
and worked her way through the English Channel. The
sighting of other ships' sails became commonplace, a vast
change from the emptiness of the mid-Atlantic. They
passed within sight of Calais, through the Wadden Zee
and down through the Zuider Zee, and finally came to
rest at a berth in Amsterdam.

To Pieter, the whole world seemed to be on an incredibly grand scale: the multitude of piers and docks; the
countless buildings, some with many tiers and levels; the
forest of tall masts pointing up to the blue sky; the march
of the city out to the horizon itself.

He disembarked from the ship with his single piece of
luggage, a case he could carry in one hand by its straps.
He walked the streets he had known as a boy, finding
them much as he had remembered. They were narrow
and dirty, the stones themselves looking worn and
wearied, having been walked over by many thousands
of feet. People seemed to be everywhere, babbling constantly, raucously, interminably, about any or all issues
under the stars—engaged in conversations that had been
going on when he had been here as a boy and had yet
to come to their conclusion.

The people had not changed: the sober, industrious ones, looking purposeful; the drunks near the taverns, singing, laughing, oblivious to everything; the old crones gathered in the doorways and on stoops, covering their shoulders and their hearts with their gray shawls, looking with displeasure on the young girls; the old, empty-eyed men who sat in windows, reduced to the only thing left— waiting for the end; the beggars in their rags and tatters, cringing and whining as they tried to squeeze a bit of copper or silver from a likely-looking prospect, snarling and spitting when they were refused. Here and there walked a prosperous man, most likely a merchant, fat, smug, looking with disdain on those who were not blessed as he was.

No, none of these had changed. He realized, however, the years had brought a great change in him. Once he had been a part of this world, another piece blending into it. But now he attracted people's attention. He was dressed in neat, quiet clothes, but somehow they were not quite right, not exactly the garb of a local resident. He was marked as a visitor from another place, an outsider, a stranger. Several times he was even mistaken for a foreigner and people made crude remarks before his face. He let it pass, never letting on he spoke a Dutch as pure as any of them.

He procured lodging at an inn, not far from the waterfront, that had been recommended by the captain of the *Hope of Orange*. He was given a private sleeping room— an indication that the owner of the inn regarded him as a man of substance with the ability to pay for his comfort. A lesser man would have been shown to the common dormitory and been forced to sleep with a dozen others who coughed and snored through the night.

He ate a substantial meal at the inn's tavern, washing it down with copious drafts of good beer and enjoying a conversation with a man of his own age, a merchant who had settled in South Africa and now made his home in Capetown, on the southernmost tip of the Dark Continent. The merchant spoke of his home and Pieter of America, and both men realized there was little difference between their worlds. Both were settlements of the Dutch and both were miniature versions of Holland. The only difference, Pieter reflected without pride, was that Capetown was still a Dutch possession and New Amsterdam was not.

He rose early in the morning, breakfasted, and took to the streets. He wandered past the guild halls, and they seemed as mighty and substantial as they had in the past. He paused in front of the West India Company building and thought of all the hatreds he had felt for this place and its arrogant burghers. But the ones he hated most—the Killiaen Van Rensselaers, the Van Twillers, the Kiefts—they were all dead in their graves, and surely hatred was meant to stop at the grave.

He came to the house where he had lived with his Uncle Jacob after his own father had died. He went to the door, and the old woman who answered told him Jacob had passed away many years ago and his sons had sold the house. They had prospered in the iron business and moved away, she said, but she didn't know where. It didn't matter. Pieter had no desire to see the cousins he had never really known.

Through the police he obtained the information he sought. He gave them a man's name and they directed him to a small square in a fashionable part of the city. When he arrived at the square, a piece of silver given to a young boy brought him to the house that was the destination he had been seeking since he left his home on the Broad Way.

This was his purpose in coming to Holland.

He stood before the house and hesitated before he knocked. He took a deep breath and then lifted the brass knocker and let it fall heavily on the wooden door.

A handsome-looking woman, in her middle thirties, with a pleasant expression on her face, came to the door.

"Does . . . is this where . . . Pieter de Kuyper lives?"

"Yes," the woman said, "do you wish to see him?"

Pieter nodded his head in mute reply.

The woman opened the door and allowed him to enter. He felt self-conscious as he stood in the mirrored hallway with a soft, rich carpet beneath his feet. He removed his hat and breathed heavily.

"And whom shall I tell Pieter is here?"

"Pieter de Kuyper."

"Yes, I know," the woman said, misunderstanding him. "But what is your name, sir?"

"Pieter de Kuyper."

Her eyebrows came up.

"I believe I am your husband's father," he said in a voice that was not much more than a whisper.

A look of understanding came across her face. "Oh . . . oh dear . . . oh my dear . . ." and then she fled down the hall and disappeared through a doorway. In seconds Young Pieter came through the same doorway.

"Father!"

Pieter stared at his son, now a man of forty years, heavier through the middle, but the face still lean and somewhat angry-looking, the same face he had known, and yet not the same.

"If I'm not welcome in your house, please say so."

"Not welcome?" Young Pieter said, grabbing his father by the shoulders and squeezing until he winced. "Don't even think such a thing."

"I wasn't sure," Pieter said truthfully. "Nor would I blame you if—"

"The past is the past. Good God, what would families be like if they didn't have their fights. Come, I want you to meet my wife," Young Pieter said, and dragged his father toward the woman who was standing in the hall-way, looking at them in wonder.

"Father, this is my wife, Carol. Carol, this is that scoundrel of a father I've told you so much about."

Her smile was genuine. "If you only knew how happy this makes your son . . . and me as well."

"And I'll never forgive myself for not learning about you sooner than I did," Pieter said with a courtliness that touched them both.

Pieter spent several weeks in Amsterdam. At his son's insistence he moved into the lovely house on the square. He learned Young Pieter was a very successful solicitor who was rising rapidly and soon might achieve a high government post. During the days, while his son was at his office, Pieter visited his old haunts—those he could remember or find—and most of them looked familiar. Christiana's old house had changed but little—a new roof and a few more flower boxes, perhaps, but to Pieter it looked much as it had forty years ago. The Van Venter family still owned it; one of the brothers or sisters, he thought, but he took no steps to find out. Without Christiana's presence it was just another house.

He enjoyed his time with his son, and he became devoted to his daughter-in-law. There was even a small grandson to complete the picture.

It was only on his last night in Holland that he and his son spoke of the old animosity that had driven them apart. Neither of them had wanted to bring up something that might spoil their present happiness with one another.

"I blamed what happened to my mother on you," Young Pieter said quietly after dinner, when the two of them were alone in the library. "I know now that I was wrong."

"Perhaps it was I who was wrong," Pieter admitted. "I had no right to bring someone like your mother to America. She never really belonged there. It would be all right today, but New Amsterdam was too harsh for her in those days. I should have known better, but I was young and headstrong and foolish."

"And in love," Young Pieter said.

"That most of all."

"I've learned not to judge people," Young Pieter said. "Only God is capable of judging what's in a man's heart."

"And what of my heart when I did my best to drive you away?"

"I think you did it because you were afraid to admit you had made a mistake."

"It was foolish of me."

"And it was foolish of me not to understand there was too much love in your heart for you to really want to hurt me."

"I would die first."

"I know that now, Father."

They grasped each other and held on for a long, long time. Neither was ashamed of the tears that washed down their cheeks. And both knew that, at last, there was peace between them.

When the ship sailed from Amsterdam, Young Pieter and his wife stood on the dock and sadly waved their good-byes.

Pieter stood on the deck and watched the shore recede until the curve of the horizon took away his view.

He was content. He had healed the wound between

himself and his firstborn. He knew Christiana was looking down with approval from her place in heaven.

Europe disappeared.

The waves rolled under the ship.

Pieter slept.

Stone Eagle, blood son of Senadondo and chief of the Wickquaskeeks, crossed the waters at Spuyten Duyvil and went to the newly built farmhouse near the field that had been staked out but had yet to be plowed and planted.

The farmer, John Archer, saw the formidable-looking Indian coming toward him as he worked on setting a new fence post. He wished he had his musket handy, because one never knew, but he had left it in the farmhouse.

"What can I do for you?" he asked nervously.

"You are my new neighbor," Stone Eagle said, using the recently acquired word in his vocabulary. "I live on the other side of the river."

"Yes?"

"I would be your friend."

"Well, say . . . I didn't expect . . ." John Archer began, and then pointed toward the house. "Maybe you'd like to come in and . . . and have a drink or something."

"My name is Stone Eagle."

"I'm John Archer."

"Our children must be friends."

"Why, sure," Archer said. "Seein' as we all got to live around here together."

"I will enter your longhouse," Stone Eagle said. As they walked the Indian kept his eyes straight ahead, but the white kept looking left and right with some apprehension.

"Before he died, the old chief, Senadondo, said my people must learn to live with your people."

"Well now, that's nice and friendly," the farmer said with an uneasy smille. "He was a smart old bird."

"We will be friends, John Archer," Stone Eagle said with great solemnity. He followed the white man into his farmhouse.

It was not a friendship Stone Eagle particularly cared about for himself. Given his choice, he would have taken his bow and his knife, gone into the forest, and lived as he pleased. But it was a friendship he wanted for the children of his tribe. He did not need it, but they did.

This is what Senadondo would have done, he thought
as he drank the white man's beer. And perhaps we will
survive.

The aldermen and burgomasters met with the governor in the meeting chamber of City Hall. Today they
were to discuss the land patents issued during the years
when the province had been under Dutch rule.

Governor Nicolls used to invite Peter Stuyvesant to
these sessions, but the crusty old fellow always refused.
He was no longer invited, because he had left the province. The States-General had recalled him to Holland to
explain his disgraceful action of surrendering the city.
Stuyvesant went back, rejoicing over the opportunity to
do battle with the burghers. He intended to prove it was
their lack of support, *their* niggardliness with money and
troops, *their* fault the province had been lost. Governor
Nicolls wished he could have been a fly on the wall when
the tough, fiery Stuyvesant took on the entire Dutch
government. He had no doubt the government would find
itself overmatched.

Pieter de Kuyper listlessly looked over the patent documents that were piled on top of the large table. If they
found nothing wrong with any of them, the governor said,
he would confirm their validity under the British Crown.

It was dull work. The men looked at document after
document, each containing a description of the property
and the name of the owner, each written in the driest
and dullest language possible.

They had been at it for several hours when Pieter began to be aware that a great deal of land was held in
the names of Jacob Adam de Kuyper and David de Witt.
More astonishing was that these two names were sometimes linked with a third one—Robert de Pauw.

His own son and the son of his old nemesis in business
together?

Pieter studied the documents more closely and realized
his son had used the imprecise wording of the Dutch charter to obtain thousands of acres of land. He hadn't exactly stolen it, but the morality of his methods certainly
left much to be desired.

The wealth of his son and son-in-law increased as he

went through more documents. He took Abraham de
Witt aside and showed him the evidence.

The burgomaster was as surprised as Pieter. "I knew
they had bought land together . . . but so much!"

"And sometimes they did it with Robert de Pauw."

Abraham de Witt shook his head. "Why de Pauw?"

"Can't you guess?"

"No. Robert de Pauw is a likable lad, but quite thick
in the skull. Why would they bother with him?"

"They didn't," Pieter said. "They must have made a
deal with Robert's father when he was still alive. That
old brigand must have financed them at the beginning.
His price included the partnership of his son."

Abraham looked at his friend in astonishment.

"Michael de Pauw and our sons?"

"It must have been what happened. Otherwise how do
you explain their connection with Robert de Pauw?"

"You must be right, but I find it almost unbelievable.
Why did the old man do it?"

"Because he knew that someday we'd find out. It's as
if he's reaching out of his grave to deliver the final blow."

Abraham de Witt shook his head. "What's done is
done. There's one good thing about all this. At least we
don't have to worry that we have fools for sons."

"Not fools," Pieter said. "Pirates."

Jacob Adam entered the house on the Broad Way in
a happy mood. He went to the kitchen, where Zilla was
preparing the evening meal. He lifted her off her feet
and twirled her about.

"Put me down, you scoundrel!" she cried, loving every
second of it.

"All right, old woman, you're getting too fat anyway,"
he said, bringing her gently to the floor.

"What caused all this?" she asked. "You don't have
to tell me because I already know. What deal did you
put over on someone now?"

"The biggest one so far! Five thousand more acres on
Long Island. That makes eleven altogether. We're going
to be rich!"

Zilla went about her business of chopping vegetables.
"Seems we're rich enough as far as I can tell."

"No one is ever rich enough. But don't worry. When

I'm the richest man in the province I'll still let you cook
my meals and darn my socks."

"You'll never be so rich I won't be able to bring
a heavy wooden spoon against the side of your head,"
she said.

"You black people are all alike. Always resorting to
violence."

Light banter was uncharacteristic of Jacob Adam. He
acted this way only with Zilla, and only when they were
alone. Even though her skin was a different color, he
thought of her as his mother. He meant no disrespect for
his real mother, but Zilla had been the one who had cared
for him all his life.

Zilla, by the same token, thought of Jacob Adam as
her son. She loved Pieter, and she loved Anne and her
children, and she had loved Young Pieter when he had
been around; but even so, the love she lavished on Jacob
Adam was special.

He held out a document.

"Is that another one of those deeds?" she said.

"Yes. Three more lots along the Hudson. Choice property. You're becoming a rich old lady, even if you can't
read the papers that tell you about it."

"I don't know why you keep giving me these things.
I already own . . . how many have you given me . . . eight
or nine?"

"This makes exactly twelve parcels of land. Some on
Manhatan. Others on Staten Island and Long Island."

"But why? I have a good home here. What can I do
with land I never even see?"

He became serious. "As long as my father or myself
are alive you have a home here. But what if we both were
to die? As long as you own your own property, you have
nothing to worry about."

"I don't want to hear about dying. I don't like that
kind of talk."

"Then we'll change the subject. But we'll take this deed
and put it with the others."

"All right, but I still think it's silly."

His voice became tender. "I could never sleep if I
didn't know that you were taken care of, Zilla. It's only
my way of telling you how much I care about you."

Zilla's eyes misted over. "Everybody thinks that you're

coldhearted. Funny, they don't even know you. Nobody knows you but me. Why can't you loosen up with other people?"

"It's a hard world."

"You'd be a lot happier if you weren't so hard on yourself."

Pieter entered the kitchen and Jacob Adam slipped back into his reserved manner.

Zilla brought two glasses of beer to the table, and the men sipped them in silence.

"I discovered something interesting today," Pieter said when the silence had become irritating.

"What's that?"

"I'm the father of a great landowner."

"I've done well."

"Are you proud of the way you've done it?"

Jacob Adam shrugged. "Only the results matter."

"And I understand you're also increasing the wealth of Robert de Pauw."

"Very little, but he serves his purpose."

"At least I can be thankful for that."

"His father was your enemy, not mine."

Pieter relaxed a bit. His son was perfectly correct in not assuming a feud of the older generation. "You'll be pleased to know that Governor Nicolls approved all your Dutch land patents."

"I'd be surprised if he hadn't. He is not a fool who would upset the province."

Already my son thinks of it as a province in the English fashion, while I am still tied to the idea of a colony in the Dutch fashion, Pieter thought. "What do you plan on doing with all your land?" he asked.

"Profit from it."

And now he brought up a subject that had been bothering him for some time. "I hope you'll have time to take more interest in the family whaling business."

Jacob Adam was surprised. "But that's your business. You don't need me."

"I'm getting old. The Lord may be thinking of recalling me," Pieter said quietly.

Jacob Adam started to speak, and then thought better of it.

Pieter continued. "What will you do with the *William* if I die?"

"I've never thought about it."

"She's a good ship and makes a good profit."

"I'm aware of that."

"Well, what will you do with her?"

Jacob Adam did not want to get into an argument with his father, and so he tried to avoid the issue. "It's not something we need talk about now."

"I want to know."

Jacob Adam sighed. His father was insisting on a showdown. Very well, he thought, I will not lie, because he will know I am lying. I will tell him the truth he does not want to hear.

"I will probably sell the *William*," he said.

Pieter was on his feet, his face flushed with anger. "Dammit! You cannot sell her! She's part of my flesh and blood!"

Jacob Adam's own face flushed. He stood up and walked from the room.

Pieter watched the empty doorway for a few moments and then slumped back in his chair.

Zilla brought him another glass of beer. "You started it, you know that?"

"I know," Pieter said grudgingly. "But why can't he bend once in a while?"

"Why can't you?"

He looked at her and, despite himself, smiled. "Dear, dear Zilla, what would we do without you?"

"Try making life less difficult around here."

"Tell my son to change his ways."

"I do tell him. The same way I'm telling you to change yours," Zilla said, walking back toward the pot of stew that was simmering over the open fire.

"I will try," he said, but he knew he was lying to make her feel better. He was sixty-five years old and it was too late for him to change. His life was set, and there would be no more turnings from the main road, no more explorations down side streets, no more dalliances down dusty, untrod lanes, no more—it hurt him even to think of it, but it was the truth—no more dreams.

He looked at Zilla, and it came as a shock to realize she was an old woman; gray-haired, slightly stooped now under the weight of years, her hands somewhat arthritic.

But as he looked the years melted away and he saw her as the woman she had once been—ebony skin that was smooth and without lines—skin that became wet with the sweat of lovemaking, skin that glistened and shone; a wonderful, taut body that was full of fierce strength.

And then he saw a younger version of himself, wordlessly entering the small bedroom where Zilla would be waiting with a lust to match his own. They needed each other and took each other. The color of their skins made no difference. Hunger was hunger. Flesh was flesh.

And then he recalled the tenderness of it all. The gentleness. And he thought about how much he really cared for this woman and how much comfort she had brought to him. Over all those years, they had never let their secret slip out. No one knew and no one had been hurt. The only result had been that the lives of two people had become richer.

He sat in the chair and smiled as he remembered it all.

She saw the expression on his face and became suspicious. "What are you thinking about?"

"Nothing."

"Now am I supposed to believe that?"

He laughed. "Very well, you caught me."

"What were you thinking about?"

"How it used to be with us."

"We're not supposed to talk about that, remember," she said sternly.

"I can't help it if I think about it, can I?"

"I suppose not," she said, some of the sharpness disappearing from her voice.

"And don't tell me that you never think about it," he said. "I won't believe it."

She sat down, and a smile came to her lips. "I think about it every now and then. But I think about other things, too. Like what a fine life I've had because of you."

"I wonder what people would think?"

"What do you mean?"

"If they knew what had been going on between the two of us for all those years."

She wagged her finger at him. "Are you turning into one of those old fools who go around bragging about their past and how many women they've had?"

He laughed again. "Maybe."

"Now you listen to me, *Mister* Pieter, there could be no good of it if people found out. Why, it could even hurt Jacob Adam and Anne, and you know I'm not going to let that happen."

He held up his hands in mock surrender. "I give up, I give up. We'll keep it our secret, I promise."

"Thank you."

"Our secret," he said quietly and smiled again. "But you have to admit it is a very sweet secret."

"Sweet enough to let me go to my grave knowing there wasn't a thing I missed," she said.

The Union Jack on the mast at Fort James weathered its first winter, but New York remained a Dutch city. The houses were unmistakably Dutch, and the faces of the people, reddened by the winds and cold, were also unmistakably Dutch. It was as if the English had taken possession of a piece of Holland.

The people ate waffles and pancakes and puddings. The adults sat piously in church and listened to their pastor speak of love and friendship with the English, and since most of them could see no difference in their lives, they agreed with their pastor and accepted the situation.

The children, of course, didn't care which flag flew over the fort; most of them never bothered to look at it. They played the same games their fathers and grandfathers had played in Holland. They would go from house to house with their *rommelpot*, usually an old stewpot whose top had been covered with an animal bladder. The bladder was pulled tight and a stick was jammed through a hole in the middle. When the stick was turned the pot gave off a deep rumbling sound and was a clear message that the children were begging for sweets. The legend was that if you did not honor their entreaties, the rumbling of the drum would trouble your dreams.

Like their forefathers, the children of the Dutch played many types of ball games—short ball and long ball, pin bowling and skittles, racquet ball games, stick ball games, and club ball games. When the snows came and it was too difficult to play with a ball, their restless, inventive minds turned to other games, and not always the kindest sort. One was called Clubbing the Cat. They would place a cat in a barrel and roll it along the ground, all the while beating it with sticks and making a tremendous racket. This went on until the terrified cat made good his escape. The process was repeated when they found another cat. In time the mere sight of a barrel was enough to send the cats of the town fleeing to the highest rafters of the nearest barns.

The people celebrated many holidays throughout the year. Shrove Tuesday, or *Vasten Arond*, was the traditional day for landlords to receive their rents, and people dressed in their Sabbath clothing and exchanged presents. St. Martin's Eve, or Halloween, was the night when ghosts, goblins, and spirits came out to haunt the roads and the graveyards. But everyone's favorite was Christmas, when there were great feasts and gatherings. They gave their thanks to St. Nicholas, the patron saint of the colony. St. Nicholas had been the patron saint of all sailors, and it seemed only fitting that he was doubly honored by these adventurous people who had left their homes and sailed a great ocean to begin new lives. St. Nicholas was the very embodiment of Christmas, the very symbol of the New World, the patron saint beloved by everyone. The people thought of him as a personal friend, the spirit of everything that was good in their lives. His name seemed too formal for someone who was part of the family, and he became known as Santa Claus.

The snows fell on this Christmas Eve, and the people stayed in their snug houses, close by the great fires that burned in the hearths. They sang songs of St. Nicholas, songs of the Zuider Zee, of Utrecht, Leyden, and Antwerp. They gave toasts learned in Amsterdam and Ghent. They drank mead wine, beer, brandy, and mugs of steaming rum. The new year was coming, and they looked forward to life in a prosperous world that was at peace with itself and with them.

After Christmas and the beginning of the New Year of 1665 had passed into history, Governor Nicolls convened the council and allowed its members to name their successors, usually themselves, as had been the custom under Dutch rule. A few months later he appointed Thomas Willet as mayor of the city. This office was more honorary than effective: the real power remained in the hands of the governor and the Council of Burgomasters and Aldermen. Willet was an Englishman who had lived in New Amsterdam for twenty years, having been granted a land patent and a business charter in 1645 by the West India Company. At that time he operated a profitable trading business between the Dutch colony and the English colonies of New England. Thus it was that the first English mayor of New York was well known to the Dutch inhabitants. He spoke their language fluently, conducted business as they knew it, and seemed more Dutch than English to most of them. His appointment was another example of the wisdom of Richard Nicolls. The governor was remaking the colony into an English province, but he was doing it in a most pleasant manner.

Due to Nicolls' insistence, the new "Duke's Laws" did not list witchcraft as a capital crime, as it was considered in New England. The Puritans of New England had a disgraceful record of witch-hunting and witch-burning, and Governor Nicolls was determined to keep this pestilence from spreading to his province. Witchcraft had never been a problem under Dutch rule, because the industrious burghers were more interested in business affairs than in hounding some poor old demented woman who often wasn't even aware of what she was being accused. The Dutch were religious people, but in their everyday lives they were more interested in their purses than their souls.

There had been a few witchcraft trials in Holland, but the last known one had occurred in 1610. There had not been a single trial during all the years of New Amsterdam.

In 1665, however, New York witnessed the first witchcraft trial in its history. A man named Ralph Hall and his wife, Mary, were brought to the city from their farm just north of Jonas Bronck's. They were charged with the use of witchcraft in the murder of a man named George Wood.

There was a trial, quite tame compared to some of the spectacles seen in New England, but interesting for other than the usual reasons.

Because Ralph Hall often sold his wheat to the de Witts, David was called as a witness for the defense.

"Have you ever seen, or heard spoken of," the defending lawyer asked David, seated in the witness box, "anything that would lead you to conclude that Ralph or Mary Hall indulges in the practice of witchcraft?"

"Never."

"How long have you known them?"

"Four years and some months," David said.

"You would say they are God-fearing people?"

"Yes."

"Would you trust them with the lives of your own children?"

"Yes."

The prosecutor was not so gentle.

"How can you say these people *never* have indulged in witchcraft?" he asked, with a sneer in his voice.

"Because I have never seen them have anything to do with it," David replied.

"Do you follow them home and watch what they do at night?"

"No."

"And you have never seen them in bed? How can you be sure they are not witches?"

"I've never seen you in bed either," David said jokingly. "How can I be sure you aren't a witch?"

"You dare to joke about a matter of the Devil?" the prosecutor said nastily.

"We're not talking about the Devil," David said, getting feisty, thrusting his jaw forward. "We're talking about two people. And I say they aren't witches."

"How can you be so sure unless . . . unless . . ." the prosecutor rolled his eyes around at the ceiling, then brought his face close to David's and shouted triumphantly, "unless you are a witch yourself!"

"I'm no witch and you know it," David said, fighting hard to control his temper.

The prosecutor turned to the judge. "I say this man is a witch!"

"Now wait a minute—" David began, but the prosecutor cut him off.

"Are we to listen as one witch gives testimony for two others?" he asked, and looked around at the silent spectators, who were enraptured by this latest revelation.

In the deathly silence a voice rang out.

"This is ridiculous!"

All heads turned to look at Anne de Witt, who had risen from her chair at the back of the courtroom.

"What kind of a trial is this?" she demanded. "My husband is accused of being a witch on no evidence—is this the sort of court we have here? Very well," she said angrily. "If he is a witch, so am I! And so are our families! And so is everyone in New York! What are you planning to do? Burn us all?"

There was a general hubbub. Faces were turned toward Anne. David moved out of the witness box and went to her side.

"The witch names herself!" the prosecutor cried in glee.

A crazed-looking woman started to move toward Anne. David pushed her back from his wife and looked around at the faces. Some of them were not friendly.

Suddenly a new voice was heard in the courtroom—a strong, demanding voice. "I wish to be called as a witness. Immediately."

Every head turned, and the people were startled to see the angry visage of Governor Nicolls.

Once in the witness box, the governor wasted no time. "I have listened to enough of this farce," he said. "There are no witches here, only men with evil minds who wish to create them."

He turned his attention to the witness for the prosecution. "I will let this pass this one time. The next time one of you so much as whispers the word *witch* I will have you put in the pillory."

The frightened witnesses shrank into their seats, trying to become as inconspicuous as possible.

The governor turned his attention to the judge. "As you can see, there are no longer any witnesses for the prosecution. Everyone who has testified says these people aren't witches. And that incudes me. Now go ahead and give your verdict," he said as he stalked from the room.

The frightened judge banged his gavel and gave his verdict in ten seconds. The charges were dismissed and Ralph and Mary Hall given permission to return to their farm.

David and Anne de Witt followed the governor outside.

"Thank you," David said.

"There is no need to thank me," the governor said. "I did it because we cannot have this plague coming from New England to New York." He turned and bowed in Anne's direction. "It is really I who should be thanking you, for speaking out as you did."

"I'm proud of you," David said to his wife. "But I was worried for a moment or two."

"Nothing would have come of it," Anne assured him. "The people of New York are too smart to believe in witches."

"It's good to be reminded of that once in a while," the governor said.

Peter Stuyvesant returned from Holland, where his anger and hard facts had silenced the States-General. This august body quickly dropped the charges of treason and cowardice. They knew as well as Stuyvesant it was their own stinginess that had prevented him from defending the city against the English. He retired to his beautiful bouwerie, which covered a large tract of land on Manhatan. He spent his remaining years happily tending his orchards and flower gardens. For his farm he paid the handsome sum of 6,400 guilders—the equivalent of 500 English pounds, or 2,500 of the Spanish-milled dollars.

The people had hoped for peace, but that summer the English declared war on the United Netherlands. It was a venal war, fought for base reasons.

At one time the two peoples had been great allies; they had a common enemy—Spain. But now that Spanish power was fading, the two countries became commercial rivals, each determined to outstrip the other.

France wearily declared her support for the Dutch, and then proceeded to do absolutely nothing to help her ally. The first Anglo-Dutch War, as part of the Thirty Years War, had been bad enough; but the second Anglo-Dutch War was pure folly, and as if God Himself wanted everyone to know it, London was ravaged by fires and plagues. These catastrophes touched the far-flung possessions of the English, New York included. The problem was money. There simply wasn't enough to go around, and what little there was stayed at home to solve the local problems. The colonials received no help from the mother country.

The people of New York wouldn't have cared, if only they had been permitted to go about their business. But it was not to be. The Dutch had the more powerful fleet, and they blockaded the ports and coastal waters of America, preventing the normal passage of trading ships and packets.

Ships coming from Europe, carrying cargoes of guns, powder, woolens, and lead, were seized by Dutch privateers and their shipments confiscated. New York received no goods to trade for the furs of the Indians. The fur trade almost disappeared, and since it was the prime source of wealth in the province, the malaise soon spread to every other business as well.

The war caused hardship for every family in New York, and the de Kuyper family was no exception.

The *William* was returning from a whaling trip, her holds filled with blubber. There had been some hesitation about sending her on this voyage because of the problems with the Dutch raiders. Pieter had not wanted to take the risk, but Lars Jorisen had insisted he could avoid the raiders. After Pieter had finally given his approval, the *William* avoided the rich coastal waters and went far out to sea, where the chances of meeting a raider were slim.

Lars Jorisen was on deck when the lookout cried out that the Narrows was in sight.

Then the lookout spotted two small Dutch frigates sailing on a course that would intercept the *William* before it could reach the Upper Bay.

There was little Jorisen could do. The *William* no longer had its cannons: fighting the armed frigates was out of the question. He could turn and attempt to flee from the Dutchmen, but the frigates were smaller and speedier and the *William* could never hope to outrun them.

He could not fight them and he could not outrun them. A third alternative was to surrender, but Jorisen dismissed this thought immediately.

He chose a daring fourth alternative.

The sailors went aloft and raised every shred of canvas carried by the *William*. Speed was essential if Jorisen's plan had any chance of succeeding. With all her

canvas spread before the brisk winds coming from the
sea, the ship drove forward, her bow biting into the waves
and sending the spume thundering along her sides. Jorisen had one great advantage over the Dutch raiders. He
knew what he was planning to do and they did not.

The course of the ships brought them closer and closer
to each other. The Dutch ships arrived at the point of
intersection and held in place as the *William* approached.

Jorisen ordered his men to show no sign of hostility.
His only chance of success depended on getting the raiders to think he was surrendering. To this end he ordered
a white flag run up on a line leading to the top of the
main mast.

The *William* bore down on the two ships. As they came
within earshot the captain of the first raider commanded
them to drop sail.

"What?" Jorisen shouted back as his ship drew level
with the other.

"Drop sail and prepare to be boarded!"

"Aye, aye!" Jorisen shouted back. He turned and issued instructions to his helmsman.

The captain of the raider waited for the *William* to
slow down. It was only when the stern of the *William*
was past his own ship that he realized his "prize" had no
intention of stopping, and the white flag only a ruse.

This had been Jorisen's desperate gamble—that he
could get past the frigates before they realized what he
was doing. The raider ships were facing in the wrong
direction. Their sails were slack. They would have to turn
around and build up to speed again, and by the time
they did all this, Jorisen was sure, he would have enough
of a lead to bring the *William* within the range of the
guns of Fort James, where the raider would not dare to
follow.

The raiders turned slowly in their traces. As the first
frigate turned it presented its side to the fleeing whaler
and a broadside was fired. However the turning action
caused the ship to pitch and rock in the water, and the
turbulence threw the gunners off their marks. Only one
shot hit the *William*, the iron ball smashing into the stern
railing and carrying it away.

The *William* sliced through the water and made it to
the Narrows with the raiders in pursuit, their port and

starboard guns useless against a target that was dead ahead. They were faster ships, but Jorisen's bold move had opened considerable water. As the raider captains gave chase they spread apart, intending to place the *William* between them, so they could straddle her with gunfire from both sides.

But first they had to catch up to her and pull alongside.

They passed through the Narrows and entered the Upper Bay. Jorisen kept one eye on the sails and the other on the pursuing ships. He noticed the *William* begin to move more sluggishly through the water. The winds in the Upper Bay were not as strong as the ones in the open sea, the surrounding hills and land masses robbing them of some power. The raiders were also suffering this reduced wind, but Jorisen suspected they would be less affected because they were lighter craft and not loaded with tons of whale blubber.

As minutes passed, the *William* came closer to the sanctuary of Manhatan and the protecting guns of Fort James. Jorisen ordered a distress flag run up alongside the Union Jack at the top of the foremast. He knew the soldiers at the fort would be watching the drama and wanted to take no chances at being mistaken for a Dutch ship.

But now the first raider, slightly speedier than the other, had inched its bow forward until it was now parallel to the stern of the *William*. Two hundred feet of open water separated them. The raider kept gaining, and the *William* began to come within its line of fire. The Dutch captain was patient; he waited until four of his starboard cannon were level with the *William*. And then the guns roared. The heavy shot whistled through the air. Two cannon balls splashed harmlessly into the water. Another one struck the *William* directly amidship above the water line, the ball pounding through the planking and burying itself in whale blubber after smashing half a dozen barrels to bits. The fourth round tore through the sails and rigging, punching a hole in a main topsail and sending some rigging crashing to the deck.

Jorisen kept his ship on the same course, driving her toward the mouth of the East River. The raider fired again and two more rounds crashed into the *William*'s hull, this time accompanied by several screams and curses. Captain Jorisen knew the raider had drawn its first blood.

It seemed madness to continue on this tack, since the Dutchman had drawn even and was now able to bear all his starboard guns on the *William*.

But Jorisen had another trick in reserve. He knew if he made a run straight for the fort the raider would be able to stay at his side and immobilize him with its guns. Therefore he had *not* headed for the fort, intentionally drawing the raider away from it. The Dutch captain, suspecting nothing, was doing exactly what Jorisen wanted him to do.

The minutes seemed like hours. The *William* took more hits, including one that tore off several spars and sent a sail crashing to the deck, impeding the sailors and causing a great deal of cursing.

"Do we have full way?" Jorisen calmly asked the helmsman.

"Aye sir, ship's t'speed."

Jorisen waited and waited. He waited until the Dutchman fired another broadside, accepting the punishment and hoping it would not do severe damage. As the shot whistled by, he ordered the helmsman to throw the wheel over swiftly. The *William*, her bow churning white water on both sides, jibed quickly to port. The sailors immediately heaved on the lines and adjusted the sails to capture the wind as it crossed the ship from a new angle.

Jorisen's tactic worked—it caught the Dutch captain completely by surprise. Before he could react, the bow of the *William* passed his stern, now heading directly toward the guns of Fort James.

The raider, after the confusion among its crew gave the *William* a head start, jibed about and set out after the other ship.

The minutes passed and the swifter raider crept up on the target. The second raider had been caught far to windward by the *William*'s shift in direction and was now completely out of the fight.

The first raider captain began to regain a position that would enable him to fire his guns. But then the sound of other cannons was heard and a spout of water splashed in front of the swift Dutch frigate. The raider had been drawn within range of the fort's guns.

The stubborn Dutchman did not break off the attack but continued his run at the *William*. The guns of the fort had gotten their range, however, and they were more accurate than any cannon fired from the rocking, swaying and pitching deck of a ship.

One, two, three iron balls crashed into the raider. A fourth splintered the mizzenmast and a shower of spars, rigging, and sails came tumbling down on the deck, burying sailors, fouling the lines, knocking the gunners from their posts.

Another round smashed into the knighthood—that great wooden block at the foot of the mainmast through which passed most of the lines used to haul the yards. The lines were cut loose and the set of the sails was lost. The raider lost way, and the *William* inched out of the range of its guns.

The raider captain knew he had lost and quickly brought his ship about, passing astern of the *William* and heading back toward the safety of the bay.

Jorisen watched from his quarterdeck. The captain of the Dutch raider looked back and saw him. He brought his hand to the peak of his cap in salute to the man who had outwitted him. Jorisen waved back.

Jorisen watched the raider, accompanied by the second frigate, limp toward the Narrows. He smiled when he thought of what excuse the second captain would give the first for failing to get his ship into position to fire a single round.

The *William* berthed at the quay. Great cheers went up from the British garrison and the townspeople who had been watching the encounter.

Three men aboard the *William* were dead, and several more had been wounded. One man had lost a leg to a cannon ball and would die before nightfall. The other wounded men would recover, although one man would never regain the use of his eyes, and another would limp through his days.

Pieter de Kuyper came aboard and congratulated Captain Jorisen for his brilliant tactics in saving the ship.

"There is one thing, however, that bothers me," Pieter said thoughtfully.

"What is that?"

"That the ships who fight against us fly the Dutch flag, and the guns that saved us are English."

Jorisen understood Pieter's feelings. The old man could not accept the situation, and yet there was nothing that could be done about it.

"I don't care about flags," he said softly. "Only that the *William* is safe."

But it was the last trip the *William* made for some time. The Dutch raiders became more numerous, and it was foolish for any ship from the English province to wander out into the hostile waters.

"I'd like some more wine," Pieter said to Zilla as they dined at home with his daughter and son-in-law.

"There isn't any more," Zilla replied.

Pieter shook his head. "This damned blockade."

The fact was, the blockade was affecting the quality of life in New York. The traders were the worst off, almost in a state of despair. They had no goods to trade with the Indians, and without furs and skins they had nothing to send back to Europe, assuming they could find a ship to take them—which they could not.

"If wine is the only thing we must do without, we're not in such bad straits," Anne said.

"It isn't only wine," Pieter complained, "it's everything that comes by ship. I never realized how dependent we've always been on Europe."

"We're not as bad off as many others," David said. "Compared to some we're living off the fat of the land."

"What do you mean?" Anne asked.

"At least we have hard money to buy what goods are for sale. Many of the poorer people have run out of cash —gold, silver or wampum. The merchants refuse to accept goods as barter because they have no market for them."

"It's true," Pieter confirmed. "If a trapper shows up with a canoe loaded with pelts he can't get as much as a peck of corn for them."

"Do you mean there are people in this town who are going hungry?" Anne demanded.

"Yes."

There was a hard glint in her eye as she looked at her

father. "And as an alderman you allow this to happen?"

"What can I do about it?" Pieter asked in his own defense. "The subject has come up at the council, but if the merchants will sell only for hard money, there's no way we can force them to do otherwise."

"Your father is correct," David said. "The governor will not permit the council to force the merchants to sell for barter if they don't wish it. He says it is the right of every Englishman—and I guess we're included in that category—to dispose of his property as he sees fit."

Pieter shrugged. "So if the merchants insist on hard money, it's hard money they must have."

"That's disgraceful if people are hungry," Zilla said.

"It's the law," David said.

While the others continued with their meal, Anne convinced herself that this was simply another problem to which there had to be a solution, if only one could think of it. She finally had an idea and touched her father's arm. "Do you have any hard money?"

Pieter nodded. "Some."

"More than our own family really needs?"

"Yes."

"And you?" she asked, looking at her husband.

David was cautious. He knew how his wife's mind worked, and wondered what deviltry she was planning now. "A little," he admitted. "Jacob Adam and I find it prudent to have some cash on hand."

She stood up and looked at them in triumph. "I have a wonderful idea!" she said happily. "We'll lend our extra money to people who need it. Only temporarily. When the blockade is over they can pay us back."

"That's crazy!" David said, partly because he thought it was, and partly because he knew what his partner would think of such a wild scheme.

"It is not," Anne said angrily. "You have the nerve to sit here, eating a fine meal, while people are starving right outside our door?"

"It isn't quite as bad as that," David said.

"Starving," Anne repeated, ignoring her husband. "While we have the means to help them."

Pieter began to consider the proposition seriously. "I've never thought of going into the banking business, but that's no reason not to consider it now."

Banking! David thought; now there's a way to satisfy both his wife and his partner. "A temporary banking business might be the answer," he said. "We could lend money at a fair rate of interest—"

"Interest?" Anne said. "Why can't we simply give people the money?"

David held up his hands. "Do you think Jacob Adam would lend money without interest?"

"My brother has the soul of a shark," she said. "Anyway, what does he have to do with this?"

"Half of my money belongs to him," David said. "I can't do a thing without his approval. I *know* he won't let us give the money away, but if we charge a fair interest he might agree."

Anne considered this briefly and recognized the truth of her husband's argument. "Very well," she said, quickly making up her mind. "But isn't it possible to charge a slightly lower rate of interest?"

"I think we can do that much," Pieter agreed.

The announcement was posted the next morning outside Pieter's office.

M O N E Y

to be loaned to good men
for good purposes for the duration
of the blockade

on which
AN INTEREST OF 10 PERCENTUM
will be charged

Inquire within

Dozens of men and women lined up at the door, eagerly signed the agreements, and walked out with clinking gold and silver coins in their pockets or else admiring the handsome strips of wampum. Anne had the satisfaction of noting the interest rate was two or three points lower than usual.

"Don't you feel good about this?" she asked her father.

"As a matter of fact, I do," Pieter answered, with a smile. "New Amsterdam had given me much and this is one way I can pay back some of the debt."

The only one who complained was Jacob Adam. He thought they should have charged an interest rate that was *higher* than usual. Why, in such times, he argued, we could well have gotten a twenty percent return. He gave up in the face of his father's stubbornness and contented himself with the idea that the family was at least making some profit from the operation. He also filed away for future use the idea of a de Kuyper Bank. Banking was a good business, he reflected, because it did away with middlemen and spoilable commodities. It went like an arrow to the heart and main function of all business—the accumulation of as much cash as possible. A clever banker could end up sitting on a mountain of cash, all his and all very spendable. This idea had great appeal for him.

Pieter knew his banking operation was, at best, only a temporary measure. The real solution was to end the blockade, and on his urging Governor Nicolls dispatched request after request to the Duke of York to bring about some action. Send ships, send troops, send money, the dispatches said with boring regularity.

"The last dispatch will certainly get results," Pieter said as the latest parcel was sent overland to Plymouth, Massachusetts, there to be sent across the ocean on a fast packet.

"I wonder," the governor mused.

"Surely they must understand!"

"Royalty have a way of blinding themselves to any truth they don't agree with."

"What do you mean?"

"No one really likes to tell a king what he doesn't want to hear," the governor explained.

"But surely they read your reports?"

"Perhaps."

But the duke and his royal brother, Charles the Second, had other matters on their minds and ignored the governor's requests.

Richard Nicolls was a man of means, and when the public treasury ran dry he paid the men of the garrison out of his own pocket. But even a substantial fortune cannot be substituted for a public treasury for any great length of time, and the governor began to write different kinds of letters, no longer asking for ships, arms, and money, but only that he be allowed to leave his post and return to England. These letters, as the others, were ignored by their Royal Excellencies.

The blockade had not affected the farmers, and they continued to bring their grain into the city. But now there were no ships to take it to Europe, and it began to pile up. The price of grain fell so low that it became cheaper to give it away if only the buyer would come and take it from the farmer, thus saving him the cost of transporting it. The warehouses of New York filled to the bursting point.

One of the men who owned several farms and did not know what to do with his grain was Robert de Pauw.

Jacob Adam de Kuyper paid a visit to the comfortable de Pauw town house, Robert's residence since the death of his father several years ago.

They drank the Brazilian coffee that was becoming very scarce now that no ships had come from South America for months. They briefly discussed the details of their land "partnership," and then Jacob Adam brought the conversation around to where he wanted it. Robert de Pauw readily assured him the grain business had fallen on evil times.

"What do you plan to do with your grain?" Jacob Adam asked as casually as he could.

"I don't know," Robert said. "I can't get two shillings for the lot of it. I suppose I'll have to burn it."

"I'll buy it from you."

"But it's worthless! If you want it, take it," Robert said.

"No. I wish to buy it. I'll give you two hundred guilders."

Robert de Pauw was astonished. Two hundred guilders was hardly a fortune, but it seemed like a lot of money to pay for useless grain.

"I won't cheat you in this way," he protested.

Jacob Adam refused to listen. "I owe a debt to your father. If your conscience is bothering you, I suggest you pay for the transfer of the grain."

"That will cost only a pittance."

"It's important for me to pay this debt."

After much argument, Robert de Pauw agreed, but he did it with a heavy heart. He truly believed he was cheating his friend and partner.

Jacob Adam next paid a visit to the oil factory, where he talked with Cornelis Brenwyck, the man who had bought it from his father.

The oil factory, like everything else, had fallen on hard times. After the last trip made by the *William*, the whaling ships had stopped operating. This, naturally, was putting the oil factory out of business. Jacob Adam commiserated with Brenwyck for a time and then generously offered to buy back the factory. Cornelis Brenwyck was a tired, aging man. He had bought the factory hoping it was the way to riches, but like all his other endeavors, it proved to be anything but that. He quickly agreed to Jacob Adam's terms, and although the price was half what he had paid, he thought himself well out of a hopeless situation. Who needed an oil factory when there was no blubber to turn into oil?

Jacob Adam's next stop was at City Hall, where he met with Governor Nicolls.

"This war will not last much longer," he said.

"I hope you are correct."

"When it ends, the price of grain will go higher, maybe higher than ever in the past. Europe has seen the worst of this war; her fields have been devastated and there will be a shortage of grain. They will turn to us for their supply. We'll be able to sell it at any price we name."

The governor nodded and waited for the other man to continue. He had dealt with him often enough to know that Jacob Adam did not philosophize without some business objective and a sound plan of action to implement it.

"If you buy grain from me now," de Kuyper proposed, "enough for the garrison and your other needs, I'll allow you to defer payment until the war is over. Of course, I'll want to be paid at the rate current then, not at the price it sells for today."

Grain? Since when had de Kuyper gone into the grain business? the governor wondered. His surprise was quickly suppressed by thoughts of his own disastrous financial position. He had been spending his own money to pay and feed the troops. If he accepted de Kuyper's offer, some of the burden would be removed. The costs would be defrayed until the end of the war—and the Dutchman was correct about the war not dragging on much longer. No one's heart was really in it.

The English countryside was a disaster, and the people wanted an end to the fighting. The French king also was applying a great deal of pressure on the British monarch to end hostilities.

"Suppose I agree to this plan of yours," Nicolls said in a manner that told Jacob Adam he already did. "How soon can you deliver the grain?"

"Can I borrow twenty of your soldiers?"

"Yes."

"Good. Then you can have the grain within the next few days."

"Why do you need the soldiers?"

"To ready my new warehouse."

"And where is that?"

"The oil factory."

"Very well, I agree to your terms," the governor said.

"This should be put down in a written form and signed by both of us."

"Don't you trust me?"

"Yes, but what if you leave? Can I trust the *next* governor?"

Richard Nicolls smiled and conceded the point.

"I'll have the document drawn up."

"The price of the grain will be set when the market rises to a point I believe to be fair."

The governor sighed. "De Kuyper, you are a buccaneer and a rascal, and the price will be set when you are assured of making a killing. Save this sort of prattling for those others you treat as children, but please, spare me."

Jacob Adam smiled. He enjoyed his dealings with the governor. It was refreshing to do business with a man who understood what was going on. It was also reassuring to know there were not too many others like him.

"Very well, sir," he said. "I'm sure we'll both benefit by this day's work."

"I'm sure we will," the governor said. The arrangement suited his needs. Without any immediate cost he would receive grain to feed the soldiers. The labor they would provide to Jacob Adam would cost him nothing. Of course the day of reckoning would come. The bill for the grain would be presented, and the governor knew it would be high. But by then the war would be over and, the governor thought hopefully, I probably won't be around. Let the *next* governor worry about paying de Kuyper.

Jacob Adam was well aware that Nicolls was hoping to be relieved of his duties. But he didn't care. Nicolls would sign a contract and his successor would fulfill the terms. The English were very fair when it came to matters of trade. It was an important source of their wealth, and they would do nothing to upset it.

The soldiers were put to work at the oil factory. The vats and stoves were stored in the back rooms, and the building became a grain warehouse, filled to the rafters.

The cost of the entire operation amounted to almost nothing—two hundred guilders to Robert de Pauw and one hundred and fifty to Cornelis Brenwyck. He had no labor costs.

There were times when a war had its uses.

Manuel Gerait could not find enough work to fill his days.

He had worked on the restoration of the *William*, but that had long been completed and now the ship was in its berth with no plans for voyages until the war ended. He had helped construct the first well within the walls of the fort, but that had not taken more than a few weeks. He had worked on his own house, but there was very little to do; and the joys of playing with his son were not the same as when the boy was younger and Manuel's time with him was limited to sojourns between voyages.

He visited his sister in the house on the Broad Way, and she would find little tasks for him, but they were only make-work projects and he knew it.

Manuel sat in the kitchen of the de Kuyper house and watched as Zilla worked at the spinning wheel. Long strands of yarn hung from pegs in the rafters above her head.

He marveled at her hands and fingers as they traced the yarn without ever making a mistake; and these were hands and fingers that were not as nimble as they had once been.

"You'd better find something to do with your time," she said, "else you're going to turn into an old man like Pieter."

"He's not himself these days," Manuel admitted.

She shook her head. "Ever since they raised that English flag, he's been acting like he's ready to die."

"I sometimes wish we had the Dutch flag back," he said.

She looked at him sharply. "What difference does it make?"

"I've been out in the world more than you. It's possible for a black man to have a good life among the Dutch. I'm not so sure about the English."

"What do you mean?"

"The Dutchman is fair as long as you give him a good day's work. I hear stories about the English that don't make me feel any better now that we live under their king."

"But we're free. We have papers saying so."

"A man's free long as he can pay for it. What happens to you if Mister Pieter dies? You can come live with me, but I'm not exactly a young man anymore. What if I die? How you going to live?"

Zilla's thoughts flashed to the land deeds given her by Jacob Adam. She kept them in a metal box, and she knew there was a record of them at City Hall. For the first time she was beginning to realize their importance. She told her brother about them.

He shook his head and smiled. "Well, that's one less worry I have to carry around on my back. Jacob Adam did that for you? I guess I never will understand that boy."

"No one understands him but me. That boy would die for me, and I'd die for him," she said fiercely, and Manuel knew she meant it.

They talked until the light of day began to fade. As Manuel helped his sister light the lamps, Jacob Adam entered the house. The two men chatted briefly, and Jacob Adam was about to go to his bedroom when Zilla said, "Manuel is bored to tears. Can't you find something for him to do?"

It had never occurred to Jacob Adam that there were men who did not have more than enough activities to fill their days. He turned to Manuel. "Do you know anything about clearing land?"

Manuel remembered the early days when he had helped clear the land for the West India Company's tobacco farm, and later when he had helped old Claes Vincent clear Pieter's farm.

"I've done my share of clearing land," he said.

"Good," Jacob Adam said. "You're now in charge of clearing the land for the new racecourse on Long Island."

"A racecourse?" Manuel said in bewilderment.

"A venture of the governor's and mine. The land is just on the other side of the river."

"When do we begin?"

"Next week. There may be some pesky Indians, but I'm sure you'll be able to handle them."

The black man grabbed Jacob Adam's hand in his own mighty paw and shook his benefactor's arm until it began to throb. Manuel was over sixty years old, but his frame still contained the strength of a bull.

He left the house and went home, wearing a smile for the first time in months.

Zilla said nothing, but she sent a silent prayer to the heavens, thanking the Deity for giving her so fine a son.

Charles Stuart, the English monarch, was finally able to conclude a peace with the Dutch. The Treaty of Breda was signed on July 21, 1667, and it brought an end to the Second Anglo-Dutch War. There were happy celebrations in London, Amsterdam, and the other major cities of Europe.

The terms of the settlement were generous to the Dutch, since the English stood to lose more if the war continued. The English kept the Province of New York, but waived any claim to the colony of Surinam. This last place, a hot, sticky land on the northeastern coast of South America, became known as Dutch Guiana. At the time, the English felt the Dutch got the better of the deal. Charles was heard to observe that he didn't think much of the New York colony and would have been willing to give it up. "It'll never be anything," he said.

The news of the Treaty of Breda flew around the world, arriving in New York in the almost unheard of time of six weeks. The ship that brought the news also brought a document from the Duke of York that released Governor Nicolls from his post, granting him permission to return to England. His replacement, the governor was informed, would be Francis Lovelace, who now was putting his affairs in order. Until the arrival of Lovelace, which might not be for another year, Nicolls was ordered to remain in New York.

The governor became a changed man. He smiled a great deal, laughed, and paid regular visits to the taverns, where he fraternized with the citizens, a thing he had not done before.

This habit of dropping into taverns, incidentally caused the permanent attachment of Staten Island to the Province of New York.

The governor was at Kock's Tavern enjoying the company of several of the younger merchants, including Jacob Adam de Kuyper, David de Witt, and Oloff Van Cortlandt's son, Stephen. A group of Englishmen were at the next table, and the conversation turned to the pressure being put on the Duke of York by Sir George Carteret and Lord Berkeley of New Jersey to grant them the lands on Staten Island.

If one bothered to look at a map, it was easy to see there was some validity in this claim of the charter holders of New Jersey. Staten Island was separated from Breuckelen by the Narrows, but the entire Upper Bay lay between the island and Manhatan. On the other hand, the Jersey shoreline followed the western border of Staten Island, separated only by the Kill van Kull and the Arthur Kill, little more than wide streams or narrow rivers, whichever it pleased one most to call them.

"It's a shame those latecomers should be allowed to take the island," said Stephen Van Cortlandt, who owned a tract of land there and was in fear of losing it.

David de Witt, also a Staten Island landowner, agreed. "Staten Island's part of New York. How can the duke just give it away like that?"

"The duke hasn't exactly given the island to New Jersey," the governor said. "He's simply set an impossible task for its retention by New York."

"And what is that?" Van Cortlandt asked.

"The duke has said that all islands in the harbor that can be circumnavigated within twenty-four hours will belong to New York. Oyster Island and Little Oyster of course present no problems. But it's impossible to sail around Staten Island in twenty-four hours. There's simply too much island."

"I disagree, sir," said an Englishman at the next table. "It can be done."

"It's impossible," the governor said.

"I can do it," the Englishman said.

Interest livened at both tables.

"Are you *going* to do it?" de Witt asked.

"I've made no plans thus far."

"But let us suppose that you were to make plans. How would you actually do it?" Jacob Adam asked, always looking at matters with a thought to action.

"It would be impossible in a large ship like a frigate or a cargo packet," the Englishman said. "Those streams on the western side are too narrow and shallow."

"So it would have to be done in a small boat?"

"Yes. A swift sloop, perhaps, one that could carry more than one headsail. And the weight would have to be kept down to allow for swift tacking. I think no more than two men should be in the boat."

"Do you have a particular boat in mind?" Van Cortlandt asked.

"I own a sloop, the *Bentley*. She'd be about right."

"And what is your name, sir?" the governor asked. He recalled having seen the man, but had never met him as far as he knew.

"Charles Billop, sir, Captain Charles Billop, late of His Majesty's service, now in the Province of New York."

"Do you have a crew member in mind?" Jacob Adam asked.

"Hardly. Until a few moments ago the idea of actually doing this never entered my mind."

Jacob Adam turned to the governor. "Will you accept Captain Billop and his sloop, *Bentley*, to represent the province in a race around Staten Island?"

The governor straightened up in his chair. "Well, I believe the island rightfully belongs to New York. I also don't think a boat can sail around it in twenty-four hours."

"But we must at least give it a try."

"Very well. I authorize Captain Billop to represent our claim to Staten Island."

Jacob Adam turned to Billop. "I recommend that Captain Lars Jorisen go along as your crewman. There's not a finer sailor in these waters."

It had started as a jest, but it was now serious business.

Lars Jorisen was sent for, and the men spent many hours planning the venture. As Jorisen and Billop talked, the men grew more confident of their success.

"We'll carry an oversize foresail for the reaching work," Jorisen said.

"And cut the reefs from the main," Billop added. "We'll not be needing them."

"Is the *Bentley* rigged for a topsail above the main gaff?" Jorisen asked.

"No."

"Then we'll put one on."

"An easy thing to do. We'll start the first thing in the morning."

"Does she carry flooring boards in the cockpit?"

"Yes."

"Are they structural?" Jorisen asked.

"I see what you mean," Billop said. "They come out tomorrow."

"I suggest we go around the island starting at the northern tip, going counterclockwise," Jorisen said. "That way we'll have more wind at our back on the final run through the Narrows."

Billop nodded his agreement. "Leaving the tacking work for the kills—and in changing tacks the *Bentley* is as fast a boat as I've ever sailed."

It was agreed that she would sail in seven days.

The governor notified the authorities in New Jersey of his plans. He wanted them present to witness the event in case it was successful.

George Carteret smiled when he heard of the attempt. Sail around Staten Island within twenty-four hours! The island was as good as his.

A flotilla of ships and boats gathered at the head of the land jutting into the Upper Bay, where the shore of Staten Island turned west and the waters narrowed into the Kill van Kull.

At exactly eight o'clock in the morning a cannon was fired from the deck of a British warship and the *Bentley* sailed across the imaginary starting line into the kill.

Governor Nicolls stood on the warship next to Sir George Carteret, and they made a wager of twenty pounds.

"I'll put twenty pounds on the *Bentley*," Jacob Adam said to the Jersey men, and five of them took him up on the bet.

"Would you be interested in making it fifty?" one of them said.

"Done."

David de Witt placed almost two hundred pounds in wagers. The deck of the warship had a party atmosphere, but there were several very serious faces. For a man like Stephen Van Cortlandt, who owned over five hundred acres on the island, the stakes on this day were high indeed.

Lars Jorisen and Charles Billop tacked the *Bentley* back and forth across the kill, pointing as high as they could into the wind, wasting as little effort and time as possible with each shift in direction. The *Bentley* was slightly more than twenty-four feet long, her beam less than seven feet across. The sloop drew only three and a half feet of water. It carried a mainsail, two headsails, and a gaff topsail. The headsails had to be unsheeted and retied with every tack.

The two men took turns at the tiller as the day wore on. The sun dipped lower and lower into the sky, and the *Bentley* passed into the Arthur Kill. The wider waters allowed them to make longer tacks, thus increasing the efficiency of the sloop. But despite their expert sailing, when the sun disappeared, they were still on the western side of the island, less than halfway through the journey. If the speed of the boat did not increase, they would be certain to lose the wager.

The winds had been steady but light during the day. Now they picked up as they heralded the approach of a storm. The *Bentley* strained and groaned as she darted back and forth across the kill, her sails stiff as boards, her rigging tightened to the point where it hummed.

It was late at night when the little sloop finally made its last tack, broke free around the southern tip of the island, and sailed into the waters of the Lower Bay.

And now the winds came to the *Bentley*'s aid, freshening until they became a mild gale.

Lars Jorisen took down the second headsail and raised the oversize "gollywobbler," which puffed out and jerked the *Bentley* into an even faster rhythm.

"Isn't that too much sail for this wind?" Charles Billop asked, his eyes nervously watching the canvas looming at the front of the boat.

"Aye, lad, far too much. But if we're to win this race, there's naught to do but raise her."

As if the wind had heard Billop's question, it struck in a powerful gust as the bow of the boat broke through a wave, the white spume filling the air and dashing back on the two men.

"Now, lad," Captain Jorisen growled, "we'll see exactly how well this fine lady can do."

The wind was now coming at an angle from behind the little boat, enabling her to sail at a broad reach, by far her fastest point of sailing. The bow sliced through the water, sending spray into the air, causing little wavelets to spread out in the *Bentley*'s wake.

Midnight came and went, and the winds increased. They whistled through the rigging and tore at the mast, but the sloop was equal to them and her bow kept churning forward.

The men were thoroughly spray-soaked. It became painful to work the lines and sheets with their numbed hands and fingers, but work them they did. The tiller seemed twice as heavy as it had earlier, and the men's faces showed the strain as they leaned their weight against the slender piece of wood to keep the boat on course.

The action of wind and wave intensified and the motion of the *Bentley* became another form of torture for the sailors. The delicate craft would be carried to the crest of a wave and then dropped unceremoniously into the trough. The rudder would clear the water and the sloop would twist sideways. The men would flap the tiller in the air, and there was always an anxious moment until it took another bite of water and could be used to bring the boat back onto its proper course.

The *Bentley* was moving swiftly, much more swiftly than before, but the men hardly noticed, being numbed beyond anything but tending to the exacting routine of running the sloop.

And then suddenly Jorisen laughed and pointed ahead.

"The Narrows!" Billop cried. He looked up at the sky, which was growing thick with storm clouds and showed no sign of a rising sun. "Damn me! I think we're going to make it!"

"Of course!" Lars Jorisen shouted to be heard above the howling wind. "You don't think I'd be here if I didn't think we could do it!"

It began to rain, gently at first and then harder and harder, adding to their list of woes.

The dawn finally came, and the sky grew lighter as the little sloop fought wind and tide and rain.

But now the *Bentley* was a racing greyhound and the two men could smell victory. They sped across the waters of the final leg, arriving at the finish line a few minutes before seven o'clock. Loud cheers greeted them from the decks of the ships at anchor—except from the men from New Jersey, who watched with disbelief as the sloop sailed a victory circle around the flotilla. The little boat had circumnavigated Staten Island in less than twenty-three hours! The island had been saved for New York!

The city was jubilant. Billop and Jorisen were proclaimed heroes and carried about on the shoulders of other men. The two master sailors were not even conscious that it was raining. They were too happy and too numb to notice anything so meaningless as a little more water.

The governor granted a large manor on Staten Island to Charles Billop. His land lay in the Tottenville section, a densely wooded tract where many flowers grew wild and perfumed the air. The Englishman declared he was going to name his manor Bentley in honor of the noble sloop that had won it for him.

Lars Jorisen was also granted a sizable portion of land on the island. But he said little about it, and those who knew him understood he would make no plans to live there. The only home he cared for was the master's cabin aboard a good sailing ship.

The New Yorkers collected their bets from the Jersey men and, all in all, quite a goodly sum passed from the western bank of the Hudson to the eastern bank. Even Lars Jorisen collected some money, although he had not placed a bet. Manuel Gerait had done it for him when he learned the Dane was going to be aboard the *Bentley*.

The lords of New Jersey were outraged, but there was nothing they could do. The Duke of York had set the terms of the wager and they had lost. Staten Island was, and would forever be, a part of the Province of New York.

Pieter de Kuyper roused himself from his bed and felt the chill of the approaching winter in his bones. It was before dawn, an hour that in recent years usually found him fast asleep; but today he was up and anxious to be on his way.

Today was a very special day.

Zilla had breakfast ready on the table, and as he ate she chided him on his plans.

"This weather is too cold for you to be going out on a boat," she said. "Why don't you wait until the spring? That's the time to make a trip."

Pieter sipped his steaming brew made from the juices of deer meat. He held the heavy mug tightly in both hands and let the warmth seep into his cold, brittle bones. "I won't be gone long," he said. "Two, maybe three days."

"A man your age should stay home by the fire," was Zilla's definitive answer.

Manuel came to the house, and the two men walked down to the *William*'s berth. As they boarded the ship the dawn was breaking in the east, a beautiful late-fall dawn with air so crisp and cold a man's breath steamed out in front of his face, looking so tangible and yet so fragile it seemed to be a living creature that could be shattered by a blow.

Lars Jorisen greeted Pieter as he came aboard. "A beautiful day for a sail," the captain said.

"The finest day of the year, Captain," Pieter answered, filling his lungs with the air, intoxicated by the joy of being alive at this moment.

As the sun moved higher, its redness changed to a golden amber and the sky became a deep blue punctuated by soft white clouds moving like hungry sheep across a heavenly meadow of virgin grass.

The *William* slipped its cables and sailed into the East River, putting on speed as the sailors climbed through the shrouds and bent on more canvas.

The swirling waters were flecked with white as they churned forward in their endless journey, hardly affecting the passage of the *William* as it moved through them with stately disdain.

Pieter stood at the bow rail and gazed at the waters. It was now called the East River, but once it had been known as the Hellegat—Hell Gate—the name he had given to the waters more than fifty years ago, when he had first sailed them aboard a tiny sloop at the side of Adriaen Block. How different was this day from that one! he thought. And yet what had changed? These were the same waters, dark and swirling and eternal, looking now as then, forever changing and yet forever the same. The passage of years cannot be measured by the swirls in a river; but for the man at the bow a lifetime had passed.

To his left was Manhatan. Manhatas, land of the Manahatas. New Amsterdam, land of the Dutch. New York, land of the English. Manhatan, island of hills, island of streams, island of his life.

On the right were the beautiful and unspoiled shores of Long Island, giving evidence here and there of the presence of man, but still a wild land with the bushes and trees growing down to the edge of the water.

Manhatan too was still a heavily timbered land, hardly less so than when he had first seen it. And the animals were still there—the birds and deer, the chipmunk and squirrel, beaver, otter, raccoon, mink, wild turkey, weasel, wolf, and bear—all still there, perhaps not as bold as they once were, but almost as numerous and as much a part of the landscape as the trees and rocks themselves.

The streams still bubbled and sang their way to the river, here and there passing a farmhouse or a barn. Trees would be missing near these places, some of them having been turned into chairs and tables, fences and posts, and the houses and barns themselves.

The *William* passed inlets and minature bays, and Pieter thought he recognized the cove where he and the others from the *Restless* had spent the night . . . the place where he had wandered off by himself and had been found by the Indians and brought to their chief. Pieter wanted to believe it was the same cove, but he knew he was only trying to please himself; after fifty years there was no way of knowing if it was really the same place. But he saw a boy standing on the shore talking to a man, and he pretended these people were Adriaen Block and himself. He closed his eyes, and he could still see the two of them. He opened his eyes again, but now the *William* had passed farther along the shoreline and he could no longer see the cove or the people.

And now they passed into the narrower waters that flowed beneath the rocky palisades, known as the Heights, north of the village of Harlem. The village was left behind as the ship moved easily up the river until the sun began to leave the sky. The sails came down, the anchor was dropped, and the *William* rested in midstream, arrogantly observing the land.

It was a night of magic. The stars came out in great numbers as if in honor of the occasion—millions, billions of them, stars beyond man's ability to count, a blinding array that formed a brilliant canopy for the passage of the full moon as it made its arc of the heavens.

Nothing could be done or said to stop Pieter from going ashore and walking to the top of the Heights. Lars Jorisen sent six armed men with him. While Pieter walked as if he owned the earth, the guards jumped at every sound that came from the woods, looking fearfully from side to side in the darkness as they imagined every known and unknown horror, gripping their muskets so hard their knuckles turned white.

Pieter stood alone on the very top of the hill, silhouetted against the dazzling sky, and he seemed to grow taller and shed the years that had passed since he had last stood on this very spot with Senadondo and watched as the old chief proudly went to his appointed meeting with the Great Warrior. On such a night as this did Senadondo know it was time for him to leave the world of men; on such a night as this did he know he would finally meet his ancestors face to face; on such a night as this.

Pieter did not sleep this night, but stood on the hill until the light of dawn had chased the stars back into their hiding places. The men who had come to guard him felt almost frozen, and it was agony for them to walk back to the ship. But Pieter, an old man who only yesterday morning had looked as fragile as a fine teacup, walked boldly at their head, unaffected by the cold, fearless of the night creatures of the forest, his head held high and his eyes as bright as the stars of the night.

The *William* shipped anchor and continued up the Harlem River until she came to Spuyten Duyvil, and again the ship was stopped on Pieter's order. Wearily the guards followed him as he walked briskly along the shore and traced his steps to where the village of Senadondo of the Wickquaskeeks had once stood. And once again Pieter conjured up men as they had been and no longer were. A tall, stately chief looked deep into the eyes of a boy whose face shone with hope and innocence. The vision faded.

There was another village about a quarter of a mile away, but Pieter did not wish to go there, because he knew these were the people of Senadondo and he was ashamed at having lost the deed to their lands. The lands had remained wild, but he knew it was only a matter of time before the white man came with his houses and barns and fences, and then there would be no place for the Indians. Pieter hoped that Senadondo understood he had done his best to keep the lands. But his best had not been good enough.

The *William* shipped anchor again, and Pieter told Lars Jorisen to make his way past Spuyten Duyvil. The captain said nothing, but he knew it was impossible to sail a ship through this body of water. The Indians called it "the false-start-place," because it *appeared* that a ship could pass through it into the Hudson, but in fact it could not.

Jorisen snaked the *William* back and forth, between rocks and boulders, gritting his teeth as he heard the keel timbers scraping bottom, but finally, through some miracle, the impossible was achieved and the ship sailed into the free-running waters of the Hudson. It had never been done before by a full-sized sailing ship, and more than a century and a half would elapse before it would be done again.

They headed down the river—the Great Ocean River, as it was called by the Indians—and Pieter stood at the bow rail, his eyes thirstily drinking in the expanse of shore he had seen as a boy, his mind again filled with wonder at this land, with its green hills and crystal streams, its sandy beaches and pearly shells sparkling under the sun.

He closed his eyes. His mind took him inland and he saw his farm and the smiling face of Claes Vincent. And there was Captain Block and Governor Minuit. Tryntje Vincent. Geertie Smit. The door of the house opened and a beautiful young girl came out—Christiana as she had been on the day she first stepped ashore on the New

World. And there were the children, his own and other children who had been born on this land and who now claimed it as their own as their fathers and father's fathers passed on to inhabit other regions.

It was almost night when the *William* berthed. Pieter took Lars Jorisen's hand in his own. "Thank you. For today. For yesterday. For a lifetime. This is the last time I will be aboard your ship."

"But Pieter," Jorisen protested, "this is your ship."

Pieter shook his head. "I've transferred the title to you. Now you are not only her master, but her owner."

"Being master is enough."

"Good-bye, old friend," Pieter said, and there was no mistaking the finality in his voice.

A dampness passed in front of the tough Danish sea captain's eyes and his vision blurred. He grasped Pieter's arm with his one remaining hand. "Good-bye, old friend. And safe harbor."

Pieter left the ship and did not look back.

He came to the house of his daughter, and was unable to speak a word from the moment he entered until the moment he left. He went to his grandchildren, putting his arms first around Emilie, then Paul. They spoke to him, but he did not answer. He gave each a rare coin of Spanish gold.

"What's the matter, Grandpa?" Paul asked, but Pieter only shook his head. He turned to David de Witt and gripped his arm.

Finally he held Anne in his arms—long moments while they could hear the beating of each other's heart. She wanted to speak, but something in her father's eyes kept her from doing so.

Pieter rejoined Manuel, who was waiting at the door, and he walked outside without a backward glance.

Anne stood in the open doorway and watched as Pieter and Manuel walked down the street, rounded the corner, and were gone. David stood silently at her side. She remained in the doorway for a long time, staring at the empty street, letting the tears roll down her face.

Pieter stopped when he came to his own house, turned, and looked out on the streets and buildings of the town. His eyes were bright, as if he understood the vastness of the empire that would be, an empire he had helped create. It would grow and go on and on, long after his own bones had turned to dust; a civilization spreading out through the woods, taming rivers and mountains, conquering deserts and swamps, building homes, raising families, living, dying; all of it.

The vision of what had happened, what was happening, what would happen, flowed through him. The streets of tomorrow, the people of tomorrow—he could see them, and in that instant he was a spirit glimpsing the seamless cloak of eternity.

He turned to Manuel, who quietly opened the door.

They entered the house, and Pieter sat before the fire. Zilla was about to speak, but a gesture from Manuel caused her to hold her tongue.

Pieter sat quietly, his eyes still bright with what he had seen, allowing the warmth of the flames to creep into his flesh and bones. A sleepy smile came over his face. He looked once at Manuel and Zilla, and then went back to staring at the flames. The delicious warmth suffused him and his eyelids grew heavier and heavier until they closed. His hands were folded on his lap. His eyes did not open again.

A long time later, Manuel came to Pieter's side and took one of the old hands in his own. He held it for a moment and returned it to the lap of the lifeless body.

He did not say anything to Zilla, but she knew that Pieter was dead. She did not cry. When he had walked into the house, she knew he was going to die.

Manuel reached down and picked up the body; a frail body, Pieter's flesh and blood departed, so it seemed, with the breath of his soul.

Without a word Manuel carried Pieter from the house. He crossed the Broad Way and climbed the small hill until he reached the knoll at the top. He turned and held Pieter so he was facing the city he had loved in life. He was dead, but a smile remained as his sightless eyes gazed for the last time on the land he had made his home.

Tears coursed down the black man's face as he held the body of this man he had loved above all others.

Pieter de Kuyper was gone.

* * *

The funeral was over.

Jacob Adam walked at his sister's side as they returned to the house on the Broad Way.

"I'll miss him so," Anne said, wiping the last trace of a tear from her eye.

"He came here to build a place for his family. I'd say he had a successful life."

"And now it's up to us to continue."

Jacob Adam pointed ahead to where Emilie and Paul walked beside their father. "That's already being done."

"What about you?"

"I'm only twenty-three."

"I don't see any particular girl in your life," Anne said, not allowing him to dismiss her argument.

"Don't worry about it," he said. "I'll marry and have children. Otherwise there wouldn't be any sense in what I'm doing."

"What do you mean?"

"I want the de Kuyper family to really count for something in New York. It's pointless to create a legacy and then find there's nobody to leave it to."

Anne knew the way her brother's mind worked. Yes, what he said would make perfect sense to him. There was no doubt he was trying to build an empire. What was an empire without an heir?

"Maybe you can come to dinner in a few days," she said impishly. "There's a girl I'd like you to meet."

Despite the solemnity of the situation, he smiled. There was a spirit to this family, he thought, a strength that would take them far.

"Why not?" he said, anxious to get on with his part.

TOWERING ADVENTURE
BY THE AUTHOR OF
HIGH EMPIRE

CLYDE M. BRUNDY

GRASSLANDS

A former riverboat gambler comes West to stake
a land claim when the only deeds are carried in a
holster—and signed with lead. His name is Will
Cardigan and his story, and that of his children
and his children's children, is boldly etched across
seven decades, from horse to helicopter, gunplay
to graft. Interwoven are three great loves, a blazing
vendetta, and a monumental disaster that forces
the Cardigan family to pay the price of empire
on the vast Colorado plains.

Avon ◆ 75449 $2.50

GL 6-8

THE BIG BESTSELLERS
ARE AVON BOOKS

☐ Birdy William Wharton	47282	$2.50
☐ Dubin's Lives Bernard Malamud	48413	$2.50
☐ After the First Death Robert Cormier	48562	$2.25
☐ From Distant Shores Bruce Nicolaysen	75424	$2.50
☐ The Second Son Charles Sailor	45567	$2.75
☐ Grasslands Clyde M. Brundy	75499	$2.50
☐ "The Life": Memoirs of a French Hooker		
Jeanne Cordelier	45609	$2.75
☐ Adjacent Lives Ellen Schwamm	45211	$2.50
☐ A Woman of Independent Means		
Elizabeth Forsythe Hailey	42390	$2.50
☐ The Human Factor Graham Greene	50302	$2.75
☐ The Train Robbers Piers Paul Read	42945	$2.75
☐ The Insiders Rosemary Rogers	40576	$2.50
☐ The Prince of Eden Marilyn Harris	41905	$2.50
☐ The Thorn Birds Colleen McCullough	44479	$2.75
☐ Chinaman's Chance Ross Thomas	41517	$2.25
☐ Lancelot Walker Percy	51920	$2.95
☐ Snowblind Robert Sabbag	44008	$2.50
☐ Fletch's Fortune · Gregory McDonald	76323	$2.25
☐ Voyage Sterling Hayden	37200	$2.50
☐ Humboldt's Gift Saul Bellow	50872	$2.75
☐ Mindbridge Joe Haldeman	33605	$1.95
☐ The Monkey Wrench Gang		
Edward Abbey	51250	$2.75
☐ Jonathan Livingston Seagull		
Richard Bach	44099	$1.95
☐ Working Studs Terkel	34660	$2.50
☐ Shardik Richard Adams	50997	$2.95
☐ Watership Down Richard Adams	39586	$2.50

Available at better bookstores everywhere, or order direct from the publisher.